"Do you trust me, Alex?"

Unwillingly, she raised her eyes to his. The Christopher Donally who looked back at her was not the heartless myth that rumors had shaped over the years. She'd looked into those same blue eyes once long ago, when she'd peered across a crowded ballroom and had seen him walking toward her. He'd been wearing his uniform then. He was young and brash, daring her with stormy eyes to dance with a man who was nothing more than a common servant of the crown. An Irishman.

He was the most exciting man she'd ever met.

She laughed at her silly mood and retrieved her handkerchief from him to blow her nose.

"There." His hand fanned out over her cheek. "I hope you are laughing out of relief. Or I shall feel sorely abused."

A new bout of unexpected tears filled her eyes. It had been so long since she had shared this manner of camaraderie with anyone.

"I should be asking if *you* trust me," she said.

Other **AVON ROMANCES**

MELODY THOMAS

In My Heart

AVON BOOKS
An Imprint of HarperCollinsPublishers

This is a work of fiction. Names, characters, places, and incidents are products of the author's imagination or are used fictitiously and are not to be construed as real. Any resemblance to actual events, locales, organizations, or persons, living or dead, is entirely coincidental.

AVON BOOKS
An Imprint of HarperCollins*Publishers*
10 East 53rd Street
New York, New York 10022-5299

Copyright © 2004 by Laura Renken
ISBN: 0-06-056447-4
www.avonromance.com

First Avon Books paperback printing: April 2004

Avon Trademark Reg. U.S. Pat. Off. and in Other Countries, Marca Registrada, Hecho en U.S.A.
HarperCollins® is a registered trademark of HarperCollins Publishers Inc.

Printed in the U.S.A.

10 9 8 7 6 5 4 3 2 1

*Many, many thanks to Jean Newlin, Linda Kampschroeder
and Anita Baker, goddesses of grammar and
encouragement, for your years of support,
and for being the best eyes I could ever have.*

*Thank you to my agent, Linda Kruger, because I think
you're the best, and my editor, Erika Tsang, without whom
this book would not have found a wonderful home at Avon.*

*To my husband, Tom, my inspiration,
my love, my heart—I love you.*

Chapter 1

~~~⁐~~~

London
Spring 1866

"**H**ave you lost your senses, Lady Alexandra?" Professor Atler dropped her report on the desk as if the papers Alexandra had given him held the plague wrapped in black ink.

"Someone in the museum is a thief, Professor," Alexandra Marshall managed without clearing the hoarseness from her throat. "I have done my research and stand by my findings, sir. This is not a case of misidentification."

"You are out of line with an accusation of this magnitude. Bloody Christ. . . ."

Professor Atler's unexpected blasphemy made her flinch, and Alexandra knew in that instant what it must feel like to face the gallows. Kill the messenger had taken on new meaning.

A dim whale-oil lantern provided the only light in a room filled with priceless relics. Mummified corpses lay in wooden boxes beneath glass away from sunlight. She'd long since become accustomed to the unpleasant musty scent that

1

pervaded this paneled chamber, and drew courage from the next breath. But as surely as her gaze dropped to the Mogul decanter in her hand, she knew that she'd sealed her fate.

Her appalling discovery would set the elite academia back on its heels if word of the thievery ever leaked to the wrong people. Someone had tampered with priceless treasures. Someone intimately familiar with the museum's routine and with antiquities.

"It is not my intention to harm the museum." She set the once-priceless artifact on the desk. "But I am the one who checked the antiquities in question when they arrived. Someone has replaced the jewels with replicas. Very good synthetics, but fakes nonetheless. Whoever replaced those jewels did so with skill."

"Some will accuse you of trying to cover up your mistakes with this manner of accusation. Perhaps you erred in your earlier assessment. Have you considered that?"

"I . . . did not err, sir." But Professor Atler's observation had done what he'd meant to do. What if she *had* erred in identifying the pieces upon their arrival? Folding her hands in her skirts, she kept them from clasping. "I made no mistake."

"But you are not sure."

"Every emerald and ruby on that sixteenth century decanter is a fake. The prongs have been tampered with or replaced." She pointed to the other examples she'd laid out on the desk. "So I went back and looked at more. The emerald elephants from China are perfect replicas of the originals. There is much more that I have not brought here. Someone has gone to a great deal of effort to make sure none of us ever found out."

"And yet, you alone discovered the deception."

The inference sent a skein of alarm down her spine. "The light, sir," she explained. "Synthetic jewels, even those grown in a dish, do not possess the same light spectrum. Behind glass, the differences aren't as apparent. I'm positive the switch has only recently taken place."

A bushy brow lifted. "How do you know this?"

"As you know, those displays are changed every three months. When I was preparing the vase for moving, I noted first the prongs, then the gems. I cross-checked that vase with my research and the inventory index." When he didn't reply, Alexandra added, "I wrote a report on my findings and wish to begin a full-scale investigation."

A pair of bronze griffins crouched on each end of the desk. Professor Atler had not looked away from the papers, a decided slump to his thin shoulders. His brown woolen jacket was wrinkled where he'd been hunched over the desk when she'd arrived earlier. Heavy sideburns the color of his graying hair framed his tired face. Alexandra felt pity for him. As the director of this museum, he faced professional annihilation. A scandal of this magnitude would ruin him. Something she'd not considered until this moment.

Heart racing, she dropped her gaze. She'd known Professor Atler most of her life. He was a colleague of her father's since they'd worked together in the British diplomatic corps. Four years ago upon her graduation from the university, he'd sponsored her at the museum. Since then, she'd already published more papers than most full-time curators had. Her cross-disciplinary studies were in physical anthropology thanks to her father's passion for exploration. She loved nothing more than to explore a dig for bones. When Professor Atler had first agreed to act as her advisor, he had just completed pioneering work in the field of Egyptology after discovering a cache of royal mummies at Deir el-Bahri near the Valley of Kings. Highly respected and knighted by the queen, he was recently appointed director to the British Museum.

She highly regarded him, which kept her ever vigilant. Alexandra was constantly struggling to prove herself to him, her male colleagues, and to the public who had made her an object of curiosity. A public that focused more on the fact that she was a woman rather than an archaeologist, as if brain matter differed in someone who had breasts.

"Has Lord Ware read this report?" he finally asked.

Unwilling to admit fear of her father's reaction, Alexandra

shook her head. "I came to you first," she said, confident that he now believed her, that he would side with her findings. "I wish to present this to the trustees before news of the thefts should leak out."

"So that each member will know where his precious donations have gone? What if you are wrong? What if the mistake is yours?"

Heat warmed her face as the implication of his words became too clear. Professor Atler's gaze flickered to the Mogul decanter. "If there has been a theft as you allege, the scandal will ruin us all." He looked at her hard. "Most certainly your father, who sits at the head of that board and in Parliament where we secure financial backing. Our livelihood depends on the benevolence of those who support what we are doing here."

"So it is better to admit to a mistake in identifying the pieces than to an actual theft?" She could barely voice the words.

Professor Atler looked at her. His slender steel-rimmed glasses softened his brown eyes. "I'm sorry, Alexandra. I truly am." He ripped the report into pieces and dropped the remains of her whole career into the garbage receptacle beside the cluttered desk. "If you wish to retain any position at all, you will say nothing at this time."

Alexandra could only gape in disbelief.

"I'll see this issue properly handled with the trustees."

Alexandra could not breathe. Anger threatened to erupt past the tightly corseted ribbing of her gown. Without a doubt, she understood politics enough to know where this was headed. Once the scandal was out, she would most likely be transcribing manuscripts in the basement for the remainder of her life, if not outright accused of theft. Everything that she'd worked for would be vanquished to the Hall of Noble Scapegoats. Someone here was a thief. Someone who knew antiquities. How could making her the sacrifice possibly find the felon and solve the crime?

"Professor Atler?"

"Go home, my lady." He shoved papers into a cracked leather satchel. "For your own sake and that of the museum's reputation, trust me to handle the internal investigation as I see fit."

Alexandra stood in front of the long window overlooking one of the most magnificent cities in the world. From the river, London took its beauty from Wren's skyline of churches, steepled towers, and elaborate stone buildings. St. Paul's rested on a hilltop. She gazed at the gray tinged dome, made almost invisible by the looming nightfall. Rain pounded the streets below her.

Turning away from the window, she leaned against the wall. Cold seeped beneath her skirts. Unconsciously, she touched the silver locket she always wore tucked beneath her bodice. She must have pulled it out in her nervousness. The silver was warm in her palm.

Drawing in her breath, she stole another glance around the corner. After leaving Professor Atler, she'd waited an hour before she'd gathered enough courage to sneak past the security guard back up to her cramped office. Worn oaken cabinets lined both sides of the corridor. Voices had driven her into hiding behind the flowing palm that had outgrown its pot last year. Now it seemed only the maid remained. Water sloshed in a bucket and the mop scraped the tile floor as she worked her way up the long hallway.

Alexandra squeezed her eyes shut, said a quick prayer, and peeked around the corner. Her corset almost defeated her as she dashed to the room across the hall. She had not returned her key to security for the evening. Mumbling about the real possibility of fainting, she bent and shoved the skeleton key into the lock, working meticulously until she heard the click. Down the hall, the maid continued to mop and softly sing, her pretty voice filling the empty corridor. Alexandra stepped inside and eased the door shut.

The area was lit by small windows, and Alexandra paused, as much to stay the pounding of her heart as to let her eyes adjust to the dimness. A cluttered desk loomed before her. Aged books and manuscripts layered the top in what could only be construed as chaos, but Alexandra had an organized system to her madness. It took her thirty seconds to find the notes from which she'd written her report. Notes that contained file numbers of various tampered pieces in the museum. Alexandra walked through the door to the adjoining storage room. The museum's accession records contained thousands of catalogued artifacts and bills of lading. Access to the room was open only to essential museum staff. After tomorrow, she would most likely be essential to no one here.

Matching her notes to inventory sheets in which she'd found a discrepancy, she flipped through the signatures at the bottom of each one. A weight seemed to drop into her stomach.

Had she been so blind?

Professor Atler could indeed make a case against her. Checked against the signature on these sheets, her name was the leading specialist, linking her to every tainted artifact.

The realization only made her feel more isolated.

Alexandra tucked each sheet of paper inside a book. Her hands trembled. She wasn't a thief. Indeed, she never walked the plank of discord, if she could help it. And now she was committing what she was sure would be a felony. But these records were too important.

Anger helped subdue her fear. A decade of studies had inched her forward in the growing field of archaeology, to where few women ever had the opportunity to go. She'd struggled to divine her place in a vocation that belonged solely to the pompous male gender.

But her stubborn persistence to work, her aptness to disappear in a crowded room during functions, had rendered her so invisible that she wondered if anyone would even miss her if she was dismissed. The realization that she had so few allies among her peers brought to the forefront the seriousness of Professor Atler's accusations. Most of her associates thought her father's influence on the board had bought her a place at the museum. Lord Ware's privileged daughter. Few would care if she was replaced.

Alexandra slid her cloak over her shoulders. She would go down the service stairway and out through the Hall of Antiquities with the crowd of patrons leaving for the evening. If no one saw her leave, then no one could put her whereabouts up here after closing.

She reached for the doorknob when it suddenly jiggled.

Alexandra's hand froze.

The security guard always did one final check of the rooms after the floor closed for cleaning, but she had already seen him leave. Professor Atler must have sent someone around again. Maybe he'd noted her missing key.

With her notes in hand, Alexandra moved behind the door's spine, her back pressed to the wall, her eyes cast toward the ceiling. She flung her gaze to the door leading to the adjoining storeroom.

"Lud, Dickie," a soft feminine voice shattered Alexandra's paralysis. "You scared the daylights out of me. What are you doing here?"

Alexandra couldn't hear the man's muffled reply above her racing heart. It took her longer than it should have to realize that the two were quite occupied in a kiss.

Without waiting to hear what would happen outside, Alexandra wedged the other door open and slipped through the adjoining storeroom. A few minutes later, she was downstairs in the main hall, leaving the museum with a throng of people. She would not be able to return her key tonight.

Outside the main door, a tableau of the African plains greeted visitors of the British Museum. Three giant giraffes, and other wildlife depicted, had enthralled young and old alike for years. A guard watched the long marble staircase that led downstairs. Easing the hood of her cloak over her hair, Alexandra covered her head. Her coifed hair did not allow much room. Since she'd never developed the skill to lie, even the simplest exchange of dialogue would give her away as a criminal. She wore her guilt like a bright red halo. A blind man would know the instant she said one word that she was doing something wrong.

Another guard suddenly joined the first. Alexandra abruptly stopped. A woman carrying a baby knocked against her, and she snapped upright. Heart racing, she stepped beside those who were admiring the exhibit on the landing, and waited for her nerve to return before casting a glance over her shoulder. The second guard's appearance worried her. Her arm bumped the man next to her. Wearing her hood pulled over her head, she kept her head downcast.

The scent of shaving spice, rich with a hint of the exotic, floated over her senses. She realized the velvety scent originated from the neighboring male shoulder she'd bumped. Strangely, as the seconds skipped past, her awareness settled away from the crowd to the man beside her and the feeling that as long as she stood here in the circle of his scent, she was safe. A solid head and shoulders above her, he had an advantage when it came to seeing the details of the display.

". . . with some resemblance to giraffes," she heard him saying to someone on his other side, and all other noise seemed to recede.

His voice was smooth, darkly masculine, and so familiar Alexandra felt her breath stop. She resisted the urge to look up at him.

"I have never seen animals so strange." A girl giggled, just out of Alexandra's sight. "I think they are taller than Uncle David."

"And better-looking. Especially the one in the middle."

The girl laughed, and Alexandra shifted her gaze. By slow degrees, she relaxed as she listened to their banter. She could see no farther than the gloved hands braced against an elegant cane. The wool frock coat he wore gave no quarter to the expensive fabric that tailored his wrist beneath. He was not a man who flaunted his wealth.

"What is an un . . . an ungulate?" the feminine voice queried. "Such a silly name."

Buried in her hood, Alexandra dropped her gaze to the plaque displayed in front of the exhibit.

"Relatives of Bessie, dear heart." The man's gloved hand thumped the plaque. "They could be twins."

The girl laughed as if the assertion were ridiculous, and Alexandra felt the tender camaraderie the two shared. "A cow does not remotely resemble a giraffe."

"Tell that to the makers of this exhibit," he said.

"I think I shall," the girl said.

"Ungulate is a general term for a large, varied group of mammals that includes horses, cattle, and their relatives," Alexandra finally said, if only to extol the museum's honor for these two unbelievers. "They are divided into two groups depending on the numbers of their toes. A giraffe is an even-toed ungulate. As is a cow."

Silence greeted her.

Complete and utter silence.

Still staring straight ahead, she could sense their stares, and, unable to contain the odd satisfaction of having shocked them, Alexandra felt a smile pull at her mouth. Self-adulation was well and good while hiding behind the hood, but she'd never have been so bold otherwise. Indeed, she despised the public eye in which she'd found herself lately with her new appointment to the museum staff.

"What did I tell you?" The man's voice was laced with humor. "Bessie does have relatives in Africa."

"And a horse? What would a horse be?" the girl asked.

Alexandra bent forward past her hood to see whether the girl had asked that question of her, and inhaled the male scent of the man beside her. At the same time, she realized that the crowded landing had thinned of people. Voices from downstairs echoed in the huge marble foyer. The guards were no longer at the top of the stairs.

She should leave now. Then her focus narrowed unexpectedly on the girl's eyes awaiting her reply. "A horse is considered one-toed," Alexandra said. "An odd-toed ungulate." That the two seemed willing to invite her into what had become serious dialogue made her add, "As is that rhinoceros." She pointed to the huge stuffed creature at the end of the display, one horn thrust fiercely toward the phantom sky. The three of them studied the odd creature in deference to her observation.

The girl grunted. "How does one tell the difference between species of elephants?"

"Asian elephants have more toenails on each foot than Africans," the man offered to the conversation.

Alexandra was impressed that anyone would know that detail. The hood had fallen back on her hair, and she could feel the man straining forward to see more than her profile. "Aye, I've counted," he gallantly elaborated.

For the first time, Alexandra recognized the hint of an Irish brogue, and her heart began to race. The girl choked back a laugh. "Surely there is a simpler way to tell the difference?"

The man's coat was opened casually. Alexandra's gaze had lifted past black trousers, a silver paisley waistcoat, and jacket. "Their ears," he said, leaning forward to better assess her. "Asian elephants have smaller ears than Africans. Asians are usually . . . from . . . India."

Eyes the piercing blue of an Erin sky at sunrise stopped Alexandra's breath. Slowly, she pulled aside her hood.

"My brother served in India. Tell her, Christopher," the girl said. The shadows left Alexandra's face and seemed to fall over his. Those familiar blue eyes froze even as hot color rushed over her face. He seemed momentarily as shocked as she.

Yet, there was something else there in his eyes. Something that was not cold at all.

If only for a moment.

"I'm sure the lady has more important things than to listen to us, imp," he answered succinctly, all that legendary Donally charm now suppressed behind hooded eyes.

"He served in the Bengal army," the imp beside him volunteered. "He was knighted by the queen for his service."

Christopher turned an impatient glance on the girl.

"Yes, I know," Alexandra said.

Christopher Donally had been an intelligence officer. She also knew that he'd been seriously injured while attached to the northwest provinces. Her gaze dropped to the heavy cane in his hand. It had taken him a year to walk again; a feat that made liars out of the doctors who had sent him home to England. But then Christopher always had a knack for defiance.

She'd been barely older than that girl when last she'd stood this close to him. His black wavy hair was cropped now, enough to still be considered in fashion. His face was hard and lean, with a masculine benevolence just beyond devastating. He'd stepped from the scarlet uniform of his royal regiment to the attire of a gentleman. Yet, there was something inherently more predatory in his appearance that would not be tamed by his civilized appearance. An incredibly handsome appearance.

His starched white collar, a stark contrast to his tanned complexion, marked the signs of a man at ease in two worlds.

Lord in heaven, how had she not known that he was in town?

She peered up at him, suddenly at a loss for words. "How are you, Christopher?"

Christopher regarded her with a distinctively ironical eye. "I've never felt better, my lady."

He didn't call her by name. "Are you ready, Brea?" He slipped a protective hand beneath the younger girl's elbow and smiled warmly into her face. "We have an engagement to keep."

Alexandra's mind whirled like one of the thousand dust motes that scattered in the dying streamers of light. By his resemblance to the pretty girl at his side, she knew that the dark-haired imp was his sister. Alexandra wondered if Brianna Donally remembered her.

"Sir Donally!" Professor Atler appeared in the corridor.

She could stay no longer. Not with Attila the Hun bearing down on her. "It . . . was nice to see you again, Sir Donally."

His eyes narrowed. Perhaps he hadn't expected the kindness.

At the top of the stairs, Alexandra's hand went to the railing. Despite everything that told her to keep walking, she stole one last glance over her shoulder. But Christopher was not watching her.

Bent over in conversation with Professor Atler as they walked through the tall doors into the museum, he had not given her a second look. The world had kept turning, when everything inside her had stopped. It was as if she had never been anything to him. Alexandra started to turn away when her gaze hesitated on the blue eyes of the brunette looking over her shoulder. Confusion marred the girl's brow.

Alexandra's mouth turned up before she stopped herself. The last time she'd seen Brianna Donally, the girl had been seven, all curls and lace, and the brightest sparkle in her blue eyes.

Ten years was a lifetime ago.

A lifetime to say goodbye to her dreams.

And to her heart.

Keeping her eyes downcast, Alexandra fled down the winding marble staircase. Long ago she'd sworn away her sadness, so she did not understand the tightness in her throat.

Like much of Britain, she'd followed Christopher Donally's life over the past years. The London press loved him: a son of Erin, born from humble roots, heir to the fortune his father made building London's first steel railroad. In the years following his return from the service, Christopher had taken the reins of the family company. He'd fought his way back from a near-life-ending injury. He was ruthless in his battle to better the working conditions for those who labored in the foundries and ironworks up north. The commoners applauded his defiance to an establishment that would crush a lesser being.

She wondered which crusade or project of his had brought him to London.

Clutching her book and notes beneath her wrap, Alexandra made her way past the gatehouse to her father's carriage. Her slippers slapped at the wet stone walkway. The pale moon gave the misty air a chalky glow. London's lamp-lighters were out, and she nodded guiltily to the young boy she passed nightly. Her heart sank at the realization that she'd been so engrossed in her own problems that she'd forgotten the wrapped bread in her drawer that she always brought for him from home. Before she could say anything, the footman stepped forward to help her inside the carriage.

Lord Ware sat reading the newspaper, the light in the carriage trapped behind the pages. "Good evening, Papa." She kissed him dutifully on the cheek, just above his mutton-chop whiskers.

Austere in his black coat and cravat, he consulted the silver watch he carried in his waistcoat. "You're late, Alexandra." He reinserted the fob into his pocket. "You know how I abhor waiting."

She settled her skirts on the richly appointed seat across from him, her notes tucked securely in the book she clutched beneath her cloak. He looked tired, and suddenly her problems with Professor Atler seemed less important.

"How was your day, Papa?"

He folded the newspaper as he read nearer the bottom. "Did you forget that we had a dinner engagement tonight?" he said, peering over his spectacles at her. The carriage jerked forward.

She had forgotten.

"It matters not," he said. "I'll dine at the club."

The rattle of carriage wheels pulled at her thoughts. Alexandra turned her chin and stared out the window at the damp streets. The carriage passed the gardens of Montague House. The east wing held the residences of most of the museum directors.

"Richard Atler was here before you arrived." Lord Ware studied her before resuming his read. "He chats like a woman."

"The Atlers are old friends of this family, Papa. Why wouldn't he say hello to you if he was nearby?"

The last thing she wanted was to bring down Jehovah's

wrath on Professor Atler's scapegrace son, especially since he was one of the few true friends she had in this life.

She needed desperately to feel something from her father just now. To have him look up at her from his wretched paper and see that she was troubled. See her as something other than an agenda. Professor Atler was his longtime friend. Perhaps if she asked her father to talk to him, Atler would not be so willing to sacrifice her to save his own job.

But another part of her warned about getting him involved in her affairs and the need to handle her problems on her own.

Her hand went to the locket.

She was suddenly angry that she hungered for something she'd never have, that she'd regressed ten years to the naïve girl she'd once been.

"Remove that thing in my presence, Alexandra."

Her gaze snapped to her father. He had not bothered to take his nose from the newspaper. Without argument, she fumbled for the latch and barely caught the locket before it dropped into her lap.

Alexandra didn't know which she hated more: That her father's moods still held the power to terrify her. Or that she no longer had the will to fight him.

Chapter 2

"This arrived for you just now, Sir Donally. From your solicitor in London."

Rain pummeled the house. Dressed casually in his morning coat, Christopher looked over the top of the periodical he'd been reading as his steward approached from the arched doorway of the library.

Christopher disliked the sudden race of his pulse, out of place in the stoic façade of his expression. Though he'd already washed and shaved, he felt the effects of a sleepless night in the stiff bent of his leg.

Last night, he and his sister had arrived home late from the dinner with Professor Atler and his son. He'd not been able to follow her example and sleep. Blaming his insomnia on his leg, he'd paced the library most of the night.

"Sir—" His servant stopped in front of the desk.

Lowering the journal, Christopher took the packet as if the contents inside had not cost him a fortune and a legion of sins to obtain. Yes, Christopher Bryant Donally, the Irish scourge of London's *ton,* had been accused of lacking most virtues, but patience was not one.

He'd finally put Donally & Bailey Steel and Engineering

on the throne for one of the most prestigious projects of this century. No man was more determined to carve his mark on this society than he. That desire was as deep-rooted as his soul. And nothing would stand in his way: not societal prejudice and not his bloody leg, which would cripple him if he allowed the pain to control him.

Barnaby discreetly turned to leave. Like every other servant in the household, his steward knew his moods.

"Barnaby." Christopher stopped the man before he'd taken two steps. "Did you invite the courier in for hot chocolate before returning him to his father? It's a long way back to the London office."

"But of course, sir." The aged servant grinned, showing a row of overlapping teeth. "Especially after your sister glimpsed Master Williams's frozen corpse thawing in your front entryway. She is with him now in the kitchen."

Christopher frowned. "Is she?"

"Aye, sir. She brightened right up—"

It was the narrowing of Christopher's eyes that stopped Barnaby's happy soliloquy. Suddenly Christopher wasn't thinking about the packet in his hands. He was thinking about Brianna.

"Did anything else arrive with the morning mail?"

"Two contracts came in from your Southwark office."

"I've already gone over them. They'll be dispatched this afternoon."

"The British Museum has sent you their eternal gratitude in recognition of your support. You've a letter from your brother in Carlisle. The managers at the ironworks in Galloway and Sheffield have sent you your quarterly accounting."

The older man hesitated, his professional demeanor bending as his obvious affection for the young mistress of the house pervaded his expression. Brianna held all their hearts. "I am sure there will be something for Mistress Brianna in the afternoon mail."

Christopher dropped the packet beside the empty coffee

cup at his elbow. "Don't patronize me, Barnaby." He walked with an uneven gait to the liquor cabinet. But did not imbibe. There was not a single bottle of alcohol in this house. He poured a tumbler of water, drawn from his own well. "I'm not blind to what is going on here. And neither are you."

"No, sir. Will you be wantin' yer cane, sir?"

Without answering, Christopher raised the tumbler, examining every facet, seeing the beautiful shimmer of expensive cut glass. But no peace of mind. It annoyed him that after six bloody years, his thigh still resisted the change of weather. London's moody climate was one of the reasons he despised coming here.

But only one.

Christ, he had not expected to run into Alexandra Marshall yesterday at the museum.

With that black thought, he tipped back the glass. "Tell Brianna we'll attend the opening at the opera. She'll not be treated like some leper."

"But you don't like the opera, sir."

Professor Atler had given him permission to use the museum box at the theater. It was time he started to make his social rounds. "If Gracie needs anything for Brianna, let me know. My sister has a week to prepare."

"Yes, sir." Barnaby's grin lit with all the subtlety of a Roman candle. "Mistress Brianna has never been to the opera, sir."

Barnaby bowed out of the room.

Turning his gaze to the empty glass in his hand, Christopher could feel the storm that had descended upon the outskirts of London with all the wrath of a mistress scorned. A fire crackled in the hearth. He leaned one hand against the polished mantel and stared into the flames.

Brianna was the youngest in the family, with five brothers. At seventeen, she possessed a love of life untouched by malice. But her sheltered upbringing in Carlisle had not prepared her for the reality of being untitled and half Irish in a gilded

world spun in fairy tales. Where Christopher had become inured to much of society's intolerance, he knew his gentle sister was not. Where Christopher battled the establishment
with as much icy calculation as he had any foreign enemy,
Brianna had only wanted people to like her.

Perhaps he'd been wrong to encourage her to come to
London with him. But she'd looked up at him with eyes that
told him he was her champion. How could a man be any less
than invincible?

Yet, he knew that he was not.

Christopher looked around him, the purveyor of this
manor, and every tree, pond, and fish within three thousand
acres. He'd filled every room in this house with the finest
crystal and furniture. Chippendale was all the rage. Chinese
water silk paper decorated the walls. His money had bought
him land and a house, but little else. He intended to buy his
sister a Season.

"Christopher?" Brianna's effervescent voice turned him
around. "Is it really true?" Her caged crinoline danced as she
ran into the room looking much like a rainbow in yellow and
violet taffeta. "Are we going to attend the opera?"

"Aye, imp." Christopher's mood lightened as he saw her
excitement.

"May I wear my new gown with the low décolletage?"

He set the glass on the mantel. "I bought you a gown with
a low décolletage?"

"Actually you bought them all." She grinned. "They're the
rage, Christopher."

With her inky tresses and clear blue eyes, there was no
doubt they bore the same sire. Unlike the others in his large
and extended family, he and Brianna carried their father's un-
tamed black Irish looks. But the resemblance ended there.
He stood over six feet by at least two inches; the top of her
head barely reached his shoulders.

Lifting her chin, she gave him a serious look. "You aren't
taking me out because you feel pity for me, are you?"

"Me?" Christopher pushed off the mantel. His mouth quirked into a grin. "You're a brat. Why would I feel sorry for you?"

"I already know my presence here has ruined your social life."

He stopped in front of her. "You've not ruined my social life."

"Haven't I?" She crossed her arms. Her skirts brushed the pair of matching leather chairs that faced the desk. "You've been larkin' to yourself for nearly a month of Sundays, brother, snapping at anyone who comes within yards of you."

Christopher brushed the black strands of her hair away from her face. "It's not you, Brianna."

"Swear on your heart?"

"I swear on my heart. And you will have your Season. I promise."

Brianna's arms wrapped around him. "I know you are determined to do this." She pressed her cheek against his chest. "Mama always talked of London when I was a little girl. I thought . . . it would be different."

Christopher tipped her chin. "Would you rather return to Carlisle?"

"No." Brianna stepped out of his arms. "I want to see London. To go to the places you've been."

She toyed with the papers on his desk. He knew she wanted to ask why no one had invited her to tea. She'd been excluded from the upper social circle. But she didn't ask, and as Christopher watched her struggle, he saw her expression change. Her gaze wandered to the desk. Then to the periodical he'd been reading when Barnaby had walked into the room. In the lengthening silence, she picked up the journal.

"I had no idea that you were a fan of Lady Alexandra's work."

Easing the magazine from her hands, Christopher watched as her blue eyes returned to his in honest bewilderment. "I support the museum," he said. "I'm familiar with everyone's work. Which reminds me"—he turned and, stretching out his arms, jerked the heavy velvet drapes shut—"I have work to get back to before lunch."

"That was her at the museum yesterday, wasn't it?"

"Yes, Brianna"—he braced his palms on the desk—"that was Alexandra Marshall."

The infamous Lord Ware's precious progeny.

Brianna's lips pursed. "I expected her to have a wart on her nose. She doesn't look like the devil's spawn. Do you think she's prettier than Rachel?"

"No, I don't think she's prettier than Rachel."

"Rachel is quite confident that you two will marry. She told me so after you danced with her at the Yule celebration last December."

"Brianna," Christopher finally snapped in exasperation. "I will see you at lunch." Her nose lifted when he dismissed her to light the lamp. "And stay out of the kitchen," he called after her. "You are not a servant here."

His sister turned in a cloud of violet taffeta, her blue eyes wide as they held his with a look far wiser than her seventeen years. "You're a good man, Christopher. No matter what you pretend."

When she left the room, the warmth seemed to go with her.

Disgusted with his temper, he leaned against the side of the desk and crossed his arms. With D&B's success, formally announcing his betrothal wasn't as far from his mind as Brianna thought. He wasn't getting any younger, and lately he'd begun to explore the possibility of children. A thought he'd not given free rein. Not in ten bloody years.

Christopher's gaze pulled back to Alexandra Marshall's article. His first impulse was to throw the periodical into the fire and watch it burn. The long hours he'd spent pacing to relieve the ache in his leg had not displaced her from his head.

And why not? He glared at the cornice in the ceiling.

He'd hardly recognized her last night from the woman she'd once been. Her ocean-green eyes had lacked the fire that had been so much of his memory of her. She wasn't beautiful in the traditional sense. She never had been. But her pouty mouth alone would have earned her a prized fellowship in the hell's fire kiss-me society for spoiled aristocrats.

Lifting the magazine, Christopher brought it around to the lamp. He'd told Brianna the truth. He'd not been reading Alexandra's article in the January periodical. It had been his luck or lack of such that he'd just flipped the page upon Barnaby's arrival. But now his eyes stayed and read the whole piece. The up-and-coming lady archaeologist had been appointed Keeper of Eastern Antiquities. No other woman had ever held that prestigious rank of honor.

Lord Ware's daughter had finally achieved her precious dream.

The icy water encased Alexandra's body. She pushed harder and harder into the murky oblivion, the sound of her pulse roaring through her veins. Kicking with all her strength, she broke through the glassy surface of the water.

And she closed her eyes, letting the frigid air fill her lungs.

Her morning swims were her only concession to frivolity. The unorthodox recreation, especially on icy spring days, added to her eccentric reputation. But she didn't care. For at eight and twenty, a woman was old enough to indulge in something wicked without censure.

Alexandra plowed through the water, continuing her brisk pace as she began her return trek across the chilly pond, finally slipping beneath the water and back into the greenhouse, where she surfaced. Inside the glass house conservatory, water steamed from heated lava rocks brought back from one of her father's excursions to Borneo. The warmth gave life to a tropical jungle in the middle of a late spring storm.

But for her lady's maid, who awaited her with a towel, Alexandra came to this place alone daily. As she did most everything in her life.

"Lordie, milady." Her maid helped Alexandra strip out of her sodden chemise before wrapping her shoulder-length hair into an exotic pink turban. "You made two minutes today beneath that water. I was thinking that you'd drowned for sure this time. Then who'd be tellin' his lordship the news? Not me, mind you."

Alexandra pulled the towel from her face. "Is Papa in one of his moods again?"

"I heard his lordship raging at some young man from all the way out here. He'll be giving himself apoplexy, milady."

"Someone is here? At this time of the morning?"

"Aye, mum. I believe the unfortunate gentleman regrets his visit."

Alexandra prayed it wasn't someone from the museum or another magazine reporter. Since her post at the museum had been awarded to a woman, she'd been the unwilling subject of much journalistic interest.

Cinching her wrapper, she hurried from the greenhouse. Her father's London mansion was a stately affair, subdued by the chilly lines of tall windows set in a stone façade. An aloof iron fence separated the house from the street. Even with the presence of the pond and the greenhouse she nurtured, an austere lawn yielded only a glimpse of warmth.

She decided not to wait for her hair to dry before dressing. She did little with her hair anyway except confine the thickness in a snood, she thought as she critically examined herself in the mirror sometime later. The black hair snood matched her customary gray gown—an unexceptional gown like every other garment she owned. As she stared at her reflection in the looking glass beside her canopied bed, housed in the mausoleum that encased her life, Alexandra watched the rise and fall of a sigh.

Her father had wanted to return to Egypt next year. Part of her was glad that he was having difficulty gathering a consortium to finance the expedition. Alexandra did not wish to leave the museum to follow him, not when she was working to carve her place there.

In this case to exonerate herself.

Having spent most of the night compiling her notes, she was struck with the horrible realization that she was connected to every missing or altered piece in the museum. No doubt her own evidence would make her suspect.

She needed an ally on the board. Someone other than her father.

And with that thought, today she'd awakened with new purpose. All she had was her own intellect to see this through. Instead of fretting, she'd contact those board members who had spoken out in her favor to hire her this year. They would be the most sympathetic to her plight and would probably listen. Her father would call her efforts politicking. She called it a bold act of desperation.

Alexandra's mind cleared and she found her gaze seriously refocused on the woman looking back at her from the looking glass.

What had Christopher seen when he'd looked at her last night?

She'd once been inclined to patronize her delicate psyche with visions of her beauty. Nothing about her was memorable anymore. Not her pale brown hair. Her caged crinoline, narrow by fashion standards, made her appear gaunt. She never noticed if men looked at her.

A fleeting knot of irritation tightened her stomach.

Except for Richard Atler. He played the gallant to the point of ridiculousness. And he didn't count, as they'd grown up together, which made the prospect of any physical contact with him seem incestuous.

She met her maid's worried gaze in the glass. "Don't look at me as if you have already planted me in my grave. There are worse things in life than spinsterhood."

"I'm not blind, milady. Ye stayed out again all night. Ye'll be makin' yourself ill." Her maid clasped the silver locket Alexandra always wore around her neck. The necklace her father despised. She tucked it inside her bodice. "I've been with you most of your life to know when something ails ye."

"I was hardly outside, Mary. I was working in the cottage."

"You know you must take care of yourself, milady."

Alexandra had slept in the old carriage house out back that she'd converted into her personal sanctuary five years ago. Looking like something out of a Charles Dickens novel, the small thatched cottage was buried in the woods that surrounded this property. She would often remain there entombed with her precious books all through the night.

She took a deep breath. "It's only that I have much to do today, Mary. That's all."

Alexandra hurried out of the room and down the stairs, her skirts flaring with her pace. Her father detested tardiness.

Bracing herself, she hesitated in the doorway of their elegant dining room and smoothed her skirts. As was her father's custom, he sat at the head of the ornate table, where saddles of ham were being trundled to his side. His gray eyes never once raised from the newspaper he was reading as she eased into the chair beside his.

"You're late, Alexandra." His morning anthem to her.

"My apologies, Papa." Her heavy skirts rustled with the movement. She refrained from explaining the need to dry her hair, especially since that was not the cause of her habitual tardiness.

Her father wore a black single-breasted velvet jacket with a high-collared silk shirt beneath. "Have you seen this trash?" Waving the newspaper like a gun, her father shook it in front of her nose before tossing the front page across the candelabra. Half holding her breath and afraid of what would greet her, Alexandra looked.

Christopher Donally's photo graced the society page, but as his dark magnetic looks held her gaze, her expression remained a sober gray.

"That black Irish bastard made a ten-thousand-pound endowment to the new museum fund. He is trying to ingratiate himself where he doesn't belong. It is the lowering of society, I tell you."

The sum was enormous by any standards. The upstart Irish heir to D&B Steel and Engineering was making his presence felt if he had ruffled her father to such a state, and she could not entirely ignore the spark of disloyalty that surfaced to see her father so flustered.

Keeping her eyes downcast, Alexandra stirred cream into her coffee—her favorite brew of the day. "Sir Donally is merely one man," she said in reverence to his mood. "You are a respected member of the House of Lords. Why do you fret so?"

The chair creaked. Her father leaned forward on his elbows.

Pinned by sudden concern for her father's wan mien, she watched him, alarmed. He was always such a stickler for class decorum, but his intense reaction over Christopher Donally went far beyond class differences. She set aside her coffee. "What has happened, Papa?"

"I cannot get financing for any future projects with the museum. And someone has called in my markers at the club."

"Papa . . ."

"The bank no longer owns the mortgage on this house and will advance me no loan this year. I still have my estate in Ware only because the land is entailed. Now I'm faced with that—" He flicked a hand at the paper. "I find out that Donally has been elected a museum trustee. Not from Atler, mind you. But the bloody newspaper."

Her own problems momentarily forgotten, she pushed her eggs around. She didn't for one instant believe that her father was suddenly the object of an attack. It was quite common for banks to buy and sell mortgages, and if her father hadn't gotten into so much debt in the first place with his travels these past years, he wouldn't be in this predicament. It was also common that markers were scooped up by an unsavory few who would then charge outrageous interests to maintain a loan. But she pointed out none of this.

"Perhaps you should have attended the trustee meetings last year," she said instead.

A hand hit the table, making her flinch. She kept eating.

"Mark my words, Donally is not on that museum board for his love of antiquities. He is in London for a purpose."

"An endowment to the British Museum will not ruin your place on the board. And it is preposterous that you still hate him so. He is probably here to give his sister her debut. She is with him. Heaven knows he will need all the support he can garner in this town."

"You saw Donally?"

Alexandra lowered her fork. The food suddenly weighted her stomach. "Yesterday . . . at the museum." She lifted her gaze.

His eyes lacerated her in wounded disbelief. "And now you are here in my dining room defending him?"

Taken aback by the accusation, Alexandra almost stammered. "I defend no one, Papa. Sir Donally has been back in England for years. Why would he wait until now to bring down London's wrath upon your head?"

"I thought you'd have more sense by now, girl." Her father tossed down his napkin and stood. His height seemed to fill the room. "You never did know Donally for what he was. Neither do you know him now. Mark my words. He despises the ground we *both* tread."

Speechless, Alexandra watched her father stalk out of the room, leaving an inert silence in his wake. The wagtail clock counted the seconds before Alexandra blinked and found herself the unwelcome focus of attention. The servants standing near the buffet hastened to appear occupied. Her fingers fidgeting with the linen napkin in her lap, Alexandra dropped her attention to her plate.

"May I pour you more coffee, mum?" her servant asked.

"Thank you, Alfred." She slid over her cup.

She was embarrassed that her father had behaved so rudely before the servants, so she simply fell silent and averted her eyes.

At once, her gaze caught and paused on Christopher Donally's face looking up at her from the paper. And all the years she had sworn to forget, all the days she had lived on with her life, fell away.

A ghost of a smile turned up the corners of her mouth. Perhaps because so many people had wanted him to fail. And he had not. She'd found pleasure in his success.

Sliding the newspaper nearer, she smoothed the wrinkles from its crinkled edges. Almost ten years had passed from the time that he had walked out of her life and never looked back. Nine years, six months, and two weeks. Not that Alexandra was counting, at least not until last night when she'd run into him at the museum.

Christopher Donally was the only man she'd ever loved.

Proficient in five languages, he'd once been assigned to the diplomatic staff under her father in Tangiers: the melting pot of cultural integration and a place where Britain wanted to exert her mighty influence. It was there that she'd met him, when she was just seventeen. There that she'd fallen in love with the dashing army officer. There where she'd married him.

But the wrath of God had quickly descended on them both, and Christopher, who had been a respected officer, was shipped away in disgrace before their elopement had been made public.

Her marriage to Christopher had only survived slightly longer than the birth of their son. Born premature after a difficult pregnancy, her baby had not lived beyond his first day of life. By then, she'd turned eighteen.

At the profound memory, her hand went to her locket buried beneath her bodice, like so much of her life hidden in shadows.

At eighteen years old, she could not fight her father's will,

or the annulment that followed. But married or not, she'd defiantly announced her plans to run away with Christopher
when he returned for her. Her father had not said a word. For
eight months, as she recovered her health, she'd kept her
trunks packed.

Waiting.

Except Christopher never returned.

And until last night, she'd thought ten years had been
enough to forget.

Outside, the dismal rain had stopped. "Alfred." She set her
napkin on the table and stood. Her servant appeared in the
doorway. Fastening her gaze on his narrow face, she told him
to find Mary. "And have the carriage brought around to the
old cottage."

It was time to lend her efforts to her own welfare. She
would fetch her notes and find the addresses of the trustees
she planned to visit.

"But milady"—Alfred looked uncertainly over his
shoulder—"the barouche has not yet been brought out of
winter storage. Lord Ware attends his club on Tuesdays."

Recalling her father's diatribe over the potential scandal of
his failing credit, Alexandra felt a responsibility to keep him
home. "You may ask him his plans once you have the carriage brought around," she hastily added on her way down
the hallway that led to an outside door.

By then, she and Mary would be gone.

Alexandra rode away from the London townhouse of the
president of the College of Physicians. Adjusting her cloak,
she remained staunchly intent to see this through. She'd just
finished attempting to see Sir Donald Owensby, who had not
yet returned with his mother from a tour on the continent.
Alexandra crossed him off her list, frustrated that she had
one remaining name of the four that she'd begun with that
morning. Two, if she counted the last name she'd scribbled
before she left the house.

Lord Wellsby and his wife lived in Grosvenor Square. They had nine adult children, all of whom Alexandra had met sometime in the last few years at various benefits. They were both devoted to charitable causes as well as the Betterment of Society League.

The drive up the long line of trees ended at a fashionable red-brick Georgian house. When Alexandra alighted from the carriage, the stiff wind ruffled her cloak and tightly coifed hair. She and Mary were shown into the corridor. As the servant took their wraps, Alexandra was relieved that Lady Wellsby would see her.

"Why, good afternoon, Alexandra. What a pleasant surprise. How long has it been?"

Alexandra's greeting faded on her lips. The older woman was dressed in black. A white cap covered her silver hair. Alexandra had not noticed a mourning wreath on the doorway. Dipping into a curtsy, she said, "I apologize if I came at a bad time."

"Do not fret, my dear," Lady Wellsby said, taking Alexandra's hands and pulling her inside the drawing room. The wallpaper and heavy curtains were red velvet and cream, a formal compliment to the striped upholstery of matching fabric. "I do so need the company. I had to cancel my Thursday salon this month. I've positively been going mad with boredom."

"My call isn't as much social as it is business," Alexandra replied.

"Women do not bother with business during teatime." Lady Wellsby waved her servant over. "Would you care for refreshment, my dear?"

"Please." Alexandra set her reticule in her lap.

After the servant left, Lady Wellsby leaned nearer. "My husband's uncle passed away three months ago. It was for the best, poor fellow had been dreadfully ill. Lord Wellsby had to go last week to settle additional matters on the estate. There were no sons or male relatives, so it appears that he will inherit the responsibilities. Of course, we will need to find appropriate husbands for his cousins."

Alexandra felt her shoulders slump. Lord Wellsby would not be back for days, maybe weeks. "It must be dreadful for them to lose a parent," she said quietly.

The servant returned carrying a silver tray laden with china. "But then, you will not need to worry about being destitute," Lady Wellsby said. "Your father was an only son and you are his heir. The next Countess Ware. It is very rare, dear, for a daughter to inherit a title. But I know that he has seen to it that you will."

Alexandra set the saucer on the tea table near her knee. She didn't need a lesson on the law of primogeniture and entail.

She'd rehearsed her mission to the exclusion of all else, so it was with much restraint that she partook in the trivial discourse that often accompanied teatime. Lady Wellsby gossiped about the upcoming social Season that usually began with the May exhibition of the Royal Academy of Arts, but this year, because of a fire, would be marked by the grand opening at the opera. Alexandra didn't care. But it seemed to mean a lot to Lady Wellsby to have someone in the house, and Alexandra didn't have the heart to appear uninterested.

Finally, the entryway clock had pealed five times before she approached the purpose of her visit. Lady Wellsby remained silent during the discourse, and Alexandra felt her stomach sink.

"I think what I really need is advice on how to proceed with my case," she finally ended by saying, feeling for one wretched instant every fatal flaw in her divulgence.

"To be frank, my dear"—the woman's gaze lifted as she laid a hand over Alexandra's—"I have always had a fondness for you. I knew your mother when we lived in Alexandria. Our husbands shared the same post. Your father doted on her. She was enchanting. You have her eyes."

Alexandra had taken her name from the city where she had been born. It was a place of which her father always spoke with great affection. Perhaps because it held his heart. Her mother was buried there.

Lady Wellsby inhaled. "But I must tell you, my husband would not have agreed to vote for hiring you had it not been for the machinations of your father."

Conscious that Mary stood quietly behind her, Alexandra folded her hands in her lap. "I don't understand."

"Lord Ware arm-twisted or blackmailed half the board to get you voted into that position you hold so dear. It does not surprise me that you may not have been qualified to do the job."

Alexandra sat in stunned silence.

"You do understand that it is better that Lord Wellsby not get involved? He is your father's friend."

"I appreciate your candor, Lady Wellsby." Alexandra finally stood. "No one else has cared to be honest."

Lady Wellsby followed her up. "You didn't know. About your father, I mean?"

"I had entertained the hope that perhaps my patronage was granted because I'd scored the highest on every field exam given me. My thesis on Eastern antiquities and the nomadic heritage of mogul craftsmen is public record. My fellowship at the university is unofficial because I am a woman. Women are not granted academic degrees."

"And well they should be granted such privileges. But these are not occupations for people like us, dear. You should be married," Lady Wellsby offered, "with a passel of devoted sons at your knee."

"Lady Wellsby had no cause to say those things to you, milady," Mary said when they'd reached the carriage.

Alexandra sat stiffly, staring outside. The dome of blue sky was so bright her skull throbbed. "She didn't mean any harm, Mary."

"You've earned your place. No one can take that away from you."

Alexandra turned her head and met Mary's gaze. Strange that she wasn't even thinking about her job.

She'd been thinking about her son.

"What will ye do now, milady?"

Her gaze fell to the last name on the list crushed in her gloved hand. She would have to come up with a more viable plan to find the thief herself.

Chapter 3

Christopher cupped his sister's elbow and led her through a throng of people up to the third level of the opera house. They'd arrived at the Season's first major event and had waited a half hour just for the carriage to inch far enough along in the line of coaches to let them out. Finding the box was simple. Brianna at once pulled her opera glasses out of her reticule and applied them to her nose, eagerly surveying the five tiers of plush boxes from her roost.

"There must be thousands here tonight," she breathed in wonder.

There was a sudden burst of thunder as the orchestra warmed up in the pits, giving notice that the audience should take their seats. "Thank you, Christopher." Brianna lowered her glasses. "Will the show be in English?"

"The show is *Die Zauberflöte,* Mozart's, *The Magic Flute.*"

"I didn't know that you speak German," she said with a laugh.

"You should like the show. It's a love story."

The rumble of the crowd increased in volume as more people filled the cavernous hall. Expensive perfume hovered like a cloud in the air.

Grass-green, brilliant purples, and pinks combined with the glitter of jewels provided a startling tableau. At first, Christopher didn't see her; then, as if from some divine hand, the crowd below parted and Alexandra Marshall stood with her profile to him. Without realizing, he tilted closer to the rail.

In the museum, her cloak had hidden her face. He searched her features now. With her chestnut hair pulled back into a thick cluster of curls, her willowy body tamed by silk almost black in the pale gaslight of the auditorium, there was nothing that should have drawn him to her.

She was standing next to a tall, distinguished man he recognized at once. And his whole body went cold.

Even separated by a thousand people in a crowded theater and ten years of a past he'd managed to overcome, he was shocked by the utterly black malice that darkened his thoughts.

Alexandra took that moment to look up and catch his stare. The contact went through him, feather-light against his sternum, and caught him unexpected. Lord Ware looked down at his daughter before twisting around to follow his daughter's gaze.

With a fatalistic indifference Christopher no longer felt, he met the force of Ware's glare. But he was no longer that man who had once stood at the edge of Alexandra's glittering world as if he were a kid at the circus, his nose pressed to the slits in the canvas tents, watching the show unfold. Christopher didn't lack for the qualities to compete in this world; since he'd been an officer in the military, he'd honed those skills as efficiently as he'd sharpened every other skill in his life. He merely lacked the enthusiasm to play the games. More often than not, he had no need to make his presence known in a room full of people. If they wanted something from him, they always seemed to find him. Yet, even while he'd scorned the social hypocrisy in which politics thrived, he knew that he needed acceptance for D&B to grow and prosper in this clime. And for his sister's sake, he needed to behave. So he walked the double-edged sword of his principles and promised to play nice.

With a brief nod, Christopher politely acknowledged the two.

"Look." Brianna squinted through her opera glasses. "There is Lady Alexan—"

Lord Ware abruptly turned away with his daughter, leaving Brianna to witness the snub.

She lowered her glasses. "He doesn't much like us, does he?"

A slow rage rose from the pit of Christopher's gut that Brianna had been included in Ware's disdain. "No, I'm afraid not."

But it was Alexandra's stolen glance back at him that gave him pause. And he wondered how she had managed to remain loyal to that arrogant son of a bitch.

Christopher put his arm around the back of Brianna's chair as the curtain behind him parted and a mismatched couple stepped into the museum's box. Recognizing the man as another trustee, Christopher stood. Formal introductions were made.

"There is quite a crowd here tonight," Sir Owensby replied, after he'd seated his mother. Mopping his brow with a handkerchief, he gazed out over the horseshoe-shaped auditorium. "Hear tell a fire delayed the opening of the art gallery," he elaborated, pointing out that the exhibition at the Academy of Arts usually launched London's Season.

Christopher pretended interest. It was truly amazing that he had lived his whole life and not known such details. "I'd heard that."

Then Owensby leaned forward as he took his seat. "Perhaps we should send these swells down to the sewer's project in the South End. Put them to work, eh?" he chuckled, and Christopher knew he'd suddenly found a kindred spirit.

"I'm quite familiar with your name over at D&B." Owensby shoved the handkerchief into his black formal jacket and settled his bulk into a chair. "I'm an architect. My company has had the pleasure of working with yours on many projects. I understand that he's in Calais."

"Donald dear," his moon-faced mother interrupted. She spoke behind her fan. "Isn't that Lord Ware and his daughter?"

A monocle went to his brown eye. "She has become quite the celebrity of late." Owensby lounged back in his chair, and regarded Christopher. "It never hurts to know the right people. Have you had the pleasure of meeting her father?"

Shooting the man an amused look, Christopher turned back in his seat. For the sake of Brianna's reputation, he wouldn't answer that question.

Passing a glance over Christopher, Alexandra raised her opera glasses and tried to rally interest in the colorful spectacle on stage. It took the first half of the show to realize that all the excitement in the theater tonight lay in the audience. She had to cover her mouth to keep from smiling at some ribald comment that flew past her from the restless crowd below her father's box.

"Bloody rubbish." Lord Ware snorted his disapproval.

Normally she possessed the ability to focus on the show. Behind her the curtain opened again as some colleague of her father's entered the box. This time her father left, and at once she shifted her glasses.

There was something wicked in the act of blatant spying, something that prodded her despite herself. Christopher Donally and his sister sat on the front row of the museum box across the auditorium, content to watch the opera. His arm was braced on the back of Brianna's chair as he whispered periodically in her ear. She knew that he understood German and probably translated freely to his sister.

Remembering her father's earlier rudeness, she lowered her glasses. Christopher had looked her father in the eye and not turned away. She smiled to herself. He was the only man she'd ever known who had never been afraid of her imposing patriarch.

"Are you enjoying yourself?" Richard Atler startled her

when he slid into the seat next to hers. His cologne overpowered her and she waved her hand as if the act would clear the air of fumes.

"What are you doing over here?" she asked.

"Visiting you, if I may. These seats are far better than mine."

She noticed that he'd left his newest ladylove stranded beside the Owensbys in the museum box. Dressed in bright red, the woman's skirts flowered like an overfertilized rose. Alexandra often wondered if Richard ventured to Cremorne Gardens to find his women.

"Your father is in his element tonight," he said.

"Parliament is in session. Alliances need to be forged."

"You didn't show for work yesterday. Everything is quite hush-hush, you know," he elaborated with a dramatic whisper. "The academic community's lady professor. What trouble have you caused now, Alexandra?"

"Me?" It was just like him to accuse her of being difficult.

He leaned an elbow on his thigh. She'd known Richard most of her life. He was a tall Adonis, and considered by most to be dashing. But she'd never gotten past the fact that she'd seen him naked once. They'd both been five. It had been a shock to learn that boys relieved themselves differently than girls.

Still they'd managed to become more friends than rivals, and he'd helped see her through more than one interview since she'd been appointed as staff to the museum. But like so many other men of his kind, he was wont to lend his efforts more to play and carousing than hard work. He'd never have made it through his university studies if she hadn't completed half his assignments. Over the years, Richard Atler had become such a harmless fixture in her life that she took little notice of his antics until he spouted off some insipid innuendo about her character.

She glared at him. "Do not think to imply that I've done anything wrong, Mr. Atler." Without referring to his poor taste in women or general lack of character, she said, "You of all people have no right to stand in judgment of me."

"Naturally, you never make mistakes."

"If you are referring to doing my job properly, no."

And she intended to prove it.

Richard's gaze went over the theater. "It's been a long while since you've been on display."

Except for the necessary formal appearances and an occasional tea, she rarely made social rounds. Her debut had taken place ten years ago in an exotic palace in a foreign world. She smoothed the silky fabric of her dress and lifted her gaze to where Christopher sat.

She wondered how much of that night in Tangiers he remembered.

Richard was suddenly snapping his fingers in her face. "You haven't heard a word I've said. Where are you?"

His gaze followed where hers had been. "I see. And what can one say about a dark Irishman who has the power to make your icy heart melt?" He waved his hand airily. "Give the museum ten thousand quid and he's almost a lord. But not quite. Bets are being wagered at the club over how long before some esteemed lord snags Donally's sister for his mistress. Because he certainly won't find her a husband among that venerable lot."

"Don't be gauche, Richard," she snapped. "Even I weary of your constant sarcasm. Mr. Donally would most likely kill any man who insulted his sister in that way. Make sure you don't take part."

"Do I detect a hint of approbation?"

"I admire a man who can build the name *Donally* into the enterprising force he has. And why shouldn't he be able to give his sister a Season? He's certainly earned the right."

"I didn't say I agreed with the antics, my dearest love. I merely pointed out the obvious. Don't forget, I'm a wee commoner, too. The only difference is that he's been knighted by the queen."

"Go away, Richard."

He straightened. "Since you're in your usual form this evening, my lady princess, I shall indeed take my leave."

After he left the box, Alexandra pulled her reticule into her lap. She half expected that everyone here would see through her façade and know her for the felon she was. Her nerves were frazzled.

Using her stolen key that afternoon, she'd entered the main storage vault of the museum and removed item 422 from its velvet case locked within a box. The authentic White Swan, an almost colorless ruby, was priceless. The one she'd stolen was a fake. The Emperor Shāh Jahān had given the original swan to his one true love. Later, he'd built the Taj Mahal in her memory. She'd been preparing to move the bauble to the upstairs exhibits last week when she'd initially discovered the thefts.

Nor had Alexandra missed the irony of the number on the box when she'd replaced the wooden container among the dozens that lined the shelves: 422. She and Christopher had been married on April 22, 1855.

With an ardent desire to see this opera end, Alexandra stole another glance at Christopher.

This time, he was watching her as well.

"Hit him, Mr. Williams! Knock him in the jaw!" Brianna yelled.

Christopher jumped nimbly from foot to foot, feinting against Williams's right hook. "Hit me right here, Willie boy." Christopher sidestepped a swing and hit Williams's jaw. The boy staggered and almost fell in the grass.

"Christopher!" Brianna clutched the rope. "You're going to hurt him!"

"No, you're . . . not, sir," Williams panted, feinting left. "I can stay on my feet . . . with the best of them. And my name isn't Willie."

"Hold up your hands. Like this." Christopher demonstrated.

Brianna paced up and down the rope line. "You just wait, Christopher Donally."

Williams's face was intent. He punched and missed twice more.

Christopher grinned. The sun had appeared over the trees like a long-lost troubadour, and he danced to the music. "You're game, Willie, me boy. I have to give you points for guts."

Sweat beaded on Christopher's chest. His muscles flexed and coiled. He'd removed his shirt before stepping into the ring he'd built last year beneath the spreading branches of two giant elms. He still wore his riding boots and breeches from his exercise that afternoon. He worked too many hours behind a desk not to stay active when he could.

Boxing was a sport Christopher particularly enjoyed. Even with his leg, he could dance circles around most any-one, except maybe his youngest brother, Ryan. From the side, almost out of the line of his vision, Christopher glimpsed a visitor coming up the long drive. Deliveries from the London office seemed a regular occurrence these days since Brianna's arrival on the estate. Barnaby was on the ter-race setting up for a late lunch.

"Brianna?" Christopher called over his shoulder without taking his eyes off his opponent. "Tell Barnaby we have an-other visitor."

She didn't budge a slipper. Defiance clung to her stubborn silence, but before Christopher warned her to go, she spun in a huff and flounced off, her pink crinoline bobbing in re-strained fury. His grin vanished as he turned his full attention on Stephan Williams.

The youth's Adam's apple bobbed. "If this is about this morning, sir."

"Your problem is timing, *Willie*."

Now that Brianna was gone, all gloves came off, meta-phorically speaking.

Christopher hit him. Hard enough to give him pause. Make him more nervous than he already was.

"But it's not what you think, sir. I really like your sister."

"You're in no position to take on the responsibilities of a wife."

A bead of sweat ran down Williams's temple. His breathing was becoming labored. "I'll . . . have my own law practice one day, sir."

"One day is not today. Today you're a courier. Tomorrow, your father can send someone else to this house. Because if I see you here again, I won't be using gloves the next time we have this discussion." He danced around the ring. "Do I make myself clear?"

Williams had made the mistake of encroaching where he didn't belong. Christopher had returned that afternoon from his ride to find the boy in mouth-to-mouth discourse or as close to what could only be construed as a kiss with Brianna.

Christopher's first instinct had been to flog the young whelp and fire his father as his solicitor. But part of the blame, he knew, lay on his sister's shoulders. Beneath her coy façade, she had a streak of rebellion that deserved to get her thrown over his knee. The poor youth didn't have a chance if Brianna had set her cap for him. Christopher blamed her wildness on being raised by five older brothers and all the nonsensical books that she'd been allowed to read over the years. She lacked a suitable feminine mentor.

"Yes, sir. You make yourself very clear, sir." Williams raised his gloves and evaded a jab. "But I don't have to like it."

Christopher actually felt a spark of respect for the younger man. He'd demonstrated courage to step into this ring today. He had heart, which would take him far in life. But before Christopher could reply, something made him pause as he looked across the span of terraced gardens toward the tree-lined drive below.

Alexandra Marshall stepped out of the cab.

The breeze caught her skirts.

Her eyes went to the lofty stone manor house with its mullioned windows framed in pilasters and steep gables, then slowly around the grounds. Grounds that belonged to him. His knowledge of botany had prompted the design. There were no hedges of thorn or quickset to lay boundaries to the yard. The terraces were artfully overgrown with just the right colors and textures that it was as if a person stepped into nature's wonderland.

She tented a hand over her eyes. He knew the instant she found him. Williams took that moment of inattention and laid a left hook into his jaw, sending him backward into the rope.

And Christopher went down.

"No one comes out to this place," a man's voice jerked Alexandra around. The cabdriver stood beside her, his eyes flicking over the manse before settling on her. "Not if 'e values 'is bloomin' life anyways."

"Whyever not?"

" 'Cause the guv'nor there"—he tossed a nod over his cloaked shoulder—"is protective of that sister of his. That's why not."

"You know Sir Donally?"

Beneath his many-caped driving cloak, the driver wore a red-checked shirt tucked into baggy trousers. "What person around here don't know the capt'n? When he bought this estate, this whole district was fairly crumblin' with neglect. He's rebuilt 'bout every tenant's house. Made 'em into functioning farms again."

The driver plopped his hat over a curly crop of black hair. "My sister lives in the village. That'll be twenty shillings, milady. That's for both ways."

"Twenty!" Alexandra gasped.

Good lord. When she'd hired him that afternoon, she'd had no idea of the cost. She would have to pay him upon her return to the city."

A gust of chilly wind set the treetops in motion. She started to clutch her cloak before remembering that she'd left it inside the cab.

"You have my cloak. Surely that counts for a retainer until we return to London."

"I charge by the half hour, mum."

It didn't matter. Depending on how long this took, her time here could be very short. Immeasurably short.

Easing her skirts to the side, she took the stone pathway away from the gravel drive. She was not naïve enough to think that coming here unescorted was acceptable by anyone's standards.

Christopher was some distance away. She recognized him easily. His black riding breeches hugged the sinewy lines of his legs. He was shoving his arms into a snowy white shirt.

Earlier, she'd felt the heat of his eyes seconds before the young man in the ring hit him. They were now both talking.

"My brother is only too capable of dealing out what he is dished."

Alexandra jerked around. Christopher's sister had walked up beside her. She looked quite demure in voluminous pale pink muslin. "It is for poor Mr. Williams that I worry. I suppose I won't see him again."

Alexandra followed the wistfulness in her voice. They both watched the young man in question climb out of the ring and march across the lawn toward the stables. His shoulders lacked width and the maturity that came with age. Unlike Christopher, whose body defined masculine perfection with the subtlety of a blaring horn in church.

"Oh, my." Brianna lowered her eyes and dipped into a curtsy. "I have been remiss." She quickly introduced herself, though Alexandra already knew her name. "Would you care for some tea, my lady?"

Did Brianna remember her from the museum, or did Christopher's sister not know who she was?

Alexandra's first instinct was to turn down the invitation, but she changed her mind. "Yes, that would be nice."

"Cook makes the absolute best tea. Coffee, too, if you like it. Christopher likes coffee better than tea."

Chatting like a small bird, Brianna took her around the house, through an enclosed stone pathway that went to the back terrace. Alexandra found herself led in such covert secrecy to the inner realms of Christopher's hallowed sanctuary. She would have considered the whole charade amusing had she not felt like a blatant trespasser. Clearly, Christopher's sister was aware of this fact as well.

Their steps resonated in the enclosed archway. The manor was beautiful and filled with life, even among the stones. Pale green lichen contributed stately character. Brianna talked about the restoration Christopher had done on the Elizabethan house.

"He has quite a creative mind, my brother does," she said. "He builds bridges and railroads. To do something like this is quite a change." Her eyes brightened. "You've lived all over the world, haven't you? So has Christopher," she said before Alexandra could reply. "Though he never talks about his time in the military. I suppose it has to do with his injury."

Unsure what to say, Alexandra asked, "You will be in London long?"

"Christopher is giving me a Season. I was presented at court last month. It's always been a dream of mine to meet the queen. The presentation was held at St. James's Palace. Have you ever been there?"

Alexandra found herself engaged by Brianna's unpretentious personality. "When I was much younger."

"You must know the grandest places in London to visit," she said after a few moments. "Will you tell me? I wish to meet others my age."

Alexandra had not ventured out on the town in years. "I haven't a favorite spot, exactly." She tried to remember anything Lady Wellsby might have said. "I do believe the next important social event of the season begins with the opening at the Royal Academy of Arts, and also horse racing at the Ascot." This she knew from her father. "There is also the regatta at Henley in July."

"Don't tell me you actually leave the museum?" Christopher came up behind her.

Even before she turned, Alexandra felt the hot essence of him. His shirt lay open to her gaze in what she was sure he'd meant to be a scandalous display of his complete lack of mores. She forced her stare past the hardened muscles on his stomach. It was just like Christopher Donally to flout propriety and smack her in the face with her own. Well, she'd have none of it.

"You'd be surprised where I'm capable of venturing, Sir Donally. And with whom."

The fact that she was here should prove her enormous daring.

Or stupidity.

"Oh, please, you must tell me everything, my lady. Christopher means well. But he's hardly a woman privileged to insider gossip."

Alexandra's gaze roamed his chest. His hardened stomach. A line of dark hair disappeared in the waist of his breeches. "No reasonably intelligent human being would mistake your brother for a woman," she shocked herself by saying. More so because she found her palms itching to slide inside his shirt in a strictly gratuitous manner indicative of the sudden insanity that had taken hold. She could smell the musk of his skin, the weight of his heat.

"My lady," Brianna said cheerfully. "How marvelously outrageous you are."

Christopher's eyes bore into her outwardly composed face, radiating the lazy arrogance she remembered so well.

Except she also knew the other side of him. His touch. The way he held her head when he kissed her. His body sliding over hers, between her legs. There was suddenly serious heat between them.

He shifted his gaze on his sister. "Give me five minutes, imp."

Brianna's expression fell. "I thought perhaps she might join us for lunch. Barnaby has almost finished setting everything out."

"She won't be staying."

Alexandra sensed rather than saw the momentary battle of wills between brother and sister, before Brianna turned and dipped into a graceful curtsy. "Then I bid you good day, my lady."

After Brianna left, Christopher turned back to her. He carried a towel and wrapped it around his neck. They stood beneath the spreading branches of an elm almost as if a decade had not separated them. "What do you want, Alex?"

"I see you still box." She attempted a polite smile. His height afforded him an unwelcome advantage, which she didn't like. "Is Mr. Williams the young gentleman with the clever left hook?"

His smile gave her a fleeting glimpse of strong white teeth. "Come, my lady, after ten years you can't suddenly be missing me?"

"I want to know why are you here in London?" She hadn't meant to sound so impertinent, but every accusation her father had made burned at the back of her mind. And she suddenly could not dismiss the coincidences of Christopher's appearance here in London and her father's recent string of financial disasters. Maybe even her own.

She had to be sure.

Amusement entered his eyes. "Have I missed some law that says I'm not allowed to visit this city?" He held up his hand. "No admittance to Christopher Donally, by order of Lord Ware"—looking at her throughly, he lowered his hand—"and his snobbish daughter?"

Unimpressed with his sarcasm, Alexandra brazened forward with her interrogation. "Your brother heads your business ventures here. Everyone knows that you handle the Northern division."

He dabbed the towel across his face. "You know that much about D&B? I'm impressed. Maybe I should have been keeping one finger on you all of these years. You have me at a disadvantage."

"Don't flatter yourself, Mr. Donally. Most of London has seen the newspapers. Your company is currently one of the few that is being considered for the engineering analysis for the Channel Tunnel project."

"Do you have a passion for English mud?"

"Do you always answer questions with a question?"

Alexandra felt his mood shift, if only slightly. "I was an engineer before I was ever anything else in this company. The Channel project analysis is mine. My ideas. My proposals." He crossed his arms. "Have you any other sordid details you would like to know?"

Fumbling with the latch on her reticule, Alexandra delved inside. She handed him the counterfeit White Swan ruby. His fingers rubbed against hers. Their eyes met. Only because she refused to look lower than his neck at the blatant display of muscled flesh and sinew beneath his open shirt. A growth of beard shadowed his jaw.

"I wish to know where one can find someone who makes synthetic gems. Emeralds and rubies, to be exact."

He rolled the pendant over in his hand. "Is your father having trouble keeping you draped in the real thing?"

"Don't be a boor, Mr. Donally."

He pressed his palm against the tree at her back. His forearm brushed her breast. "What's happened to you, Alex?" His sky-blue gaze raked over her, taking in her plain gray gown.

The tree backed her spine. "I don't know what you mean."

There was nothing tame about his perusal of her person. He reminded her of a hawk trapped in a cage, his instinct checked only by the bars that gilded his life. "You used to like me hot and sweaty. And wearing far less than this."

"Oh!" She raised her arms to keep her breasts from touching his sweaty chest. The last barrier of ice in her demeanor melted. She burned with a flush. He smelled earthy and pagan, all things coarse. Sunlight splintered the shadows on his handsome face.

Her gaze flicked over him, then fled. She stared pointedly at the house. "You're crude, Mr. Donally."

"What are you really doing here, Alex?"

Her eyes snapped back to his. "My name is Alexandra."

"Maybe to your stuffy upper-crust colleagues, but not to me."

"I told you why I'm here."

A gust of wind teased his shirt. "Ah." He slid his thumb over the jewel. Alexandra was not unaware of the soft menace in that movement. "You wish to learn who manufactures synthetic gems. Then I don't need to worry. You're not here to plead for that fancy career of yours."

Alexandra went cold inside.

"Atler already told me he's opened up an internal investigation to clear up some recent disparities in the inventory." He stood back and bounced the swan in his hand. "Strange that your name happened to come up. Is this one of the pieces in question?"

"Professor Atler would rather accuse me of incompetence than accept the scandal that the museum has been blatantly robbed."

His eyes took on a darker shade of blue. "Because any gems stolen will probably never be recovered. Think of your sacrifice as the lesser of two scandals. If this gets out, the reputation of the museum will be destroyed. But if the museum is guilty only of hiring someone of inexperience, the issue is altogether different."

"Whoever tampered with those relics knew that I had inventoried each one, to be so precise with what he took. He must have also known that Professor Atler would do exactly what he is doing now."

"Then my guess is that your well-earned profession is in jeopardy of burning to the ground."

"No!" She wanted to strike him. "My job is the only thing that matters in my life, Mr. Donally. I have nothing else." Lifting her chin, she met his gaze, now hooded in the shadows. "I will not let everything I've earned be taken away from me because of politics."

"Politics?" His eyes narrowed. She didn't understand why he'd suddenly gone all cold and dangerous. "Welcome to the real world."

"I will not let them win."

"What is it you want from me?"

Her heart raced. Everything that mattered in life depended on her catching this thief. "All synthetic gems bear hallmarks of their laboratory origins. I want you to find out who makes this kind of jewelry. There can't be many people who have that kind of capability. I know this will take time. I'll pay you."

"Don't bloody insult me."

"My offer is not meant as an insult. I'm desperate. I have to find the thief and recover the jewels. Surely that should not be difficult."

His wry amusement seemed to dissolve her plan. "Why haven't you gone to your father with this?"

"If he interferes now, before I have all the facts, no one in the industry will respect me again. They'll think he bought my way out." She threw him a furtive look. "But you . . . you know people."

His laughter stung. "That's bloody ripe. You think that I have connections to the criminal element of our society? By virtue of my *Irishness*? Or something else?"

She watched the breeze stir his hair. "Both, if you must know." That and the fact she had no where else to go. "You must still know people who . . ."

"Let me open your eyes, Alex. It takes a knowledgeable chemist to perfect this art. Such men sell their wares to the wealthy. Men who conceal mistresses and don't wish to hand down family heirlooms in return for the sexual favors granted them."

"You would know that from experience, I suppose."

"I don't give my mistresses fake emeralds or rubies." His grin was white with all manner of arrogance that made her bristle. He flipped the gem back to her. "But if I should find a clue buried in the opium dens or pleasure palaces of London's underworld, I'll be sure to let you know."

Clearly, any warmth he was capable of feeling was reserved solely for his sister. "You were always such a high-minded prig, Christopher Donally."

"Me?" He had the audacity to look offended.

"You can rot. I don't need you anyway."

Eyes narrowed, Christopher watched her march off, her back ramrod straight. "Aye," he almost yelled back. "That was always the problem."

She'd never needed him.

And she'd certainly never fought for him as she did that bloody job. Hell would freeze before he'd ever allow himself to step into her life again.

"Barnaby?" Christopher tied the cravat around his neck. He'd washed and changed. He could bear his smell again. "Do you still have a brother who works on staff at the Marlborough Street magistrate's court?"

"Yes, sir."

"Doesn't the Metropolitan Police force handle museum security?"

"For five years now." Barnaby brushed the jacket before helping Christopher slide it on. "I understand her ladyship works at the museum. Mistress Brianna showed me a fine piece she'd written in the periodical."

Christopher met his steward's gaze in the looking glass. "You've discussed all of this in the time I was outside?"

"Naturally, sir. We would not discuss her in front of you."

"Naturally." Christopher turned away from the glass. He was willing to allow that Alex was a curiosity. But he was not willing to abide the rattle of gossip. It was bad enough that he endured that from his sister.

His room was richly appointed with lingering traces of the history of this house in the high ceilings and four-poster bed. The bed hangings and drapery fabric were from Clarence House. Armless chairs were covered in fabric from Scalamandré. All of this went unnoticed as he opened a carved jewel box to retrieve his watch fob.

"If you have time next week"—he tucked the fob into his waistcoat pocket—"I'd like to drop by and speak to your brother."

"May I send a message to warn him, sir?"

"I would appreciate that," he said with polite amusement. Clearly, his steward thought him an ass and indulged him his mood.

"Mistress Brianna is already at the table, sir," Barnaby said as Christopher left the room, his steps silent on the thick carpet. "She insisted that she was too starved to await your convenience."

"Furious, more like."

But so was he. She was due for a serious lecture before he left today for his London office.

"Young Williams did seem like a nice chap," Barnaby added. "Dashed annoying at times, these young folks."

"Young Williams is exactly that, Barnaby. Young."

Brianna was halfway through her meal when Christopher arrived on the terrace. Sunlight lay a carpet of fragrant warmth over his senses.

"I hope you don't mind that I started," Brianna said. "I waited and waited until I thought the sudden spring zephyr would carry away my bones."

Annoyed as hell at his sister, Christopher pulled out his chair. He was in one of his quiet rages, and could not seem to rein in control. "What were you doing out there, Brianna? Inviting her ladyship to tea."

She continued to eat, but her chin dipped lower. "I like her," he thought he heard her say.

"Excuse me?"

"I like her." She snapped up her eyes. "I think she's nice."

"Hell, you think Williams walks on water. What do you know about people or their character?"

"More than you do. Mr. Williams happens to be a nice boy, who also happens to look up to you. Heaven knows why, since you insist on pummeling the lights out of him just because he likes me. You deserved being knocked onto your arse today. And as for Lady Alexandra, I do know her. A little," she amended.

Christopher accepted a cup of coffee from the servant. "You met Lady Alexandra?" His tone was doubtful.

"It was a long time ago. She came to Carlisle."

"When?"

"Just after you returned from India. It was when you were ill. No one would allow her near you." Brianna sipped her tea. "Papa told her that he would have the magistrate arrest her for trespassing no matter whose daughter she was. I was curious who she was." Brianna drew in a breath. "I followed her."

"You need to understand something, imp—"

"When I came upon her outside the gates, she was crying. She asked if I was your sister. She said that I looked like you. Then she said that she was sorry. I didn't know why. I still don't, except her father has something to do with your past. A past that no one will ever talk about."

Brianna folded her hands in her lap. "I understand that you will marry Rachel. After all, it's what Papa wanted. But it wasn't until I saw the way you looked at Lady Alexandra in the museum that I realized I'd never seen you look that way at another woman. A look like that bears investigating. Don't you think?"

Christopher dragged his hand through his hair. "Don't romanticize some glimpse you thought you saw into something it wasn't."

Brianna shrugged prettily and picked up her fork again. "I still like her. Even if you don't."

"Sir." Barnaby entered the dining room. A grizzled man carrying a tattered bowler followed. "This is the cabdriver who delivered Lady Alexandra here. He says he's been waiting long enough and wants to return to London."

Christopher looked first at one man, then the other. "The lady in question left an hour ago."

"Perhaps she did, perhaps she didn't," the driver drawled. "But she didn't go with me. And she didn't pay me fer bringin' her here."

"The gent's been playing the dice with some of the stable hands, sir," Barnaby explained. "He had an axle bearing loose and I'd given him permission to see it fixed. I had no idea he hadn't left with the lady."

"Pay him." Christopher tossed down the napkin and stood. "Her ladyship hasn't come back here, which means she's on foot."

The driver snickered. "Imagine someone that blue getting those dainty slippers dirty."

Christopher turned slowly. The little man blanched. "I didn't mean nothin'—"

"There's only one road to London," Christopher told Barnaby as he helped him into his greatcoat. "Have my carriage follow it. I'm taking Caesar. I'll meet the driver on the road."

With that, Christopher left the house.

Chapter 4

 ~~~⟨Oෙ⟩~~~

The wind had grown increasingly brisk. Christopher pulled back on the reins, sending his agitated stallion in a circle. He'd reached the crossroads that dissected the edge of his estate. The trees had thinned. He looked left, before electing to pursue his current course. Alexandra was too intelligent to take the wrong road. Overhead a bank of clouds blanched out the late afternoon sunlight. A shadow crawled across the fields. In the distance, he saw sheep.

With an oath, he nudged his horse. Alexandra was either the fastest woman on foot he'd ever known or she'd gotten a ride. The latter possibility annoyed him. It was bad enough form that she'd hired a cab to bring her out to his estate. He knew why she had. She didn't want her father knowing that she had come to visit him today.

He wanted to laugh. Some things never changed.

The just irony of it all was that the magnificent gossip mill would most likely have her in his bed before the month was out anyway.

The horse topped a knoll and he saw her in the wooded distance. A gust pulled at the folds of his cloak. His tall boots hugged the girth of the horse, staying his movement. The sun

came out from behind the clouds. He watched her turn and
shade her eyes, recognizing the frisson of awareness that
went through him when he knew she'd found him on the rise.
His hands tightened the reins and he allowed Caesar to take a
few prancing steps forward, before kicking the horse into a
gallop.

The road dipped for a hundred yards. When Christopher
topped the second hill, Alexandra had vanished. He found
the place easily where she'd left the road. Narrowing his
eyes, he surveyed the woods, listening for any sign of her.
The woods were too thick to follow on horseback. Her departure had all the sophistication of a quick escape.

So, the lady would prefer to walk the five miles back to
London rather than see him.

Christopher's mouth curved faintly.

He'd always enjoyed a good chase.

Alexandra stopped for the third time in as many minutes to
empty a pebble from her slipper. Her corset didn't allow the
freedom to bend and retrieve her shoes with any ease. She
was thirsty and chilled. She cursed Christopher. First for
turning down her plea for help when he could see her desperation, then for daring to have the audacity to follow her after
her wretched cabdriver left her stranded.

She glared at her muddy slipper. A hole had formed in the
sole. Her gaze moved in disbelief to her skirts. The tear in the
gray silk fabric reflected her dash to escape an ornery goat.
She'd lost a glove on the fence. Her hair hung in tangles to her
shoulder. For the first time in years, her thoughts did not reflect
kindly on the less fortunate masses. It was deplorable that her
driver had chosen to leave, for now she would not pay him, she
thought defiantly. Besides, he had her fur-lined cloak.

Alexandra gauged her direction. Shoving through a thicket,
she set her course toward the pub that she had passed on the
road that afternoon. She held her reticule close to her chest.
Surely someone would be heading into London. Once in the
city, she would hire another cab.

A plop of rain splattered on her cheek. Alexandra tented a hand over her eyes and looked at the ugly sky. The fragile warmth of the previous hours whimpered beneath the building clouds. A cold wind swept across the fields and beneath her skirts.

Rain spattered the moist leaves at her feet. Stepping over a fallen log, she picked up her pace. Already she was wet and cold. Over the frigid gust of wind, the whinny of a horse alerted her, and her head snapped up. She shoved the hair out of her eyes. A dilapidated barn filled the clearing, its sagging thatch roof having seen better days. Probably during the Middle Ages, she thought sourly as she gingerly bypassed a mound of questionable substance.

Limping now, she was nearly inside the barn when she saw him. Her heart choked off her gasp.

Christopher leaned in the doorway. Arms crossed casually, looking every bit as if he'd just stepped out of a man's fashion plate, he watched her with a cocksure expression.

"Oh!" She wanted to hurl a rock at him. How did he know where she'd be coming out of the woods?

The folds of his greatcoat whipped around his mud-splattered boots. He looked at the sky. "Are you planning on a bath, Alex?"

Her teeth had started to chatter in earnest. She couldn't breathe. "My name is Alexandra, Mr. Donally." She ran past him into the shelter of the barn. "This is your fault. If I p-pass out, I'll never forgive you!"

Life wasn't fair at all to throw him in her face like this. She hadn't done anything wrong to have her whole existence turned inside out. She bent over her knees to catch her breath. Lord, she was going to swoon. The wind billowed beneath her skirts.

He stripped off his riding gloves and walked toward her. "Turn around."

She struggled to straighten. "I w-will . . . not."

"Oh, for Christ's sake." His hands were on her shoulders and he spun her around. "You haven't anything I've not seen before. Or would you rather swoon in my arms and have me undress you while you're unconscious? Your stays are too damn tight."

Shivering violently, she felt his heat at her back. He unbuttoned her gown, his hands working swiftly as he began to pluck at the laces on her corset beneath. He unquestionably knew his way around a woman's garments. Sweet, icy air filled her lungs. Her nose captured the warm masculine scent of his body.

"In case it has bypassed that intelligent brain, madam"— his hands smoothed away the hair at her neck—"I am bloody furious."

"No m-more so than I, M-mister Donally."

A horse snorted and stomped, and Alexandra peered up through a tangle of hair. A stallion balked at his quarters, his long head hanging out over the stall.

Christopher's coat enveloped her. Two hands on her shoulders pulled her around, and she was looking up into his handsome face. She pretended he didn't smell like shaving soap and sunlight. Or that she didn't smell like this barn. He clutched the cloth of the coat and looked down into her pale face.

"How long did you think that you could keep walking?"

"I have n-no trouble walking."

Despite her feeble protest, he moved her to an overturned barrel. Her bulky crinoline made it impossible to sit comfortably or fight him when he knelt at her feet. She looked at the top of his head bent over her shoes. His short crop of black hair was a contrast to the white of his collar. "Where did you think to go?" he asked.

She buried her chin into the fabric of his coat. "There is a pub not far from here. That was my destination."

Bracing an elbow on one knee, he raised his face. "And you'd have asked a stranger to take you back to London rather than return to me?"

Grudgingly she conceded to the flaw of her strategy. Still, it had been the best plan available.

"You should have gone back to the house, Alex. My driver would have taken you wherever you wanted to go."

His coat had already warmed her and her shivering had stopped. She also had the wisdom to realize that he was right to loosen her stays. Though she would never in a thousand years ever tell him that. "Had I known I'd be strolling the countryside today, I'd have dressed accordingly," she said. "Exercise is not going to kill me."

"Aye," he said admiringly, and stood.

The horse snorted, and Christopher pulled him from the stall.

Christopher's gaze ranged the length of her and the quirk in his lips deepened into amusement. "I had expected to see you in a dead faint alongside the road three miles back. You've impressed me."

She narrowed her eyes but could not sustain her anger at him. It seemed like a moot point anyway. He was here, and she was warm. "So how did you know where I'd be?"

He walked the stallion to the barn door. Outside, the rain drummed against the ground. The air smelled of damp straw and meadow grass. "I own the land," he said. "I had the advantage. I simply rode ahead to the first logical place you would end up."

"This is all yours?" Alexandra pushed off the barrel and went to stand beside him.

Christopher wore a charcoal woolen waistcoat, black trousers tucked in boots. His hand went beneath his jacket to his hip, a man of the world, confident, yet so vulnerable, as if he were a boy and had just been handed a fragile gift.

He turned his head, his love for the land etched in every line of his expression. "Not so bad for an Irish lad," he said.

An aching tenderness welled up inside her. Christopher had come far from the younger man he'd been. Despite her anger, despite everything between them, she felt pride for his achievement. "It's truly beautiful," she said quietly.

The beat of the rain filled the empty space between them; then she watched his eyes change, as if he'd allowed her to see a part of himself that he didn't share with people. Certainly not with her.

He took a step away from her. Water dripped in the barn someplace. "I should spend more time here, but I don't. I have an estate in Carlisle more suitable to raising children. I don't like the politics here."

"Do you *have* children?"

The improper query lifted his gaze. His hands went gently over the black's long muzzle, and he said something soothing to the animal. "Not that anyone has told me about."

Watching the gliding movement of his capable hands, she frowned. Of course, he wouldn't have remained celibate all of these years, but the thought of him in another woman's bed twisted like a knife inside her.

"Brianna remembered you," he said. "She said that you went to Carlisle shortly after my return from India."

His jacket had casually opened to the waistcoat beneath. He watched her intently. Everything about him was boldly masculine and dangerous, and her thoughts were too intimate, too personal to share with a man who was now a stranger to her. Yet, she and Christopher had had a son together. They'd shared laughter and dreams and, for their brief time while they'd lived in Tangiers, they'd shared carnal intimacies that put her girlhood fantasies to bed forever.

Perhaps, in a way, her past needed more closure than she'd realized. But she was not going to tell him that she'd gone to Carlisle all those years ago because she'd wanted to start where they'd once ended. Or that she'd tried to bring their son home to England. Christopher's family despised her, and she wanted only to forget.

"That was a long time ago, Christopher. I hardly remember."

"She thinks that the two of you should be best friends."

"I hope you don't think that I encouraged her."

"Trust me. I believe you." Just as quick as the rain began, it slowed to a drizzle. Christopher walked to the barn entrance. "It looks like the cloud is passing. When was the last time you ate?"

"I need to get back to the museum. As soon as possible."

As if on cue, the muffled rattle of a carriage sounded from up the road. Christopher told her to remain in the stables. When he returned ten minutes later, he no longer had his horse.

"To the museum, then," he offered. "It's not too far out of my way. If that's all right with you?" He raised a brow.

Alexandra's first instinct was to pull away, but it would have been silly to argue when she was in need of the ride and the hour had grown increasingly late. Her hands clutched the coat tighter.

"After you, my lady."

She dashed ahead of him down a wooded path that led to the road. A black, stately carriage, drawn by two equally impressive black horses, restlessly straining their bits, waited. Right behind her, he helped her inside. The carriage was richly appointed in black leather seats. Everything about Christopher seemed starkly shaded in blacks and whites.

Except his eyes.

Alexandra squeezed into the opposite corner. His knee touched hers. Totally aware of his presence, she brushed at the water stains on her skirts and was suddenly very tired.

The coach jolted forward in a sluggish scrape of wheels and the jingle of harnesses, and she turned her gaze out the window. A dreary cloudy afternoon had replaced the bright sunlit morning that had greeted her when she'd awakened. The warmth of Christopher's heavy coat made her drowsy, and despite her awareness of his presence so close to her, she closed her eyes.

Alexandra was jolted awake when the carriage splashed through a puddle. She sat straight, her gaze going around the interior of the carriage. The lamp had been dimmed. The coach rode past thatched cottages with picket fences. They'd long since passed through the outskirts of London.

Christopher sat in the corner. His elbow on the ledge of the seat at his back, he leaned his head against his fist, his eyes hooded in the shadows. Heat rose in her face. Alexandra had the notion that he'd been watching her sleep for a long while now, and she barely resisted the urge to look down to reassure herself that her modesty was intact.

"Have I been asleep long?"

"A half hour."

She must look ridiculously disheveled. Outside, the streets were sloppy wet. She hugged the coat to her.

"What has he done to you, Alex?"

She snapped up her gaze, alarmed. "Who?"

"Who do you think? Or are you still making excuses for him?"

"My father is one of the most intelligent men I know."

"Don't confuse arrogance with intelligence, Alex. Or manipulation with compassion. You've become exactly what he wants."

His attitude was quite indicative of all the problems that had ever been between them. She dropped her gaze to her hands and brushed at her skirts. Christopher never truly understood about her father. Papa had lost the only woman he'd ever loved when her mother died giving her birth. All of her life, he'd taken Alexandra everywhere with him in the world, never leaving her with governesses or tutors. He'd defied protocol and allowed her a real education when women were not schooled in anything but social discipline. He may have arm-twisted the board to get her the job at the museum, but he'd done it because he loved her.

Which didn't excuse his atrocious behavior, but it did make her more sympathetic to the reasons behind his actions. Anything he ever did, he did to protect her.

Christopher's eyes reflected black in the dim light. He dropped his gloved hand. He held the White Swan, rolling the piece in his palm. She sliced her gaze toward her reticule on the seat beside her.

"How much are we talking about?" He held the Swan in the light, meeting her shocked gaze over the gem. "What do you estimate the value of what has been stolen?"

As her heart quickened, her mind fumbled for a response. "In the past year?" She mentally tabulated the market value of the missing jewels, most which were in fact priceless. "Maybe seventy thousand pounds."

Christopher sat forward. "Jaysus." He bent over his knees. "You aren't joking?"

She folded her hands in her lap. "I wouldn't joke about something that serious, Christopher."

"No." He eyed her critically. "I suppose you wouldn't."

"All you see is the money," she said, insulted that he would take everything that meant so much to her lightly. "Those artifacts were ruined, and for what?"

"That comment sounds like it came from someone who has slept in wealth her whole life. There's a lot worse things people do for money."

"That's not what I mean." Christopher didn't see the priceless, ageless antiques that had been destroyed for greed. "If someone wanted money he should have just robbed a depository. Those artifacts were hundreds of years old. Created while this country still lived in the Dark Ages fighting with swords and arrows, while cultures in China and Egypt had already survived over seven thousand years."

"Bravo, Alex." He studied her. "Then how is it that these thefts went undetected for so long?"

"Everything is kept locked and catalogued in a room. Every three months the pieces are rotated and put on display. It may be fifteen months before the same pieces are seen again."

"Then the thefts have been going on for a long time."

"I didn't notice until this last grouping went on display."

Christopher's eyes were not unkind as he finally sat back against the plush seat and crossed his arms. The cloth of his coat pulled at his shoulders. "I'll think about what you said today."

"You either believe me or you don't."

"I said I'd think about it."

"What is there to think about? I told you everything."

"It's not that simple, Alex."

She turned her head to stare out the window. "There is nothing new about that sentiment," she said with a laugh. "When has anything in life ever been simple?" The wind outside stirred the leaves in the street as the carriage passed.

"Do you like art?" he suddenly asked. There was unexpected affection in his voice and she lifted her gaze. "I understand that the opening of the exhibition at the Royal Academy of Arts was postponed until the end of next month."

She blinked owlishly. "Are you inviting me?"

The leather seat creaked. He sat forward and placed his elbows on his knees to look at her, his eyes so blue that Alexandra felt the sheer starkness of their color. "This is not some underhanded scheme I have to seduce you. As a matter of fact"—he turned his head, before bringing his gaze back around—"when you left the house this afternoon, I was quite glad to be rid of you."

The corners of her mouth lifted a little. "I hadn't noticed."

"My sister needs an introduction into society," he said as if arriving at a decision of great preponderance. "I know little about the machinations of your London Season. I've never had a need or desire to join in the fanciful politics of the *ton*. Brianna needs to be seen with the right people. You can get her into places I can't."

"Me?" Refraining from telling him that she was the most socially inept woman in all of Great Britain, she shivered at the mere thought of playing nursemaid to anyone.

"Let's say I think you're a capable woman if you choose to be."

"My debut was hardly a sterling example of success."

His gloved fingertip caught her chin. "You're wrong, Alex." His thumb slid over her bottom lip. "Look at what you've accomplished with your life since. Don't demean yourself. Not in front of me."

Unable to dismiss his intent gaze and the tingle that went through her, Alexandra felt her skin grow warm. One touch and he'd ruthlessly shattered all of her defenses. "You want to make a bargain with me? My help with Brianna for yours?"

"I'll grant you one better." Christopher's mouth curved faintly, but there was no mistaking that every inch of him was coldly somber. "I'll find out who your thief is."

"You're not feedin' me some of that famous Irish blarney, are ye, Christopher Donally?" She affected the accent he hid so well. "No one can ever know that I gave you this information."

His mouth crooked as if to tell her some things never changed. He'd taken all the risks once before. "Don't worry, your secret is safe with me." He slipped the White Swan into his waistcoat pocket. "You tend to your side of the bargain and I'll tend to mine. I'll leave the decision to you. Either way, Brianna needs a mentor," he said flatly.

Alexandra considered this. She dropped her gaze to her lap, unsure of the race of her pulse. Unsure of Christopher. But mostly unsure of herself. She was not a social butterfly and was entirely unsure of her ability to help, not hinder, his sister's cause. "If I were to help Brianna, then attending the art gala would be the best place to start," she agreed.

"Are you seeing anyone?" he asked after they'd begun to settle into silence.

She laughed at the less-than-subtle question. "Are you concerned that I'll not find an escort if I should choose to attend the gala?"

He flashed her a white grin. "Unless you think Papa Ware will approve of my showing up on your doorstep," he said, ignoring her glare of disapproval at his sarcastic use of her father's name. "So, do you have a beau?" He brushed at his trousers. "One who keeps your mind occupied with other matters . . . of a less intellectual nature?"

His voice shivered all over her. "Of course I have a beau. As a matter of fact, I am seeing someone," she flat out lied to his face.

She cast her gaze outside before he saw the blush crawl

over her face. It was none of his business whom she saw or didn't see.

"And you?" she asked after a moment. Lamps from passing coaches winked in the approaching darkness.

"I have no beau, Alex. Frankly"—his silky voice lowered, pulling her around—"I never did go in for that sort of sick entertainment."

"Oh." She untangled herself from his lecherous gaze. "Your wit is as dull as your humor, Christopher."

In truth, their dialogue was strangely liberating. She wasn't looking to be seduced by him anyway. She loved her work with the museum, and needed his help.

A tap on the window alerted her that the carriage was slowing. "We're here," Christopher said expectantly, as if awaiting her answer.

Alexandra bent forward to look out the window at the museum. Montague House and the newer wings of the museum claimed the whole city block. Outside, the busy streets were in motion.

"Oh, my God," she gasped.

Christopher followed her gaze to the corner, where Lord Ware paced not twenty feet from where the carriage had stopped. He wore his coat and hat, the newspaper in his hand, tapping his thigh.

Alexandra fell back against the seat. "He's probably wondering where I've been. What will I tell him?"

Christopher removed his coat from her shoulders. Her eyes widened in alarm. "What are you doing?"

He flung open the door. "I'm not riding around the block to hide from your father. Sooner or later he'll know you've been with me today."

He descended the carriage before Alexandra could push past him and escape into the crowd. Once on the street, he shoved his arms into his coat and shrugged it on his shoulders. She was paralyzed.

Propping one boot on the wooden step, he returned to fill the doorway. "Try telling him the truth for once, Alex."

"You don't understand. . . ."

"You're right. I don't. Do we have a bargain or not?" he asked.

"You have to let me think about it."

He smiled faintly. Before she could stop him, he placed his hands possessively around her waist and lifted her out of the carriage. Her palms pressed intimately against his chest as he swung her around, setting her in front of him. The full shock of his body against hers stripped her breath away. "I will give you until the end of the week." Persuasively wide shoulders blocked the street as he brought her hand to his mouth.

The effect was the same as if he'd kissed her full on the lips in front of God and all of London to witness. His eyes danced with lively amusement, and Alexandra jerked away from him.

"Oh!" she rasped. "You did that on purpose, Christopher Donally."

"Did I?" She watched his gaze lift and touch her father, who remained as if frozen by the last ice age.

"My lord," Christopher said dryly, his courtly bow no more servile than David ever was to Goliath. "My lady." He gave her a knowing look. "Until we meet again."

Speechless, Alexandra watched Christopher climb back into the carriage.

Damn him!

She whirled.

She strode past her father. "It's not what you think, Papa." Without waiting for a footman, she hiked up her torn and battered skirts and climbed into the waiting carriage.

Whatever ailment festered between her father and Christopher Donally, she refused to be the bone between them any longer.

By the time Christopher reached his office, he was lost to his mood. He shut the door behind him and, stripping off his greatcoat and gloves, walked to the windows that overlooked the Thames. The city was alive with lights, just waking up. Fog was setting in.

His leg ached, and he sat in the large wingback leather chair.

Photos of D&B's projects, framed in teak, lined the walls. A potted fern in dire need of a drink sat atop a bookcase. Its leaves littered the floor.

A knock sounded on the door. His secretary peeked around the corner. "Will you be here long, sir?"

Christopher lit the lamp on his desk. "I have to stay late tonight."

With Ryan gone, he had more than one bid to go over this week.

"Yes, sir."

"Stewart—" Christopher stood and removed his jacket, tossing it on top of his coat. His casual attire was hardly indicative of a man who headed one of the most prosperous corporations in Britain. He rolled up his sleeves. "Send a note to my man of affairs. There are some business matters I wish to discuss with him on the morrow."

Stewart looked over his wire spectacles. "Does this have anything to do with his son, Stephen?"

Christ . . . did everyone in London know his bloody business? But in truth, this business had nothing to do with the younger man.

"Your solicitor was here less than an hour ago, sir," Stewart explained, "to profusely apologize for his son's forwardness toward your sister. Would you like for me to recite the exact words?"

"No thank you, Stewart."

"Also, the RFQ for the next phase of the embankment project arrived from the Southwark office. I placed the drawings on your desk."

"Has Ryan sent word when he will be back from France?"

"No, sir. But your brother did leave an extra key to the townhouse. I can remain longer if you need me, sir."

"Go home to your family. No sense in your being out in this sludge."

"Thank you, sir."

The door closed behind the man.

Christopher turned his chair, his gaze steady on the distantly fading lights. He should be basking in his long-sought-after success at some prestigious club, rubbing shoulders with Parliament members who welded the funding ax over most projects in Great Britain. Yes, and a smart man would have learned long ago that entangling himself with royalty's pedigreed spawn would get him hanged at the scaffold of social blunders.

A ship's horn bellowed from somewhere downriver. In the muffled blare of the room, Christopher withdrew to the cherrywood cabinet and poured water on top of the fern from a decanter he kept there.

Later, he walked the empty hall, his boots sounding loud on the floor. D&B owned the three-story brick building with fifteen offices that fronted the Thames. He entered the long room at the end of the hall. Rows of drafting tables formed the center of the room. This was the heart of his firm. Where ideas were born. Where projects were put to paper.

Ink filled his senses. This was the one place in his life he felt truly at home with himself. Not the sprawling estates he owned. Not the world he'd bought with his money.

It was at the last table, nearest the window, that he set up his work space for the night. He pulled out the embankment project notes. And now, through his and Ryan's efforts, the firm was a major contender for the job of preparing the engineering analysis for the Channel Tunnel in the Straits of Dover. An engineer's dream.

If D&B was approved to head the project, no professional would ever again look down at the brash Irish upstart who not only stepped up to the ladder after his father's death, but continued to climb every rung to the top. The only loss was that his father was not here to see the success of the company he'd built.

Christopher never doubted that his father had believed him capable of doing the job. Even if Christopher had doubted himself. But some things ground into a man's psyche never went away, and he'd been crushed into mincemeat enough beneath authority's bootheel to know when to heed caution.

But a decade of lessons learned had not cooled that inner core of him that had so often fueled his dreams as a younger man.

He stared out into the fog-bound night. In the beginning of his career, he'd been an engineer who'd built bridges and roads for the army. He'd served on General Windham's staff in the Crimea, a young idealist, before he began working in intelligence under the foreign secretary. Before he went to work at the consulate in Tangiers.

The worst mistake of his life.

As his mind pulled away from his work, he slipped the White Swan from his pocket and dropped it on the drafting table beside his inks.

Christopher set his teeth and cursed the day he'd looked across a glittering palace ballroom in, of all bloody places in the world, Morocco, and saw Alexandra Marshall. The daughter of one of England's greatest diplomatic miracles, she was one of few women present. Strange, that he remembered to the stitch the platinum silk gown she'd worn. In a room bathed golden with candlelight, she'd looked like a moonbeam. What had started out as a bet by his friends to walk across that floor and ask Lord Ware's icy daughter to dance had hastily burned into a romance that ended when Alexandra became pregnant.

That ended when he'd married her.

There had been no special dispensation given to him. She'd been seventeen. He'd been twenty-one, untitled, and Irish, and so bloody in love that he would have waltzed barefoot through fire to have her.

God, he'd been a fool.

And Alexandra Marshall had not changed.

She could no more stand up to Ware than she had ten years ago.

Even with Alexandra carrying Christopher's child, he was transferred out of the diplomatic corps. Though Lord Ware

had spared him the disgrace of a court-martial, he'd seen to it
that Christopher never went near Alexandra again. With the
death of his infant son, he'd walked away from Alexandra's
glittering world and never looked back.

Christopher despised the aristocracy's vain and pretentious, holier-than-thou morality. He despised butting brains
with the narrow hierarchy of a government that chose to label
a man's worth more by the titles he carried than his deeds. In
Crimea, he'd witnessed the Earl of Cardigan send six hundred men to their deaths at the Battle of Balaclava in defiance
of the intelligence supplied him. The light brigade charge
never had a chance against fifteen thousand. He'd watched
the same arrogance in India when command after command
fell to a rebellion perpetuated by the simple conceit of the
elite.

Ironically, it was his very service in India that had won
him a knighthood. Not that he wished to carry the memory.
Christopher had returned to England with the prognosis that
he would never walk again.

His father's belief in him and a year's emotional healing
helped him rejoin the human race. In time, he went back to
doing what he did best: building bridges and roads.

Because of the patent his father held on the process that
created molten pig iron into steel, his company helped lay the
first steel rail at Camden Goods Station and Northwestern
Railway in 1862. D&B had been responsible for laying a
thousand miles of rail and building or designing over a hundred bridges across Great Britain since.

Now, at thirty-two years of age, Christopher was the head
of D&B Steel and Engineering. He was a member of the
Academy of Sciences, the British Royal Society of Architects, and had been awarded the Gold Cup from the Institute
of Civil Engineers just last year.

His company was up for one of the most prestigious projects of the century; yet, he still needed peer sponsorship to
get into the finest clubs in London. His bloodlines lacked the
proper color to see his sister welcomed into upper society.

Worse, he was Irish. But proudly so.

He'd told himself that Alexandra would provide the bridge he needed. After all, that was what he did best: build bridges.

But involving Alexandra again in his life, even for Brianna's sake, had been something more that a perfunctory bargain or the internal war he waged against her bastard father.

Christopher wasn't sure what exactly, as he pondered the science of his reasoning, or lack thereof. Maybe it was learning today that Alexandra had once gone to Carlisle and, despite everything, had faced his family to see him.

Maybe it was realizing that not one damn person had ever told him that she'd gone there.

Chapter 5

"My hair has dried, Mary." Alexandra adjusted her locket inside her bodice. "Do what needs to be done. I have to get to the museum."

"You're in a might hurry, milady." Mary worked Alexandra's hair into a thick bun at the nape of her neck. "His lordship has been up here twice this morning to speak to you."

"I'm well aware of that."

He'd attempted to speak to her last night before she went to the carriage house to work, and again before her morning swim. She and her father had barely spoken ten words since she'd climbed into his carriage looking as if she'd been pulled from the river. She'd explained that she'd been caught in the rain and that Christopher, with all the gallantry of a rat, had returned her to the museum. Naturally, she'd refrained from using the word "rat," but she'd been thinking it just the same, considering the unbelievably rotten nerve of his departure. Her father, wearing a stare she didn't like, had sat back in the carriage and said nothing.

In truth, what could he say?

He didn't own her. He didn't own her heart. Or her future, if she didn't give it to him.

Alexandra gave herself up to the spinning emotions inside, deeply aware of Christopher's hand in her mood. She'd hardly slept in days. The strange sense of excitement had truly lured away all common sense for her to feel anything but trepidation over accepting his proposal. She'd already sent him a note.

He was trusting Brianna to her care and tutelage. Toward that end, her first task was to find Richard Atler and ask him to attend the art gala with her at the end of the month. She would do that while at the museum today. He worked in the anthropology department.

"Mary." Alexandra critically assessed her reflection, lowering her gaze to the practical muslin gray dress that she wore. She turned away from the tall-looking glass and pulled her cloak off the bed. "I'm about to join the social scene this Season."

"You, milady?" Mary ran after her into the corridor.

"Lady Wellsby has a reading salon on Thursdays." Alexandra swung her wrap over her shoulders. "Surely, arranging my own introduction there can't be too out of protocol."

"No, milady. Seeing as how you do enjoy reading."

The stairs curved around the elegant marble entryway. A crystal chandelier twinkled. Somewhere in the house, a window had been opened, and Alexandra felt the scented chill of a breeze. Her gaze went to the tall clock at the bottom of the stairs. She was anxious that Alfred had ordered the carriage brought around before her father heard her in the corridor.

"Drat it all." The hands on the clock had not moved from last night. "It's stopped again."

Was she early or late?

Mary said breathlessly from behind her, "The thing hasn't worked correctly since his lordship balanced the weights last year."

"The pendulum isn't swinging."

"Don't ye be opening the case, mum," Mary gasped. "You know how his lordship fancies the thing."

"It's a beautiful clock," Alexandra retorted. "It should be

working." The glass door was locked. She lifted her gaze to the clock face. She would need a chair to reset the hands anyway. "Tell Alfred if he can't get this clock to work, then find a clocksmith. I will not see such a fine antique so ill-kept."

Mary's jaw dropped slightly as Alexandra swept out the front door. "Yes, milady."

Every day for the past five years, Alexandra had arrived at the museum before the doors opened to the public. Today, she was late.

Greeting the guard, she swept through the employees' entrance. Halfway up the stairs, she debated the best place to find Richard.

Her office door was unlocked. Swinging it wide, she came to a halt in the doorway. The very person she sought was sitting on her desk when she entered her office.

"My lady." He slid to his feet.

A playful lock of blond hair fell across his brow. He wore a shirt with a stand-up collar, silk cravat, and blue-checked trousers. His dress always bordered on the outrageous for a man who worked with antiquities.

"You are fashionably late today," he said, pointedly examining his silver watch fob. "Are you ill? Do I need to call a physician?"

Alexandra walked past him, her eyes raking her small office for any signs of disturbance. She would know the instant anything was remotely out of place. "What are you doing out of your dungeon, Richard?"

He raised a brow. "Maybe I've been concerned about you."

She stripped off her gloves. The room was a small airless chamber and his cologne overpowered her. She'd warned him a hundred times not to wear the stuff around her. It made her sneeze. "I think that you just want me to tell you what dastardly deeds are afoot," she said pleasantly.

He leaned a thigh on the desk. "Is that too much to ask from my future bride?" His eyes twinkled in mirth. "Besides, what man could you marry that would let you walk all over him the way I allow you to trod on me, my lady?" He bowed deferentially.

"Richard." She stopped him. "What are you doing up here so early?"

He made a production of studying his sleeve before lifting his gaze. "Actually, I needed your help downstairs. On a particular shipment that just arrived."

Instantly alert, she straightened. Excitement accelerated her pulse. "Has the Cairo shipment come in?"

"Last night." He nodded to the photos on her desk, which she had somehow missed.

Her hands splayed the photos in disbelief. She still smelled the chemicals on the paper. "These just came out of the darkroom?"

"I thought you'd want to see them. The pieces are magnificent, but the fellows who packed everything weren't exactly careful. I need an anthropologist who knows how to document everything for the display. But obviously you are too busy—"

"Wait." She stood. Richard turned, a bored expression on his face, as he clearly awaited her to prostrate herself in apology. "I'm not used to anyone showing interest in my skills. If I've trod on you . . ." Clearing her throat, she hurriedly said the words. "I apologize."

His eyes widened in mock disbelief. "She apologizes," he praised the ceiling. "Lord in heaven, I should document the occasion."

"Do you want my help or not?"

"I'm always interested in your skills. And naturally, your work, too."

Ignoring the innuendo, she decided to get to the subject at hand. "Do you like art? I thought perhaps you'd like to attend the gala."

His brows raised.

"This will be a strictly platonic arrangement, Richard," she warned. "We'll be in public."

"You mean you'll be using me so you can attend with the museum's newest trustee." At her shocked expression, he crossed his arms. His bright blue jacket pulled at his shoulders. "Father told me that Donally was seen bringing you back to your father. And that you were in rather a state of shocking disrepair. People have already started to talk."

"You would be in disrepair, too, if you were caught in a rainstorm."

"Ah, then he was merely acting the gentleman."

Alexandra sat. "I've accepted the task of introducing his sister to society. Mentoring her, so to speak."

"You?" Richard laughed, and Alexandra was beginning to get annoyed at him. "What do you know about society, dearest?"

"Posh! I've lived and breathed the air my whole life, and I don't mean the kind you suck into your lungs."

"Do you honestly believe that people will accept Donally's Irish kid sister?"

"They just *have* to like her, Richard."

"Why? So big brother will be nice to you?"

She glared at him. "This has nothing to do with Christopher."

"Christopher is it, now?" He sauntered to the door and propped a shoulder against the frame. "What better place in the world is there to watch the drama of the *ton* in all its glory unfold but at the opening of the art gala. Anybody who is somebody attends. This will cost you." He grinned. "I'll be expecting you downstairs every evening to help me catalogue that Cairo shipment. Maybe share a dinner or two with me."

The door slammed shut behind him, and she winced. Miserably, she kneaded her temples. Her pulse increased as her thoughts progressed to the broad-shouldered form of the newest board trustee.

Richard was wrong. She wasn't mentoring Brianna for Christopher's sake. She was doing it for her own. Christopher would help her find the man or men responsible for the thefts.

Turning in her chair, she set her focus on her work. The Cairo display was scheduled to go up at the end of the month. Her hands spread the photos over her desk. Recovering her magnifying glass from her desk drawer, she began sweeping the photos. Richard's enthusiasm was infectious. A dazzling display of skulls, seeds, pollen, and an array of urns and statues lay across three workbenches. These specimens were fantastic. She went to the next set of diagrams and photos. She was deep in concentration when a knock sounded on the door.

"Lady Alexandra?" The knock sounded again before the door opened.

Alexandra recognized her secretary's timid voice. "What is it, Sally?" she asked without looking up.

"Professor Atler was up here earlier looking for you. He said for me to tell you to go to his office when you arrived. The constable's here to see you, milady."

"The constable?" Alexandra set down the magnifying glass.

Surely Professor Atler could not know about the stolen Swan. He hadn't had time enough to do an inventory.

"Are you in trouble, mum?"

"No." Alexandra stood and brushed down her skirts.

But the sharp knife of fear slicing into her stomach brought home the fact that she trod on precarious ground. For theft was a felony, even if the object stolen was counterfeit.

A few moments later, Alexandra arrived downstairs. "My dear." Professor Atler guided her inside his office as if she were incapable of noticing the black wooden chair placed in front of the desk. Oaken cabinets stretched from the floor to ceiling. "I'm glad that you could finally make it to work today."

His tone was unmistakably brisk. Glancing at each of the two men present, Alexandra took the empty chair. She felt as if she'd just been invited to sit before the Inquisition.

"Milady." The constable bowed slightly.

He was a tall, thin man in a dark blue uniform. A monocle

hung from a chain around his neck. Holding a tablet, he introduced himself by name.

"What is this about?" she asked him.

"Are you acquainted with a woman named Bridgett O'Connell? She was a maid on your floor."

"Bridgett?" She looked at Professor Atler, confused. "I see her every night."

"She's been missing for nearly a week, milady. We are questioning everyone who works on the floor."

"A week?"

"When did you last see her?"

Alarmed, she folded her hands over her reticule. "Before I left the museum. Last Monday night."

"What time was that?"

She cleared her throat. "Seven o'clock."

He consulted his notes. "You were at the museum that late?"

Alexandra didn't glance at Professor Atler. She'd disobeyed his orders to leave that day. She'd stolen museum inventory sheets and still had her key. "I heard her outside my office door talking to a guard. I think she called the man Dickie."

Again he consulted his notes and the long list of names on the top. "Dickie?" He glanced over her head at Professor Atler. "Did we miss someone? I see no guards by that name."

Professor Atler was looking at her hard. "Are you sure that was the name you heard?"

Alexandra was disgusted with his constant doubt of her. "I'm not mistaken."

The constable closed the tablet. "She was talking to this Dickie?"

Their dialogue was more than friendly. "She seemed to know him very well. Do you think anything has happened to her?"

"We have to look into all leads, milady, but if you want my opinion, she wouldn't be the first woman to run off with a pretty face." He turned to the professor. "We can only hope she won't wait too many more days before she contacts her family."

Perched primly on the edge of her chair, Alexandra watched him leave. Men were such arrogant morons. What did they know of a woman's heart? Maybe the woman had family who disliked the match. She absently thrummed her fingers. If the maid had run off, Alexandra wished her the very best in life.

The door shut, and the room suddenly seemed to shrink by half. Professor Atler returned to his place behind the scarred and cluttered desk. She marked the chilly repose of his countenance, feeling as if all the blood in her veins were beating a tattoo on the drum of her ears.

"You did not sign out of the museum last Monday night. Why not?"

"I must have forgotten."

He crossed his hands at the wrist. "You were also in the vaults on Thursday."

"I am always in the vaults. I work here."

His cheeks flushed. "I'll be bringing in a team of experts from the university to oversee the necessary inventory." The look in his brown eyes was rueful. "It is my sincerest hope that you haven't tampered with evidence. By God, you could be brought up on ethics charges at the very least. I don't care who your father is."

Alexandra clamped her jaw. She studied the small strap of lace on her sleeve. Despite everything between them, her father had believed in her talent. But he was also a respected member of the House of Lords. A scandal of this magnitude would destroy him.

Professor Atler's power over her life suddenly seemed omnipotent. Drawing in a breath, she refrained from adding to the fire by telling Atler that every altered piece in question came from her department. He would find out soon enough and arrive at his own conclusions.

"I'm assigning you to the reading room until after the investigation," he said. "I must do the same with your staff."

"My staff has done nothing wrong," she whispered. "They're students. Please assign them to someone else's department. Something like this could ruin them."

"Not until all the facts are in." He looked down at his clenched hands. "I'll need your key. The one you have yet to return."

Alexandra's mouth tightened in anger. In spite of the air of calm she exuded, her stomach churned. She dug through her reticule. She didn't bother to make excuses for the fact that the key was in her possession. In horror, she felt the hot burn of tears behind her lids.

"I expect I'll be hearing from your father," she heard Atler say.

Ignoring the hint of misgiving in his voice, she stood and slapped the key on the desk. "This is an incident that I wish resolved as much as you, Professor. I have no desire to see my father sweep down to my rescue. But neither will I allow myself to be implicated."

Something flashed in his eyes, and he came to his feet.

But she held her ground. "I have not misidentified artifacts. Someone in this museum is a thief. Someone who has signed in and out of the vaults for months. You should be placing every Keeper in the reading room until your investigation is concluded."

After leaving Atler's office, Alexandra had rushed to find her staff and tell them the news. Sally was a mother of three. Her two aides were young men from the university who, despite her gender, had elected to intern with her. Then she'd watched as her office door was locked by security. Alexandra stood alone in the marble gallery with its huge glass window casements, and felt a tug of desperation.

The museum and all its staid elegance no longer held the power to cleanse her mind or lift her heart. She passed the giraffe menagerie out front and ran down the marble stairs. Wearing her cloak, she left the museum grounds. Her mind and body were numb, but she slowed and forced herself to walk, not run. Remembering her wretched corset incident, she found her mind unconsciously drawn more to Christopher's presence than the relevant fact that he'd practically undressed her in that barn.

He was the only one who'd agreed to stand by her.

The streets were busy. The *clip-clop* of horses' hooves registered ever so gently in the back of her mind. She passed curio shops, and bakeries, and little girls selling spring flowers. Someone bumped her. The air smelled brackish, and she lifted her gaze to find that she'd reached the Thames. Seagulls floated in the sky.

That she'd walked the streets alone gave her pause. She'd never been to this part of London, and shivered in distaste at the poverty. Without thinking, Alexandra continued to follow her feet. Attempting to escape the lewd stares and comments that came her way, she turned down the busy street and walked past miles of warehouses and teamsters driving huge wagons.

She found the brick structure at the edge of the business district in Westminster where she knew it would be. Entering the office building, she lifted her heavy skirts and climbed three flights of stairs. DONALLY & BAILEY STEEL AND ENGINEERING was engraved on the smoky glass door.

Inside, the room was alive with activity. A bespectacled man with wiry limbs and corncob hair looked up over the papers he was reading. He sat at a cluttered desk to her left. "May I help you, mum?"

Alexandra let the door swing shut behind her. She sensed rather than saw that people had become aware of her curious presence. The hood of her cloak still covered her head. "Is Sir Donally in today?"

"He is in a conference, mum. Do you have an appointment?"

Christopher's deep voice came to her from the corridor just off to her right. She turned her head. A transom opened at the top of a door.

"Mum?" the little man questioned.

"I . . ."

Alexandra had never been to a place like this. An element of raw energy filled the place. This was territory intimately connected to Christopher. Her gaze went to the photos that lined the wall. Half-built bridges, men carrying picks and shovels, the pictures drew a world far beyond anything that she'd ever known.

People like Christopher Donally built worlds.

"Mum?"

She turned to look at the speaker. "I . . . perhaps I should return at a more convenient time."

Down the hallway in Christopher's office, the talking stopped. The door opened and three men stepped into the corridor. "The plans look in order, Sir Donally," the taller man said. He slapped a brown bowler on his head. "I look forward to bringing your proposal to the committee."

Alexandra met Christopher's eyes, and saw him hesitate. Something close to a thrill shot through her when their gazes touched. Heat rose in her face. He was dressed casually in a snowy white shirt with his sleeves rolled up his tanned forearms. He wore a black waistcoat and trousers, and a gray necktie.

At the same instant, she recognized the shorter man who had exited the office, Lord Somerset. He was her father's whist partner on occasion, and had more than once visited the house. Heart racing, Alexandra turned back to the photos on the wall. "We will meet next month, then," Lord Somerset said. "With a decision."

Footsteps passed behind her. Out of the corner of her eye, she watched the door to the corridor close with a relief that nearly folded her knees.

"What are you doing here, Alex?" Christopher stood beside her.

Her gaze chased up to his face. She had been so sure of all of her reasons for finding herself in this building. Now she felt only embarrassment and a sense that she had intruded where she didn't belong.

"You have the ear of two very powerful men," she offered. "That can only be good for business."

His brows drew inward. "Are you alone?" A glance over

her shoulder confirmed that she was. "How did you get down here?"

She crossed her arms. "I walked."

"All the bloody way from Bloomsbury?"

Aware of his anger at her, she plowed on determinedly. "Have you had a chance to check out any leads yet?"

"No, I haven't."

"But why not?" It was impossible that he had not already looked into the matter. She had sent the note yesterday.

As if suddenly mindful of the attention they'd drawn, Christopher led her out into the corridor and down the stairs. She was acutely aware of his hand on her arm where the heat of his palm warmed her through the fabric of her gown. An array of plant life grew in profusion and filled the narrow entryway. Everything smelled earthy.

"Now, what is this about?" he asked when they'd reached the landing at the bottom of the stairs.

She leaned her back against the wall. "You've had my reply since yesterday."

He laughed aloud. She shot him a furious glare.

"Exactly, Alex."

"And you're busy."

"As a matter of fact, I am. But that's hardly the point." Outside, the rumble of a fast-moving wagon vibrated the floor. "You're going to have to trust me. This is not an overnight endeavor and will take time."

Alexandra knew she was acting irrational and sought to bring her panic under control. "In point of *fact*, Christopher Donally, I do have a right to ask questions. This is my life we're talking about."

He crossed his arms and leaned a shoulder against the wall. His arm brushed hers. "I have an appointment Monday to see a man."

"But that is days from now."

A brow lifted, and, aware of his displeasure, she examined a dead leaf at her feet. "Who?"

"I've arranged to talk to a man in the police force who

knows people on Bow Street." He tilted her chin. "I will be discreet."

"Do you swear, Christopher? On your honor?"

"My honor?" His voice softened. "Such as it is. I swear. If it makes you feel any better, I also spoke to my solicitor this morning, and he is compiling the names of all the known jewelers in London."

She started to cry. She leaned her forehead against him. He was too close not to touch. She didn't know what was happening to her. Her emotions had been tilted completely off center and now traveled as if on a runaway train. She was happy one instant, harried the next, crying in the next. It was as if the instant Christopher had stepped back into her life the floodgates broke.

She was not a weepy person!

His arm went around her. "Why are you crying, Alex?"

Alexandra huddled more deeply in her cloak. This whole scene made her feel childish. "I'm sorry." Her words were muffled against the fine white lawn of his shirt. "I should not have come here to bother you. I'll not do so again. I know it's fodder for gossip."

"Alex." His voice beckoned her gaze. "What else has happened?"

Her shoulders wavered on a sigh. She withdrew a handkerchief from her reticule. "I've been removed from my position at the museum, if you must know." She sniffed indignantly. "Professor Atler has delegated my talents to the reading room, where I will sit over tourists and students for the remainder of my life."

Christopher took her handkerchief and tenderly blotted at each cheek. "Do you trust me, Alex?"

Unwillingly, she raised her eyes to his. The Christopher Donally who looked back at her was not the heartless myth that rumors had shaped over the years. She'd looked into those same blue eyes long ago, when she'd peered across a crowded ballroom and had seen him walking toward her. He'd been wearing his uniform then. He was young, and brash, daring her with stormy eyes to dance with a man who was nothing more than a common servant of the crown. An Irishman. He was the most exciting man she'd ever met.

She laughed at her silly mood and retrieved her handkerchief from him to blow her nose.

"There." His hand fanned out over cheek. "I hope you are laughing out of relief. Or I shall feel sorely abused."

"I should be asking if *you* trust me," she said, recovering bravely. It had been so long since she had shared this manner of camaraderie with anyone.

His long-sleeved shirt was stark white against his dark waistcoat and trousers. He was beautiful half bathed in sunlight and shadows. "You never did explain the arrangements between your sister and myself."

Christopher's mouth curved wryly. "No, I guess we haven't progressed that far in our bargain."

"We'll need a place to meet."

"Naturally." He brushed the wisps of hair off her temple. "I wouldn't expect you to make the daily trip out to my estate."

"This should be fun, don't you think? Where do you think we should meet?" Her eyes widened as if just remembering something of import. "She will need clothes—"

"I'm sure she will." Christopher smiled faintly, and wondered if she realized that she'd just insulted him by implying that he'd not provided for his sister properly.

But then he no longer cared. She'd lifted her head and he looked down into her face, a strange tenderness engulfing him. He was holding her easily, his palm resting on the nape of her neck. They stood in the middle of this stairwell at Donally & Bailey Steel and Engineering, in a world that he had built.

"We have a great deal to accomplish," Alexandra prompted the silence, jarring him back to earth.

Upstairs a door slammed.

Footsteps tapped down the stairwell. Christopher took her elbow and pulled her with him outside into the bright sunlight. He shoved his hands into his pockets and, after admiring the crisp dome of blue sky, slanted his gaze at her. An iron bench out front of the building separated them.

They were standing casually on the walk, each excruciatingly aware of the other, when Stewart emerged. "Sir." He nodded to Christopher. "We have an appointment in Southwark."

For five minutes in that stairwell, he'd forgotten everything. "Thank you, Stewart. I'll be up shortly."

"Yes, sir." Stewart gave Alex a stern once-over before turning to go back inside.

She caught Christopher's gaze. Her brown hair was pulled back into a bun at her nape, her features too delicate for such a harsh coif. In the sunlight, her eyes were unmistakably green. "I should go now, so you can get to work," she said.

Neither of them moved. Her hand traced circles on the bench. "I was looking at the pictures hanging on the wall. Very impressive."

"Thank you." Something deep inside him stirred at the compliment. "My brother is in Calais," he said after a moment, detailing the fact that Ryan sought to obtain the feasibility analysis project for the joint Channel Tunnel. "Which is one of the reasons why I'm here in London. I'm working with the British finance and planning committee."

She nodded as if she'd understood everything he'd just said. Hell, he didn't even know what he'd just said. He gave himself a mental shake. Hailing a hansom cab, he placed her in the seat and leaned his foot on the step. "Ryan and I share a townhouse in Belgrave Square. Not quite West End but close enough to be considered respectable."

"Papa and I do not even live among society. We live near the university." She laughed, clearly an attempt to put him at ease on the subject, a gesture he didn't need but nevertheless appreciated. "I would like to get to know your sister a little before we attend the gala."

"You found an escort, then, did you?"

"But of course I did." She fluffed her skirts. "I told you I was seeing someone."

"Of course." He leaned an elbow against his knee and grinned. "And you never lie."

Turning to the driver sitting behind the cab, he patted his waistcoat, realizing at once that he'd left his money upstairs.

A smile twinkled in Alexandra's eyes. "Don't worry, Christopher." She thumped the ceiling of the cab. "It's good to know that some things haven't changed."

Before he could reply, the driver clicked the reins. His hands going to his hips, Christopher watched her ride away.

Alexandra stopped in the entryway and handed her servant her cloak and gloves. A glance at the clock made her flinch. At least it was working again.

"He's not home, milady," Mary said from the stairs. "We have been told to hold dinner."

"I'm not hungry," she said, without elaborating that she had just spent the whole day riding around London unchaperoned. She was too exhausted to explain. Nor did she care.

Standing in her room at the windows, she threw the curtains wide to the moonlight. Across the pond, the old carriage house shone through the trees as stainless as carved ivory. Her glance passed over the dove-gray bed hangings and drapery fabric, the shadows that laced the light like cobwebs that needed to be dusted away.

Until today, she'd truly not noticed how colorless her world was.

Chapter 6

"Hey, Mister Donally. You want I should smash that pretty face?"

Christopher flashed a grin. "You can try, Finley."

Dancing around the ring, Christopher ducked a gloved swing, and landed a punch across the big man's square jaw. "Not bad for a lightweight, eh, Finley, me boy?"

More than the need to exorcise the ghosts inside him brought him here tonight. He wanted to fight. Unlike Merryweathers across town, Gilliland's Academy, though no true academy in the formal sense, did not train the wealthy elite in gentlemen's boxing. At Gilliland's there was nothing gentle about a pugilist encounter. Coming here to Holywell Street to work out with the common masses was one of Christopher's many social vices. To London, Holywell Street and obscenity were synonymous, a visual cluster of Old London in the heart of the capital.

Home.

A place that he swore Brianna would never know. He'd not lived here long those years his father had first brought the family to London, but the time spent on this street had shaped the man he would one day become.

"That's twice you've let me hit you, Finley." Christopher snatched a towel off the rope that boxed in the ring. The heat in the gym made it impossible not to sweat. Neither he nor Finley wore shirts. "You've grown soft since I was here last."

"I missed you, too, Mister Donally." Finley accepted the towel to blot his face. "And here I been goin' easy to let you catch yer steam."

They'd sparred vigorously for the last half hour. Attempting succor for his uneasy conscience, Christopher had come here tonight, his mood strangely disordered. Hell, he'd not produced a rational thought since he'd watched the hansom drive away.

Seeing Alexandra in his office today had done something to him. The fact that she'd foolishly walked to his office to see him only added to her allure. He realized that he liked her idiosyncrasies and had always been drawn to her originality. Perhaps because his own restrained personality suffered the same damning quirks.

Nor had the confining years completely buried that man beneath the respected veneer of his job. He just hadn't realized how shallow the grave had been dug. Or forgotten the satisfaction gleaned from bucking what equated to a feudal caste system.

Or maybe his desire for Alex stemmed from that libido-rousing way she smelled when his nose was in her hair, without strong perfumes, or the way she'd smiled when she'd told him that his work had impressed her.

She was one of the few women on this earth who actually understood what it was that he did. Or, for that matter, showed any interest.

Christopher rubbed the kink from the back of his neck. The lessons of an ill-spent youth could not bank the restlessness that swam through his veins. He was already planning an excuse to see her again.

Someone brought over a bucket of water, and he dropped a ladle of the icy stuff over his head. Finley did the same.

Christopher turned his attention over to the man sitting on a barrel and leaned a foot near the Irishman's thigh. "Finley."

His wrists on his knees, he bent nearer. "I'm in need of a footpad."

The big Irishman grinned white teeth. "Are ye accusin' me of livin' a life of sin, Mister Donally?"

"What is life without sin?" He lowered the towel from his face. "Besides, anyone who takes kids off the street even for a few hours a day has my vote for sainthood." His glance led Finley's about the large room. The noise was deafening as groups of shabbily dressed kids sparred.

"The program's grown since you bought us them gloves," Finley observed before pinning Christopher with an inquiring glance. "What can I do for ye, Mister Donally?"

He lowered his voice. "If I gave you a job, could you be discreet?"

"As discreet as your shadow."

Christopher regarded Finley with solemn interest. He and the big Irishman went as far back as childhood. "I imagine that the buying and selling of stolen gems are handled by a certain few in this town?" Christopher asked. "I want to know if there has been a sudden influx of gems on the market and who has handled the flow."

Finley suddenly looked relieved. "I was worried for a time there, Mister Donally. Thought I was going to have to set you back on the straight and narrow."

Someone yelled from across the room, "You gonna come to the fight next week, Mister Donally? Most of the usual hobnobs will be there. Finley could win a hundred quid on this one."

Christopher eyed Finley up and down. "Are you going to win me back my money this time?"

Finley shoved to his feet. Not many people were taller than Christopher, but Finley was one. "Yes, sir, Mister Donally."

"So, you were worried that I'd suddenly become a jewel thief?" Christopher raised his gloves. "You've insulted me, Finley."

Finley's mouth turned up. "Yes, sir, Mister Donally. I think I'm going to like working with you again."

* * *

Alexandra pored over the storage shelves that contained periodicals, running a finger over plates detailing the dates of issue. A dull hum gathered in the aural chamber behind her. Rows and rows of leatherbound tomes filled the other cases for as far as she could see. Fumbling for her reading spectacles in the white apron that protected her dress from dust and ink, Alexandra applied them to her nose. She stepped upon a stool to further assess the periodicals stored on the top shelf.

Arriving at the museum early, she'd taken up her place in the reading room, and promptly decided, after sending off a brief letter to Lady Wellsby, that despite everything, Professor Atler may have done her a favor by putting her here. The Season was about to officially arrive. She knew in her heart of hearts that she would just shrivel up into the floorboards if Christopher discovered how completely out of her element this whole bargain situation between them had put her.

She'd perused every social column in every London newspaper printed in the last month, searching for pertinent gossip, names of prominent citizens, and events to which she could secure an invitation.

It was during her scan of the London *Times* that she'd uncovered an article detailing the scope of the Channel project. Christopher's name caught her attention, and everything else fled to the netherworld of the insignificant.

Christopher had been mentioned prominently as a contender to lead the project. Pulling out archived geological journals, she soon lost herself in reading about the rock formations in the Straits of Dover. The whole undertaking fascinated her, and that Christopher might play some part in its planning left her in awe.

Everything about him was stimulating, and she found herself wishing that they could talk about his work. She also knew that he was a private person and what he didn't want the press to know he certainly wouldn't share with her. Still, reading about chalk strata was far more interesting than parading around Hyde Park on Sundays.

The hollow echo of approaching footsteps intruded. Alexandra pulled her nose out of the periodical. Vaguely aware of the cadence of the steps heading in her direction, she bent and glanced through the cracks that separated the shelves.

Her heart stammered to a halt.

Christopher!

Wearing a dark woolen overcoat that fell below his knees, he walked with a predatory grace that exuded confidence. Heads turned as he passed. There was no denying the fact that he was dangerously attractive. Of course, she was biased and possessive, and the fact that she'd known him for over ten years gave her more tenure over him than anyone else.

She blinked. Realizing that he had not deviated in his course, she struggled to replace the periodical she'd been reading, then jumped off the stool and, patting her hair, rushed back to make herself look busy at the table.

The society columns were still spread out where she'd left them. Hastily, she refolded the pages.

By the time she'd gathered up the papers, Alexandra was convinced that he'd changed his mind about their bargain. What else could have brought him here?

Smoothing her skirt, she listened to his steps close in on her hiding place and straightened her shoulders. Christopher's gaze swept past her from down the length of the walkway. Stopping abruptly, he stepped back into the aisle. The stark shade of the coat turned his hair nearly black in the dull light. He was tall and nearly touched the lower ceiling where the periodicals were stored. There was heat in his eyes when they met hers.

"Mum." Sally's voice startled her. "I've found three other technology manuals on the Sommelier boring machine. . . ." Her tongue slowed as she looked up at Christopher's approach. "Sir Donally—" she dipped into a clumsy curtsy. A flush stained her round cheeks.

"Thank you, Sally," Alexandra managed, annoyed at her secretary's untimely arrival. "You may put them on my desk."

"But you don't have a desk."

"The table, then. Here." She wagged her hand when it seemed Sally wouldn't move. "Put them down here."

"The Sommeiler boring machine?" Christopher cocked a brow, not looking too unsettled to see her reading a periodical that contained his work. "You really must be bored. Those periodicals are practically technical manuals."

"What are you doing here, Christopher?" she asked.

He didn't attempt to charm or apologize for his presence. "I fully appreciate your ability to traipse three miles and not pass out. This museum is an exercise in exertion." He pushed her spectacles back up on her nose. "You are a difficult person to find."

Horrified to realize that she still wore her spectacles, Alexandra snatched them off her nose and shoved them in her apron.

"So, this is the infamous reading room?"

She grabbed his arm. "You walked *through* the reading room. This area belongs to the staff. You shouldn't be back here."

Removing his gloves, he glanced at the cluttered shelves. "I recall having this same conversation with you at my office." His gaze came back around, and despite her resolve to remain aloof in his presence, her heart skipped and thumped like a failing piston. "I thought that I would return the favor," he said.

"You have news?"

"Patience, Alex."

Patience was not one of her virtues. She would have told him if she weren't positive he didn't already know. And knowing Christopher Donally, he had analyzed all sides, oiled the machine, and put it on the street to work. She had only to trust him.

His gaze dropped to the newspapers in her arms. "Do you need help shelving those while we talk? I can't stay long."

"Do you have a meeting?"

"Among other things."

Consumed by an awkward restlessness, she straightened her shoulders and told herself to get back to work and quit acting foolish. His business with her was just that. Business.

Christopher followed her past shelves of newspapers and onto a catwalk, unconsciously bringing her slim ankles to his full view during the climb to the second tier of shelves housing every edition of the London *Times* ever printed. The acrid scent of printer's ink emanated from the dusty collection.

Christopher's teeth were exceptionally white as he grinned. "Impressive." He looked around at the tiers of shelves, giving her the same term she'd given him.

"Yes, I suppose it is." Her gaze met his. Their eyes held before she caught herself and turned away. "Except I don't belong down here," she retorted, putting away two newspapers. "I belong upstairs."

"Do I detect a hint of elite snobbery?"

"How would you feel if all of your talents were delegated to building the royal hound house?"

"If it pays." He shrugged eloquently. "Hounds need shelter, too."

Rejecting his comment, she slanted him a smiling glance. "So, I can hire you to build my doghouse?"

"Somehow I have difficulty picturing you with a dog. A piranha maybe. But only because of the novelty of owning a flesh-devouring predator." He grinned. "You won't have to wait two thousand years to study bones."

Alexandra could not repress a smile at his jest. In passing him, she let her skirts brush his legs. "I'll have to remember that."

"Does anyone ever come back here?" The full weight of the crowded shelves muffled his voice.

"Rarely."

"Then we're alone?"

"Hmm." She read the plaque in front of her nose and deposited another newspaper. "Better here than the vaults. Especially since you have an aversion to dead things."

Crossing his arms, he leaned a broad shoulder against the

shelf and watched her work. "You'll have to show me what you do in the museum someday."

"It's truly exciting work." She edged another step and filed another paper. "One day I think I'll write a book about it all. I've had work published in various science journals." Hoping to hear him extol some of her genius, she turned expectantly, to find him smiling down at her. "Have you ever . . . have you ever dug up an archaeological site when building a road?" she asked, aware of the fluster in her voice.

"A D&B construction crew came across old Roman ruins earlier last year while working on the Holborn Viaduct."

Like all attempts at improvement here in London, work on the famous viaduct had been preceded by mass demolition. A world of relics had been found. "Yes." The thrill of such a discovery lent animation to her voice. "The Romans were once a strong presence in the British Isles. Their form of government. Their engineering skills." She shelved another paper. "We are still discovering old coins in sheep pastures even today."

"You always did have a passion for history."

Alexandra looked up to find his blue eyes on her face. And suddenly the whole world stopped spinning.

"So did you."

At one time, anyway.

It was one of the things she'd loved most about being with him. They shared an interest in history.

"You never married again." He tucked a wisp of her hair behind her ears. "Why not?"

The question startled her. Her hand went to the place he'd touched on her ear. "Neither have you."

With an aloof shrug, he said, "I've been busy building a company."

"You're very rich, Christopher. You could have married a highborn bride for who you are. Have you thought of that?"

"An impoverished lord who would overlook an Irish commoner as a son-in-law for the pocketbook he brought to the family coffers? No, thank you. I like my life the way it is. Uncomplicated. You haven't answered my question."

"Pah. I'm too old to worry about such nonsense," she returned, her eyes full of gaiety. She may not desire marriage, but she had no qualms about enjoying Christopher's company.

"I imagine some young swain would have had to go through your father first," he said.

"My father has never been disagreeable to my marrying," she said offhandedly. "He was only disagreeable toward you."

"As I remember, I didn't inspire distaste in you."

He was behaving poorly and knew it; she read it in his eyes. Her heart thumped wildly against her ribs. Once, while they'd lived in Tangiers, he'd boldly stolen her away from her father's house. They'd picnicked in the ruins outside the city, the soldier and the diplomat's daughter. He'd been wicked and daring, and so beyond the strictures that bound her world. He'd made her laugh and feel unafraid, and after they'd eaten dinner, he'd pressed her back into the hot sand and kissed her. She'd never told him that his had been her first kiss, but he'd guessed just the same. He had the same look in his eyes as he studied her face now.

Tenderness.

And she felt something deep inside her respond.

Did he know that she had never been with another man except him?

He cleared his throat and studied the black tip of his shoe before lifting his gaze. "I came here today to tell you that Brianna is in town. I'm warning you now: She'll be a handful. Are you sure that you're up to this task?"

Her earlier fears put a brake to her thoughts. Would he tell her that he didn't want her? Her eyes glanced off his. "I am sponsoring her, not mothering her, after all. If anything, I was a young girl once, and probably know Brianna's heart better than you do."

"Indeed." His lips twitched briefly. He brushed his hand over her hair. "My concerns are about your father's reaction, Alex."

"Oh." Her response waned beneath the weight of his gaze.

She turned abruptly and, standing on tiptoes, struggled to re-place the last paper in her arms. "My father doesn't own me, Christopher. I will do as I please."

Moving behind her, Christopher took the paper from her hands and shelved it in the slot above her head. Alexandra stiffened as if bee-stung. The heat from his body, his scent, pinned her to the case. Every inch of her awareness focused, heightened on the movement of his hands as they braced the shelves next to her head.

"What are you doing, Christopher?" She strove to keep her voice calm.

"I don't know, Alex. Maybe I don't believe you." His voice was a hoarse whisper against her hair. No part of him touched her, yet she felt his presence over every inch of her flesh.

"Or maybe I want to tear down that prissy bun you wear." From over her shoulder, he lay a knuckle against her jaw and tilted her face. Her eyes widened on his. "Or just back you up against these shelves and shove my tongue down your throat."

Appalled at the primitive thrill that shot through her, Alexandra opened her mouth to reply. As if in slow motion, he lowered his head and covered her mouth with his own.

His lips were startling against hers, breaching the fragile barrier of her mind with a brand of flame. Her hand found purchase against his shoulder as if she would catch herself from falling. The masculine scent of his shaving soap melded with something deep inside, something aching to be set free.

Then he was turning her in his arms. His coat fell open around her. She felt the taut, hard muscles of his chest. In-stead of a starchy cravat, a tie disappeared inside his dark burgundy waistcoat. Somehow, she'd reached beneath his vest to the warmth beyond the fine cloth of his shirt. She opened her mouth to the sweet, minty taste of him, answer-ing the thrust of his tongue.

And wanted more.

Echoing his deep, feral groan, she kissed him hungrily.

Greedily. Then he was pressing her into the shelves, framing her face with his palms, and they were both deepening the kiss. His mouth was demanding, relentless, soft, and glorious all at once. The earth could fall into the sun and burn to a crisp. She would not know, nor care. Her skirts enfolded his legs. Her arms slipped around his neck, until she stood on her toes, her breasts crushed against his chest, giving even as she took, feeling erotic places in her body she hadn't felt in so long.

His thumb drifted over her cheekbone, a feather-light touch.

Slowly, his lips retreated.

Slowly, she opened her eyes.

And held his in a restless communion forged from the cold illogic of their actions. Awareness threaded like electricity through the air between them. She was cognizant of the heavy thudding of his heart, while her own raced in a maddened flight.

Whatever it was they'd once shared between them, whatever passion had been theirs, neither pride nor prejudice nor the years that had passed beneath their feet had vanquished it. The spark thrived and burned as if yesterday had never come to pass. Her blood burned with the fire. He'd tasted of daring and danger, and so much more.

He touched his bottom lip with his knuckle, and she saw for the first time that both were slightly swollen. "You've hurt yourself."

"I'll have to remember to duck faster."

She didn't know if he referred to her or to Brianna's Mr. Williams punching him the other day. His mouth curved wryly. "It wasn't Williams."

Then it was she.

There was no halting the flight of her courage and in its wake she felt only panic and confusion. He tilted her chin. "Listen to me."

"Don't you dare apologize, Christopher Donally."

"Trust me, Alex." His gaze laughed into hers. "An apology is the last thing in my thoughts at this moment."

"It is?"

"Aye."

Gathering her shattered poise, she drew in her breath and looked away. Her eyes widened in alarm.

"Richard!"

Alexandra practically shoved away from Christopher's embrace, his stillness uncanny as he yielded no room to retreat. He pulled back, but his arms were slower in releasing her.

"Richard." Her flustered hands smoothed the dusty cloth of her apron. "I didn't know anyone was around."

"Obviously."

She hastened past the sudden chill in the air. "Richard, this is—"

"We've met," he said flatly without extending his hand.

Christopher's smile was amused. "Atler," he replied in greeting.

"There are patrons downstairs asking questions that I can't answer," Richard said. "I think you should get back to your station."

Christopher looked from Richard to Alexandra, his eyes dispassionate. In the time it took her to breathe, his composure had returned. "I have a meeting to attend." He handed her a card. "The Belgrave address. I'll let Brianna know that she can expect to hear from you."

"Thank you."

Nodding politely to Richard, Christopher left the catwalk. Alexandra leaned against the rail, listening to his footsteps recede, until she glimpsed his tall form disappear around the shelves.

"I'm shocked." Richard's droll voice spun her around.

"You didn't have to be so rude. What is wrong with you?"

He took a step toward her. "While he had his tongue in your mouth did he by chance mention to you that he's betrothed?"

Alexandra's reserve cracked with a familiar mixture of

shock and dread. She looked away, angry with herself for giving Richard the satisfaction that his words hurt. She didn't know any such thing.

"It's true," Richard said. "She's an Irish lass, a longtime friend of the family, the daughter of the other half of D&B. The announcement hasn't been made public yet because your black knight is busy with two major projects here in London."

"How do you know this?"

"Donally is a museum trustee. Gossip is rampant among the ranks since he walked in to see you. Everyone loves an underdog as much as they do a good scandal."

"Are you planning to tell anyone what you saw?" She crossed her arms. "Because if you are—"

"Let me court you." He grinned, and the cavalier Richard she knew appeared in a burst of white teeth and sunlight. He wore a jaunty blue-checked jacket and red waistcoat. His pants were yellow. "I could serve as your protector, vanquish your foes. Make an honest woman of you before Donally sinks his claws into you."

"Trust me." She edged past him. "We've been friends too long for you to ruin everything between us. I don't need another protector. And there's nothing wrong with my honesty."

He stopped her before she reached the stairs. "The man's cold-blooded, from what I hear. If you don't believe me, ask him what he did to receive those medals that graced the chest of his royal uniform."

Alexandra remained riveted in place. Finally, she lifted her chin. Richard, who had never behaved so wretchedly physical toward her, awaited her response. And suddenly she became aware that the man over whom she felt a slight superiority was sorry for *her*.

"I have work to do, Richard."

"You're naïve," he called after her, "to think that Donally isn't enjoying this game. What other reason would he have to suddenly show up in your life again?"

It was true that Christopher had thought up the bargain between them. But not once since that day in the carriage had she considered that he'd gotten the better end of the arrangement. Whatever reason he'd had to invite her back into his life again, she needed him more.

With that thought in mind, she left the reading room. Cornering Professor Atler outside his office, she told him to cut her hours, explaining that the only reason that she consented to present herself even for four hours every morning was because her staff needed her. She was helping her two aides complete their dissertation for graduation.

After quitting Professor Atler's stunned presence, she walked out of the museum, hired a cab, and did something she hadn't done in years. She went shopping.

One elbow propped on the desk, Christopher toyed with the pencil in his hands. He was not normally susceptible to distractions, or daydreaming, or any other form of comatose behavior, yet he'd long since abandoned the columns of numbers. He stared out the large picture window overlooking the busy street in front of the townhouse. The heavy velvet drapes had been pulled back, leaving the sheer muslin beneath. He could see the dull glow of lamplight and hear the clip-clop of traffic. The rain had started to fall shortly after dinner. Drops pebbled against the eaves of the house and dripped on the outside sill.

With an oath, Christopher pinched the bridge of his nose and refocused on his work. He should shut the damn curtains so he could concentrate. He had a fist-high stack of papers to go over tonight—all written in French.

Ryan had forwarded the financial report on the Mont Cenis tunnel project currently being undertaken in the mountains between France and Italy. The enterprise was the forerunner to the Channel project. One that D&B had vested economic and personal interest. He flipped through the pages of his tabulations. The world had leaped forward since the days Hannibal had marched his hundred-thousand-man army and fifty elephants over that pass in 218 B.C. to attack

Rome. Now a Sommelier boring machine had the ability to cut through solid rock. Think what something like that could accomplish beneath the English Channel.

Voices outside in the hall drew his head up. He thought he'd heard the front doorbell. A moment later, a knock sounded on his door.

"Beggin' your pardon, sir." Barnaby stepped around the door when Christopher bade him to enter. "This telegram arrived from Calais."

Knowing that it was from his brother, Christopher popped the seal and read the message. Excitement tightened his chest.

> LOOKS LIKE WE'RE IN FROM THIS END. STOP.
> DEPENDING ON YOU NOW, BIG BROTHER. STOP.
> BE HOME SOON. R.

"Good news, sir?"

"Very good news." He cleared away the papers from the clock that sat at the edge of the desk. "It's still early." He could have most of his work finished before midnight.

Christopher had already had the first interview with the planning board. The second meeting was scheduled next month. With the French approval for the project analysis, D&B had more than a toehold in.

He looked up to see Barnaby still standing in front of the desk. "Is there anything else that you need?"

Footsteps padded down the hall. "Christopher!" Brianna burst into the room and waggled a note. He tilted his head, slightly recognizing at once the owner of that penmanship. "Lady Alexandra will pick me up tomorrow. I have been invited to my first tea."

Christopher walked to the window and drew aside the sheer drapes. Lamplight washed over the wet surface up and down the busy roadway. "That's nice, imp." A carriage was waiting to pull away from the curb and into the traffic. He could see the pale outline of a woman inside. She wore a hood. He thought he saw her pull away from the glass. "Who delivered the message?"

"The lady's driver, sir," Barnaby said.

"If you don't mind, I shall retire." Brianna whirled in a swish. "I'll have to be rested for tomorrow."

Christopher lifted his gaze to see his sister's purple skirts disappear around the doorway. "Gracie goes with you at all times."

"But of course," she called over her shoulder. "A lady always brings a chaperone along."

A seed of admiration for Alex took root. Until this moment, Christopher hadn't been convinced that she would go through with her part of their bargain. Eyes narrowing, his gaze went to his jacket behind the desk.

"Sir—"

"Wait here, Barnaby."

"Sir." His steward seemed to brace himself. A globe framed by an ornate wooden trestle sat near the desk. "You've a lot of work to do tonight. With the rain, your leg must be bothering you. Perhaps you would care for a cup of hot cocoa? They say chocolate does wonders for one's constitution."

Christopher's hands had frozen around the jacket, the urgency driving him a moment ago fading. He was not a man prone to spontaneity, yet he'd been about to race out of the townhouse to catch the carriage.

And Barnaby had seen it all over his face.

"Thank you, Barnaby. Chocolate would be a . . . wise choice."

"I'll leave you to your work, sir." Barnaby shut the door behind him when he left.

Christopher remained standing with his coat still in his hand. Bloody hell!

He tossed the jacket back on the chair, and found himself returning to the window, watching the carriage rumble out of sight. He hadn't maintained such a monkish lifestyle that he should be straddling the brink of his restraint like a randy neophyte fresh out of the schoolroom.

Yet, his will betrayed him. The memory of her scented hair, the taste of her in his mouth, her softly curving form, had whetted his appetite to no small degree. He shut his eyes.

And it was with a flailing sense of awareness that he realized his decade-old dissension with Lady Alexandra Marshall had ended at the museum, the moment his lips had touched hers.

Chapter 7

"**R**otten Row." Brianna laughed and turned in a circle. "What a wretched name for such a beautiful place."

Fashionable people arrived in Hyde Park during the hours of eleven and two to take in the air, Lady Wellsby had told Alexandra.

Indeed, people coalesced like colorful butterflies, others strolling the flowered walks, their unhurried pace due in part to the warmth and hour of day. In the years since Alexandra had first emerged in society, she was surprised how little protocol had changed. She absently straightened her sleeves, patted her hair, and gazed at the surrounding skyline. For the past week, Christopher had taken other transportation around London and had left Brianna the carriage.

Turning back to Gracie, who remained in the carriage with her feet propped and her expression downtrodden, Alexandra smiled in sympathy. "We'll make our rounds and should return in a few hours."

"Thank you, mum," poor Gracie said. "My feet are killin' me dead from yesterday. And the day before. They are." Her voice lowered. "I don't see how ye can keep up with the lass, milady."

Brianna had already walked toward the path, her eagerness having become contagious in a disjointed way, if only for the fact that somehow Christopher's impish sister had escaped the corroding prudery that enshrouded almost every aspect of life in Queen Victoria's England. Brianna took color from her surroundings. And to her family's credit, she was remarkably schooled in the social graces, a vision of the Paris fashion plate, and quite adept at holding her own in any crowd. With little preamble this week, she'd played whist with the masters at Lady Biddleton's, croquet at Lady Pomroy's, and archery in Lady Blasedale's backyard, defeating a crowd of shocked debutantes by a bull's-eye.

"Is it wrong that I should play to win, my lady?" Brianna had asked later, clearly disturbed by how some had treated her.

"It's never wrong to perform your best," Alexandra had replied. "Do not allow someone else's doubt to cheat you of your victories in life."

Even if Christopher's sister had not won political points for humbleness, she did win Lady Wellsby's attention and an invitation to join the reading salon on Thursdays.

In the distance, scaffolding had been erected over a church steeple. The staccato of beating hammers rose over the street traffic hovering like an unseen cloud above the park. Brianna had told her that Christopher was attending meetings around here today.

And at once, her whole mood shifted and warmed her all over. Alexandra smoothed her skirts. Since that day in the museum, her awareness of him evoked something illicit, something exciting and forbidden as sin. She'd not been prepared for the feelings he'd evoked. Or the restless yearning she did not recognize in herself.

Indeed, she had not been prepared for him.

She and Brianna strolled the park, stopping as the occasion invited to greet someone they might have met this past week. Her beautiful charge drew the interested eye of more than one young swain, but Brianna, the practiced flirt, ignored them all. Except one.

"Look, oh, look!" She pointed before Alexandra could catch her arm. "It's Mr. Williams. What is *he* doing here?"

The young man turned, as did a dozen others. But it was Stephan Williams's tall form that held Brianna's gaze. The young man was walking a handsome roan, clearly on his way toward the exit across the park. He was dressed casually in the manner of a delivery boy, and Alexandra saw that the saddlebags on the horses were full of packages.

"You are here as my chaperone," Brianna whispered, her excitement barely contained. "There can surely be no harm in saying hello."

Except Christopher would personally put her in the boxing ring himself if she allowed Brianna's reputation to be compromised. But something in Brianna's bright gaze warmed Alexandra.

"Control yourself, Miss Donally," Alexandra said. "You may greet him on our way past. And if no one hears you, you may tell him that we'll be walking the park tomorrow at the same time." She smiled sweetly through her teeth. "Because Lady Wellsby is headed our way."

Christopher rarely left the office until after seven. The first to arrive and the last to leave, his employees had often wondered if he might sleep on the rosewood conference table in the adjoining room. But today he'd left before five. He'd been finished with his work or good portion of it, when his solicitor had dropped by the office. He'd been too restless to sit in traffic, so walked the last six blocks to the museum. What he'd seen of his sister this week, she'd never looked so happy.

He shouldn't have felt anything but calm. Certainly not the uneasy feeling that had solidified into the restlessness that drove him now.

Christopher reached the museum. Pigeons roosted beneath the eaves of the main entrance. Bypassing the messy steps, his feet carried him over the pebbled concourse, past the private residences. Scaffolding had been built up and down the length of the building, its neoteric presence a monument to progress. After all, this was the decade of the betterment of life. It was ironic that while Alex served to preserve the old, he made his living destroying it. And he'd always done so with a mercenary zeal, as if scraping away the past would somehow improve the future.

Yet, some things, he'd come to learn, were worth preserving. The estate he'd purchased outside London was one.

"Lady Alexandra left an hour ago, sir," the uniformed guard at the back entrance informed him after he'd trekked through a pile of rubble to reach the desk. "Professor Atler escorted her home."

"Atler?" Christopher's tone betrayed more than surprise.

"His son. Richard Junior, if you may. Though I would never call him that to his face. He hates the name."

"Why is that?" Christopher found himself asking despite the fact that he didn't give a roach's ass what Atler liked or didn't like.

The guard leaned forward on an elbow. "He's nothing like his father. He'll be the first to dress a man down for calling him Professor Atler."

That was an interesting tidbit. The kind of information that should be filed away, he was thinking when his gaze fell on the pass-key box behind the desk. A quick scan of the room followed. Some measure of security had been taken to prevent entrance into this room from the outside. A metal bar this side of the exterior door provided an added measure of strength to sturdy English oak. A window built high on the wall was too small for any mature adult to squeeze through.

"Who has access to those keys?" Christopher asked.

The guard turned to look at the glass-encased box. "Only a handful of staff." He pulled out the manifest. "No one takes a key without signing for it. Even for an hour."

Christopher held out his hand. "May I look at that?"

The guard handed over the tablet to Christopher. "I suppose, seeing as who you are, Mr. Donally."

Christopher flipped the papers back and forth. Names and times listed went back only a month. "Where are the rest of these records?"

"The old tablet sustained water damage. As you can see, much of this room is under construction and will be part of the new museum."

"How convenient to lose everything." Christopher noted that Richard Atler was predominately listed. So were Alex and a half dozen others. "Does someone man this desk at all hours?"

"Yes, sir. There is also a night watchman on duty outside at the gate and two in the museum."

Christopher handed the tablet back. If someone were stealing from the museum, the thief certainly wouldn't sign out a key. Would he?

"You going to the fight tomorrow night?" the guard queried, and Christopher suddenly focused on the question. "I've seen you at the gym on Holborn," the man explained. "You're not like most fancy gents what pass through here, sir."

Christopher pulled out his card. Borrowing the guard's ink and pen, he scribbled his address on the back. "Do me a favor Mr. . . ."

"Potter," the guard said.

"I want to know if anything interesting has happened here in the past several months. Employee gossip. Think about it and pay me a visit."

"Yes, sir, Mr. Donally." The guard accepted the banknote Christopher added to his card.

Walking outside, Christopher looked at the blue sky. It was as much his business as anyone's on the board to root out problems with security. The more he rooted, the more concern he had for Alex. Why had she been the one targeted? Was it her perceived inexperience that made her an easy scapegoat? There was nothing intellectually weak about Alexandra Marshall.

His coat restlessly batted at his knees as the breeze swept through the courtyard. Children played to his right, and turning his gaze at the happy sounds, he stopped, his pensive mood vanishing as abruptly as if the sky had just dumped a tub of ice water over his head.

Alex stood with Richard Atler on the porch of the massive residence across the enclosed courtyard. Greek columns bracketed their tender display of affection. Christopher watched her laugh as Atler showed her some waltz movement with his feet, the loving tableau played out in front of God and the whole world to observe. Her laughter made her delicately boned face radiant, an image of breeding and serenity, that had always attracted him to her. Christopher shoved his gloved hands into his pocket.

A surge of possessiveness stunned him almost as much as the recognition that he'd been chasing after her. The notion was unbelievable to a man who had prided himself on a certain amount of ruthless control. He had survived a decade without seeing her and two contemplating the possibility of marrying another woman. That Alexandra Marshall should encamp in his mind now reeked of more than the absurd.

It reeked of bloody irony.

He started to walk away—then changed his mind abruptly, when Atler took that moment to look up and catch Christopher's stare.

Neither moved. Only now Christopher took in the couple with detached interest. The man bent his lips near Alex's ear and said something that made her turn expectantly.

Shadows drew across the courtyard as a cloud passed before the sun, so he beheld little of her expression. But he'd felt the warm touch of her eyes. Felt it go through him.

Lifting one side of her skirt, she hurried down the stairs to where he stood below the branches of a tree.

"Christopher." Cheeks flushed, she drew alongside him. "You should have sent word that you would be here tonight."

His gaze lifted over her head to find Atler watching them.

"You're quite fortunate I'm still here." She plucked a piece of plaster from his coat sleeve. She was remembering their kiss. Or maybe it was only he who was remembering.

"Richard and I are working on a project together. Perhaps next time you're here, I'll show you what I do," she said.

"I don't think that would be wise, Alex."

Her smile had begun to fade, and he was disappointed to see it go. But there was nothing he could do for that. Traipsing around the museum with his ex-wife was the worst possible move he could make. He regretted making the suggestion earlier.

"Have you any news, then?" she asked.

He gave her a brief rundown of what his solicitor had told him. There were four hundred jewelers and pawnbrokers in London proper alone to interview. "My guess is that after everything is said and done I believe your jewel thief is conducting business outside of London. Until the interviews are finished, the news may be slow. I wanted to warn you."

Her gaze suddenly embraced his. "This is the first time that you've actually told me you believe someone else is the thief."

"Do you think I'd allow you within an inch of my sister if I thought you guilty?" He cupped his gloved hand to her chin. "Whatever has happened here is not your fault."

"Thank you." She leaned her cheek to his palm. "I know this must sound terribly unsophisticated. But thank you for believing in me."

Her presence, her smile, the sunlight in her leaf-green gaze suddenly left him wading through animosity he didn't understand.

"That was never the problem between us," his voice lifted her gaze. Then he pulled away his hand, aware that they stood in the rose-scented courtyard surrounded by the sound of children playing. Aware that Richard Atler watched them from the sprawling porch of his residence.

She stepped awkwardly away and the distance between them tripled. "No, I suppose it wasn't."

He glanced at the street. He'd never lacked for confidence, yet even now, when life flowed all around him, there was that part of him that remained cloaked in doubts. He'd torn away and rebuilt so much of his past that it shocked him to see the fist-sized hole that suddenly gaped before his eyes. "I need to go," he said.

"Don't you want to know about your sister?"

The words stopped him. Somehow he'd forgotten that had been part of his reason for coming here tonight.

"Perhaps if you were home once in a while you could share some of her triumphs." Her voice hinted suddenly of reproach. "Small as they are at the moment."

He laughed at her gall. "Is that a reprimand?"

"As a matter of fact, it is. You hired me to do a job. . . ."

As she continued to speak, his gaze eased down her throat, touching the pulse that beat at the porcelain-smooth base of her neck, then ambled over the curve of her perfect breasts. Perfectly fit to his hands.

"Christopher!" She arrested his attention. "Are you listening?"

His eyes settled on hers with mercenary precision. Having been caught with his hand in the sugar bowl, so to speak, he merely lifted his brows. "No, I'm not," he said flatly. "You were saying?"

"You can expect my report on Monday," she said diplomatically, clearly wanting to do the right thing by their bargain, yet, in typical fashion, reading everything all wrong.

"Your what?"

"You do wish to be apprised of her progress, do you not? I have recorded everything of importance in a ledger for you to go over."

He restrained the urge to roll his eyes. "Why am I not surprised that you would write a report on my sister and submit it to me for review? Why not just an outline?"

"Because a report is more thorough."

She'd crossed her arms, and even while he knew he was acting the ass, he didn't have the power to stop himself. "And will this feasibility analysis be complete with a conclusion and recommendation?" His gloved hand swept the air. "*The Social Trials of Brianna Donally.*"

"Of course not." She'd rallied sufficiently to narrow her

eyes. "I would title it *The Social Blunders of Christopher Donally*. Chapter One: 'Don't Kiss the Sponsor Then Ignore Her Existence.' I don't know what you expect from me, Christopher."

He knew precisely what he wanted from her at that moment. A quiet corner would suit him fine. Fixing his eyes on her face, he raised a brow. "Have you missed me, then?"

Alexandra's spine snapped to attention. "You have a pontifical opinion of yourself, Christopher Donally, to think that I would be mooning over you all week."

"Is that correct?" He grinned, unabashed despite the insult. "Pontifical?"

"Pompous, arrogant . . . self-important."

"Is Richard Atler your lover?"

Alexandra's chin went up. "Is Rachel Bailey yours?"

He continued to look at her, his blue gaze unrelenting. But Alexandra had seen something flicker in his eyes.

"She is the other half of Donally and Bailey, is she not?"

"The last I heard she was."

"I suppose men have no qualms about taking lovers," she said.

"If you're asking whether or not I've been celibate for ten years, the answer is no. If you're asking if I've taken Rachel Bailey to bed, the answer is most *adamantly* no. She's barely older than my sister."

"I was your sister's age when I met you."

He bent nearer, his eyes blazing. "You were *never* Brianna's age."

Turning on his heel, Christopher stalked away.

Alexandra stared at his back, thoroughly alarmed by the magnetic pull of those words and his dismissal of her all in one hot raspy breath. She didn't know what she'd done to anger him. Especially since he had been the one to seek her out.

Richard joined her moments later. Christopher passed through the iron gates that separated the busy street from the private residential grounds, broad shoulders shifting beneath his coat as he hailed a cab. He was a few inches taller than most of those who surrounded him, and her gaze followed him easily.

Richard tilted her chin, his mouth tightening into a thin line. But there was only compassion in his eyes when he finally spoke. "There can't be any two people more mismatched than you and Donally," he said quietly.

"Don't you think I know that?" she snapped, angry with herself for losing control. "I'd also forgotten how impossible he could be!"

Except being near Christopher was akin to standing on a bridge during a lightning storm. Alexandra found she could no longer just think about him without feeling some jolt to her sternum. Drawing in a deep breath, she welcomed back her old routine, even if it was only a few hours each week. Richard had asked her to help prepare the Cairo exhibit. Brianna had pleaded to come to the museum to see what it was that Alex did, and Alex had momentarily experienced a shameless urge to parade herself in front of Christopher's impressionable sister.

On the downside of her morning, four men were currently taking inventory in *her* department, sitting judgment over her work, and Christopher was clearly refusing to acknowledge the attraction between the two of them. That one single passionate kiss had reduced her to a witless half-brained Nereid should have been impossible.

Christopher was no longer present when she arrived to pick up Brianna in the mornings. She had not seen him in days. Perhaps men were more adept at emotional castration, or maybe his clear-cut methods of duck and avoid were more honed than hers. For the moment, her mind itched to escape the condition in which she'd found herself mired.

"You must have gone to school for years just to learn what everything is in here." Brianna's voice held amazement as they threaded through the labyrinthine hallways that made up the upper and lower levels of the storage vaults. Even with the size of the museum, every square inch of space seemed to be utilized by some artifact.

Few people realized how little of the museum was actually on display compared to what remained in storage.

"Everyone has a specialty." Alexandra turned up the lamps around the storage room. Light chased away the shadows. She ran her fingers down the line of specimen containers on the shelves. "In my case, it helped to have a father sitting on the board of trustees for two universities."

"Christopher couldn't get into Oxford or Cambridge." Brianna traced a gouge in the workbench. "But he lets very little stop him. My whole family is stubborn in that way."

Christopher was Catholic. It was a known fact that if a man didn't belong to the Church of England, some doors would always remain closed. He had graduated from the Royal Military Academy at Woolwich, earning his commission by merit, not by purchase.

Alexandra pulled out a tin box containing samples that she'd been cataloguing. She set them on the bench, and leaning against the table's edge, she looked at Brianna. "Do you ever see anything of your brother?"

"As little as possible, if you please." Brianna wrinkled her nose. "One would think he walks on needles these days." As if realizing her error, she lifted her sheepish gaze. "I must sound terribly ungrateful."

Just the opposite. Alexandra sympathized.

"I fear that my presence has burdened him overmuch."

Alexandra removed pen and ink from the shelf below the workbench. "I know that he cares enough about your happiness to give you a Season. What we're doing now is only a prelude." She tried to make it all sound exciting. "Soon we'll attend soirees where you'll meet gentlemen."

Brianna's reticule swung from her wrist as she plopped on a stool. "I don't know why having a Season meant so much to me. Perhaps I felt as if this were my last chance."

"Good heavens, you're only seventeen."

"It's not that. Not entirely," she amended with a tiny frown. "Christopher has been trying to make the company a success. He has been torn between the two ends of the operation. Between living here in London and living in Carlisle. I want him to be happy."

Alexandra watched her young charge's face. "You love him very much."

Brianna's expression faded. "Christopher may not be fond of the social scene, but he'll work in places no one else will go and teach kids no one else will have anything to do with. He'll even give me a Season. The pride in it is rooted deeply inside him. You have no idea how much a name affects everything about a person's life. The road has been all uphill. Now the family wants him to marry. He is the only one of my brothers left unattached. Even Ryan will wed by summer's end. When Christopher marries, who will have time for me? I'll just be in the way."

Alexandra returned her attention to the shelves and closed her eyes. "And how does your brother feel? About marrying?"

"Marrying Rachel Bailey would be like sealing a treaty between our families. It's what her father and mine wanted. But I don't think that's what Christopher wants."

Alexandra turned. "How do you know?"

"Because he would have married her by now." Brianna peered at Alexandra with blatant interest. "You and Christopher are old acquaintances, aren't you?"

Thrice before, Brianna had probed her on this very subject, but this time the inquiry slipped beneath her guard and she let Brianna read more than she'd intended to share.

"How much of an acquaintance were you? I mean, why else would you agree to help me?"

"We knew each other a long time ago," Alexandra said, relieved that Christopher had not elaborated on their bargain. It would have hurt Brianna to learn that Alex was helping her in exchange for Christopher's help.

Except something had changed these past weeks, and as Alexandra had gotten to know the young woman, an odd kinship had begun to grow. If life had wielded a different sword, Brianna would have been her sister-in-law in truth and Alexandra would be performing this very same function.

She certainly wouldn't be hurting at the very thought of Christopher marrying anyone else.

"Lady Alexandra knew your brother when she lived in Tangiers," Richard said from the doorway, having been introduced days before.

Brianna's blue eyes widened on Alexandra. "You knew my brother while he served in the military?"

"Yes," she said distractedly, glaring at Richard. "He was an attaché assigned temporarily to my father."

"Truly?" She turned to Richard. "Did you know him, too?"

"I was still in boarding school." He walked into the room and leaned a hip against the bench. "Your brother was a top government cryptologist."

"A *spy*?"

"That means his job was cracking codes," Alexandra explained.

"He can speak more languages than her ladyship here can."

"Christopher? My brother Christopher?" Brianna was clearly impressed. "And I thought he'd only built roads through deserts and jungles. You must have lived an exciting life in such a place. I wish I could go to places you've been. How wonderfully exciting."

Turning away to retrieve the last of the plates, Alexandra sought to comprehend the turmoil raging in her heart.

She did not regret her life. Her world, from the time she could toddle, had been filled with exotic travels, history books, tutors, and diplomatic affairs. She'd met princes, sultans, and kings.

Yet, she'd never been allowed to join the children who laughed in the protected stone courtyards in the residences where she'd lived. They'd been servants' children. And often from the shadow of her bedroom curtains she'd watched them play as curiosity of them held grim parley with solitude. Dubbed the ice princess as she'd grown older, she could only pretend indifference to the unflattering tribute to her character.

For by her father's act to set her apart, he'd helped make her an outcast who fit into nobody's world.

Richard had befriended her, and Christopher had dared to treat her as if she weren't royalty. Christopher, with his insular family and his penchant for defying rules, was the only person who'd ever worked for her father who didn't pay homage to her, who'd repeatedly hurled his gauntlet smack in the teeth of authority.

Alexandra felt the kick of something akin to enmity.

His insufferable opinion of himself certainly had not changed, for him to think that he could press her back against the bookcases in the reading room, give her a soul-rending kiss, then walk away without even a by your leave. The last time he'd done that to her, she'd found him in the compound stable and nearly run him through with a pitchfork.

Tossing all emotional introspection into the garbage, Alexandra focused on the bench with the realization that she had finished setting up the boxes.

"I've been busy since I last saw you," Richard said, opening the first book for Alexandra's perusal. "You would be proud. I've not been to one club all week."

"What is it that you both are doing?" Brianna asked.

"Cataloguing specimens that arrived in a recent shipment. These are the leaf and pollen samples," Richard said, thumping the table. "Everything here was found buried at a dig near Cairo."

"Who drew the pictures? They are very good."

Alexandra nodded at Richard. "He did." She lifted the book to the light, noting the details of each drawing presented on the various pages. "You've missed your true vocation, I think, Mr. Atler."

He snorted. "And embarrass my father more than I already do?"

In the awkward silence that followed, Alexandra felt the deep-sprung impetus behind his remark; then all at once he said, "Do you like the cut of my new jacket?"

The candy-striped abomination could catch all manner of

rodents, it was so bright. But she refrained from comment. Who was she to cast stones, when she was just as guilty of her own rebellion against her father? She and Richard were certainly a pair.

"Father is out of the museum this morning on another one of his merry jaunts." He grinned conspiratorially. "So we'll not be disturbed."

For the next hour, while Alexandra diligently worked, Richard introduced Brianna to the storage room, detailing the contents on the shelves. And later, as Brianna sat prettily on a stool, he relegated away the gloom of the basement with a recital of the *ton*'s most recent events.

"I had a wonderful time at the opera," Brianna said to his comment about the show. "Wasn't LaBella Scilloni divine?"

"Everywhere, apparently." Richard leaned a hip against the specimen table. "Just last week in Paris, during the death scene in *Nibelungen,* she fell on the stage with her feet toward the audience. . . ."

"What happened?"

"Her crinoline ballooned up, offering the spectators a splendid view of her drawers. They were red, no less. Now everyone in Paris is wearing red."

Brianna lowered her head to muffle her laughter. Alexandra gave Richard a reproving look. "Such flaws, it makes them all seem so human, don't you agree?" he said with a grin.

Alexandra washed her hands in a pitcher of water and removed her apron. "I think you've entertained us enough for one morning, Mr. Atler."

"Ah." He straightened and bowed gallantly over his arm. "That is my cue to leave, Miss Donally." To Alexandra he said, "I would ask you for a kiss, but we are not alone."

"Have a nice day, Richard." If he'd stayed another second, she'd have thrown the apron in his face.

Once outside the museum, the cool hyacinth-scented breeze washed over Alexandra. The walkways were crowded. Carriages rattled past.

"Sunlight!" Brianna held up her arms to the sky. "And fresh air."

Alexandra pulled her gloves on and smoothed the soft leather. "We should attend to the printers and see if your calling cards are ready." Looking down the row of carriages, she found Gracie talking to their driver. "Lady Wellsby said it should not take more than a few days."

Hastening down the steps, Brianna scattered a bevy of pigeons pecking the ground. "Must we?" She tied the poppy-red silk ribbon of her straw bonnet and hurried for their carriage. "I wish to get to the park. If that's all right with you? We're late."

Surprised to see her charge less than enthusiastic about the calling cards, Alexandra decided that she could pick them up herself. Parliament had a late session tonight. Afterward the clubs would be full. Her father wouldn't miss her.

They wore no cloaks. The sun had grown hot by the time they descended from the carriage at the park. Brianna's face suddenly brightened. A white horse-drawn phaeton rattled past, but Brianna only had eyes for the one person who had appeared on the path in front of them.

Looking absurd in an oversized black suit, Stephan Williams tried to appear casual. "Good day, my lady." He bowed to Alex, but his eyes were for Brianna. "Miss Donally." His barely suppressed adoration was conveyed in that one stolen glimpse.

Alexandra suddenly looked away. Christopher had surely been blind to have missed the look on his sister's face when these two came within a thousand yards of one another.

Alexandra should have been more concerned that all of Christopher's well-laid plans for his sister might come to naught. But hadn't she been seventeen once? And so completely in love that the moon and the sun rose and fell over her heart?

Caught by something she could not define, Alexandra waited until her heart stopped pounding, until her emotions refolded themselves back into their tidy compact little square where she could tuck them neatly away. But she could not tuck them away.

They would no longer be contained.

Chapter 8

"**Y**ou're home early, Christopher." Brianna leaned in the bedroom doorway, watching him shave in the dressing room. "Especially since I've hardly seen you for days."

Rolling the razor across the strap, he met her gaze in the glass. His shirt hung open at the neck. "This is the busiest time of the year for the company, imp."

Brianna fluffed her pink wrapper. Seeing the movement, he felt a pang of remorse for not displaying more interest in her activities. "Talk to me." He bent back to the razor. "I'm not in a hurry to go out tonight."

He wasn't. He'd had one damn meeting after another.

"You didn't tell me you were a spy during the war. How romantic. Is that why the queen knighted you?"

Christopher turned. "Who told you that?"

"Lady Alex said you were a cryptologist working for her father. I imagine shades of *Arabian Nights* meets Emily Brontë."

He returned to shaving his face. Clearly, he'd allowed his sister to read too many novels. Reaching for the lamp, Christopher turned up the light. Since that day he'd seen Alex in the courtyard at the museum, he'd purposefully relegated her morning and afternoon arrival here to Barnaby and Brianna's maid, Gracie. He didn't expect Alex and his sister to share life stories.

The razor paused in midair. "Cryptology is not spying. And imp?" His gaze held hers in the glass. "What I did as an officer in the military is not something that I care to have bandied about. Do you understand?"

"Is it a secret?"

Only the fact that he was nearly court-martialed, and that he'd disgraced the hell out of his parents. "There are some things that I'm not proud of."

"Does that include your past *acquaintance* with Lady Alex?"

He barely missed cutting his throat. Leaning a palm on the commode, he swished the razor in the bowl of water beside him. "No," he said.

"Lady Wellsby was quite pleased to learn that Lady Alex would be attending the art gala at the end of the month. She said that it is high time for her ladyship to join the living. Don't you agree?"

He rinsed the soap off the razor. "You spoke with Lady Wellsby?"

"Quite extensively. We went to the printers' last week and ordered calling cards. But I must say, in the beginning I don't think she was pleased that Lady Alex brought me to her house for tea. Lady Alex introduced me for the express purpose of gaining entry into Pritchard's Clothier on Regent Street. You know anyone who is somebody attends there, and she is Lady Wellsby's couturier. Anyway . . ." Brianna waved her hand, and Christopher had to focus on the numerous threads of her dialogue. He scraped the razor over his cheek. Somewhere he discerned that his sister was discussing two major events, past and present, simultaneously. "It was most discomfiting at first to be looked over like so much sausage strung up in the butcher shop until Lady Wellsby found out who I was. She seemed quite pleased to learn that I was your sister, and chatted endlessly about meeting you last year in Edinburgh. Frankly, I think Lady Wellsby likes you."

That pleased Christopher. He'd met Lord and Lady Wellsby when he'd lectured at the university in Edinburgh. The Wellsbys were proud benefactors of education, which was probably why he had allowed them to monopolize most of his time that night. It had been through them that he had found the physician who had diagnosed the problem with his leg.

"She spoke of the new museum and was quite glad to know of others who felt obliged to help with the undertaking. We even talked at length about the recent find in Cairo. Lady Alex may not know anything about fashion, but she's no cottonhead. Her vocabulary of big words that none of the rest of us can understand might even put you to shame. Anyway, I have decided that milady is much too interesting a person to be alone."

Christopher found himself in awe of his sister's animated discourse. "You decided all of this in how many weeks?"

"Lady Alex is nice, Christopher. And it wasn't as if I stumbled upon Lady Wellsby and came up with a plan. It was only a passing thought. Besides, she has a beau. I met Mr. Atler when she took me to the museum."

Christopher finished splashing water on his face. Tossing the towel down, he turned. "You went to the museum? When?"

"This morning."

Before he could say anything, Brianna leapfrogged into another topic. "You're getting all dressed up tonight. If I weren't your sister, I'd think you looked quite dashing."

Leaning a palm against the doorframe, he raised a brow. His bedroom window was open to the sounds of the busy street below. "Is all of this a way to work up to asking me for something?"

Her slipper made circles on the floor. "I want a new bonnet."

"You already have more bonnets than most girls in London. I told you last night that you don't need any more money for clothes."

"Other girls carry money."

He looked at her hard. "For what purpose? We have accounts in half the stores in London. What can't you buy?"

She crossed her arms. "I do hope that you're not the manner of man who gets dressed up just to spend money and time on a . . . a demirep. When I haven't a farthing to my name!"

Christopher's brows soared incredulously. "Demirep?"

"Don't be such a bluenose. I'm seventeen and quite the modern woman. We don't shy away from conversation at the lady's whist table on Fridays."

"Does Lady Alexandra allow you to speak so freely of prostitutes while playing whist?"

"Of course not. I was with Lady Wellsby's ward. She's twenty and smokes cigarettes."

Christopher slanted a critical look at his sister. "Is this an example of high society, imp? Smoking cigarettes and talking about strumpets?"

"N-no." She lowered her chin. "But you treat me like a child."

"You're seventeen, Brianna. You *are* a child."

"I'm a grown woman. Why must you always be so protective?"

"You can stop the tears." Turning back into the dressing room, he changed out of his shirt. "I'm not going to wash out your mouth."

"Are you cross with me?"

"Stay out of the museum from now on."

Stark silence followed. "But why?"

"Because I'm asking."

Because he didn't have a fondness for Richard Atler, nor did Christopher trust him. So little, in fact, that he'd hired someone to do a background investigation on the man. And because Alex had seemed to like him. Alex, who couldn't tell a cockroach from a gerbil unless it was fermenting in a speciman dish.

Christopher buttoned the clean shirt. He'd thought only of avoiding her at all costs. When he had something to report to her concerning his side of the investigation, he would send her a note from now on. She was dangerous to his resolve, his character, and his peace of mind. And he was dangerous to her reputation, whether she willed to think about that or not.

Knotting his tie, he returned to the doorway. Brianna remained against the other doorframe studying the lace on her sleeves.

"I have a lot on my mind, imp. I don't mean to be sharp."

"Will you be out late again tonight?"

"Yes." He shrugged into his vest.

"Good night, then," she said.

Clipping the silver cufflinks onto his sleeves, Christopher walked through his bedroom and looked down the hall. Gracie came out of Brianna's room. He yanked down his cuff. "Is she all right?"

"Why, yes, sir." Gracie reassured him. "She is curled up with a book and will probably go to sleep shortly."

He looked behind him out the bedroom window. The sun had barely set. "At eight o'clock?"

"She always retires to her room this early, sir."

Christopher's eyes went to his sister's bedroom door. "Does anyone check on her later?"

"Yes, sir. I always peek in before I go to bed."

"Make sure that you do." He turned away to retrieve his jacket from his room and shrugged into his coat. "I'll be back late."

"Ye have an important meeting, do ye, sir?" Gracie beamed.

"Sir." Barnaby met him at the top of the stairs with his coat. "Lady Alexandra is here."

"Here? Now?"

"Your sister is unavailable so she inquired about you. I put the lady in the library, sir."

He should tell Barnaby to send her away. She had no sense

of protocol, coming to this townhouse so late in the evening. Even he knew that casual social calls ended before six P.M.

"Beggin' your pardon, sir," Barnaby queried when Christopher didn't move. "Do you want me to send her away?"

"I'll handle the problem." Christopher walked down the stairs. A carpet runner muffled his steps. He stopped in the doorway of the library.

But moved no farther inside the room.

Alexandra stood with her nose bent over the globe, rotating the orb by slow degrees. Framed by the window behind her, the cloudless sky was aglow with the fading indigo twilight of a spring day. She wore gray silk as unfashionable as a farthingale, and a shock of protectiveness wrapped around him. Crossing his arms, Christopher leaned a shoulder into the doorjamb.

For all of Alex's worldliness in the intellectual world, she possessed an aura of social innocence that he had always found appealing. Having donned nothing so provincial as her magenta-and-fuchsia-clothed counterparts attending London's soirees, she could walk into a roomful of swans looking like a goose and notice nothing different about herself.

He didn't want her to be vulnerable to ridicule.

Or to him.

Then her eyes snapped up at some noise he must have made, and time in all its unerring eloquence stuttered to a halt.

It had taken him years to gain the direction over his life that he now enjoyed. She was a threat to that. And still he could not pull away.

Was his struggle to gain the one worth risking the other?

Stepping into the room, Christopher shut the door and realized just how perilously close he was to making the second biggest mistake of his life.

"Mr. Donally."

So, she was back to calling him by his last name. "Miss Marshall." Folding his arms, he leaned his back against the door.

She put her hands on the globe. "I've interrupted your evening." Her gaze went over him. But for his white shirt and silver paisley waistcoat, he was dressed impeccably in evening black.

"But surely you knew if you came here at this time that you would."

Alexandra's cheeks burned. "That's not a nice thing to say."

He continued to watch her with eyes the color of twilight. "My humblest apologies, madam. Then allow me to simplify. *Why* are you here?"

"You weren't at your office." Painfully conscious of his nearness, she clamped down the urge to turn away. Unnoticed, her fingers walked over the globe, spinning the sphere. "I brought Brianna's new calling cards," she said, as if he would believe for one instant that was her reason for visiting. "I put them on the desk. Along with my repor— A schedule of upcoming events that she will be allowed to attend. All of which you will have to begin making appearances."

He pushed off the door. "All of which you could have given to Brianna." Walking behind her, he shut the curtains with careful precision. Then he turned. Reaching across her, he placed a hand on the globe and stopped it from spinning.

The intensity in his blue gaze surrounded her, touched her intimately. Even as he radiated danger, she felt drawn to him.

His shadow covered her. She lowered her face. His hand took her chin. "Are you pursuing me, Alex?" Humor and something far more laced the words as his eyes burned into hers. His palm was callused and warm against the tender flesh of her cheek.

"Perhaps it's the pressure of the investigation . . . and my impatience," she acquiesced, conceding some of the truth.

"And the fact that your neck is in the noose," he said with thinly veiled sarcasm, his tone so emblematic of his temper. "Should I be honored or amused?" His palm eased over her hair, forcing her head back. "You think of stolen jewels and I always seem to come to mind. There is some pleasure then to know that I am in your thoughts."

Her hands clutched her skirts for fear of touching him. "You mock me, Christopher."

And just that fast, she felt the change inside him. "It is not my intent to mock." His gaze riveted on her mouth, then slowly rose to her eyes. "Maybe to understand you. But never to mock."

For a long time, as she stared into those penetrating eyes, a sort of despondency grabbed hold. "You are mistaken if you believe that I came here for any other reason except to see you. I . . . I have found it difficult not to think about you," she whispered unsteadily.

He made a sound before looking away, then back at her again. This time with solemnity. "*Is* Atler your lover?"

Alexandra stared at him, realizing that he meant to know. For whatever reason, he had deliberately turned the conversation back to their dialogue in the carriage when she'd told him Atler was her beau. But something in his eyes stopped the urge to throw his own lack of celibacy in his face. Something about Christopher, the man she knew him to be, told her his reasons for asking went far deeper.

The hot sting of tears touched her eyes. "I don't have a beau. I lied about Richard because I didn't want to be seen as this person no one wanted to be around."

She drew nearer into the circle of his strength. Gone was the carefully constructed barrier she'd erected against him. Gone were the years that's she'd despised him for walking away. Gone was her desire to run from him when all she wanted was to know him again.

"With the exception of you, I've never had a lover." Her voice was raw. "I think about you and all the wonderful things you've done with your life. I think about what it would have been like to have remained your wife and shared those dreams. I wish that I'd never seen you at the museum that night, but I did, and now here I am asking if you've missed me the way I've missed you."

For too long, he said nothing. Her heart pounded its chaotic rhythm in the chasm of silence that grew between them. His gaze was on her face. His fingers no longer wandered through the heavy coil of her hair but framed her face. Her own heart was throbbing.

"How did you get here tonight?" he quietly asked.

Surprised by the sudden tenseness in his voice, she searched his eyes. "I came by cab. My carriage is waiting for me at the museum." She lifted her chin. "I no longer care if Papa knows where I go—"

He brushed his thumb across her mouth. "Perhaps, but there are some complications I'd rather avoid just now." He laughed lightly, a sound that came from deep in his throat. "This is bloody insane."

But he wanted her.

She could see his desire in his eyes, the way he kept looking at her. Heat pooled in her abdomen and between her legs. She felt giddy, as if coming to life after a long, cold dormant sleep.

He slipped his fingers in her hair in an act of possession so hot that she could see the glitter in his gaze an instant before his parting lips covered hers.

The kiss seized her starving senses and stole her breath, divesting her of any questions about his intent.

Or hers.

Her arms wrapped tightly around his neck. He splayed his other hand over her breast, and with a fierce certainty of the rightness of her actions, she pressed against his palm. Opening her mouth to his with such hunger, she was oblivious to the rudimentary dignity of her unschooled passions. Her need for him was overwhelming.

Her hair tumbled to her shoulders. Christopher pulled back and raked his gaze slowly over her face. "You cut your hair." He breathed against her brow. "I like it."

The scent of him filled her nostrils. Wanting to touch him all over, she rasped against his mouth, "You still kiss like sunlight."

The heat of him surrounded her. He looked deeply into her eyes, his gaze laced with perplexity. "I don't know how I feel at this moment. But if wanting you is any indication . . . hell, Alex, every instinct is telling me that we should not be doing what we're both thinking of doing."

A soft sigh feathered his lips. "But when did that ever stop you before, Christopher Donally?"

He dug his hands into the thickness of her hair and pressed his nose into its fragrant softness. "We need to go someplace . . . more private than this townhouse."

"Yes." She felt wanton and wicked. They were planning a tryst, and Alexandra could barely breathe past the anticipation. The fact that Christopher seemed as affected as she lent warmth to her limbs.

A knock sounded on the door and Barnaby entered after a moment. Christopher and Alex stood separated by the globe. She considered the irony of that as she lowered her gaze and listened to Barnaby tell Christopher that his carriage was ready. For it was as if the whole world did indeed stand between them.

She could bring him to her private sanctuary. No one ever went to the carriage house when she was working late. The nights were too chilly for her father to take in the air. Heart racing, Alexandra looked up at Christopher through the veil of her lashes. The gray-haired servant had left.

"I have an engagement tonight," he said. "Business." He shoved his hands into his trouser pockets. "It's not something I can miss."

Already she felt Christopher withdrawing.

"I see." She wouldn't cry. The notion was ridiculous.

"No, you don't see." He pulled her into his arms. His chin rested on the top of her head, and she squeezed her eyes tight to keep from clutching his shirt. She would surely shatter if she did.

"Christ, Alex. You need to think about this," he finally said. "Really think. Hell, I need to think."

He had no need to tell her the consequences. But he needn't have worried that she could get pregnant. The doctors had told her she would probably never be able to con-

ceive again. A lump in her throat choked her. She didn't want
to think about that.

"There is a place I go. A secluded place that is mine," she
said, telling him about the carriage house where she spent
so much of her time, willing him to follow her into the
night.

His strength, palpable beneath her cheek, enveloped her.

He'd come to her once before. But would he do so again?

Turning down the lamp in her carriage, Alexandra looked
out over the wrinkled face of the fading sky and descended
into reverie. Christopher had paid the cabdriver to return her
to the museum, and to keep silent, by the look of the tip he'd
received.

Her carriage pulled out into traffic for home. London's
serrated skyline was vivid against the ethereal layer of clouds
that embraced the horizon. A southern breeze curled through
her hair from the small window above her head. She'd left
her hair down and free to bounce around her shoulders. Then,
without willing it or knowing what had fallen over her,
Alexandra ordered the driver to take her to Pritchard's on Regent Street.

After allowing herself to be led into a back room, she
stared at herself in the long glass, wearing a downy wine-red
bodice over her shoulders. Tiny pearls festooned the cloth in
a sophisticated picture of refined elegance. Alexandra stared
in awe.

She'd never been to a place like this. Her seamstress came
once a month to the house with dull designs, dull fabrics.
But Alexandra wanted something different. Something
alive.

"You need not hide your bosoms, mademoiselle." The
modiste readjusted her bodice lower. "You have a lovely
shape, *oui*?"

Alexandra caught the woman's encouraging nod in the
mirror.

"Bosoms are all the rage," she confirmed.

Alexandra had always prided herself on her pragmatic approach to life, and didn't entirely understand this sudden desire to add new evening and carriage dresses, riding habits, and morning gowns she would never wear at the museum. Still, she could not hide the unbidden sense of daring to waltz on the wild side of life. It had been so long since she had cared about the way she looked, or lounged in the cocoon of silks and satins and muslin so soft to the touch the fabric felt like gossamer. She would buy more than a bonnet tonight.

"I do wish to add color to my wardrobe," Alexandra said. "But not so much that I shall glow in the dark."

"Naturally." The modiste regarded her politely. "How soon would you like your gowns, milady?"

The modiste flushed in anticipation when Alexandra decided on the purchase. "I will be drawing payment off my own funds," Alexandra said, wishing her father's name to remain out of these transactions. In truth, she'd never done anything like this on her own initiative before. "And I will pay you extra if you can have this order ready in a week."

The modiste met the seamstress's gaze, then clapped. "You heard her. Pronto, it is time to get to work. Yes, madam." She turned to Alexandra. "I think we can do that."

That evening she ate at a restaurant, watching snowy seagulls swoop and drop on restless wings over the masts of ships moored off the riverbank. She watched the lights from Christopher's office building across the river wink out and wondered if, wherever he was tonight, he was thinking about her.

Alexandra walked out of the restaurant and nearer to the river. She listened as Big Ben faintly chimed the hour of eleven. The sounds and pungent smells of the night climbed over rooftops and bridges. The day was gone, but London had seemed to come alive.

And she had awakened with it.

When Alexandra arrived home, she swept past the butler and raced up the stairs into her bedroom. Ladylike grace had run the way of her heart and abandoned that staid place in her comportment. She didn't know how long functions lasted. Except that, by her father's example, most concluded near dawn. She doubted Christopher would stay out that long.

Shoving aside the mental tapestry of jovial music and dancing, she gathered together books and paperwork that she could concentrate on tonight. After telling Mary that she would be working at the carriage house, Alexandra found the path into the woods.

Nourished by the pond, just before the ivy-wreathed stone wall, the alders and willows had overgrown the bank and provided a thin screen of cover from the main house. She let herself into the cottage, then once inside turned the key in the lock.

Behind her, the muslin curtains, blown from their fastenings, cracked in a gust of rain-scented wind. Broken moonlight shining through the study window glinted off the ghostly furnishings. A Grecian marble Athena lay on the mantelpiece near a clock. Richard had designed that clock and given it to her as a gift last year. From the cluttered oaken bookcases and desk to the awards and numerous newspaper articles framed on cedar-planked walls, this room was filled with all the pieces of her life.

Kneeling beside the fireplace, Alexandra attempted to coax the peat to flame. She shut the curtains against the night. Another fireplace stood against the back wall in the adjoining bedroom. In the shadows, a chintz-covered lounge, bed, and rosewood armoire filled the small chamber. But before she could light the lamp, a carriage rattled to a stop in front of the cottage. Nervously brushing her hands on her skirts, she walked to the door.

Her father stood on the threshold, his gloved hand outstretched toward the door latch. She looked past him to the footmen standing next to the carriage. "What are you doing here, Papa?"

Peering at her over his spectacles, he seemed to study her unconfined hair. Her chin tilted slightly. She tamped down the urge to excuse her state. Nor would she succumb to guilt. They'd made a pact years ago when she'd returned to live with him after Tangiers that he would not dictate certain boundaries of her life. He would not comment on her appearance, he would not tell her how to dress or how to do her job at the museum. He would not tell her that she couldn't work here all night if she chose, or sleep here when the occasion warranted. Yet, in the past few weeks, he had violated most every accord of peace they had ever reached. Perhaps not by words but by his manner. She had not been so aware of the breach until this moment.

"May I enter?" he queried.

She stepped aside as he walked past her into the cottage. "I saw the light on here." He looked at the clock behind her on the mantel. Then at her desk piled high with books and a sundry of clutter before turning back to her. "I have been rather late in coming home recently," he said.

She lit the second lamp on her desk. "Parliament is in session. I don't expect that you'll be home every night for dinner." Without elaborating on her day or her reasons for starting work here so late, she simply asked, "What did you wish to speak to me about, Papa?"

He took in the fire she'd been attempting to light. "You didn't tell me that you were interested in joining the social scene this year."

"I'm twenty-eight years old, Papa. I have hardly *joined* the scene. I thought that I would attend Lady Wellsby's Thursday afternoon salon. Play whist on Fridays—"

"You've never had the social stamina for that manner of poppycock. You get heart palpitations in crowds, for God's sake."

"My heart is beating fine."

"Alexandra." He turned on her. "I've never forced you to partake in this *ton*'s Season. Nor have I cared in the past that you chose not to spend your time with a flock of gaggling geese."

"Lady Wellsby is not a goose. And Papa . . ." She hesitated. "This is what I choose. So please don't interfere."

"Professor Atler dropped by my London office this evening."

Alexandra bit back her shock. "Why?"

"He is concerned that you will be coming up for evaluation in three months. And that you are not ready."

"How considerate."

"If you're having difficulties coping with your responsibilities—"

"Papa—"

"If I have put too much on your shoulders with my expectation—"

"I will not fail my evaluation."

The last thing on this earth she wanted was for him to try to fix her life. Her decision not to involve him in her problems leaped higher up the forefront of her resolve. She tipped on her toes and kissed his weathered cheek. "I'm all right."

Her father shoved a hand into his pocket. "Everything I've done . . . I've tried to protect your interests, Lexie."

Her father's childhood endearment for her caught her unexpectedly. "I know, Papa."

He cleared his throat. "Perhaps, since you have decided to step out this year, you would care to accompany an old man to the art gala? It has been a long time since we've attended the show together."

Alexandra felt her cheeks grow warm. "Yes, it has, Papa. But I'm already attending the show with Richard."

"Atler?" He frowned.

She turned away, suddenly worried that her eyes would betray her heart. That she might somehow betray Christopher. Dropping to her knees, she worked to start the fire, aware that her hands now trembled.

"I've always been fond of Richard," she said.

But not in the way that she'd implied, and she'd never felt so rotten in her life for the lie.

Her father's steps sounded hollow on the wooden floor as he walked to the doorway of the other room. She had not been here long enough to light the lamp beside the bed. The room was dark.

"Is there anything else, Papa?" She fanned the flames and watched them take hold of the peat.

"Have you eaten supper?"

"I've eaten."

He scanned the room. "Very well, then."

Awaiting his departure, Alexandra didn't look up when the door closed. But when he was gone, an awful weight seemed to lift from her shoulders. She stabbed the peat with the poker, sending sparks up the stone chimney. Finally, she stared into the flames. A few moments later Alexandra listened to the clip-clop of horses fade toward the main house.

What was happening to her?

A glimpse at the clock drove the anticipation from her heart. As she contemplated the midnight hour, her heart bounding madly, she had not allowed herself to think that Christopher would not appear.

She stood, then went to the front door and twisted the key in the lock. Walking into the adjoining chamber, she dropped to her bed and lit the lamp, replacing the etched globe. A moth fluttered in its light. Then, all at once, she lifted her head. And turned. Christopher was standing against the wall.

His face thrown into the shadows, he stood unmoving, pinning her with only the touch of his eyes. The starched white collar of his shirt was loose against his neck. His coat hung open.

Breathing his name, Alexandra came to her feet.

"Am I still welcome here?"

His guarded impenetrable mood held no sway over her, and unable to temper the haste of her pulse a second longer, Alexandra flew into his arms.

Chapter 9

Christopher wrapped her close to him. Yet for all the power behind his restraint, he buried his fingers in her hair and slid his mouth down her throat. Alexandra's lips found the shell of his ear. "You . . . came," she breathed hoarsely.

"No." A curve softened the line of his mouth. "But it is my sincerest aspiration that before this night is through"—his strong hands went to the curve of her waist—"the promise of those words will bear true."

Then he was kissing her in earnest, drinking in her gasp. And she was pressing him back against the paneled wall, her hands sliding to the buttons on his waistcoat. He was kissing her as hard and as desperate as she was kissing him. She swept aside the waistcoat, effectively relieving him of that hindering cloth between them. Exploring the hardened curvature of his chest beneath the fine lawn of his shirt, she'd attempted to keep her dignity the same as she'd tried to restrain her hands from ripping off his clothes.

She'd failed at both.

"Do you have any idea of the height of the fence around this property?" his voice whispered against her hair.

139

He smelled of tobacco and the essence of expensive bay-berry. "I should have been more precise in my directions." She grinned up at him. He'd stolen onto these grounds for her. "There is a gate at the bottom of the hill in back."

"My carriage will return at two A.M."

"That's only two hours." She stood on her toes and kissed his jaw, her palms roaming his arms. Beneath his shirt-sleeves, his muscles flexed. His flesh was warm against her touch. "Two hours is not time enough, Christopher."

Their breath mingled, shallow and hot between them. Half undressed, he stared down at her with heavy lids. Dark, crisp hair curled over the vee of his shirt. Laughing softly, he bent and kissed her lips, nibbling a slow path to her ear. "I imag-ine we could do much to ruin each other in that amount of time," he said in a dark husky voice that betrayed his desire. "I think we need to take this . . . slower. I'm seriously in dan-ger of humiliating myself."

Lifting her skirts, she unlaced her crinoline and let it bil-low to the floor. "I will do no such thing, Mr. Donally." She bent her chin over the hooks on her bodice. "We cannot waste a moment."

His scent all over her filled her nostrils. Her skirt fell to the ground, followed by her bodice. She still wore her stays and underthings, stockings and slippers, which she hastily kicked off her feet. Her gaze lifted expectantly.

His eyebrows were raised. He removed his tie with a jerk of his hand and worked his fingers over the buttons on his shirt. He did not fumble with his attire as she fumbled with hers. "You leave me breathless, Alex."

He looked magnificent. "Do I?" She took his palm and placed it on her chest. "My heart is racing, Christopher."

Taking the full measure of her breast, his lambent gaze locked on hers with lazy ease. "Shall we debate our physical states?" He pressed her other hand over his pants, his arousal evident beneath.

His wickedness enflamed her. "And what does the winner get, Mr. Donally?"

Edging her toward the bed, he bent his mouth over hers. The mattress hit the back of her thighs and she tumbled backward, with him following her down to the comforter. He caught himself above her, barely touching her, their breath mingling, their gazes locked, face to face. His eyes, like chips of blue heat, lowered to her lips.

"I get this." He lowered his mouth to hers, a blatantly sexual invitation that made her groan. "I get you, Alex."

With a murmur that was her name, he pressed her back to the confines of her mattress. Her hands gripped the flexed strength of his arms. Her eyes closed and her lips parted to his, to the insistent pressure of his kiss as he opened her mouth and thrust his tongue inside. Whatever control she had imagined that she'd possessed vanished. She had enough to do just to breathe. He still wore his pants, but his erection pressed hard against her, and she moved against him. His hands went between the slit in her drawers, easing her apart to his hungry probe. Dissolving around him, she wrapped her arms around his neck. Her knees fell apart against the welcome onslaught. A vague sensation of falling took hold of her stomach, twisting and gliding against her pelvis.

"Christopher—"

A groan tore at his throat. "Damn . . . Alex . . ."

The bed ropes groaned. Her hands went to his shoulders. He slid his mouth down her throat over her collarbone. She was dying. Her body arched to get more of his fingers inside her. Christopher pushed back to gaze down at her. Every nerve ending sizzled in wicked anticipation.

"Have I ever told you how beautiful you are? Everywhere?"

Her eyes glided open. She should have felt mortification, to be so exposed. But her body burned where his eyes touched. Where his mouth was about to do more as his gaze traveled lower.

"Wait," she gasped.

He was moving down on her.

"No." His dark gaze drilled into her, his voice unrecognizable.

Struggling to sit, she pushed herself up to the bed's edge. Her hair tumbled over her shoulders.

She couldn't breathe.

"I want to see you," she rasped, pushing him aside as she stood. He stepped backward and hit the chintz lounge. His shirt draped opened as if he'd been in a brawl. "And I want out of my clothes," she said.

His eyebrows shot up. Warm rough fingers pushed aside her hands and unhooked her corset up the front. His forearms were corded beneath her fingertips as she leaned on him. "Why don't you do away with that contraption?" His voice was husky.

"Then none of my gowns would fit." Bracing against him, she stepped out of her drawers.

"Buy bigger gowns."

"Christopher!" She edged him backward and he sat abruptly in the lounge.

Her breasts fell free into his hands. Her head fell back as his mouth plied each nipple and she straddled his lap. He bent her backward over his arm. Her necklace had somehow twisted around her neck and become entangled in her hair. His hand caught in the chain and it took her a heated minute to realize that he was no longer kissing her. She pulled back, aware that the locket lay in the palm of his hand. His gaze lifted slowly to hers.

The expression in his eyes widened with bewilderment, and Alexandra moved defensively as she swiped the locket from his grip and held it protectively to her. She did not move from Christopher's lap.

"How long have you been wearing that?" he quietly asked.

"Since you gave it to me."

It was as if the heated moments before had not occurred. A lifetime lay between them. A lifetime of questions and anger and accusations all unresolved, now suddenly remembered.

"Why?" he asked.

Her breathing had not yet settled back into her chest, nor had his. She still wanted him, wanted to touch him, but she

dared not move her hands from the locket. It was as if by doing so, she would expose her heart and give away all of the
precious secrets she'd held so close. She wasn't prepared to
surrender what she'd guarded inside either her heart or the
locket.

"You and I are no longer those people we were, Christopher," she whispered. "I don't care what happened in the
past."

Christopher looked away. When his eyes came back
around to hers, they were neither angry nor cold. "Maybe *I*
do." He brushed the hair from her face. "Maybe there's a lot I
don't understand at the moment."

"The fact that we're both here should explain something to
you."

"What?" His eyes went over her face. "That I find you incredibly attractive? That I haven't managed to think ratio-
nally since you stepped back into my life? That I've wanted
to shove you up against the wall and fu—"

"Don't you dare say that crude word to me, Christopher
Donally!" She poked a furious finger against his chest.
"Have you considered that whatever we had between us is
still here?"

"What did we have, exactly, that wasn't so easily tossed
into the gutter of bad mistakes?"

Perhaps he hadn't meant the words to cut her, but they did
nevertheless. "I don't care if you did walk away all those
years ago." Her hand slid through the tangled thickness of his
hair. "I understand why you did what you thought—"

He lifted her like so much thistledown off his lap and set
her on her feet. Looking at her as if she were the many-
headed Hydra, he stood and followed her to the armoire as
she whipped out her wrapper. "Your father threatened me
with a court-marital. Christ, Alex, I didn't walk away. I was
sent away. You know that!"

"You never wrote." She knotted the belt. "You never inquired about your son. You *left* me!"

"*I* never wrote?" He was incredulous. "I thought you knew

that I would come back for you. They couldn't keep me in India forever. Then I received the news about our son in the same mail packet that I received notice that you had not contested the annulment. By that time, we had been unmarried for nearly a year."

"I was barely eighteen years old by then, Christopher. We'd married outside the Church of England without Papa's permission. I couldn't have contested the annulment had I wished."

"You didn't even try." His voice broke.

She snatched her locket to herself and held it there protectively. "Don't you dare tell me what I did or didn't do. You have no right to pass judgment over me." She wanted to shout at him, but she kept her voice low, too terrified that someone in the house across the pond would hear. "After the birth of our son, I was ill. But I waited for eight months with my bags packed for you to return for me. I would have run away with you."

"And gone where, Alex?" His voice suddenly sounded tired. "You weren't just the daughter of some vicar or country squire. You were Lord Ware's offspring and heir. I thought about that when I'd kissed you the first time. You tested my judgment even then."

Tears filled her eyes. What had been passion ten minutes ago had frozen inside her chest. "When I was well enough to travel, I left my father and returned to Ware. There was a mutiny on in India. A war. I could not reach you. Later, I went to Carlisle because I'd heard that you'd been injured and released from the service. But your family thought me too evil to allow me to see you. I went home to Ware for a year after that. You never contacted me. Then my father returned to England. We made our peace, so to speak, before I agreed to go back to London."

"What did he offer you?"

She wrapped her arms around herself. "My education."

"Aye." Christopher stared at the ceiling, his mouth flat.

"You had privileges handed to you that people could only dream."

"I earned every accolade that I ever received."

His gaze touched hers, evenly, gently. "I don't doubt that you did."

"Is that so wrong?"

"Honestly, I don't know," he said, scraping his fingers through his hair. "I don't know what is right here and what is wrong."

"*We* are right together. I've never known anyone like you."

He traced her jaw with his palm. "You've not known many people, Alex."

She turned and, bending low, pulled out a dusty box from beneath her bed. Removing the lid, she dumped the contents on the bed. Every news article or photo she'd ever read and clipped, old letters, their wedding document, all lay in a pile as if the years had just crashed down on them both. She raised her gaze and let her eyes go over his face as he looked at the sundry items of misplaced affection, the years she'd followed his life.

"Tell me you haven't thought about me at all," she challenged.

For a long time, Christopher said nothing. He hurt in places that he had shut away years ago. He didn't want to know that Alexandra had pined away for him, when he had ripped her so completely from his life. He didn't want to see hope in her shining eyes, when all he felt at this moment was the sense to quash it down. He didn't want to feel what he was feeling for her at all, as if the years had not taught him a lesson in equality and fortitude.

Christopher lifted his gaze and found her watching him. He knew the instant that she recognized the bleakness and the truth.

"You never thought of me, did you? Not even once?"

"Does it matter? That I didn't spend my every waking moment regretting the past? I would be lying if I told you that I thought of you with anything akin to kindness."

Without replying, she looked at the floor as if suddenly lost.

"Should I have died more than once, Alex?"

Tears filling her eyes, she lifted her gaze. Then stepped against him and wrapped her arms around him. "But nothing changes the fact that you came here tonight," she whispered against his chest. "Does it?"

Except he didn't know if he could do this all over again with her. Outright lust he could deal with. What she was wedging open with her words and her heart, he could not. Still, his arms went around her and they stood thusly embraced.

"You're afraid for your reputation and that of your family if anyone should ever find out about us, aren't you?" she asked.

"You didn't drag me here, Alex."

She pulled back, her eyes bright. "No, I didn't. You came of your own volition."

Suddenly he laughed. "Do you think so?" He smoothed the tangled hair off her face. She'd always had the ability to do that to him. Make him laugh when he should be focused. "It seems to me that we've already discussed that point."

"We've discussed many points, Christopher." She rubbed her cheek against his chest. "We still have an hour."

In frustration, he lifted his gaze to the rafters. His hunger for her had not lessened. He wanted to strip off her wrapper and bury himself inside her. But where minutes before his mind had been possessed, nay, staked to her thighs, reality had intruded. "You could end up pregnant again, Alex," he finally said. She smelled of flowers and summer breezes and he buried his nose in her hair. "Have you thought of that?" He pulled her to the chintz lounge and into his lap. "Have you?"

His shirt fell open and she turned her head against his chest. "I know only that I've been told I could never have any more children."

The words startled him. He tilted her chin and forced her to look at him. "It's something that I accepted long ago," she whispered. "There was . . . scarring . . . inside."

She told him what the physician had said after she'd borne her son . . . his son; then she laid her cheek on his shoulder.

"How does someone know whether a woman can conceive or not?" he asked, inexplicably angry for Alexandra.

"I don't know. I've little experience with delivering babies. But my father brought in the very best physician."

"I'm sorry . . ."

"For what?" Her eyes met his in the shadows. "You could have done nothing." There was a short ragged pause. "He was buried in the small churchyard where we were married." Her voice was distant. "I tried to get him moved back to Ware. I wanted him there. But—"

"Shh," his fingers whispered over her lips. "No more."

Christopher didn't know what to say. He despised helplessness. Despised that another man had stolen away his role as father. Christopher had not allowed himself to think about his son in years. He had always thought that one day he would have more children, and the pain that came with the thought of his firstborn would forever fade. He was shocked to realize that little had faded at all. That there were feelings inside him so tightly locked away he didn't want them out.

"Christopher—" Alexandra's cool palm scraped his cheek, turning him to face her. He looked into her uncertain green eyes. "Do you always have to be so coldly reasonable about everything?" she asked. "You're here, I'm here. I don't want to talk anymore."

She kissed him. Her sexuality drilled through his defenses. He tried not to respond. There was something inherently wrong with being here with her.

And yet, there was something so inherently right.

Christopher's arms went around her and pulled her closer against him. He deepened the kiss, opening her mouth to his, caressing her lips. He threaded his fingers in her hair tilting her chin, loving her mouth with each touch of his. Stripping away the wrapper and her chemise, he twisted with her in his lap and laid her flat against the lounge. His hand found the soft swell of her breasts. His mouth inhaled the small sounds she made. And all rational thought fled. All thought of gentleness and tender words vanished.

He pulled her to her feet.

"Look at me," he whispered.

Glazed with passion, her eyes focused slowly on his face. He wanted her. Wanted her sheathed around him.

He removed his shirt and his pants. Her widened eyes went over him and he saw pleasure in her gaze. She moistened her lips and that one movement with her tongue went over him like a current of electricity. He also saw her gaze hesitate on the ragged scar that marked his thigh. Her eyes snapped up to his stark face.

"Christopher—"

A finger went to her lips. "I'm finished talking."

"But . . . your injury must have been horrible."

"It wasn't pleasant." He walked her backward. "Certainly not a subject I wish to discuss now, when I'm about to make love to you."

He didn't bother to remove her stockings. The amber lamplight fell over the smooth curves of her body. Vivid images of scented gardenia-laced moonlight on sand and a hot desert current swamped his senses. She had not changed except to grow more rounded in all the right places.

She was no longer just his past.

Holding her gaze, he followed her down to the mattress. Her hand hit the pile of clippings, scattering them as if a gust of wind had blown through the room. He thrust solidly inside her, his eyes never wavering from hers. And for a heartfelt instant, his control vanished. He drove into her unchecked by the rigid boundaries that encased him. Boundaries that he'd built to survive. That kept him from ever needing anyone.

Her head fell back.

"No," he rasped. "I want to see you."

He wouldn't allow her to look away. She was tight and wet, and so hot he clenched his teeth until she took all of him inside her body.

"Christopher . . ."

Alexandra wrapped her legs around his hips. One hand bracing her round bottom, the other leaned with the force of his weight against the bed, he tilted her against him, rocking his body with each powerful surge of his. The roughened sound that came from his throat might have been a growl, might have been surrender. Hell, he could have died content.

But all of that ceased to matter as Alexandra's soft cries filled the room. His own urgency roared through his blood. He kissed her hard.

Hungry.

The bed ropes groaned. He braced his palms on the mattress to keep from crushing her. With her eyes half opened and glazed, he watched her come beneath him, felt her rippling around him. His own release rocked him hard. His muscles tensed and corded in his neck. Drained of the will to move of his own accord, Christopher dropped to his elbows.

They remained, looking at each other. Unguarded and uncertain for the raw sensation that had burned so hotly between them. And he knew in that moment that he was lost to her.

Alexandra blinked, her voice carrying to him in a muffled rush. "If I am dreaming, please Lord stay Your hand and let me sleep."

The words were so out of character that Christopher felt his lips quirk faintly. Except a part of him wished that it *was* all a dream and tomorrow he would awaken and find the last ten years had never happened.

Alexandra woke to pounding on her door. She stirred and groaned as she lifted her head off the pillow. Her eyes blinked. Clutching the sheet to her throat, she sat up and looked around the room in a daze.

Christopher had gone hours ago. Realizing at once how late it was, she dragged her gaze around the sun-baked room.

She didn't dare allow anyone in here!

The flames in the fireplace had burned out. Blankets and clothes were scattered like the carnal vestiges of some Roman orgy. The room smelled of one as well. The perfume of lust pure and simple. She and Christopher had not been gentle with each other or the furniture.

The knocking came again more forcefully.

Alexandra snatched her wrapper from the floor. Hastily, she threw open her windows. Sunlight pierced her skull. She was suffering from a sensual hangover. Every muscle in her body ached.

"Mum," Mary's voice sounded on the other side of the door, and Alexandra realized the key was still turned in the lock. Christopher must have left through the window. She remembered last night that it had been opened when she arrived.

"Milady—"

Combing her fingers through her hair, Alexandra opened the door.

"Oh, mum, I was beginning to worry."

The bright sunlight hit her in the face. "What is it? Has something happened?"

"His lordship has sent me to fetch you. He is waiting breakfast on you, mum."

Alexandra was not prepared for the resentment she felt at her father's demands. But she knew from past experience that he was stubborn enough to hold breakfast until noon if needed.

"Tell him I'll join him after my swim."

"But . . . milady."

A warm-grass-scented breeze whisked around her and through her hair. "Tell him, Mary. You are *my* servant. He would not dare dismiss you for being cheeky. Besides, you are only the messenger."

"A messenger is not a safe occupation. Especially in this household." Mary's eyes narrowed on Alexandra's flushed face. Then she looked around her into the carriage house. Alexandra stepped sideways to block her view.

"Very well, mum. But you best never let his lordship know you had someone here last night. And don't ye be denying it, milady." Mary wagged a long finger at her nose. "My guess, it be that Sir Donally, from all the rumor flying about."

Alexandra paled. "Rumor?"

"You've been seen with him twice in public, milady. And don't think his lordship don't have his suspicions. There's bad blood between those two, mum. I was there that day when they nearly came to fisticuffs over ye and they took Lieutenant Donally away and put him on a ship to India. That or a court-martial, milady. A man just doesn't forget."

"I'm not asking him to be my husband, Mary."

"Then you'll be satisfied playing his mistress while he takes someone else to wife? Mum." Mary clasped both Alexandra's cold hands into her own. "You've the book learning of a scholar, but you don't have the sense God gave of a goose when it comes to people."

And it was the truth. She'd failed miserably at relationships her whole life. Except with Richard, who was more patient with her than most. She didn't know how to read people and too often took what they said to be what they meant. Besides the major fact that she was not thinking at the moment and that she would not be marrying Christopher in the Church of England, which posed its own set of problems, he would have to *want* to marry her first.

Alexandra wrapped her arms around her torso, the glow of last night suddenly fading with reality. It wasn't in her to be rude to Mary because of her own distress, so she said nothing.

Mary's smile was a generous effort at a positive front. "I will see you in the conservatory with a towel. Then I'll clean up over here. You'll be needin' your linens washed and ironed, milady. I'll need you to leave the door unlocked."

Unable to hide the heat that came to her face, Alexandra turned back into the cottage. Her gaze fell on the windows. "Wait," she called after Mary. "Don't you have the other key to this cottage? You were in here sometime yesterday. The windows were open last night; someone left them open."

"No, mum. Maybe the wind blew them open."

Her gaze went around the room. "Yes, you're probably correct."

She must not have secured the windows properly. Either

way, she was glad because Christopher had found a way into the cottage.

Still, after Mary left, she walked to her desk and knelt over the bottom drawer. Removing the false bottom, she flipped open a book hidden there. The inventory sheets were nestled securely between the thin pages. She lifted her lamp off the desk and walked upstairs to the attic. Holding the light aloft, she skimmed the crates and boxes. A breeze played with her toes. Curtains flapped in the wind.

She walked to the window. The latch was broken. Outside, a heavy tree limb pressed against the side of the cottage. Even now it banged softly in the breeze. Last night there had been a storm.

She started to turn away when a leaf in the center of the room caught her attention. She knelt and brought it nearer to the light. There was no reason for the niggling concern. It belonged to the tree just outside her window. It had probably been blown in here by the wind.

Still, she kept the leaf.

Alexandra finally replaced the lamp on the desk, then proceeded to change into her chemise for a swim on her way back to the house.

Alexandra entered the dining room and sat in the same place at her father's right hand where she'd sat since she was a little girl in every house they'd ever lived.

Her hair was still wet when she finally pinned it on top of her head. She reached up to check the hastily set pins and snood. At once, a plate of eggs was set before her. Alfred filled her cup with steaming coffee. She suddenly had an urge to ask for tea or lemonade, anything to break the monotony. Nothing about this routine had changed in years.

"Are you feeling well?" her father queried before finally lowering the paper to the table and accepting his plate. "You have never slept late unless you were ill."

Her gaze lifted to assess his expression. There was no suspicion in his gray eyes. "My health is fine, Papa."

"That's good, Lexie." He shoved a stack of invitations toward her. "You've received over a dozen today in the morning mail."

"I have?" Despite her unwillingness to show excitement over something so silly as a few invitations to soirees, Alexandra fingered the edge of an envelope, aching to tear one open.

Her father's stoic expression suddenly looked perplexed. "This is something I would have expected from you at twenty. Not now"—he flagged an agitated hand—"when you're nearly thirty. Have you considered that you're merely a novelty to them? A topic of discourse for the bored?"

"Most women find what I do interesting. As for the others? I don't care what they think of me." Her stomach falling, she picked up her fork. The curtains billowed slightly as a warm breeze swept into the room. "Besides, age is irrelevant, Papa. I'm not looking for a husband."

"You're a bloody heiress, Alexandra. Every no-account in this country will be knocking at our door when your mother's trust publicly reverts to you in another year. They won't care about you. They won't care about your interests."

Feeling the weight of his judgment, Alexandra watched him return to the paper to finish the market news.

"Why do you say those things, Papa?"

He looked up at her over his spectacles and sipped his coffee. "What things?"

"Am I so ugly that you think I have to buy a man's presence in my bed?"

Choking on his coffee, he nearly spewed the brew over his neatly pressed slacks. "Good God Almighty, Alexandra. We're eating breakfast."

"You do, don't you?"

"Don't I what?" He set down the cup with a clink.

"Think I'm ugly. Poor, senile Alexandra. It just so happens that I like what I do, and I'm not so old that I can't still enjoy myself."

"If you were hurt by something you think I implied, that

is your own doing." He dabbed his napkin over his mustache and eyed her warily. "Men marry for one reason. Legitimate heirs. . . ." His ruddy face became flustered as she imagined that he was trying to explain to her the facts of life. She would be unable to give a man an heir, which left only the decrepit, insolvent elite as potential husbands. Or scoundrels.

No wonder he allowed her to pursue an education.

"Is that why you married Mother?" She observed him over her cup. "So she could be Lord Ware's brood mare?"

She knew bloody well that her father had loved her mother.

"God blast it!" He threw down the napkin. But she didn't flinch. She'd finally received a response worthy of her hostility. "I know where this is stemming from. Donally shows up and twists bloody love knots in your veins. He is already manipulating you."

Alexandra's hand tightened on her cup. "That's not true."

"He's an opium-addicted bastard. Everyone is just waiting for him to fall on his arse."

"That was a long time ago when he came back from the war injured. He is a good man, Papa," she said stubbornly, aware that she trod across uncultivated ground now. "He was always a good man."

"You were an impressionable young girl with an inordinate amount of curiosity. He took advantage of you in the worst way."

"No more than I allowed. You blame him for sins that were my fault."

"Yours?" her father scoffed. And a man who rarely shared more than a dozen sentences in any one sitting suddenly loomed over her in fury. "What did you know about men? You were barely out of the schoolroom."

Swallowing her pride, she didn't allow herself to look away. He was well into an apoplectic stew.

"Your *paragon* was already a hard-drinking, hard-nosed Irish bastard before he walked into your life. He'd already escaped manslaughter charges for killing a man with his bare fists. A fight at the academy in Woolwich. Did you know that? Lord Pierpont sent Donally to the Crimean, where it took him only four months to land in the brig for disobeying a direct order from a superior. But some higher-up liked him, which was the only reason Donally wasn't shipped back to the last ice age. He was brilliant in languages, a promising strategist, and they sent him to me to work in intelligence. He could have been the best had he chosen."

"He didn't choose. You sent him away. You did that because of me."

"Bloody hell, yes, I did." The chair squeaked beneath her father's weight as he sat forward. "Donally did what he had to do to survive the uprising in India. I won't judge him for that. But no matter the veneer he has managed to build for the world to see, a man doesn't walk away from his past, Lexie. He is what he is."

Alexandra would not listen.

It was true that she'd glimpsed the steel of Christopher's personality in dealing with all matters of his life, his business, his sister, and her. Without such strength, Christopher would never have survived his ordeal in India or his injury; he would not have built D&B to its current size and presence.

Her father peered at her from over his coffee cup. "To the best of my ability, I have seen that your intellect and drive were nurtured, and until now you had far exceeded expectation. Perhaps I was wrong in allowing you so much freedom. Or in not speaking my mind earlier. You're my only daughter and I care what happens to you."

Because he loved her, or because he believed no one else could? She didn't even know the difference any longer.

She didn't even know herself.

Her father had rallied around her in the wretched guise of protection for so long that she'd allowed him to dominate every inch of her life. Yet in truth, a part of her whispered that she had let him buy her off. For as surely as her validity for being at the museum might be convincing to her, she'd always known her father held power over her world. She'd despised her lack of control, and had used whatever means she could to punish him.

Had her past relationship with Christopher been that act of rebellion? Was it now? She'd not been as blind to Christopher's character as her father believed. Then or now. She found herself aching to throw her affair in her father's face. The sheer vengeance of it shocked her.

She shoved her fork into her eggs. What manner of creature had she become, to even think of flaunting Christopher before her father?

Withdrawing his silver watch from his waistcoat pocket, her father flipped open the lid. "I'll be taking the carriage." With a sharp glance at the watch, he snapped shut the fob. "As it is, I am already late."

And she knew how he despised tardiness.

Alexandra refused to utter the apology that leaped automatically to her lips. After he left, she took her first deep breath, and hastily finished the uneaten bowl of peaches and cream to her right.

The room grew quiet. Finally, with a resigned sigh, she wrapped the bread in a napkin. It had been a long time since she'd seen the urchin lamplighter that she used to pass at night. Tonight she'd be working late at the museum. Perhaps she would see him again.

She suddenly had a need to return to some manner of normalcy.

But not as much as she had the need to run barefoot in the grass, or smell the sunshine in her hair and clothes. . . .

"And by the by." Shrugging into his coat, her father returned to the archway. He snapped the lapels straight before accepting his hat and cane from Alfred. "The barouche is under repairs and unavailable. As it is, I have no time to drop you off at the museum."

She struggled to stand. "Papa, I have work to do."

"Obviously you don't care enough about the responsibilities you've been given or you would not have been so tardy to breakfast." He peered down his nose at her as he applied his gloves to his hands. "It looks as if you'll be spending today at home."

Chapter 10

❧

A tap on the cottage door lifted Alexandra's head. She wore her spectacles while observing beneath a magnifying glass the leaf she'd found earlier in her attic. "Milady?" Mary peeked around the door.

Alexandra had found an old jar earlier filled with trinkets that she'd collected when she was a child. Upending the container on her desk, she carefully placed the leaf inside and turned in her chair.

Having taken the pragmatic approach to her enforced captivity and escaped her sudden popularity with callers this morning, she'd walked to the carriage house. She forced herself to pull out her unread science journals and, after spending the morning reading, went to work on her paper for an upcoming periodical. By accident, her gaze had fallen on the leaf that she'd found in her attic and had placed on her desk earlier. What had interested her was the mud she'd found on the leaf, which would mean the leaf could not have arrived inside the cottage via the wind.

"Milady?" Mary stepped into the room. "You have another guest."

Alexandra covered the top of the jar. "I told you—"

"She said that you missed your appointment with her this morning and would not leave until she knew that you were all right. She is most persistent, milady."

"Brianna Donally? Where is she?"

"Here, mum." Mary moved aside and let Brianna step into the room.

"My lady." The younger girl curtsied. "I'm sorry that I've bothered you. I know it was most impertinent to insist that I see you."

Alexandra stood at once. "It's all right, I quite assure you."

"Would you like for me to prepare tea at the house, mum?" Mary asked.

Alexandra looked at Brianna. The younger girl dipped her head. "If you don't mind, I would rather stay here."

"Thank you, Mary. But that won't be necessary."

"Very well," Mary said. "But I will warm a pot just in case."

After Mary left, Brianna gazed at the pictures and news articles on the walls. "Look at all of this, my lady." Her voice held awe. "You are truly an inspiration."

Alexandra followed the younger woman's gaze. "To most a scandal."

Brianna pulled her gaze away from the walls. "Are you all right, my lady? When the carriage returned this morning from the museum without you, I was worried."

"My apologies for not sending word. But I've ended here with no transportation today."

And an unspoken mandate from her father that she not leave the house. Never more than at that moment had Alexandra ever wanted to strike anyone as she had her own father when she'd walked past him and up the stairs. The horror of her emotions had left her trembling.

In truth, she'd wanted to be alone to regroup. Her father dangled affection like a carrot, and when she got just close enough to nibble, he yanked back as if terrified of emotional intimacy. She was not accustomed to the gamut of her emotions of late. Or to the reality that she was very much in love with Christopher and didn't quite know what to do about it.

Would that she could learn to seize control of her personal life as efficiently and as focused as she attacked her professional one.

Yet, now that Brianna was here, Alexandra realized how much she wanted company and how unsatisfying she'd found solitude. "I fear I have worried you needlessly," she said.

"I'm glad that I came here. I wanted to see where you lived, especially since you are so far from the West End."

"We've stayed nearer to the university. When my father is not at Parliament, he spends his time there."

"Your home is bigger than Christopher's country estate. 'Tis truly magnificent."

Alexandra squirmed uneasily beneath such praise. "And here I don't have a place for you to sit comfortably."

Brianna turned a slow circle. "Is this where you work?"

Alexandra showed her the carriage house, where only twelve hours before she had lain in bliss with Christopher. She climbed the stairs into the attic. Brianna looked at the old books and various personal artifacts stored there. Then Alexandra took the younger girl outside, where, penned by the half-crumbling brick wall, they gazed at the Greek statue of a naked Aphrodite lounging in the midst of cloves and ivy.

"Christopher collects such statues," Brianna said quite matter-of-factly, though Alexandra sensed her interest was quite lively. "You should see the four he brought back from India." Her voice lowered. "They are quite engaged in very explicit activity, too. It is nearly impossible for an intellectual mind not to blush scarlet."

"*Kama sutra,*" Alexandra managed with a straight face, remembering the first time she'd seen such statues while standing in a roomful of appalled professors. "There are many such stone carvings found in India's historic subculture."

"Christopher has no idea that I even know where they are. Next time you're at the house, I'll show you."

Alexandra suddenly couldn't decide whether to laugh or cry. She did both. Brianna's spirit, her cheer, the expectation that Alexandra would again visit Christopher's country manse, all served to hit her square in the heart. She turned and plopped down on the stone bench overlooking Aphrodite and the beautiful pond.

With a rustle of fabric, Brianna sat down on the bench beside Alexandra. "My lady!"

"I'm sorry." Alexandra waved off Brianna's concern. "I'm unduly emotional." Clearly, she was unraveling. At once, she sniffed and, straightening her shoulders, regained control. "I have a lot on my mind." Wiping a tear from the corner of her eye, she looked at Brianna. "Did you see your brother this morning?"

"We actually sat down and ate breakfast together. He was later than normal coming down. But do you know what else has happened since I saw you last? I received *nine* invitations for balls next week, my lady." Brianna ticked off the names of the senders. "All from those who attend our reading salon. I had three callers this morning. And Barnaby received a telegram from Ryan, who is due home any day now. He wants the family to get together. I have six nieces and nephews. Did I tell you that?"

Alexandra folded her hands in her lap. "No." She imagined Rachel Bailey would probably be invited. Conversation slowed.

"You need cheering, my lady," Brianna suddenly said. "Have you ever been to the fair?"

Peering at the younger girl, she realized Brianna was dressed quite charmingly in casual blue muslin. A little hat perched on her curly head. "Have *you*?"

"Oh, yes." Brianna smiled. " 'Tis routine every year where I come from. There is one outside of London. I heard about it last week while at the whist table," she whispered as if the golden willow beside them had ears. "There are quite a few ladies who attend. It is magnificent fun."

"Truly?" Alexandra laughed.

"Of course, their husbands and brothers would be scandalized should they learn. After all, true ladies do not attend such places where only the lower masses enjoy themselves. There are cockfights and wrestling. You must allow me to take you today."

The properly raised daughter inside Alex recoiled in alarm. Realizing the forgotten fact that she had hardly set a sterling example for her young charge as it was, Alexandra thought it best to decline. Christopher would have a seizure if he learned that his sister was responsible for taking her someplace as notorious as the fair.

Then again, there was the idea of flagrantly snubbing her nose at authority, the world be damned.

She squared her shoulders. "So, what does one wear to a country fair?"

"This is not a soiree. This is an adventure, my lady. Wear something practical and comfortable."

If Brianna had held any misgivings about introducing Lord Ware's privileged daughter to the country fair, they surely faded the instant Alex descended from the carriage. It was as if the bird had walked out of her gilded cage and into sunlight.

The late-day crowd was a mixture of a few daring members of high society, lower-born individuals, and a criminal element of pickpockets that Brianna seemed to have the ability to detect of anyone who crept within five yards of them. Her parasol took care of three.

Tumblers and rope dancers wound through the busy aisles. Theatrical booths were occupied by giants and dwarfs who waved patrons into tents for magic shows that featured men who swallowed swords and fire. Alexandra gawked at it all.

By the time evening rolled over the grounds and rushlights dotted the fields like blinking fireflies, she had visited almost every booth. Even the din of voices and the threat of a thunderstorm did not diminish the thrill of adventure when Alexandra found a chipped stone Buddha and a battered silver fork that dated back to Rome's occupation of the British Isles. "Only you can treasure a bent three-pronged fork, my lady," Brianna said with a laugh.

A nearby crowd erupted in boisterous cheers.

"A pugilist match," Brianna said above the roar. "Do you want to see a fight?" Brianna dragged Alexandra toward the crowd.

"Wait." Holding her hands aloft she shook the remnants of dinner from her sticky fingers. "Everything is sticking to me."

Christopher's sister had introduced her to lemon ice and taffy, custard tarts and gingerbread cookies. She'd just eaten braised chicken with her hands and, laughing in horror at the delicious grease rivulets that dripped down her fingers, she'd proceeded to wash everything down with common ale. Lots of ale.

"I've ruined my gown."

Looking around for a place to clean her hands, she finally gave up and swished her hands in a watering trough.

"Have you never been impractical, my lady?" Brianna said from beside her.

"Four hours ago, I would never have dreamed of performing such a private ablution in a public place that served water to livestock." She shook water off her hands. "Look at me." She held out her arms.

Noting that Brianna's dress had remained spotless and cheerful throughout their adventure, Alexandra frowned.

"I will share a secret, my lady." Brianna's eyes gleamed with mischief. "We Donallys eat with our fingers. Yes, shocking but true. It is an acquired skill mastered in childhood. Sometimes when we get together and mind you there are a lot of us, we haven't the inclination toward refinement."

"You have no one to look over your shoulder?"

"Quite the opposite. We all look over everyone's shoulder. And you won't find a more opinionated, busybody, physical bunch. Last year one of my nephews knocked his older cousin right out the second-story window. Thank goodness for hedges. Neither could sit for days after my brother Johnny got hold of them."

Alexandra wondered uncertainly if that's what it was like having a family. "I have always had servants." She hiccuped and covered her mouth. "Even when I accompanied my father on a dig once in Algeria, servants brought us tea and crumpets."

Her life suddenly seemed incredibly boring.

"Is Lord Ware an archaeologist?" Brianna asked.

"A hobbyist. He would rather attend a dig than be in England. He is not a fan of society, and adventure has been forever in his blood." Alexandra bent and wiped her hands on the grass. "He and Professor Atler have always shared that passion. They worked in Cairo together before I was born. Though I've never understood their friendship," she murmured half to herself as she worked to clean her dress.

"Why not?"

"They are nothing alike."

Having failed to clean the grease from her bodice and skirt, Alexandra bought a quaint apron from a nearby booth and settled the matter of her appearance. Looking down at herself, she turned to and fro, admiring her new look. "I could be your maid, Miss Donally."

"You could plop a mobcap on your hair, and you would still never be mistaken for my maid." Brianna took her arm and started walking. "My lady, even foxed, you have a certain noble air about you."

"I am not inebriated, and I am not . . ." She searched for the correct word. Her eyes suddenly widened. They had stopped in front of a stall filled with beautiful fans. Spread like colorful peacock tails across the wooden walls, the fans boasted a tapestry of elegant and subtle artwork. "Oh, look." Alexandra pulled Brianna to the booth.

Laughing like schoolgirls, they waggled and snapped open dozens of fans, all of which Alexandra purchased and had delivered to the carriage. Liberally fluttering a bright lemon-yellow fan in front of her nose, Alexandra batted her eyes. She was suddenly swimming through her senses and quite unnaturally giddy. "You will have to teach me the fan language of ladies, Miss Donally."

They walked arm in arm away from the booths. "That means that you wish to dance with me, my lady."

And it was in that moment Alexandra realized that being with Brianna was a little like belonging to Christopher's rowdy, unpredictable Irish family. No one knew that they weren't related or that she wasn't a servant or governess. Wearing an apron over a grease-riddled gown, Alexandra stood in complete anonymity, duty to her father and to herself cast off with the stirring earth-scented wind of an approaching thunderstorm.

"Indeed." She laughed quite heartily, curtsied, and dropped back onto the grass. "I love to dance."

Brianna gasped. "My lady!"

"Oh, my."

Alarmed and a little frightened by what she'd allowed to happen, Brianna hastily knelt. "Are you all right?" Lady Alex was receiving attention from a group of ill-kempt men nearby.

"Except for the small matter of my stomach, I have never felt quite so . . . interesting, Miss Donally."

The pugilist match forgotten in the wake of the hour and Lady Alexandra's state, Brianna wished now that she had not stayed so late. No matter what her reasons had originally been for coming here today. At least her driver and Christopher's footman were at the carriage, and she could see them across the busy fairway. There was some security in that. "Let us go home, my lady. I think it's time that you're tucked into bed."

Brianna possessed a wretched guilt for not taking better care of her ladyship. Mussed to a state of disrepair, Lady Alex was like one of those exotic statues Christopher had in his home, fascinating and intriguing by virtue of beauty, yet fragile to the touch. For all of Lady Alex's accomplishments and the sterling example she represented to repressed womankind, and though Brianna yearned to be like her, Alexandra was not at all worldly. Beyond the narrow confines of her society or her brilliant academic career, she was very nearly helpless in the real world.

The Donallys of the planet would endure hardships and slay their dragons with far more proficiency than the Alexandra Marshalls ever could.

But the moment Brianna had visited Lady Alexandra that afternoon, the vulnerability beneath her façade had become something more. Something that Brianna had seen the day when she had watched Lady Alex sobbing outside the Carlisle manse all those years ago.

It was such a long-ago tableau, Brianna was surprised by the vividness of the picture that returned with her memory, that she'd never forgotten the image of the woman behind the black veil.

Or that Alexandra Marshall and Christopher could not be in the same space together without the air crackling around them. There was something long-standing between them that went back even before that day.

Having removed her shoes, Lady Alex wiggled her toes in the scraggy patch of grass. She still wore her stockings and managed to wet her feet in the dew-dampened weeds.

As Brianna was debating waving to her footman for aide, Stephan Williams, riding his tall horse, suddenly trotted into view. Her heart raced at the sight.

"Stephan," she whispered as he dismounted at the carriage. Recognizable by his crop of blond hair and his height, he wore a riding cloak that swirled around his boots.

He'd made it after all.

Brianna's gaze went back to Lady Alex, and guilt for what she'd done to her ladyship assailed her with a piercing intensity.

The romantic picture she'd painted earlier of *accidentally* running into Mr. Williams tonight suddenly fizzled, only because Lady Alex was so unspoiled and had not been the least pretentious at all about this adventure. Indeed, she'd been a jolly good sport about everything.

"Come, my lady." She helped Lady Alex to her feet. Behind her, a rushlight flickered in the breeze, casting shadows over the ground. "I fear that I have allowed you to get intoxicated. I will be severely reprimanded for this by the lordly powers that be at home."

"You have not *allowed* me anything, Miss Donally. I'm perfectly capable of taking my own blame for imbibing too much ale." She stumbled slightly. "I will not permit Christopher to chastise you for something that was not your doing."

"Yes, my lady." Brianna steadied her. "But *I* knew better. And I fear my brother knows us both enough to appreciate that fact."

From the corner of her eye, she saw two men break away from the group and walk toward her. Heart racing, she recognized the look of a footpad when she saw one. "Come, my lady. Let us hurry."

Then two things happened at once, as Brianna walked with Lady Alex across the uneven grounds. On the fairway, a grumble of thunder exploded, followed abruptly by a bolt of lightning that was not lightning, Brianna realized instantly. The detonation had occurred in the fireworks stall. Horses reared and bolted. People screamed. Whistlers zinged past her.

At once, the throng around her leaped to life. Someone shoved hard against her and knocked her forward to her knees. The force ripped her grip off Lady Alex. All Hades broke loose and suddenly the crowd turned into a panicked mob.

Christopher bolted up the tiered marble steps to the massive front door with a sense of icy determination. He'd already been to the cottage. Vaguely aware of the savage knot that gripped his chest, he'd handed Caesar off to a pair of Ware's footmen, who now sought to calm the high-spirited stallion. His quirt tapped his high boots splattered in mud from the passing storm that had only just let up a half hour ago. Suddenly conscious of his appearance, Christopher glanced over his shoulder at the short line of expensive black curricles on the driveway. He wore no coat over his riding breeches and shirt.

He was not expected here. Indeed, he'd be the last bloody man on earth Ware would expect to show up on his doorstep.

Inside, the tall clock struck midnight.

The door swung open. Male voices inside rose in laughter. Glasses clinked. "Sir—" The tall gaunt butler peered over his nose and a flash of alarm flared in his brown eyes. "Sir Donally! You shouldn't be here."

"You know my name. How?"

"This is not a good time, sir."

Christopher stuck his boot on the threshold and stopped the door from shutting in his face. The images that passed through his mind only added fuel to the realization that for one instant just now, he'd actually considered Lord Ware had somehow harmed Brianna.

"I assure you this is not a bloody social call."

The old man gasped when Christopher stepped into the foyer, his gaze briefly scanning the tall clock and massive elegant stairway. He abhorred feeling like an interloper. He had no desire to step into Lord Ware's secluded sanctum, especially in the middle of a private gathering. Cigar smoke wafted freely from the opened portal, leading into the drawing room.

"I was told my sister came here today. That Lady Alexandra did not show for her scheduled appointments."

Voices spilled into the corridor. "Alfred, ol chap," a voice called from the drawing room. "If that's Owensby, send him in." Drink in hand, Lord Somerset appeared around the corner. "Donally!"

"Lord Somerset." Christopher nodded his head.

Somerset was a short man, distinguished by his bulbous nose. "What are you doing standing out here, son?"

Christopher's fist clenched the riding crop. The last time he'd seen the man, they'd been in a conference at the office. A bloody important meeting. He was looking at Christopher oddly, perhaps recognizing his attire and realizing that he was not here on invitation.

"Send Owensby in," someone bellowed from behind Somerset. "So we can harangue him for being late."

"Sorry, ol chap," Somerset quietly offered. "This is a bit awkward. Don't know what could be holding up Owensby."

Muscles taut, Christopher followed Somerset into view of the drawing room.

"I do believe you know everyone present."

Christopher stood in the arched entryway. Professor Atler, who had been leaning with his elbow against the polished white marble mantel above the fireplace, straightened. Lord Ware's hand, holding a drink, froze midair. The satin lapels on his black smoking jacket glimmered in the firelight. The look on the man's face bordered horror, and might have been comical if Christopher were better dressed—or had been invited.

All of the men present sat on the museum board. They were philanthropist, scholars, and British policy makers. Christopher knew each one personally or professionally in some capacity.

"Sir Donally." Lord Wellsby stood and extended a hand. "Sit down and grab a drink. Owensby still isn't here. We were just talking about the pugilist match last weekend. Quite an event."

A round of conjectures and comments followed as each man boisterously returned to whatever argument Christopher had interrupted. Christopher's gaze remained momentarily locked on Ware.

"We have a differing of opinion on the final call," Lord Somerset said as a servant filled his glass with scotch.

"The call that gave me your purse." Wellsby chuckled before turning to Christopher. "Met your sister last week at my wife's salon. The girl wagered on the match herself. She knows more than ten men about the favorites. Must get that from you, ol' boy."

Christopher shifted his interest to Wellsby and attempted to digest what had just been said. "Indeed."

"Heard tell in your day you used to be the pugilist champ

at Woolwich." Somerset observed Christopher over the rim of his glass.

"Did you see the match, Donally?" another queried.

Christopher's gaze assessed each man. "No," he said tonelessly, aware that an odd undercurrent had begun to trickle around the room.

Lord Ware came to his feet, brittle gray eyes on Christopher's, and as the knee-jerk reaction to stand at attention grabbed at his spine, Christopher was suddenly thrown back ten years. Except he was not the young lieutenant who had been paraded before Ware like a criminal.

The butler reappeared in the corridor with a woman behind him. Bowing slightly at the waist, Christopher aimed his statement at Ware. "Your lordship. If you'll excuse me for interrupting."

The crystal chandelier tinkled softly. Light fluttered on the stark blue walls. Someone had just opened and closed the front door and when Christopher entered the corridor, the woman had vanished.

"My daughter is asleep, Donally." Ware followed him. "And you are insulting her by coming here at this hour."

With brutal restraint Christopher finally turned, the indifference he strove to hold around him shattering against him in waves. He knew Ware's voice carried a stabbing invasion that implicated Christopher as a social climber who didn't know two shillings about propriety.

The fact that the other men in the drawing room were also his colleagues on the board of trustees tempered Christopher's response. That and the fact that Somerset served on the Royal Commission for Public Works in Great Britain.

And all at once, a niggling uneasiness surfaced that had nothing to do with his worry over Brianna's disappearance. It was after midnight. Suddenly Christopher didn't want this man or those inside the drawing room knowing that his sister was unaccounted for.

He would go through Alexandra's damn window if that was what it took to talk to her. "Good night, my lord."

"I will not allow you to influence her." Ware's voice had lowered. This was between them now. Ware leaned on his heavy cane. "I swear, I will not."

Ware was afraid.

Of him.

"I beg to differ, my lord," Christopher said with quiet deference, pinning Ware with his gaze. "But you have no bloody say over what I do anymore."

"Stay away from my daughter, Donally."

Dismissing him, Christopher didn't slow his pace as Alfred opened the door. His boots clicked on polished marble.

Christopher bounded down the stairs. His leg ached. His stomach clenched as tightly as his fist on the quirt. Closing his mind, he thought only of his task. Alexandra's room was probably in the left wing of the mansion overlooking the pond. Nature was like a work of art to her. She would want the best view in the house. He walked on the gravel drive and took the reins of his horse from the footmen when a woman's voice stopped him from mounting.

"Sir Donally."

Christopher lowered his leg from the high stirrup and caught his weight on the injured leg. Honeysuckle filled the moist night air. It took him a moment to find the shadow in the darkness.

"I be Mary, sir." The woman stood within the hedges and out of sight of the front door. "Alfred told me why you've come here. Milady isn't here, sir. I couldn't allow Lord Ware to know. He'll probably dismiss me with no references, he will, for the lies I've told today." She wrung her hands and peered through the trees toward the massive stone house. "You see, Lord Ware and Lady Alexandra had a terrible row, and Miss Donally, she came by this afternoon. . . ."

His boots crunched gravel. Somewhere he heard a door shut. "Where are they, Mary?"

"There was some sort of fire, sir, and a riot, quite predictable for Londoners, if ye be askin' me. Stephan Williams took yer sister home straightaway. But—"

"Willie?" Christopher gripped the woman's shoulders. "You aren't making bloody sense."

"Miss Donally, she took milady to the fair." Mary held up a note. "Alfred intercepted it. It was meant for you in case you came here tonight. There was some manner of brawl. They arrested milady, sir."

Christopher refolded the note and spun away. Fury laced every boot step. Except it wasn't an anger that sprang from rage.

"Milady had never been to the country fair," Mary managed. Alex should have known better than to follow the judgment of a fresh-out-of-bloomers, self-emancipated seventeen-year-old.

One who possessed the street savvy to wager on pugilist matches, who played whist with women who smoked cigarettes, and talked openly about demireps.

Christopher put his foot in the stirrup, swinging the horse around as he mounted. "Thank you, Mary."

Mary stood at the edge of the walk, her white mobcap brilliant in the moonlight. "What will ye do, sir?"

"You mean after I turn my sister over my knee?"

And thrash Stephan Williams?

His gloved hand gripping the reins, Christopher dug his heels into the horse's flanks and left the drive.

Somehow he'd lost control of something vitally important here.

Like his whole damn life.

Chapter 11

‿‿‿‿‿◯◯◯‿‿‿‿‿

Alexandra lifted her head and stared with blurry eyes around the wretched cell. The straw mattress lay shredded in the dank corner and she'd sat on her crinoline. Her cheek was resting on her drawn-up knees. Heavy boot steps marked someone's approach.

Her guards didn't wear hard-soled riding boots.

"The bawd's lucky a bloomin' peeler didn't drop on her fer tryin' to steal that man's goods," a raspy voice said from outside the door.

Keys grated in the lock. "Threatened us with a bloody fork." The guard snorted. "Bloomin' airs fer a tart." He laughed.

"Open the goddamn door."

Alexandra pushed herself off the cot, tripping as she tried to stand. She didn't know whether to be cheered or alarmed by the prospect of facing the owner of that dark, compelling voice. Mostly she was just glad that someone had come here to get her out of this pigsty for the criminally inept. She looked down at herself aghast. Her ruined appearance was a sure parallel to her whole state of being. This moment would have benefited from a swig of brandy, she pondered resentfully.

The door squealed wide. Her heart leaped at the sight that greeted her. Wearing his greatcoat, his hair disheveled as if by the wind, Christopher stepped over the threshold and into the pale light of her cell. A dark shadow rimmed his jaw.

Never more than at that moment had she loved him so much. Maybe it was the way he looked at her. Maybe it was nothing at all, except the powerful chemistry between them that they shared even now, as they faced each other across the lantern light.

Then he had to ruin it all with his priggish arrogance!

His nose wrinkling at her smell, his gaze strafed her attire in what could barely be construed as astonishment. "You have enjoyed your night out?"

"Why don't you just laugh and get it over with?"

Amusement kicked up one corner of his mouth. "I wouldn't kick a dog when it's down, much less a highborn lady." He stepped toward her. His fingers took a strand of her hair and tucked it behind her ear. "Are you all right?"

She managed to school her response. His sister's action that night stood between them like a stubbed toe. Alexandra turned and looked at her crinoline spread out over the cot; then decided to leave it. "Have you been home?"

"Brianna admits bringing you to the fair under false pretenses. And tearfully added that you had nothing to do with Williams's presence." His voice touched her with the same thoroughness as his eyes. "She and I will have a long talk when I return."

"Please don't bother on my account." Alexandra swiped the back of her hand across her cheek, and whatever weakness she'd allowed him to glimpse vanished in the set of her shoulders. "I'm quite all right."

She strode past him into the stone corridor and stumbled over her skirts. "No thanks to this doddering gossoon. You—" she poked a furious finger into the bony chest of her errant

captor. "I shall see you drawn and quartered, you disrespect-
ful little scarab."

"Alex . . . for God's sake. He isn't the man who arrested you."

"Damn you, Donally." She poked him in the chest next. "I'm
through taking orders. I've just suffered *the* most humiliating
night in my life, and you lecture to me about formalities?"

Christopher propelled her through the smelly offal-ridden
tank of evildoers snoring against the wall. "Be grateful you
had a private room."

She stumbled again. He caught her arm, but his leg wasn't
strong enough to hold his weight and hers. They both stumbled against the wall. The ride here had sucked the strength
from his thigh.

Turning to the man bringing up the rear of their little column, Christopher reached out a gloved hand. "Give me your
bloody knife."

"Bloomin' 'ell, guv'nor." His rheumy eyes widened in
horror. "Are ye going to slit her throat?"

The knife in his hand, Christopher pressed Alex against
the stone wall. "How much have you had to drink?"

She gave him a reproving glance. "Surely you aren't going to murder me because I've imbibed in the local distilled
spirits?"

The patience left his eyes. "I can't carry you, Alex. And I
don't think you want to be thrown over anyone else's shoulder and carted out of here like a sack of grain." He knelt, his
coat folding around his feet as he bent over her dress and
sliced through her skirt.

Her hands fisted at her side. Looking down at Christopher's
dark head, she forced herself to remember that he was a Donally. Hence, his sister's brother. And the current opposing
force in her life. "I am guilty of tippling," she admitted, her
voice explicably pious. "But I am innocent of the crimes of
which I'm accused. That one"—she glared with vengeance at
the monkey-faced guard who had dared frisk her earlier—
"can attest to the fact that I had no stolen baubles on me."

The sound of rending cloth filled the mildewed corridor. "Did you attack a shop owner?" He'd relieved Alex of almost a foot of filthy fabric. And stood.

"Calling that wretched beast a shop owner is too kind. Besides, I hardly attacked him. I was pushed." Christopher was standing so close she had to tilt her head to look up at him. A hint of warm bayberry surrounded her senses. "He had the White Swan, Christopher. Or a facsimile thereof. His booth was near the end of the fairway. He was packing before the mob stole everything. My response was perfectly reasonable in the heat of battle, and if I hadn't been carrying the Buddha, he probably wouldn't have been knocked unconscious."

Christopher tilted her chin. Watching him in disbelief, she thought that he might actually laugh. "Alex," his voice whispered. "Why didn't you just get the name of his business?"

"Because . . ." The hot sting of tears burned her eyes. "*That* would have been much too simple."

A searing awareness of his restraint flashed through her. "Then unless you want to be arraigned tomorrow for battery, you'd best move."

Looking up at him, she had the sense to appreciate her dire circumstances. Unhampered by her skirts, she marched determinedly past him, her skirts swishing with as much dignity as her awkward gait allowed. She felt Christopher's eyes on her back, his presence looming like a tall winged bat all the way up the narrow stone stairwell. She prayed that she would not embarrass herself further by tripping.

In the main room, the night watchman nodded to Christopher. Without a glance at her surroundings or waiting as Christopher stopped at the desk, she strode out into the chilly night air, aware that dawn roosted on the horizon. A tight knot coiled in her chest.

The footman stood beside Christopher's carriage and straightened abruptly when he saw her approach. "Milady."

Ignoring him, she climbed the step he'd pulled out and turned to face Christopher as he walked behind her. "I wish to go home. Now."

With an agility that impressed even her, she slammed the door in his face. The door flung open and Christopher climbed into the carriage. His hand gripped her chin and she was suddenly looking into furious eyes. She dropped her palm to the taut, unyielding muscles of his thigh to keep from falling forward when the carriage started rolling.

"Don't for one moment think that I've allowed my sister off the hook for her part in this fiasco. Mobs are a nefarious, brutal lot, Alex. Much worse could have happened to you. And if you'd stop pouting long enough, you might decide to be a little more grateful that at least you can walk out of there to a clean bed."

Her hands shook. "Don't you dare turn this into a social indoctrination lecture on the wealthy elite versus the unwashed masses." She gave him her back as she struggled out of her filthy gown. "It just so happens that I like having clean linens to sleep on. I want a bath. If that's a sin, then so be it. I'm going straight to hell."

All in one exciting night, her wonderful adventure had reduced her to a sniveling, self-centered prat. She couldn't help it and was powerless to stop the tumble of her emotions.

She should have known that to tread outside the narrow circle of four hundred could only mean disaster for someone as socially inept as she. She'd been out of her element tonight with no measure of common street sense to guide her.

A shiver went through her body. There was a time that night when she'd been afraid. "You needn't make me feel like an incompetent idiot, Christopher. I already feel like a brilliant one without your help." Opening the door, she tossed her gown outside and watched it roll to a swooning lump in the middle of the road. "Leave it to me to make a complete ass of myself doing something so *simple* as going to a fair."

She twisted to face Christopher, daring him to insult her.

His gaze went slowly down her to return with bemused interest to her face. An eyebrow lifted. "Not that I'm one to complain about a half-naked woman in my carriage, but you do realize that I haven't a change of clothes in here."

She lifted her chin. "I wish to purchase your overcoat."

"With what, may I be so bold to ask?"

Speechless, she stared at him. She was exhausted, demented, and likely to hit him if he joked any more at her expense. Not in her whole life had she felt so . . . common.

"Come here."

"No." She moved to the opposite seat. "I'll get you dirty and smelly."

"Indeed." He reached across her to turn down the light. His coat enveloped her and she was filled with the scent of him. "I've not the aversion to filth that you have," he said, pulling her stubbornly into his lap.

"Let go of me." His arms were like unrelenting bands of iron. "I probably have fleas, Christopher."

His hand slid up her thigh. "You haven't experienced true squalor until you've worked the lower-level sewer beneath the Thames embankment. Nothing else truly compares."

"What a wretched thing. You've actually been in a place like that?"

"Believe it."

Finally giving up her resistance, she surrendered her cheek to his warm shoulder. Streetlights winked over the leather seats as the carriage ambled along the empty road. Christopher was watching her. "I must seem like such a snob to you," she said quietly.

"You *are* a snob." His voice was soft in her hair. "I think you've never seen a flea that wasn't embedded in plaster first."

"This is very funny to you, isn't it? That I should look like something dragged up from the depths of one of your projects?"

"No." His fingers fanned across her cheek, bringing her lips nearer to his. And a carnal thrill shot through her. He'd removed his gloves. "Never in all of the years that I've known you have I ever seen you with a hair or a stitch out of place. Unless I'd just rolled you in bed. Or in the straw. Or the sand. Or wherever else you and I managed to come together." He lowered his mouth. "I think you're sexy as hell even if you do smell like something dredged up on the Thames. And if you stopped talking long enough, I'd kiss you."

Alexandra buried her face in her hands. Her shoulders shook. She laughed because she wasn't entirely sure if she should feel insulted or relieved. She chose the latter.

Finally, she stole a glance at Christopher. "I'm truly sorry that I made you worry about me." She trailed her hand beneath his coat and down the sleek line of his muscled shoulder and biceps. "Everything would have been just fine had that fireworks display not blown up. What happened last night was not Brianna's fault."

"You and my sister scared the hell out of me, Alex."

"I'm sorry." Her emotions held the first startling glimpse of desperation that had crept nearer since they'd made love at her cottage house.

"Brianna is upset, and rightly so," he said, laying her back on the seat. He lowered his lips to her neck. His coat trailed to the floor of the carriage. "It is not every day that she misplaces the future Countess of Ware only to find out that her idol got into a brawl." His gaze encompassed hers. "I've attained the name of the man who filed charges against you," he said in the silence. "I'll make inquiries tomorrow."

Hope widened her eyes. "Then you know the name of the shop?"

"Not exactly. Alex"—he cupped her face—"the White Swan would not be the first reproduction of a museum treasure the public has ever seen." His hand tangled in her hair. "He probably designed the pendant after he saw the thing on display." He kissed her. "But it's the first real lead I've received." He placed his lips upon hers and kissed her again, longer than the last. "There has not been an influx of stolen jewels into the market."

"What does that mean?"

"That everything was probably disposed of on the continent."

"Christopher?" She opened her eyes and arched her neck to glimpse outside a pale sky. "Where are we going?"

His mouth tilted into a roguish grin. "My house."

"We are?"

Like lovers.

She wondered if he'd ever taken anyone else there.

And couldn't bear the thought.

"I sent Barnaby ahead. A bath should be waiting." He pressed his mouth against her throat and back to her lips. "I can't stop the sunrise, but I should have you back to the museum before lunch. If I don't find myself too preoccupied to look at the clock"—he tasted her deeply—"every so often."

His lips covered hers in a long, lingering feast of the senses. Slow and deep. Deep and slow. Over and over his mouth came back to hers, the powerful weight of his chest crushing her into the soft leather seat. The rush of a long reckless night, ebbed into the white-hot heat of a reckless morn. Her fingers tensed in his scalp. Returning his kiss with all the urgency of her pent-up emotions, she imbibed in his taste and the wondrous sensations of his touch. His palm slid to her waist. Scraping her fingers into his hair, she groaned into his mouth, felt her name whispered against her lips, and surrendered to the bone-melting fire.

She spread her legs to allow him access, and dragged air into her lungs as he pulled away to work his trousers loose. Her underclothes were no impediment to his touch as his hand found its way inside her pantalets and against her, tending with intimate detail to her pleasure. His finger delved inside her, spreading her apart.

The hair on his chest grazed her nipples. He banged his head on the door. "Shit. . . ." There was a slight tugging as he adjusted his knee between her thighs and hit his head again.

Her eyes slowly opened, mesmerized. "Have you ever done this in a carriage?"

"No." He looked down at her face with grim amusement. "Have you?"

He knew that she had not. "No." She laughed, unable to resist the lure of his body and wanting so much more at the moment. "Hurry."

She squirmed lower on the seat, her knees braced against the opposite side of the carriage. Christopher slid inside her. Thrust again, impossibly deep. "Tight . . . wait, Christopher."

He'd pinned her body beneath his, sheathing himself. "You're correct about that, Alex. You feel . . . hot."

Outside, the sunrise had peaked over the treetops. His shirt was unbuttoned and hung out of his trousers. He raised up to lower the shades, hesitating. She followed him up, pulling his mouth back down to hers. "Don't leave," she whispered.

He answered with a rasping oath. Yielding a moment longer to her mouth, to her movements, his strength was unexpected as he lifted her into his lap, then bent to look outside. "Damn."

A thump on the carriage made her start. She followed his gaze out the window and saw the house with its high sloping roof and gable windows discernible through the trees.

"Double damn," she whispered and pulled down the shade.

"We're here," he said, a groan in his voice.

Still lodged on his lap, impaled by his erection, she cupped his jaw between her cool palms. "It's a beautiful house." Pressing him back into the seat, she continued with her kisses and manual exploration of his very hard body. This time she was on top, his long legs trailing along the bench seat. "But I *like* it out here."

Alexandra wanted to consume him. His hands found her breasts, then her waist. The coach came to a shuddering halt on the drive.

"Christ. . . ." She heard the low feral moan of a growl. "Any moment . . . that fucking door is going to open."

She suckled his neck, her knees drawn up to his hips. "Christopher?" She was melting around him. "Are proper Irish Catholic boys . . . supposed to use that kind of language?"

His hand curled in her hair at the nape of her neck and brought her down to his mouth. "All the fooking time."

His tongue swept inside her mouth. Without letting her up for air, he held his other hand against her bottom, moving her with a thrumming intensity. On some base level, she recognized the startling primal possession. His response balanced her need. Her blood hummed. Hot damp air filled her lungs. Her lips were demanding on his, never wanting more than at that moment. He couldn't be deep enough inside, or hard enough. She wanted all of him.

Then, with a low growl, he took the initiative from her, flipping her. He clasped her bottom, holding her against him. They hit the other seat, his coat tangling beneath her back. Her hair flared around her. Their gazes touched and locked briefly, his dark and searing before his lips possessed hers. His feet kicked the door, then a knee, and an oath followed. Her heart pounded violently. Dimly, she realized that she clung to his powerful shoulders, rocking in restless abandon, all thought narrowed to the feel of him inside her. He rode her hard, his movement shoving her against carriage door; then she was climaxing around him. His eyes heavy-lidded, he watched her, her body convulsing around him, until, mindless as she, he drove into her, shuddering in release.

"Do you think they guessed what we were doing?" Alexandra asked after they'd managed to arrange their attire into some semblance of appearance. Christopher had removed his coat and placed it around her.

The carriage remained where it had been left on the front drive. Standing elbow to elbow on the front drive, they both looked around for the driver and footmen. Alexandra turned to look up at him. And for the first time in more years than Christopher could remember, he knew by bringing her here that he'd put his personal life before his business concerns. Perhaps he was momentarily deranged.

Or just exhausted.

He pulled her against the length of him. "Has it occurred to you that I might not have anything for you to wear here?"

"I feel daring."

The sun on her face, his coat draping possessively over her to the ground, he eyed her state of undress with renewed interest.

With a gamely squeal, she cut around him through the garden. He watched her flight around the side of the house before he took off after her. He caught up to her in the middle of his sprawling yard.

"Why don't you strip naked and join me in a bath?" She smiled as he walked her slowly toward the terrace, his intent clear in his eyes.

There was a growing sense of alarming depravity in his actions. "We're bloody insane, Alex."

His mouth covered hers, lingering in mutual bliss. She climbed his body, wrapping her legs around his hips. He turned in a circle with her in his arms. The trees whispered above them. He readjusted her weight. His arms tightened around her. Beneath the coat she wore, he planted his hand firmly on her bottom. He was shocked by the primal sense of male possession, the satisfaction that he could take from his lordly foe his most precious belonging. That Alex would be his if he wanted her to be.

She pulled back and their gazes held. His emotions scared the hell out of him. She was wanton and beautiful, and for a moment he was caught by the inexplicable need to keep her here.

The thought was like ice water in his face.

She framed his face with her palms. "You do realize that true gentleman of leisure are, well . . . leisurely. One cannot be paid for his services. You'll have to retire to this house so that I may stay with you . . . on occasion, of course. I would not want you to get bored of me."

"Unfortunately, some of us cannot live in a manner to which we've become accustomed if we are not paid for our services."

"I would pay you for your services, sir."

He regarded her impish grin with a wicked one of his own. "I'll pretend that you didn't just offer to keep me."

Her eyes widened in mock innocence. "Men do it all the time. I'm very wealthy, sir." She wiggled seductively. "Or I soon will be."

"Indeed."

"You wouldn't *have* to work." Her palms slid over him. "Except in bed, of course."

"That's not work, Alex." With a low growl, he bent to take her lips. Movement on the terrace stopped him.

The smell of biscuits and ham wafted on the warm gardenia-scented breeze. It took him an instant to realize that all the glass doors at the back of his house stood open to the air. The windows were open.

All senses leaping to alert, he let Alex slide to the ground, his gaze following the wooden terrace toward the gazebo. "Uncle Fer!" a little girl's voice cried out excitedly.

His four-year-old niece.

Over a dozen people sat frozen around a table. Silver gleamed from steaming chafing dishes and crystal. Disbelief checked his response as he stared in what he could only assume was as close to horror as one might feel facing the blanched faces of his brothers, their wives, and their many, many children.

"Your family?" Alexandra gasped, snatching together the coat.

His arm had raised in greeting before his actions caught up to his brain. "Bloody hell."

Alexandra's hands trembled. "Do you think they saw us kissing?"

He buttoned his coat on her. "Is that a rhetorical remark?" She had to lift the heavy folds as he guided her stumbling back toward the front of the house where the carriage had let them off. "Or a question you seriously think needs answering?"

He slammed the front door of his house, drew a deep breath, and paused as he turned back to her. He drew her into his arms. "Bear with me on this. I'm at a loss here."

She managed only a nod. "What are you going to do?"

"I'm taking you to my room. A bath should already be drawn."

Halfway up the wide staircase, a masculine voice snapped Christopher around. "Do you think that wise?"

Wearing riding boots, the man stood with one foot on the bottom stair and one on the landing. Unlike Brianna and Christopher, who possessed the same blue eyes, this man's were almost black. His stature, though slightly shorter, was no less broad in the shoulders than Christopher's. "Rachel is here." His gaze passed over Alex. "And so is my fiancée. Their things are in your room. What are you doing, Chris?"

Christopher pulled Alex behind him, where she plopped down on the top step. "Good to see you too, *Ryan*. Do you think you could have bloody warned me first?"

"How many telegrams do I need to send you?"

Christopher walked down a step. "How about one telling me that you are planning a goddamn family gathering here instead of at Carlisle?"

"I thought, with negotiations on for the Tunnel Project and considering this is the busiest time of the year for us, it would be better that everyone come to London. My mistake, obviously. Had I known that you were planning a—"

"Say it, Ryan, and I'll guarantee you won't have any teeth left when you finish."

Her forehead leaning on her palm, her elbow on her knee, Alexandra felt queasy. Movement downstairs brought her blurry gaze to the rail, where she peeked through the spindles into the hallway below. Two of Christopher's other brothers had stepped into the corridor.

Ryan tossed a negligent hand in her direction. "The *lady's* father is in the bloody House of Lords, for bloody Christ's sake," he whispered. "You don't need the kind of trouble that bastard will bring down on you. On us. Where's Brianna?"

"She's at the townhouse." Christopher started back up the stairs, then turned and retraced his steps. "On bloody bread and water, confined to her room until my return."

Ryan looked at Christopher as if he'd suddenly grown three heads and a tail. "Are you insane?"

"At the moment? Insane is an enormous understatement. You have no idea what it's like living with a seventeen-year-old newly liberated woman of modern means, who, by the way, thinks I have reduced her to the equivalent of a Roman slave because I expect her to behave like a lady."

Ryan took a step up. "Oh, that's bloody ripe, coming from someone who hasn't exactly displayed the sterling qualities of a gentleman."

As Alexandra watched the corridor fill with people, an auburn-haired woman moved quietly forward. Her interest piqued, Alexandra followed her progress. She wasn't beautiful in the traditional sense. Indeed, she was something far more interesting. She wore a pale yellow morning dress, with white lace trim. At home among the tall dark verbose Donally clan, she radiated confidence. Even as Alexandra instinctively knew that this was Rachel Bailey, the woman, as if sensing Alexandra's stare, lifted her gaze.

Their eyes held. Without a word, the woman squeezed through the male-ridden corridor. Upon seeing her, Ryan's voice stuttered to a halt. Pulling aside her skirts, Rachel Bailey walked past him up the stairs. "Ryan." She nodded coolly, then eased past toward where Alexandra was sitting. Stopping in front of Christopher, the girl narrowed her eyes. "Where are your manners, Christopher Bryant Donally? You should be ashamed of yourself." She took Ryan into her glare as well. "Were ye not thinkin' that it might be wise to inform your brother of our arrival?"

Alexandra watched the arrogant Ryan Donally transform into a docile lamb. Christopher, whose ruggedly handsome features had looked stark and dangerous only a minute before, now dropped his gaze to Alexandra.

As he started to move forward, Rachel stopped him. "Oh, no, ye don't, sir. I will take her to her bath. And perhaps while ye wait, you will do us all a favor and take a swim in yonder icy pond."

The matter effectually settled by an oath from the master of the house, Rachel turned. "Come, milady." She helped Alexandra to stand.

Stumbling slightly on Christopher's coat, Alexandra clutched a handful of woolen fabric in her hand. Looking over her shoulder at both men, who remained where they'd been verbally incinerated on the stairway, Alexandra reluctantly allowed the other half of Donally & Bailey Steel and Engineering to lead her away.

Chapter 12

Christopher rubbed a towel over his damp hair. Walking through the servants' entrance and up the back stairwell, he managed to escape his family. He'd finally decided that he could salvage little out of the events of that day and would not attempt to do so. He wore a clean pair of trousers but little else as he padded down the carpeted hallway toward his room. The door was opened a crack.

Rachel stood when Christopher entered the room. Pausing midstep, he lowered the towel. She'd been sitting in a chair, one of his books in hand, reading. Rachel was an incredibly beautiful woman. He wondered when she'd suddenly grown up.

"I found her asleep on the bed," she said. "So I covered her."

At once, his gaze went around his room. Alex slept in his bed. The sheets were damp, as if she'd crawled into bed after her bath and went directly to sleep. From the servants' reports, he'd heard that she'd gotten sick.

Walking past Rachel, he placed his hand over Alex's pale cheek, and felt some of the tenseness leave his body. She was on her side, curled against his pillow, oblivious to the world, the state of her appearance, and the fact that half of London could be looking for her at this very moment. Her hair lay over the pillow, the locket just above her breasts.

He lifted the locket and let it lay in his palm. "She never could handle her drink." Pulling his hand away, he found himself ready to leap bonfires to defend her. "She's had a rough night. Let her sleep."

Rachel eyed him with raised brows. "Apparently she wasn't the only one."

And as her gaze went over him, Christopher was aware of his state of undress. He wore no shirt. Water dripped from his hair onto his shoulders. He stepped past her and padded into the dressing room.

"But not too rough," her voice followed him. "I'll be wagerin' my next annuity."

He yanked a fleecy white shirt from among a dozen that lay neatly folded on the shelf. "I apologize for the scene that you witnessed—" He stopped himself and rephrased before shoving his shirt in his waistband. "No, I regret that all of you saw what you saw. But I don't apologize for anything."

Outside the closet, Rachel had moved beside his armoire. He heard the squeak of the door as she leaned against its frame. "Ryan really was thinking about you when he arranged this gathering today. Perhaps you should be more diligent in reading your memos."

With a grunt, he applied socks to his feet.

"He's gone to fetch Brianna," she said a little louder, as if he couldn't hear her. "Did ye catch her sneaking out of her window? Is that why you've got your nose in a snit?"

Christopher's hands paused. His gaze sought refuge in the plaster cornices overhead. "What do you know about Brianna?" He shoved his feet into a pair of tall riding boots.

"That's always been her habit. She and I used to swim naked in the pond outside my house."

He rolled his eyes. "I don't want to know that, Rachel."

"About swimming naked? Or that she snuck out of the house?"

Working the cuff on one sleeve of his shirt, Christopher returned to the doorway of his closet. "Neither."

"You should talk to Ryan when he returns."

"Ryan was out of line today."

"So were you, Christopher." Rachel's voice tightened. "I'm a shareholder of D&B as well. And if ye don't understand our concerns, then frankly you've gone and lost your mind. Or maybe your memory. I know your brothers haven't."

Suddenly welcoming the distraction, Christopher worked to fasten the cufflinks on his shirt. He'd left his collar open. "I don't know, Rachel. Maybe I have."

"Were you once married to her?"

Arching a brow, Christopher worked the other sleeve.

"One of the Donally skeletons, I think," she said when he didn't reply.

"Are there more?"

"I imagine there are a few more," she said noncommittally.

Christopher wondered just how much of his life she knew.

"Do you think you'll be able to hold on to her this time? And still be alive when the bullets stop flying?" Her expression grew serious. "Or is this something else entirely?"

His gaze found Alex, naked beneath his sheets, in his house. Inappropriate as hell, and as vulnerable as his heart. An hour hadn't passed that he'd not considered the seriousness of his actions or the consequences of his fickle mood. Or how precariously close his control had crept to the edge. Yet, even as his mind sought to justify the vengeance aspect, he knew his reasons for being with her went far deeper.

After all these years, she still fascinated him.

When he was twenty-one, he'd been so in love with her he couldn't see straight. She'd been all the things forbidden to someone like him. At thirty-two, he could see clearer, yet she still made him feel things a dozen more suitable, more beautiful women never could.

"It isn't anything else." Shifting his gaze back to Rachel, Christopher knew with absolute certainty he could say those words.

Whatever else it was he felt, it wasn't vengeance he sought.

Maybe it was peace. Or some manner of closure to his past.

A fresh start. A chance.

He knew that Alex was his. He had been her first lover. Her husband. The father of her child.

He had been all those things.

Yet, still it hadn't been enough to hold on to her.

Rachel's hazel eyes gentled on his. "Go downstairs and join your family, Christopher. You need to be with them, I think."

Christopher tilted her chin. "Why are you being so nice?"

"I figured I owe you a little something back for teaching me how to ride a horse when I was five. Even if you did ignore me something wretched the rest of the time."

Crossing his arms, he leaned a shoulder on the doorjamb. "You remember that? And you were all of . . . how old?"

"There were at least six screaming little girls all eager to scare your horse to death that day you came to see your da at my house. It was a matter of your survival that you allowed us to ride. You put me on your horse first."

He did remember. Six screeching little girls wearing curls and flounces and covered in cocoa. They'd nearly caused him to be thrown from his horse. He'd been sixteen and had just received notice of his acceptance to Woolwich. He'd gone to her house wearing his new uniform to find his father.

"You broke my wee heart when you joined the regiment and left me to be tormented by Ryan. How do you think he learned to box so well? He used me for his punching bag."

"Why can't my sister behave more like you, Rachel?"

"I'm not your sister, Christopher."

He let his gaze touch hers. "You are to me." He knew that it had been their respective families' wishes that they marry. That it was something everyone had assumed would one day happen. He'd not missed Rachel's puppy-love glimpses, and had chalked her infatuation up to a case of hero worship. He did now, as well.

With a sigh, she raised on her tiptoes and kissed his mouth before slowly pulling away. "Go see to your family, Christopher."

Alexandra awakened to the sound of children playing outside. Her hair was still damp from her bath. Somewhere, crystal chimed softly. The vague scent of bayberry hinted of Christopher. Snuggling deeper into the pillow, she brought the scented sheets to her nose and lay in slumbering bliss another dozen heartbeats before her eyes snapped open.

Her breath froze as her mind assimilated her surroundings. She'd fallen asleep. A breeze whispered against the damask emerald curtains and set the crystal lamps beside the bed to music. She lay in a vast four-poster bed that was draped in the same emerald damask framing the large opened windows.

She'd lain down for only a moment after her bath. Underneath the sheets, she wore nothing.

She sat up, her hair tumbling over her shoulders in damp tangles. Her hands went to the dull throb in her head. The room was somber with the shadows of an approaching dusk.

Good lord. She was in Christopher's bed, in his house, with his family downstairs. Twisting to find the gilt-framed clock she'd seen earlier on the nightstand, she froze.

Brianna sat perched on the edge of a white damask chair, hands folded in her lap. She wore an uncertain smile. "My lady."

"Brianna." Wrapped in the sheet, Alexandra drew her knees to her chest. "The last I'd heard, you were confined to your room on a diet of bread and water."

Her black hair coifed in ringlets, Brianna wore a dainty little hat that matched her fashionable violet-sprigged traveling dress. Hastily dabbing at her wet nose, she sat straighter. "Ryan brought me here a few hours ago," she said as if in apology for not changing her attire. "Christopher was asleep downstairs in the salon. . . . I don't mean to intrude, my lady. But I needed so desperately to talk. So I waited."

Unable to bear the agony on the younger girl's face a moment longer, Alex said, "It's not necessary to apologize."

"Oh, but it is. After everything you've been through because of me." Brianna's chest rose and fell. "I was not entirely honest when I asked you to go to the fair. I should have told you the truth."

"Yes, you should have."

"I was hoping Mr. Williams would show. But I didn't think you'd go if I had said anything, and I wasn't even sure if he'd show. So, in a way, I wasn't completely deceitful."

"You were, Brianna."

Brianna's white teeth nibbled at her lower lip. "What is life without a little adventure?"

"Happily boring, thank you very much."

"You mean oppressed."

Groaning to herself, Alexandra dropped her forehead on her knees. Now that Alexandra had met Rachel Bailey, she didn't feel entirely responsible for Brianna's liberal social philosophy. Introspective books were obviously in abundant supply wherever it was the younger woman had spent her impressionable youth.

"Does Christopher know that I've allowed you to see Mr. Williams almost every day these past weeks?" Alexandra raised a brow.

Brianna lowered her gaze, shamefaced. "I told Christopher that you didn't know anything about Stephan. Please don't tell him otherwise. Or he would be doubly angry. My brother is a tyrant, my lady, on the level equal to Nero of that once-noble bastion called Rome."

"Yes, so I'd heard." Alexandra scraped back the heavy folds of her hair that had fallen forward. "I thought you said he was asleep when you arrived."

"He was until Ryan woke him up."

"Then you argued?"

"Sort of, my lady." Brianna toyed with her sleeve. "I announced that I would run off with Stephan and get married if he so much as thought to banish me from London."

Alexandra groaned.

"And I accused him of having never been in love. For no heart ever having known love could be so cruel!"

Alexandra's breath stilled. "Then what happened?"

"Nothing." Brianna traced the flower motif on her skirt. "It was Ryan who told me I wasn't ready to have a Season, and that I would return to Carlisle. Then he told me to come up and relieve Rachel until you awakened."

Rachel was in here? As Alexandra had learned earlier, Rachel Bailey was not the simple child-creature that Christopher had once implied.

A heavy weight settled in her stomach. She looked down at her hands, realizing that Brianna no longer needed her. What about her bargain with Christopher and the great start she'd had introducing Brianna to society? She'd actually begun to enjoy herself. Then there was the realization she would now have no excuse to ever don the beautiful clothes she'd purchased.

"My lady," Brianna moved to the bed and sat. "I couldn't bear knowing that you might hate me."

Alexandra took the girl into her arms, pressing the desolate countenance against her shoulder, and resting her cheek on the girl's forehead. "I understand more than you think."

A breath shuddered through Brianna's shoulders and she sat back, lifting a furtive gaze. "Then we're still friends? Even if I have been acting quite the daft fish?"

"Love has never contributed to the intellect of anyone."
Christopher's tenderhearted sister, if she was anything at all,
was endearingly melodramatic. "When will you be leaving?"

"I don't know." She shrugged. "When Rachel is ready, I
suppose."

"I see."

"My lady." Brianna wiped the heel of her hand across her
face. "Now that we've settled the matter of our friendship . . ." She sat back and primly folded her hands into her
lap. "If I may be so bold as to ask? Why is it that you arrived
here with no gown?"

Alexandra looked down at herself, reality now replanted in
the forethought of her brain. "I fear that what remained of the
hideous thing is somewhere between here and Epping. Much
to my outraged self-respect, I threw it out of the carriage."

"My lady! Whatever did Christopher do?"

"He gave me his coat."

Then she'd waltzed in front of his whole family looking
like a dollymop. Behaving as one, too, and she having just
been released from the gaol. Death by humiliation alone
would have put her out of her misery. But no. God in all His
infinite wisdom had decided to keep her alive so that she
could further disgrace herself by getting ill all over Christopher's beautiful carpet.

"I'm glad that you are here," Brianna said, clearly laboring
under the misapprehension that Christopher had invited her
for anything distantly resembling a wholesome afternoon
with his family. "And I've already set something out for you.
I shall return in a moment."

The door shut and with a resigned sigh, Alexandra found
herself alone in Christopher's bedroom. Her wrists crossed
over her knees, she looked around her. From outside, children's laughter skipped in and out of the room.

Christopher possessed expensive taste in furnishings.
Ferns and fragile greenery flourished prominently on the Chip-
pendale dresser and atop the armoire. A collection of spicy
Chinese watercolors brought a small grin to her lips. She'd

never known another person who shared her passions for the exotic as equally as did Christopher.

Another burst of laughter outside the window piqued her curiosity. The tap-tap of wooden balls clicking against each other followed. Dragging the sheet with her off the bed, Alexandra walked to the window and cautiously pulled aside the curtains.

Five children of different ages played croquet off the terrace. The shadow of the vast stone house fell across the gardens. She fixed her eyes on the archway of elms where the passing day had begun to gather in the mist, and found Christopher standing beside the gazebo overlooking the pond. Wearing tall riding boots, he looked as if he'd just returned from the stables, and appeared as at ease in his casual attire as he did in the boardrooms of London's business elite. He held a little girl in his arms. Another clung to his leg. A tall man dressed in similar attire stood shoulder to shoulder on one side of him, another man and woman on the other. Christopher's hand rested lovingly on the little girl's dark curly head, his affection apparent for both children.

"Those are my brother Johnny's twins." Brianna joined her at the window. "Christopher holds idol status over all of his nieces. Johnny is fourth in the pecking order. His oldest is seven." She pointed toward the other couple beneath the elms. "That's Colin and his wife. Colin is a banker." Brianna then proceeded to locate his brood of four children. "My other brother, David, who is just below Christopher on the Donally family tree went into the priesthood a few years ago. He is not here today. Ryan, his affianced, and Rachel are out riding. He and Christopher had a wretched argument, I fear. And for once, I wasn't the cause."

Pulling away from the window, Alexandra let the curtain drop.

"It's all a little overwhelming at first," Brianna said in utter sympathy. "At least there have been no bloodied noses today or broken windows." Brianna turned to the clothes she'd laid out on the bed. "But then this is Christopher's house." She gave Alexandra a pointed smile. "Knowing my brother, he's put the fear of God in Nathaniel and Matthew, Colin's two oldest. They are the worst for breaking things. Tonight we will all go to mass. Tomorrow everyone will leave."

Alexandra pressed her fingers to the growing ache in her temples.

A strange sort of hysteria had begun to unfurl inside her. It was not simply the fact that she could not attend his church.

Or her desire to avoid crowds.

Or the certainty that she had nothing in common with these people except her affection for Christopher. They'd once been cruel to her. And she didn't like them.

This was all so foreign to her, this part of Christopher's life. And so contrary to her perception of him, of the man who had made love to her that morning in the carriage: the man who spoke with such an eloquent flair for profanity and made her climax twice.

She'd always known Christopher's family and faith were an integral part of who he was, the impetus behind his recovery long ago. But she'd never seen any other side but the one he'd shared with her. Observing it now lent insight into his character, and a deeper understanding of what they both faced. Her stomach knotted.

It was a strange sensation, realizing that he belonged to a world completely separated from hers.

Where rampant mischief was the norm.

Where people ate with their fingers and thought nothing of pummeling a sibling to a pulp, or throwing one out a second-story window. Even if it was accidental.

Yet, there was no doubt of the loyalty and love for each other. Stand against one, and a person would find himself facing all.

She'd only had her father her whole life. In her household, even the servants' children maintained proper decorum. Lord

Ware was more intimidating than the wrath of God any given hour of the month.

But what would her father have been like today had his grandson lived to leave the handprints of his passing in the huge empty houses where they'd spent their lives? Perhaps Christopher's son would have softened the edges of her father's world.

She would never know.

"My lady? What do you think?"

Alexandra's gaze lifted. She didn't remember sitting down on the bed. Brianna was holding up a fluffy pink creation that looked like something out of Regent's Flower Shop, and Alexandra's eyes widened in alarm.

"Most of what I have here might not be something you would ever wear. But this dress is certainly festive. No one will even notice that it is too short."

And just like that, as if the sunlight had melted away the chilling doubt, Alexandra's tension began to change into something more palpable.

"It's certainly pink. Isn't it?"

Brianna eyed her. "You won't let them cower you, my lady?" Perhaps she was remembering the last time Alexandra had faced the Donally clan alone. "Please, my lady. Come as my friend."

Would she shame Christopher by appearing in front of his family?

Alexandra fingered the silky cloth of the gown. "You've never asked why I showed up that day in Carlisle all those years ago," she quietly said. "Why not?"

"You were in love with my brother." Brianna's blue eyes were earnest. "Maybe I need no other reason than that to like you, my lady."

More than anything she'd wanted to hide the tears. She'd already decided that she would not cower. But Brianna's words convinced her that neither would she apologize.

Whatever it was that had happened between Christopher

and her father—for she suspected the rift between the two went far deeper even than the current facts affirmed—she would not remain in the shadows.

And after her exhibition that afternoon with Christopher, it would be worth it to see the shock on everyone's faces when she appeared looking like a freshly cut spring flower.

"Don't ye have a bloody bottle of anything to drink in this house?"

Listening patiently as Colin foraged through every cabinet in the library, Christopher sat with his boots propped on a leather ottoman, his head resting on the seat back as he pressed a cool glass of lemonade against his temple. His head ached. He had just started to drift to sleep when Colin's voice jerked him awake.

Over the rim of his glass, he watched his brother stalk across the room to the desk. "You're not going to find anything in there, either."

An older version of Ryan, his younger brother's physical resemblance was the only attribute he shared with any of the family. Colin was the least mechanical person Christopher had ever known. But he was a good father, at ease with people, and a genius with numbers. Unlike David, who'd abruptly abandoned the family business to go into the priesthood, Colin was D&B's chief financial officer.

"And there be no sin in staying sober today, Colin Donally," a woman's voice said from behind Christopher. Fiercely protective Meg. Colin's fiery wife rustled past and thrust a glass of lemonade into her husband's hand. "Since when have the Donallys needed fortification to get through any day? Where's your backbone?"

"Withered to dust," Colin grumbled. "Aye, like Johnny's and Ryan's. Do you see them around? Probably gone for respite at the local pub."

Christopher closed his eyes and continued to massage his temple. Alex's presence was like a thick ambient fog circulating through the house. He didn't know if he felt annoyed by his family's lack of charity or in perfect harmony with their mood. For now he settled on neither. Accepting that he was not in his right mind, he elected political prudence over the impulse to defend himself against yet another family member.

Besides, Meg was ardently protective of Rachel.

His gaze attached to the new glass of lemonade his sister-in-law just handed him. "So when are ye going to marry Rachel and be done with this silly nonsense?" she said pointedly, her green eyes flashing.

"Meg," he warned.

She plopped two small fists on her hips. "And don't ye be blowin' smoke in me face, Christopher Donally. What's everyone supposed to say or be thinking, with you bringing that . . . woman here?"

"Nothing, Meg. You're not supposed to say a bloody thing."

So the conversation fell off and drifted to the reports he had lying on his desk, a subject he wasn't particularly interested in, either.

Gathering up the glasses, Meg stopped at the window. "Ryan, Johnny, and Rachel are not getting befuddled at the local tavern," she announced. "They are outside on the terrace. Brianna brought her highness down."

Christopher walked to the window. Standing head and shoulders above his diminutive sister-in-law, he looked over her red head out the window.

Colin's and Johnny's boys had stopped their croquet game to stare. At first he didn't recognize Alexandra. Her fair hair was pinned loosely on her head and fell in curly wisps around her profile. But it was the outrageous gown she wore that captured his attention. The significance of her wearing virginal pink flounces did not escape him.

Following her hand as she pushed a wisp of her hair behind her ear, he watched her gaze lift and lock with his through the glass. At the touch of her eyes, everything in the world stilled. The corners of his mouth slowly lifted.

He recognized a war zone when it stared him in the face.

He had not expected it of her.

And a part of him wanted to bury his nose in all that pink bravado. Now, in front of God and his whole damn family.

That was the problem, he decided, all within seconds of his glance as he forced himself to turn away from the window. He was not thinking past his erection.

Meg was watching him. He knew by the worry in her eyes that she'd read the look in his. "The children have never been so close to royalty," she said.

"She isn't royalty, Meg." He turned to leave.

Meg's fingers grasped his arm. "She'll never be one of us in a country where you've just barely earned the right to vote. And she may as well be the devil for the trouble she's already brought down on you—"

"Margaret." Colin's gaze held Christopher's in apology. "Please."

"Those are not just my words, Colin Donally." Meg turned on her husband. "Ye weren't the one who sat at your brother's side for nigh on four months when he almost lost his leg. *I* don't forget."

"Meg," Christopher said softly.

She jerked away. "Now, if you will excuse me, I'll be in the kitchens if the two of ye are not mindin', thank you very much!"

"Meg . . ."

His brother rushed after Meg. With a quiet oath, Christopher braced his fists against the window casement and closed his eyes.

"Uncle Fer?" A little hand tugged at his trousers.

Christopher looked down between his arms and straightened.

Johnny's little girl looked up at him, her blue eyes wide, her dress smudged with grass stains. All of the youngest children called him Fer. She tugged again.

"What is it, Katherine?" He lifted her.

"Rachel telled me to fetch you out to play."

"Did she?" He could only guess what disaster had struck now.

"Yes." Blue eyes even with his, she twined her finger in his hair and nodded. "And she telled me to tell you *now*."

Chapter 13

"**R**achel—" Ryan crossed his arms. "Do ye think perhaps you could show some modesty in front of our guest?"

"The day you wear a crinoline to play croquet, Ryan Donally, is the day I wear mine." Rachel tossed her thick auburn braid over her shoulder. "Now turn yer face away if you're embarrassed."

From her place on the terrace, Alexandra watched as Rachel removed her crinoline, then wrapped the length of her yellow silk skirt in her waistband, revealing white stocking-clad ankles and yellow slippers. Her gaze touched Alexandra's shocked one. "Do ye play croquet, milady? As ye can see, we were just starting a game."

"I'm sure she's not interested." Ryan shoved off the stone wall where he'd been leaning. "Brianna and Johnny are my partners."

"Impossible." Brianna fluffed her skirts as she sat next to his fiancée on the terrace. "Since I am officially confined to bread and water"—she accepted a glass of lemonade from the servant—"having fun would certainly be out of the question. Besides, you and Christopher can leap off the roof of this house for all I care." Her nose sniffed. "I'm not speaking to either of you."

"Wonderful." Ryan rolled his eyes. "I can see how much your time in London has softened you, Brea. You're a regular powder puff."

Rachel tapped his arm. "Her ladyship can be on your team."

"Rachel . . ." Ryan swung around as she sashayed out onto the lawn, his gaze plowing into Alexandra's. He stiffened as if snakebit. "Milady"—he nodded—"can you at least *hold* a mallet?"

Alexandra bristled. Even if Ryan Donally did possess the kind of decadent looks that might make women look twice, he had the manners of an ape. He'd been rude to her since Brianna had brought her downstairs. "Croquet is the entertainment staple among ambassadors worldwide, Mr. Donally." Her chin lifted. Having dealt with his ilk before, she'd not run now if he were the wrath of Christendom. "I was weaned on a mallet."

His dark gaze raked her up and down. No hypocrisy, just a good old-fashioned undressing of the soul. "Were ye, now, milady? Somehow you don't look the type to play in the grass."

"Truly, Ryan"—Rachel picked up a mallet and clicked a ball—"could you be more of a bore?"

"Aye, I could be. But I'll restrain myself." Ryan swept Alexandra a manly bow. His dark hair was bound in a queue. "My apologies, Lady Alex." He was laughing at her and not really apologetic at all. "But if you were weaned on a mallet, then I was most certainly weaned on a silver teat."

"Leave her be, Ryan," a man's voice sounded. "Ignore him, Colleen."

Brianna had introduced Alexandra to John Donally earlier when she'd met his girls. He walked over and handed her a green mallet. Three years younger than Christopher, he was tall, with black curly hair and dark eyes beneath a fringe of thick Donally eyelashes. Even standing one step above him on the terrace, Alexandra had to look up into his face. "We are impressed with your courage, colleen," he said. "No one else in all of England will ever play with us."

"Don't let them scare you off, my lady," Brianna cheered her on. "Donallys always play for no less than world domination."

Alexandra clutched the mallet. These people were insane.

Ryan suddenly looked at a point over Alexandra's shoulder. She didn't have to turn around to know that Christopher had walked up behind her, nor did he need to put his hands on her for her to feel the heat of his nearness. His presence fell over her like the hot desert simoom. He was everywhere.

"Grab a mallet, Chris," Johnny said as if attempting to alleviate the sudden tension. "A game's abrew."

There was a moment's silence, during which Alexandra finally stole a glance at Christopher. "Have I missed something?" he asked her.

"I've been invited into your championship croquet match."

Christopher's wordless gaze went over his family. Ryan held up his hands. "*I* didn't invite her."

Relieving her of the mallet, Christopher tossed it to Johnny. "If ye will be allowin' me a moment with her ladyship?"

She advanced with him into his house, her eyes on his profile. She'd noticed that about him, the way he'd slipped into the familiar dialect of his family.

He was different around his family than when he was at his place of business or with her. Alexandra felt a faint twinge of jealousy.

Walking her through the French doors, he ushered her into the bright sky-blue drawing room. Everything was blue and white, from the curtains to the carpet on the floor. She looked around her in awe. The settee and plush chairs were the blue and white of fresh out-of-the-kiln delft. Christopher shut the doors behind her, startling her. She turned.

He was leaning against the mullioned glass with his arms crossed. His eyes seemed to have captured the stark blue of the room. "You don't have to do this, Alex. I can take you home. I'd intended to take you home already. You're late and probably unaccounted for—"

"No."

"You have nothing to prove here."

"I most certainly do. Mr. Donally, Ryan, that . . . that person out there has besmirched my honor. This is a matter of principle."

Christopher squeezed the bridge of his nose between his knuckles as if willing himself not to groan. Finally, he looked at her, saw the stubborn set of her shoulders, and at once softened his gaze on her. "Do you really know how to play croquet?"

She plucked pink fluff from her sleeve. "If I can dig civilizations out of dirt, surely I can hit a wooden ball around the lawn with a stick. How hard can that be?"

"A mallet, Alex. You need to call it by its proper name."

Some of the tension left his body. His glance eased down her dress and finally back to her flushed face. There was a subtle hint of restraint in the action and her pulse kicked up. "You look none the worse for everything that has happened." He stepped forward until she had to tilt her head to look up at him. "How is your stomach?"

"Brianna gave me some soup and bread. I feel much better. Even if I did humiliate myself—" Her eyes suddenly widened as he pulled her out of sight of the glass. "What are you doing?"

"I don't know, Alex." He braced his palms against the wall at her back. "It's difficult thinking about what I *want* to do when you're wearing my sister's dress." Tugging his finger in her bodice, he looked down her top.

"Christopher!" She shoved against him, furious that he found humor in the same situation that had her tied into a thousand knots.

He crossed his arms over his chest. Something akin to tenderness touched her in his gaze. "Why are you so intent on going out there?"

Despite the contradiction of her emotions, some dormant

part of her had awakened and raised its head over the iceberg of complacency. She wanted to be accepted the way Rachel obviously was. Squirming beneath that morning's memory, Alexandra allowed that she had not helped boost anyone's opinion of her. But that mattered little. More than anything she would not be intimidated.

"They have a right to their anger," he said, reading the intent in her heart as easily as if she might have opened the book for his perusal. "I don't defend their behavior, but I understand their feelings. I've felt the same way."

"Do you still?"

His elbow touched her forearm. "I don't know." He tightened his jaw before he angled his head away. "Maybe."

"My father did something to all of you, didn't he? That's what this is about. It's not that they saw us kissing today."

"It's more complicated than that." Shoving his hands against his hips, he leaned his head across his shoulders as if plagued by some pain. "More than you know, Alex."

"Don't protect me. This is my fight, too—"

"No"—his finger went to her lips—"it isn't."

"Christopher." She touched the buttons on his shirt, wanting to quell the tension that suddenly lay between them. "I'm not my father."

Someone pounded on the door. Alexandra jumped, nearly biting her tongue. Christopher pulled away from the wall.

Ryan stood at the glass. "Are you two coming out or not?" His voice was muffled through the door. He'd stripped off his jacket and waistcoat and wore his white shirt opened at the neck.

"Give us a moment." Christopher returned his attention back to her.

"Bloody hell, Chris. Sometime before Christmas would be nice."

Ryan's dark sidelong glimpse touched her before he threw out his arms and walked away.

Alexandra narrowed her eyes. "He has a foul mouth and a rotten temper."

Christopher's fingers brought her face back around to his. "Alex . . ."

She looked up into the bluest eyes and felt a smile tug her lips. "He reminds me of you."

Shaking his head, he finally quit whatever argument he'd been about to raise with her. "Come here." He walked her to the window and edged back the drapery. "Ye see those wickets set in the yard?" Placing an arm over her shoulders, he pointed at the other end of the yard. His scent covered her. She forced herself to concentrate on his words and not his mouth so close to her cheek. "In our version of croquet we play on teams. That way we don't beat the hell out of each other. And at least three of us survive."

"I see," she said, wondering nervously if he was jesting. Then decided he wasn't. Obviously all of the Donallys sprang from the same tree.

"The object is to hit your ball through each wicket. Touch the pole at the other end, then return to your respective pole before the other team. No team can win until everyone is in. So it behooves everyone to cooperate."

"Hit the ball. Not your teammates."

His grin lost none of its dullness as he returned his gaze back to the yard. "If another ball touches yours, that player receives a free shot, the same as if ye went through a wicket."

"Right." She nodded, studying the playing field with all the seriousness of a gladiator preparing for battle. "I can do this."

His roughened knuckles came back to slide along her jaw and turned her face an instant before his mouth settled across hers. The kiss was warmly possessive and plied away her will, her nerves, and all of her doubts until she was returning his affection with equal ardor.

Her eyes slid open to find his amused gaze on her lips before raising. "What was that for?"

His lips crooked into a licentious grin. Splaying her waist, he pulled her against him. "Because I have to go out there and obliterate you." He looked down into her face. "We won't be on the same team."

"I see that you are not above your usual conceit in these matters." Her mouth opened in a coy grin. "But I'm not that easy."

Except she was.

She'd always melted like wax in his presence. And the look in his eyes just before he took her back outside told her that he knew it.

From her perch inside the fountain, Alexandra wedged her mallet between two stone cherubs, studying the best angle to dislodge her ball from its current captivity. Across the yard, Ryan and Rachel were having another heated dispute. Colin joined them. Ryan, being closest to the post, was the current target of the offending team. Alexandra's gaze passed over the back of Christopher's dark head bent near Rachel's. A breeze flattened his shirt against his shoulders.

Ignoring the knot in her stomach, she concentrated on the view of her ball from her position. She'd been open-minded about Rachel's affection for Christopher. Theirs was the kind of familiar ease that came from knowing each other all of their lives. Perhaps even hero worship.

She'd been open-minded when Christopher sent her ball skating off into the wilds of his azalea garden and again into the fountain.

And if anyone would have told her a month ago that she would be standing in ankle-deep water straddling a stone cherub just to hit a wooden ball with a mallet, while other normally intelligent adults ran around the yard doing the same, she would never have believed it of herself. Not in a thousand years.

Her crinoline, long since gone the way of Rachel's, sat abandoned on the terrace. Grass stained her knees from crawling through the shrubbery. The rest of Christopher's family, the sane ones, had left an hour ago for mass. No one had even noticed as the sun dropped behind the trees, and Ryan looked up from his place in the petunias to see that they were playing by moonlight.

The teams were divided: Alexandra, Ryan, and Johnny versus Christopher, Colin, and Rachel. And with complete certainty, Alexandra knew that she had never experienced anything remotely close to a family who enjoyed beating up on each other with such relish. Who functioned in the other world as highly educated engineers, architects, and bankers. Who had all seemed almost normal hours before.

As for her opinion? She didn't care who was winning as long as it wasn't the other team. "Do you think anyone would notice if I moved my ball?" Alexandra casually asked Johnny, who stood with his ball in the mulch, watching the battle.

An amused glance over the rim of the fountain brought him closer. "I won't tell if you won't, colleen."

Suddenly the combat across the lawn ceased as all eyes were trained on them. "You wouldn't be cheating over there, now, would ye?" Colin called.

"I take offense to that slander," Johnny snorted before she could open her mouth and confess her sin. "Particularly since we all know you moved your ball at least a foot the other side of that rhododendron."

"The bush is on a bloody hill. Gravity moved that ball—"

"Aye, with the aid of yer boot." Ryan squatted on his haunches as he studied a rut in the grass. The sleeves of his shirt were white in the moonlight. "Besides, *thinking* about cheating is not the same as actually cheating. One cannot be hanged for a thought."

He hit his ball through a wicket, then played twice more before his ball bounced on a rock and veered left, missing the yellow ball in his path. He swore.

"Quite the contrary, Ryan." Rachel bent over her mallet. "There was a man from Bristol just last month hanged for that very deed."

"For what? Cheating in croquet?"

"Murder," she said succinctly. Her ball clicked against Ryan's.

"Goddammit, Rachel. Do ye think ye can pick on someone else? This is the fourth time you've hit me."

Ignoring him, Rachel squeezed between his body and the ball. She took the extra turn to go through a wicket, then hit his ball again. "The man's wife had keeled over in the henhouse dead as can be," she continued, placing her slippered foot daintily on her ball to hold it in place. "Two days later, the husband was caught in a rather compromising position with the milkmaid. In that very same henhouse, mind ye."

"Better there than the hog pen."

"When asked about his wife's untimely demise, he claimed he'd merely been thinking the deed. They'd been arguing, after all. What man wouldn't think about murder in those circumstances? he'd claimed. That was enough for guilt." Rachel swung her mallet. Ryan's ball shot off into the mist. "One cannot explicate male arrogance, I suppose."

"Or the fact that his wife's brother was the sheriff. I read about that trial in the *Times*."

Christopher crossed his arms and glared at Johnny. "Next time put those two on the same team."

Rachel turned. "It's your play, Lady Alexandra."

"And the winner gets the privilege to gloat," she reminded herself.

"There once was a young man from Bristol," Colin broke into her concentration, "who wanted to show off his pistol."

Alexandra stopped her mallet and laughed.

"All sleek and smooth. It went off too soon—"

"Crimeny, Colin," Ryan complained. "Get yer bloody brain out of the privy and let her play."

"It's only a ploy, colleen," Johnny said from beside her. "Don't let them shock you. You hit when you're ready."

"Aye," Christopher replied. Unlike the others, he'd said less than ten words this whole game. "You'll have to pardon the crudity of certain nameless gentlemen on this playing field."

"Profane judgment coming from the overlord of moral degeneration himself," Colin scoffed. "What was the one ye told about that elephant from Nantucket?"

An eruption of groans followed.

"Or that emerald-eyed Lorelei and what *really* happened to all those hapless sailors," Colin said.

"Spouting it all in front of our poor wee Rachel, too." Ryan walked past Rachel to search for his ball. "And her being fresh out of nappies."

"Say what ye will, Ryan Donally." Rachel's shoulders stiffened. "But I'm not the one exiled to the wilds of Christopher's yard. And *I'm* not the one who is going to lose."

Alexandra's gaze shifted to her ball and back to the game. She might lack the outrageous Donally spirit and verbal dexterity for the profane, but she did not wallow in her humility. Having been the most abused this day, she had managed to learn the game. Surprisingly, it took her only one undercut swipe of the mallet to escape the fountain where Christopher had sent her. The ball bounced over rocks downhill and, amid groans from the other team, rolled onto the grass.

Ignored by the enemy as a nonthreat, Alexandra worked the back half of the wickets unmolested, all the while keeping her attention on Christopher's approach. He clicked his ball directly in her path.

Alexandra lifted her gaze to Christopher's face. He stared back at her a sensual grin tugging the corners of his handsome mouth. A current of lust swept through her bones and showed in her eyes. He almost made her forget they were standing fully clothed in his yard with his family looking on. He was so cocky. Especially when he knew she was aching to annihilate him on the playing field.

"Tell us, milady." Colin tapped his ball. "How is it that a woman of your pedigree became interested in digging up bones? It is an odd occupation."

"Why?" Rachel plunked a hand on her hip. "Because she is a woman?"

"Hell, Rachel, I don't mean it as an insult," Colin protested.

"Rachel is sensitive because she found a fossil once." Ryan made champing sounds. "Big teeth."

"You should know." Colin chuckled. "Cost you fifty bloody shillings to buy it off her."

Rachel laughed. Alexandra was aware that everyone suddenly seemed interested in her response. Her gaze remaining locked onto the smug challenge in Christopher's eyes, she thought of Champollion laboring over the Rosetta stone, and the excitement he must have felt when he'd finally deciphered hieroglyphics, or what Schliemann hoped to one day accomplish in his search for Troy.

And all she wanted to do at that moment was have her turn at croquet so she could slam Christopher's ball.

Without elaborating on the disastrous curve her career had taken, she managed to evade the question entirely. "What I do is more academic than actual fieldwork. Quite interesting if you enjoy massing together leaf samples. Teeth would be even more fascinating."

"Christopher likes to collect a lot of that old stuff." Johnny took his turn. He straightened. "What is it D&B found two years ago at one of the construction sites in London? You had to come down from Carlisle personally. Isn't that how you got involved with that Atler chap from the museum?"

"Aye." Ryan groaned. "The peelers thought we'd uncovered a mass murder site. They shut us down. Turned out to be a burial chamber beneath the foundation of what used to be an abbey infirmary. The whole episode would have been amusing had it not cost the project thousands with the halt in construction."

But neither she nor Christopher were listening. His obnoxious blue ball stared up at her from the grass like some cycloptean eye.

And it was her turn to play.

Christopher gave her a wicked grin. "You will have to be a very good shot to hit me."

The conversation around them came to a grinding halt.

As if seeing the green and blue balls close together for the first time, Ryan stopped the game. "Halt!"

At once, Ryan and Johnny descended on her for a team conference. Their strategy was brief. Her goal clear. Listening to Ryan, his breath on her temple, she nodded. World domination was serious business at the Donally homestead.

But somewhere between the time Ryan and Johnny had made her part of their team and the moment they'd stepped away, something else unexpected had settled in her heart. Alexandra felt a strange and fierce shift in her universe. She felt envy.

In all the years that she and Christopher had been separated and she'd tried to move on with her life, a frightened eighteen-year-old who'd failed her one attempt at independence, he'd had his family around him.

No one had put arms around her. Or wiped the fear from heart. Richard had been away at school. She'd healed herself.

Perhaps she was stronger for it. Perhaps not. Until now, she'd liked her solitude. But being here with Christopher, with his family, was like discovering an oasis in the middle of the Sahara desert. She wanted to drink from the spring.

"Any day now, milady," Colin said.

Her concentration broken, Alexandra's fingers loosened on the mallet. Ryan waved his arms, stopping the game as he and Johnny took her to the side. She laughed because both Donallys treated her as if she'd been run over by a carriage.

"You're not going soft inside, are ye, milady?" Ryan asked.

Alexandra glanced between them at Christopher. He looked very good draped in moonlight. "Absolutely not," she reassured them.

"Colleen"—Johnny's voice was serious—"his job is to distract you."

"Quite right," she said with much gusto, rallying herself for victory.

That settled between them, Alexandra took up her stance behind her mallet. She aimed, hit her ball.

And missed.

Just like that, she'd missed her quarry. And as quick as her moment of triumph arrived, it vanished.

With the tip of his finger, Christopher closed her jaw. His smile was slow and sensual. Hot and possessive as his gaze went from her ball back to her face. "That's very bad, Alex," he commiserated, and knocked his ball against hers.

Alexandra was so angry she wanted to pick up his ball and throw it across the grass. No, she wanted to hit him between the eyes!

Christopher couldn't win like a normal person. He was the most smug, self-satisfied, gloating man she'd ever known in her life. She hated losing to him. She'd just forgotten how he used to pummel her in chess, and how furious that would make her. Once she'd dumped a whole game in his lap because he'd thought it so amusing to take her queen.

"You've already hit my ball off twice." She gripped her mallet.

One dark brow rose as she walked him around the wicket. "That many times?"

"I suppose I can't convince you to let me pass on to the post?"

Lining his ball beside hers, he grinned. "Would you like to try?"

Suddenly aware of her behavior in front of the others, she leaned nearer. He smelled like clover and grass. "It's my job to distract you."

Christopher smacked the mallet into his ball, sending hers skittering into the garden. Except her ball ricocheted against a rock, shot off like a projectile, and crashed through the beautiful mullioned glass window that overlooked the gardens.

Alexandra covered her mouth with her palm.

"Shit," she heard Christopher swear.

"Well, Christopher," Brianna's cheerful voice greeted the stunned silence. "I guess that officially makes you one of the children."

It took Alexandra a moment to realize that everyone else had returned from mass and watched from the terrace. Her gaze found Christopher. Colin slapped him on the back. "That will teach you to import your glass from Venice, brother."

"I'm consumed with admiration for your skill." Ryan walked past Christopher, shoulder to shoulder. "You should most assuredly win the game now."

Three turns later Ryan's words became reality. The game was over. Alexandra watched as the other team celebrated their victory, though slightly subdued, with laughing and backslapping.

Ryan draped his arm around her shoulders. "There is nothing worse than winners who gloat. Naver, naver gloat. That's what Da used to say."

"Aye." From behind, Johnny's arm joined Ryan's. "You've been a real sport today, milady," he said. "A real good sport."

Ryan's head angled roguishly. "Next time I'm at the museum I'll even let ye take me on a tour. Maybe donate my fossil for study."

She laughed. Warmth settled in her chest. Even if it was all in the spirit of competition, she enjoyed the camaraderie.

Colin stopped in front of her and bowed over her hand. "Milady." His grin was white.

It was the one feature combined with the dark hair and eyelashes all the Donallys shared. Each sibling possessed perfect white teeth. "I like your temper. You can be on my team any day." Colin shifted his gaze to his brothers. "And you two can polish my boots when you're finished here."

Ryan made an obscene gesture with his forearm. Wordlessly Alexandra watched Ryan and Johnny separate and begin cleaning up the game. Clearly, they were used to the routine.

Off to the side of Colin, Rachel lifted her gaze and, almost by accident, was caught as she looked at Alexandra. They had spoken around each other all night. In the golden glow of light spilling out from the house, the young woman did not look nearly so certain of herself as she did that morning or on the croquet course. Alexandra realized that she liked her.

"Thank you for inviting me to play," Alexandra said.

"You're welcome, milady." Rachel accepted Colin's crooked arm. With a backward glance, she said, "I hope that we were not too overwhelming." The soft lilt of her voice seemed more pronounced, and never more than at that moment, had Alexandra felt so *English* in comparison.

How quickly the glow faded.

Christopher stood with his arms crossed, his hip leaning against the lower stone wall off the terrace. Alexandra's heart picked up its pace. Colin and Rachel slowed on the stone steps in front of him. Only after the two proceeded onto the terrace did Christopher turn to watch them leave. Alexandra glanced up at his profile. Light from the house bathed half of his face. Johnny walked past and Christopher tossed his brother the croquet mallet. "Nice and neat," he instructed.

"You've not complained yet, have ye?"

Moving beside Christopher, Alexandra touched the rock wall. The stones were damp beneath her palms. She looked up to find his eyes on her. He'd rolled his shirtsleeves up for the game, and for one unguarded minute her awareness of him, as a man, a lover, her former husband, made everything else fade. She wanted to go upstairs to his bedroom and lie naked on his big bed, surrounded by emerald satin and him.

"You played all right tonight," he said.

The breeze sent wisps of her hair dancing across her face. "So did you. It's unfortunate about your window."

He twisted to look at the shattered picture window that overlooked his yard. He'd made no move to touch her. Suddenly feeling awkward, Alexandra pretended to focus on a square corner of quartz.

"What's another trip abroad?" His laugh lacked amusement. "Venice is a romantic city. They make nice glass."

"Do you go there often? To Venice? For the romance?" Suddenly mindful of where this conversation was heading, she looked over her shoulder. The yard was almost empty. "I should help clean up."

"Leave them." He stopped her. "They know the routine."

The smell of braised chicken and fresh bread pooled in her senses. She'd eaten very little all day.

It was on the tip of her tongue to invite herself to dinner.

There were a hundred reasons why she wanted to stay and be a part of their festivity. But one that would keep her away.

Christopher had not asked her to join the more private family gathering. Neither had Brianna.

Or anyone else, for that matter.

She pulled her hands from the wall. "I admit, I've had an interesting last two days. I like your family."

"Fortunately, we're only together for weddings, baptisms, funerals, and an occasional gathering. That leaves three hundred other days of the year free." His gaze dropped to her bare feet.

Laughing, she wiggled her toes in the grass. "I'm all wet."

"Is that right?"

Her gaze snapped up. He raised a brow, and she resisted looking around to see who might have heard. "From the fountain, Christopher."

From someplace inside the house, children's laughter erupted over a game they were playing. A cold mist had settled over her arms.

Struggling with her confusion, she knew without even realizing how she'd gotten there that somehow they'd reached an impasse. The whirlwind emotions that had surrounded them dissipated in the cooling currents of reality. Brianna wasn't going back to London for the Season. Alexandra had failed with her half of the bargain.

"There's no need for you to escort me home," she said quietly. "I'll have your carriage returned in a few hours. When will I see you again?"

"Ryan and I have preparations for next week's meetings on the Channel project. I'll be in contact."

"Christopher . . ." She'd not considered that he might not really contact her again. "We'll need to discuss our bargain. You won't forget?"

"Jaysus, Alex. Is that all you care about?"

The hostility in his voice shocked her. She fought against the stinging in the back of eyes. "Surely you must know it isn't."

"You had nothing to do with my sister's indiscretions. I don't intend to abandon my end of the bargain. Ryan and I really do have work."

"You don't owe me anything."

"The hell I don't."

"Christopher . . ." She scraped the hair from her eyes. "I'm saying all the wrong things. I don't understand what is happening."

"Don't you?" He took a step off the terrace, and took her into the circle of his arms. "I feel like an ass, Alex." His voice was a harsh whisper against her hair. She held him tightly. Her cheek pressed against his heartbeat. "I can't invite you inside for dinner. You think all of this is easy for me? It isn't. You think a game of croquet fixes everything? It doesn't. You are you. I'm me. There's not a lot of common ground between us to happily frolic. Today is a perfect example of how bloody fucked the world is."

"Chris." Carrying a cloak, Johnny stepped past him. Looking from Christopher to Johnny, Alexandra wiped a hand across her cheek. "They need you inside," he said. "Now."

Christopher pulled away from her. But in the flounces of her gown, their fingers held. "You'll have to do without me. I'm taking Alex home."

"I don't think that would be wise."

Rachel and Brianna stood this side of the doorway. Alexandra sensed a stillness inside the house. The kind of stillness that gathered before a storm.

Or a battle.

"It's time to go." Johnny laid the cloak over her shoulder.

Something was happening. Christopher turned as Ryan and Colin raced from the house, tension coiled in their expressions.

"Lord Ware is here." Ryan was shoving his arms into the sleeves of a coat. "He rode in a few minutes ago."

"Bastard," Colin hissed. "He has a lot of nerve coming here."

Her father?

Here?

Her heart pushed against her ribs.

Johnny put his hands on her shoulders. "It's best that you go through the yard, milady."

Nodding, she turned to slip her feet into her shoes.

Christopher remained where he was, his stance neither hostile nor assertive, as he made no move to stop her. Dragging her gaze from his face, she hurried two steps, and froze.

Her father stood on the lawn watching them. Wearing his greatcoat, he looked formidable in the moonlight and rising mist. Cold alarm raced up her spine, tightening her chest. She saw Ryan's hand go to Christopher's arm.

"Get into the carriage, Alexandra," her father said in a voice grinding with rage. "I will tend to you when we get home."

"What are you doing here, Papa?"

Her father took a step toward Christopher. "You black Irish bastard. By God, I will have you—"

"Papa!"

In a frantic effort to stop him, Alexandra grabbed his arm. She knew that Christopher would not fight her father. He certainly would not raise his fists to a member of the House of Lords, or probably any man in front of his family. But she was not so sure about Ryan or Johnny. "Do you intend to walk into a home filled with children and make ridiculous accusations?" she whispered. "Attack Christopher? For what?"

He dropped his gaze to hers. Then to her fingers clasped on his arm. He wore a top hat, the rim low over his eyes. She had never seen eyes so filled with rage.

"Get to the carriage, Lexie."

"We will leave together, Father."

Alexandra kept her hands firmly locked on her father's arm until he finally turned. They walked back to the front of the house. Rachel and Brianna had gone through the house and were standing near the carriage. Rachel had changed earlier into a blue satin dinner dress and looked every bit the lady. She also looked frightened. Colin and Ryan came out of the front door and slowed on the steps.

"My lady." Brianna dipped into a curtsy. Her lashes were

spiked with tears. "I have so enjoyed your visit. Thank you for allowing me to bring you here today."

Alexandra couldn't bear to look the girl in the face. Turning away, she climbed into the carriage. By the time the horses reached the edge of the drive, only Ryan and Brianna had remained to follow the progress of the carriage until it finally disappeared from sight.

Squeezing her eyes shut, Alexandra tried to remember a day when she had been more humiliated by her father's actions. Or that she had watched him publicly demean someone else the way he had Christopher just now. In a frantic effort, she swiped the back of her hand across her face.

"He doesn't deserve this from you." The flickering light from the lamp framed her reflection in the glass. "You were wrong."

Her father tore the hat off his head and threw it beside him. "I have dismissed Mary and Alfred. I don't tolerate disobedience or lies. If they are still in the house when I return I'll have them arrested for trespassing."

Alexandra pressed her back against the plush velvet seat, furious that he would take that manner of liberty with her servants. "Tell me, Father"—she clasped her hands into her lap—"what did you do to make Christopher's family hate us? To make them afraid of you?"

"Have you slept with him?"

"How dare you! Will that make me part of the unwashed masses no longer clean enough to be in the presence of the great Lord Ware?"

"Have you let him bed you, Alexandra?"

"Answer me, Father!"

"He's making a fool of me and a slut of you."

"Stop it!"

"That is what the Irish bastard wanted, isn't it? To make a public whore of Lord Ware's daughter?"

Alexandra slapped him.

Recoiling her hand in horror, she breathed in huge gasps. Tears stung her eyes. Never in her whole life had she ever struck or been struck by anyone. The violence of her emotions appalled her.

Without a word, her father calmly reached inside his jacket and, withdrawing a brown packet, tossed it on the seat beside her.

"Read it." He blotted his lip with a handkerchief.

Hands trembling, Alexandra removed a handful of documents. She flipped through each page, her heart racing, the clamp around her throat tightening. "This makes no sense, Papa." Her voice was quiet with panic. "The kind of money to do this . . . why?"

"Two of my investments are in ruins. He owns the bloody mortgage on our London house. Money I had borrowed to finance my last expedition to Borneo. He owns my reputation at the banks and at the clubs—"

"Then why hasn't he called in your markers? The mortgage?"

"My political influence is clearly more valuable to him." His jaw clenched in restrained fury. "I cut my bloody teeth fighting in the northwest frontier. Donally has no idea with whom he is dealing."

"Borrow money from my trust, Papa. There's no reason to be in debt. I'll buy everything back before anyone knows. Or let him have it all, I don't care. We can live someplace else."

"Even if I could touch your trust, I would not. This is about power. This is my reputation, which is far more valuable than any money."

"I don't believe it." She threw down the packet.

A chill went over her, not because she believed Christopher guilty of any sort of vengeance or blackmail; indeed, she knew staunchly in her heart that he was not guilty. But the timing of this tied in too closely to her problems at the museum. Everything coming down on her was like some horrible cosmic coincidence. Christopher's reappearance in her life, the museum thefts, his presence on the board of trustees.

She stared at her hands clutched in her lap. She didn't

know why everything connected to Christopher. But she was
suddenly sure that someone was playing a horrible game
with her life.

She started to tell her father about the thefts at the museum. But stopped. She knew him too well. He would find
some way to connect that to Christopher as well.

"Lexie . . . we've always managed to work through our
differences, you and I," her father said distantly.

Plowing the hair away from her face, she lifted her gaze.
His heavy cane braced between his knees, he rested his grip
on the lion's head. His hands trembled. "I've done what I
could to see you happy, and in return you've made me proud.
It's always been a satisfactory partnership. For your information, I never allowed myself to think about what happened in
Tangiers. You were young and impressionable and not at
fault. But you are not that susceptible child any longer."

"I was never a child," she whispered.

"I will not be the ass of your follies." He shifted his attention out the window. "If you choose to make a fool of yourself, I cannot stop you. But you'll not live in my house,
beneath my roof, while you do so."

He turned to look at her stricken face.

"And if you think that you don't need me in your life,
you're wrong. You enjoy the level of independence and respect you do because I've trusted you enough with the responsibility to stand up for you."

"I love him, Papa," she said, willing him to look into her
heart and see Christopher for who he really was. "Don't
make me choose between you. Please."

"Are you so needy that you cannot see what is before your
nose? He will marry another. Don't think I haven't started
my own investigation into his activities. I know more about
the kind of man he is than you could in ten years. He won't
choose you over responsibility to his business and family. He
won't, Lexie. He's not to be trusted."

"You go to the devil, Papa." She pressed a fist to her
spleen. "And if you do anything to Christopher, anything at

all, I swear on my life that I'll never speak to you again as long as I live. I'll ruin you myself. I swear I will."

Her father leaned nearer. His eyes were wet in the pale light. "You want to go to war with me, daughter?" His voice was a rasp. "So be it. Try surviving on your own. The choice is yours."

Chapter 14

⟨⟩∞⟨⟩

At nine o'clock in the morning, four days later, Alexandra walked past a pair of forbidding Corinthian columns into the marble and granite lobby of the First Bank of London. Until a few days ago, Mr. Tibley, her account trustee, had been on his yearly trek to Italy. She had not wanted to speak to anyone else.

Alexandra checked in at the desk and waited to be escorted upstairs. Few women were in the bank, and her presence had drawn the stares of most men in the lobby. Her stomach already in knots, she pretended interest in the various paintings that lined the tall walls. The Axminster carpet muffled her steps. She studied the walls filled with Antonio Zucchi artwork, recognizing the hunting leitmotif prevalent in his work, because his artwork hung in her father's library.

Her eyes were gritty. Christopher had returned to London, and she knew he was in important meetings all week. She'd not seen him, though he'd sent a message via the staff, inquiring about her welfare. Twice. She'd only learned of the notes after unpacking her trunks. Clearly afraid of Lord Ware, someone had placed the notes in her trunks when she'd

225

left the manse. She'd not slept last night. She had not slept since she'd moved out of her father's house.

Alexandra had made her decision.

For the first time in her life, her choices had never been clearer.

Most of her belongings were now crammed into a townhouse Richard had helped her find near the back entrance of the museum. At nights, she slept with a chair beneath her flimsy door latch. Even with the fact that she lived only a few blocks from the whole of the Metropolitan police force, every noise and shadow felt sinister in her new surroundings. Of course, it could also be the fact that she was physically alone for the first time in her life.

Looking at the clock on the wall, Alexandra remembered her interview with the *Vanity Fair* writer at noon. Her gaze went up the stairs to her left. She'd kept busy at the museum. To her surprise, Professor Atler had included her in the opening of the Cairo exhibit. A projected ten thousand people this weekend alone were expected to view the exhibit. Tomorrow another writer was due to visit for yet another interview. If she was going to survive, she could no longer remain separated from society. Christopher had a life, and so would she. As for Mary and Alfred, she had posted a letter to a sister's address in Devon that Mary had left her.

"Lady Alexandra?"

Alexandra turned abruptly to the voice. Mr. Tibley stood beside her. Shorter than she by at least two inches, he still projected an air of authority that, much like Professor Atler's, had intimidated her at one time. Today, however, she could not afford to be anything less than confident. Presenting her gloved hand, she politely demanded to speak to him.

"Your presence here is not a surprise," he told her after he took her upstairs to his office. "I've been expecting you. Most people due to inherit such a sizable income have usually visited me on a regular basis, and far sooner than this."

"Yes, that is one of the reasons I'm here." Accepting a leather chair that faced his desk, she set her reticule in her lap. She had never been responsible for her personal expenditures, much less a household income. "You see, I am living on my own now."

Mr. Tibley didn't seem surprised by the revelation. "Your father was in this bank last night."

Alexandra stilled. "Then you've seen him?"

"He stopped your allowance."

Alexandra fingered her reticule. Even knowing that her father would cut her off, the news still brought home the reality of her situation.

"My lady, if it's any consolation, I advised him against it. You could fight him. You are his legal heir with certain rights."

Her father must know that as well. He was making a statement. Daring her to need him for anything.

"Did he touch my personal account?"

"No, my lady. Merely cut you off from receiving any more."

"Can my father block when I will receive my inheritance?"

"The trust reverts to you on your thirtieth birthday." The leather chair creaked as he leaned forward. "Your father would have to have you declared mentally incompetent for you not to receive access to the inheritance left to you by your mother's family. But allow me to warn you, my lady. By law, your father can maintain control over your inheritance the same as a husband. But in my opinion, if he wanted your money, he could have had access to it already in any number of ways as executor of your grandparents' estate."

"We are not impoverished aristocrats," she quietly insisted. "Why is he in such debt?"

Mr. Tibley sat back in the chair and, crossing his legs, rested his elbow on the chair arm. "Lord Ware has been forced to put a substantial portion of his income back into his estate in Ware. In addition, there were massive debts incurred from his expedition to Borneo. Then there have been endowments to the museum and trust funds to the university. He has paid substantially to see that you had every opportunity at success, my lady."

Her fingers tightened on the reticule. How could the same man who had done so much for her life have destroyed everything else?

Mr. Tibley sat at his desk waiting for her to say something. "My lady? Is there something specific that you came here to ask me today?"

Perched sideways on the chair, she sat erect. "I wish to know if it is a common practice for individuals to purchase someone else's mortgage and gaming debts."

"It's done all the time, and though it may be unethical, it is not illegal."

"What is the purpose?"

He observed her over the rim of his spectacles. "Investment."

Or blackmail.

Alexandra digested this information. Her earlier anxiety returned. What if someone did want to ruin her father as he suspected? "I wish to pay off Father's debts," she finally said.

Mr. Tibley cleared his throat.

"And do not tell me that it's impossible. Or that I will injure his sensibilities. Or any of a hundred other excuses because I'm a woman. I can take out a loan against my trust."

She owed her father what he had invested in her. She would see that debt paid.

Then she would never speak to him again.

"Of course, my lady. I wouldn't presume to tell you what you could or could not do. But until the trust legally reverts to you, your father must be notified on all financial matters."

"He will not be notified. Surely I have enough in my current account to cover most of the interest for a year."

"I could not in good conscience allow that manner of expenditure. You would seriously deplete your resources."

Alexandra stood. "This is utterly impossible to comprehend." She despised the archaic laws and bureaucracy that would put that rope around her neck and choke her to death.

"Lady Alexandra . . ." Mr. Tibley stepped around his desk to block the door. "I have worked at this bank for thirty-five years. If I did what you asked, I would not only lose my job, but I would never be hired by another bank as even so much as a clerk."

"You don't need to explain."

"It is my sincerest hope that you understand my position." He watched her warily.

She wanted to stay angry with him, but her fury was with her own helplessness. She understood his situation all too well.

Alexandra glanced at the clock on the wall and knew she'd have to hurry to her interview. "I have just one more question, Mr. Tibley, if you will. Is it possible that someone could purchase a mortgage note for someone else and that other individual not be aware?"

"I don't understand what you are asking. If you are asking if that individual needs to be present to purchase the note, he does not. Such business can be conducted through his man of affairs."

As Alexandra stepped into the hallway, she turned. "Then theoretically someone could buy a note and put it in someone else's name?"

"Theoretically, yes, my lady. But why the costly subterfuge?"

"I don't know, Mr. Tibley." She turned away and left him in the hall staring after her oddly. But she intended to find out.

As much as Christopher despised Lord Ware, he was not the man behind the financial attack against her father. Christopher was a left uppercut-to-the-jaw sort of man, and would not hide from making a frontal attack.

"Do you enjoy burying yourself in the catacombs beneath London?"

Richard's cologne drifted over Alexandra. Glancing over the golden rims of her spectacles, she observed him standing at the laboratory doorway where she sat hunkered over a plaster cast. He was dressed unusually in a somber black suit. "No one can find you," he said.

Alexandra shifted her gaze back to the plaster cast. White dust covered the workbench and the floor. "*You* found me."

Richard dropped a magazine on the workbench. Pausing only a heartbeat, Alexandra averted her gaze and went back to the scalpel in her hand. She wanted to bury her face in her hands. The magazine had hit the streets this morning. Christopher would do more than throttle her, and Providence above, he had the right. This new disaster couldn't have come at a worse time.

"That's what I thought," Richard said. "You gave that *Vanity Fair* writer an interview that had nothing to do with the Cairo exhibit. How could you let yourself be trapped in that way?"

"Go away, Richard. I'm working."

All week, pieces of her life had been floating about the gossip columns. As if by virtue of her father's embattled status in the House of Lords, her whole existence was of some import to the public. First, the Cairo exhibit, where she'd demonstrated that she actually had a brain, only to discover that the color of her gown was of more import; then there was the art gala, where she'd dared to attend without an escort.

And why shouldn't she be able to go without a man on her arm? Or a chaperone? She was a spinster, after all.

Now this fiasco.

All because she'd been seen in the company of Christopher's sister at Lady Wellsby's salon.

Richard flicked the magazine. "Now that the whole of society assumes that you are continuing an affair with a lowly Irish soldier who once worked under your father, do you think this hinders or helps pave his acceptance into society? The poor, wronged husband, who is no longer quite so poor, quashed by autocracy again, as he attempts to gain entrance through you. And fails. The poets will be writing sonnets."

"Christopher hasn't failed at anything."

"He did yesterday afternoon."

Alexandra stopped working. "What are you talking about?"

"D&B is no longer in the running for the Channel project. Your lover's company has been cut loose, as they say. He's been here twice today looking for you."

Alexandra rested her forehead against her hand. Christopher had worked so hard for that dream. It wasn't fair.

"But from what I saw of his expression, it's probably best that you missed him. He did not look like a man seeking out his ladylove."

"I truly hate your sarcasm, Richard."

"What are you doing anyway? Casting mud?" He leaned over her shoulder and snorted. "A very scholarly endeavor for a brilliant mind. Did you dig up plants from the herbarium? Or is this a personal project?"

"Personal." She slid off the stool and walked to the sink that held a bucket of cloudy water, where she washed her hands. "And as you can see, I'm very busy."

Richard put his hand on her shoulder. "Why don't you look at me and tell me what you're doing?"

"Leave me alone, Richard." She hit his hand away, frightened by her own actions. "I did nothing wrong except grant an interview with an unscrupulous writer. I didn't know how to answer the questions he'd asked."

"It didn't help that you then went to the art gala unescorted. Right in front of your father. I thought that you weren't going. You caused quite a sensation in your red gown."

She didn't look up to assess the truthfulness of his words. She'd wanted to wear that beautiful gown just once before she perished of old age. "Did I?"

"But then, draped in red satin, I'd think my own mother smashing."

"You're mother *was* smashing."

"My mother was a whore who dumped my father for some sculptor in Florence. I don't even think about her, except red was her favorite color. I hate red."

"The gown was burgundy."

Richard leaned a hip against the workbench. "I'm not surprised by anything, considering this rampage you're on. How long before my father is forced to discharge you?"

"Let me think." She laid the paper flat over her cast and began rubbing the charcoal. "Any day now, I'm sure."

Wiping the hair off her face with the back of her hand, she walked over to the shelves to retrieve more charcoal. Books and various field journals were piled in enormous stacks against the wall. "At least, if my father attempts to block funding for Christopher's other projects, everyone will know why."

Folding his arms over his chest, Richard shook his head. "Except Donally runs a corporation. He doesn't need help to bring a case against your father if he thought he was wronged. Your father despises scandal. By practically admitting that you and Donally were once married, you just humiliated him in front of his peers."

"I can't help it if the truth hurts," she whispered, rubbing the charcoal over the paper.

"Unfortunately, you're not a man. Just because you've become inured to social and legal proprieties does not mean that they don't exist." He lay his palm over her hands. "How long before the wrong people learn about your child? Or that the head of D&B has a multitude of other sins under his belt that he would rather keep hidden?"

She'd pinned her hair back into a tight bun, but without Mary's help, she'd done a poor job. Strands of her hair fell forward over her shoulder. "Does that sound like concern for him? I thought you didn't like him."

"I changed my mind when I saw him today." Richard shoved his hands into his pockets. "Is he going to marry you?"

"It's not that simple, Richard." She laid her head against her hands.

She wished that she'd never seen Christopher at the museum. Or agreed to any wretched bargain. Or played croquet. Or committed a thousand other vices since he'd stepped back into her life. She was shocked at how easily she'd lost herself all over again to him.

"I have no idea who I am or what I'm doing anymore, Richard."

He removed his hand from hers. "What *are* you doing?"

Blinking the moisture from her eyes, Alexandra pulled the paper off the cast where she'd been rubbing. She had a noticeable identifying mark. Blinking past her surprise, she held up the design.

"The plaster cast worked!" She pulled the paper into the light. "It looks like—"

"A lion's head," Richard remarked, unimpressed.

"Quite right." She recognized the mane. "But what an odd mark."

"It's the trademark of Earnhart Baggins & Sons. They put that mark in the heel of every shoe or boot they make."

"Truly?" Alexandra lifted her gaze. "You know people with shoes that have this mark?"

"Any man who is wealthy enough to buy a pair like that is from your peer group, dear, not mine. Baggins & Sons caters to exclusive, very wealthy clientele."

"I found this print near my cottage window." She turned a jar upside down. A leaf dropped to the workbench. "This leaf was found upstairs in my loft." She pushed her hair behind her ear. "See how it fits exactly into the heel mark of this footprint?" She wedged the leaf onto the plaster heel. "The man who made this print is the same man who tracked this leaf upstairs."

He angled his head to look at her better. "A leaf is a leaf, my lady." He shook his head. "Your father could have gone into your cottage. Who knows? The leaf could have been in there for days. Why are you so concerned?"

Distractedly, she ran her hands through her hair, dislodging her bun. Christopher was also wealthy enough to afford Baggins & Sons footwear. The window had been open that night. She hadn't thought to ask how he'd gotten into the cottage. Maybe he'd been curious about the place and walked upstairs. Somehow he didn't seem the type to be so careless.

"I'm not sure. I suppose you're right."

Everything seemed more logical now that she knew the type of shoe that had left the print. Besides, all she'd had in the cottage were old books and worthless relics.

Richard pushed away from the bench. "I need to go." He'd taken out his gold watch and now shut the lid. "I actually have something important to do these days. I'm speaking at the university all week."

"You?" She turned on her seat. "That's wonderful."

"I know. The idea of working is a novel concept for me." Hands in both pockets, he settled his eyes on her. "I needed the extra income."

Alexandra raised a brow, impressed. "Indeed."

"Do you want to go with me? I could use the moral support."

She looked down at herself covered in dust.

"You're right." He nodded before she could speak. "Don't worry about it."

She started to ask if he had time for her to change.

"Oh—" He turned back into the room. "A constable came here looking for you earlier."

Her head snapped up. "Did he say why?"

"Something about the maid that you gave a deposition on back in April. They claim to have found her."

"Where?"

"In the Thames."

Chapter 15

The rattling of omnibuses and cabs mixed with the hum of voices as Alexandra pressed through the evening crowd to get home. Even the pickpockets, who seemed to be a fringe of unwanted children, had attempted to get to her reticule today. Gathering her skirts in her hands, she hurried down the flight of narrow stairs and, fumbling for the latchkey in her reticule, finally unlocked the door to her townhouse. The more she thought about the purpose of the constable's visit, the more frightened she became.

The door slammed behind her.

Alexandra whirled. Her reticule clutched to her chest, she stifled the scream in her throat. "Christopher!"

He stood with his back to the door, his arms folded over his chest, a look of iron restraint in his eyes. "I would greet you with a hello, but I haven't been invited in yet."

She lowered her palm from her racing heart. "You scared the life out of me."

"That's good, Alex. Maybe that will inspire you to get better locks for your door."

"How did you find me?"

"Your secretary at the museum."

He remained with his back to the door, his arms crossed, his perfectly creased trousers in tandem with everything else about him. His expression, insolvable in the shadows, clearly took nothing on trust, a characteristic that betrayed itself in unmistakable traces about his eyes. He'd read the magazine article.

He was furious.

Raw sensations washed over her. She was aware of trying to hold to her dauntless determination to accept the consequences of her acts and failing. But as she stood facing him, neither would she surrender to shame.

"Do you like my townhouse?" she spoke defiantly, as though challenging the verdict in his eyes, knowing he was not impressed.

Her desk and chair sat against the far wall. With the exception of her bedroom, and the small parlor to the right, she had little furniture. Stacks of dusty books and old relics that had once filled her private carriage house now filled the room here. She had not moved anything upstairs yet. Despite the current skimpy conditions, the walls boasted new paper and paint, the floors needing only a good coat of varnish; this place was hers.

"What happened with you and your father after you left my house?"

She carefully set her reticule onto a stack of books. "My father and I have parted ways."

"Like hell you have. You're attached to him by a damn umbilical cord. You always have been."

Color drained from her face. "You have no right to say that."

"I have more right than anyone alive." He reached beneath his jacket and pulled out a magazine. "This certainly makes sense now. Naturally, you had no qualms about spilling my life out to a journalist to get back at him."

Alexandra was startled, more at his conclusion than at the magazine he tossed at her feet. "And this was all after my visit to the morgue," he said. "Why didn't you tell me someone was missing from the museum, and that you were the last one to see her alive?"

"Until an hour ago, I didn't know that she was dead!"

"Brigett O'Connell, or what was left of her, was found at one of my work sites yesterday. She either jumped or was dumped into the Thames. The body wasn't recognizable, except by portions of a uniform she still wore. The authorities are only guessing. She could be an old woman who fell off the embankment drunk, for all I know."

"It's not hard to conclude the age of a body. Or the manner of someone's death," she whispered, sick to her stomach, "if the signs are there. I do it all the time."

He shoved off the door. "I don't understand you, Alex. There's a jewel theft at the museum. Within hours of its discovery, a woman disappears and you're the last one to see her. What does that make you? But a goddamn suspect? Or a prime witness?"

"How could I be a witness to anything? The last I heard from Bridgett O'Connell, she was quite occupied with a security guard!"

"I know what she was doing."

"How is it you know so much, anyway?"

A dark look entered his eyes. "The constable who asked you questions that day at the museum is Barnaby's brother, who works on staff at Marlborough Street court. He's one of my contacts. Very convenient if I want access to the court docket. The Metropolitan Police force also handles museum security. That interview you gave to *Vanity Fair* last week has made it incredibly difficult to remain discreet about this investigation."

She couldn't think. Her gaze dropped to the magazine curled at her feet. Her stance, the erectness of her spine as she attempted to maintain her fortitude, was complicated by the depth of her emotions. Suddenly she turned to the cherry-wood table set against the wall. Lighting the lamp, she felt Christopher's gaze on her but resolutely refused to meet it.

"I don't care if the world knows about our past." Almost in frenzy, she went about lighting the other lamps to dispel the awful gloom. "I don't, Christopher. I'm weary of hiding the facts as if I've committed some horrible sin. I'm sick of hiding between the shadows of everyone else's life!"

She turned and collided with Christopher. He'd moved like a ghost behind her into her bedroom. The heat of his scent pooled in her stomach and in her knees. She inhaled the crisp scent of his laundered shirt, everything about him that was safe and familiar.

She stepped around him and he caught her arm. "If you wanted to get at your father, you couldn't have chosen a better way than announcing our past to the world. Or moving here." His callused thumb caressed her bottom lip. "Have the last few weeks with me been your vengeance as well? Have I been your dirty little sin, Alex?"

Fighting a flare of rage, made all the more potent by the strong arms that blocked her escape, she could not hide her desperation. "You don't believe that."

His fingers threaded in her hair. "This is not just about me, Alex. D&B employs thousands of people across Great Britain. Me . . . my family *is* that company."

Barely able to stop the tears, she held herself erect away from him. "I sent messages to your office. Every day I sent messages, trying to tell you. That writer knew about us, Christopher."

He swore softly, his breath stirring the hair on her temple. "The instant I let you out on the town with Brianna, I should have guessed that it would be a matter of time before you attracted interest." Tilting her chin, he pushed his hand through her hair, dislodging the last of her pins. "This is turning into a serious mess, and I've already made too many mistakes in my life that other people have had to clean up. I shouldn't even have come here."

"Is that what I am to you? A mess?"

"You tell me. I'm having an affair with the daughter of one of the most powerful men in the House of Lords. An unfriendly bastard who would as soon have me impaled on a stake as look at me. My investigation for you might very well turn into a murder investigation. D&B has lost the Channel project, and I've lost the biggest opportunity I'll ever have to make a name. This week has not been the brightest candle in the stack." He leaned his head back against the doorframe. "That's why I haven't been in the office to get your messages until today."

"I'm sorry about the project. I know that it was important to you."

She sensed the shrug in his voice and knew what it cost him to pretend indifference. "The whole project was a gamble from the beginning. Something happened. Our company wasn't established enough, perhaps. I wasn't experienced enough."

Alexandra swiped the back of her hand across her face. She turned into her room. "I'm truly sorry, Christopher." She smoothed the white eyelet over her bed. "I should never have gotten you involved. . . ."

She began straightening things, her hands blindly touching familiar trinkets. On a triangular pedestal beside her bed, an hourglass filled with sand from Giza had been turned and now trickled toward its monotonous end. Christopher had been in here earlier.

He'd been in her room.

Touched her things.

Her gaze swept the room. The reckless extravagance of a world collector showed in marquetry cabinets loaded with miniature statuettes and intaglios carved by lapidaries during the reign of Caesar. Beside her bed stood an exquisite gold lamp, shaped like a vase and inscribed with Arabic. Few people understood the curious cryptography inlaid in gold. She touched the lamp.

"*Peace is the dove upon whose heart she lays.*" Christopher read the words aloud.

Alexandra turned to face him. Shifting his gaze to hers, he shrugged a brow. "The lamp used to belong to me," he said to the expression in her eyes. "It was in my quarters along with the Murand hourglass when I was shipped off to India."

All of these years that lamp had been sitting in the same place next to her bed since her return to England. All these years it had belonged to Christopher. Alexandra took in the rest of her room.

Everything she had, laid in the moldering remnants of someone else's past. Relentlessly and without pity, anger struck like a dagger to her heart, as she reviewed her existence down through the murdered years of her life.

Walking to the window, she leaned against the casement. A large golden feline lounged on the brick ledge outside. "The first time I ever left my father and returned to England, it arrived with my belongings." Alexandra looked at Christopher through the reflection in the window. "They must have packed up your quarters and sent everything with me."

Sliding her fingers across the delicate glass lamp, she found her focus drawn to the script. "Do you think it means that the dove brings peace to the heart or the heart brings peace to the dove?"

"The thing was written by a poet." Christopher's voice was tired. "It's not supposed to make sense."

She turned. "'Pompous philosophy' is what I remember you used to term such works. Of course, that's why you have volumes of such flowery prose in your library." Declining her head, she awaited a denial. "Brianna showed me your library."

Christopher leaned a palm against the doorframe. "It was an interesting lamp. I bought it from an Arab trader. I don't want it back."

His jacket hung open. He was tall and filled the doorway as easily as his presence filled her room. She realized now that he wasn't going to move any closer into her room.

For all the ease that he'd walked away from their past, from artifacts that she'd give her right foot for, she wondered if he'd ever allowed himself to become attached to anything outside the safety or sanctity of his family. She'd caught glimpses of hunger in his gaze when he'd spoken about the land he owned, and his work. But only a flash of something raw, as if he were afraid to ever truly love anyone or anything.

She wanted to look into his eyes and see the man he once was. The soldier who had walked across a crowded ballroom dance floor and defiantly invited the diplomat's daughter to dance.

"Look at what we're doing to each other, Alex," he said. "You walk back into my life and we're suddenly caught up with everything that went wrong in our past. Maybe we're both seeking absolution. Who knows? A lot was left unfinished."

"It doesn't have to be," she whispered. "Left unfinished, I mean."

"I went to the museum today to find you." His blue eyes fastened on her. "You weren't in the reading room."

"I was in the basement. . . ." Her hand lifting to her mahogany bedstead, she suddenly dropped her attention to his shoes as a thought struck. "May I see the heel of your shoes?"

The look on his face betrayed serious doubt as to her current state of mind. "Please," she asserted. "One shoe will suffice."

Christopher raised his ankle over his knee, displaying the heel of one shoe. The maned lion's head was there. "Baggins & Sons."

His hooded gaze dropped to her breasts, and he suddenly looked interested in her examination. "Why the inspection?"

"I made a cast of a shoe print that I found in the garden at the cottage last week. I discovered it after the night that you had visited. Near the window."

Instead of laughing at her needless worry, he studied her. "Only an idiot would have gone through a window that faced your house. I entered through your door."

"You're that adept at breaking and entering?"

Waggling his fingers at her, he raised a brow in cocksure arrogance that gave her a precious glimpse of that other man beneath the polished veneer. "Dexterity reaps its rewards. There isn't a lock made that I can't pick. And you have a flimsy excuse for all of your locks. The window was opened when I'd arrived that night. Was that normal?"

"It's not unusual that Mary leave the window cracked."

"No footpad would wear shoes like this. If he wasn't murdered first by one of his cohorts, he'd be caught by any bobby worth his salt on the street. The shoes are too heavy to run in. Does your father have many visitors to his house?"

"Some." She crossed her arms at the thought of being accosted by any of her father's friends. "You're frightening me."

"You *should* be frightened. You know enough about London to realize the danger in being alone."

"Mary and Alfred will be here soon."

Sweeping the front of his jacket aside, Christopher shook his head at the ceiling. "Heaven save me from aristocrats." He walked through her downstairs as if to check the locks on the windows. The light accentuated his blue-black hair. "Only *you* would think to bring servants into a townhouse where everyone around you works twelve-hour days to put meals on the table."

She sensed that he spoke for not only himself but an entire class of citizenry that she had never so much as associated with except to look at from her carriage windows or to pass in the hallways at the museum. The fact that his words were mocking made no difference. He was correct. But as he'd so aptly put it on the lawn of his house, she was who she was and he was who he was. That didn't leave much ground between them to happily frolic.

Still, a sliver of common ground was enough upon which to stand.

Maybe that was all that it would take to nourish the seeds they'd planted so long ago.

"Do you know how to pump your water and light the stove?" he called.

She stood in her bedroom doorway. Cabinet doors opened and closed in the kitchen. He was going through every drawer and shelf. "Of course," she boasted. Even if she had just figured out how to do both.

"Is this what you call a larder?"

"I have to go to the market." She squirmed, unwilling to admit she'd never gone to the market in her life.

He returned to stand in front of her, his battle stance obvious as he surveyed her new homestead in displeasure. "You've never *been* to market."

"I'm capable of learning."

He looked at the ceiling and laughed, a dry, hollow sound.

Always on guard. Then his eyes swept downward to where her bodice molded itself to the curves of her breasts, making her aware of the touch of his gaze. They stood unmoving, serenaded by distant voices, the rumble of a heavy omnibus, his startling blue eyes holding hers. She thought that he would kiss her. Unhappy with her or not, he was still here.

Concerned about her.

"I've missed you." Even as her palm slid to the buttons on his waistcoat, she could feel the restraint coiled in him. She wanted him. She wanted him to kiss her. "Stay with me tonight."

"No." She sensed a surge of passion between them, hot, as he bent his mouth over hers. "I can't, Alex," he whispered against her lips.

"You can't? Or you won't?"

The look he gave her when he pulled away told her the problem wasn't with performance.

"You must know how I feel about you, Christopher."

Nothing flickered in his eyes. Then he shook his head and looked away. "We share incredible sex, Alex. Don't confuse what we have with anything else. We did that once before. Remember?"

Christopher never ceased to shock her. "You behave as if I don't know the difference between lust and love. I'm almost thirty years old, not some virginal innocent who thinks she's in love with the first man who gives her a . . ." She blushed profusely. "An *orgasm*!"

He regarded her archly. "Aren't you?"

"Oh! You are so utterly arrogant!"

His gaze held tightly to hers. Blue. Pensive. "Have you ever tasted opium, Alex? Felt it warm your veins?"

She managed to keep her chin high. "You know I haven't."

He bent forward. "You surrender your soul to the magic. It puts you someplace where you don't care about consequences. You don't care who gets hurt as long as you get another shot. I used to drink it with whiskey. It would be too easy for you to become that kind of obsession."

When he stepped away, she crossed her arms. "Go away, Christopher."

He opened the front door. Looking over his shoulder, he hesitated. "Someone will be around in the next few hours to reinforce your doors with new locks. His name is Finley."

There was a brief second when she could do nothing more than breathe. "Why?" She stood in the middle of her living room.

"Because you have shitty locks, Alex."

With that, he shut the door.

Furious, Alexandra stared for a full minute at the door before she remembered that she'd forgotten to tell him about her father's accusations. Disbelief laced her thoughts. She walked across the room and twisted the key in the lock. "Damn! Double damn!"

Alexandra walked to the kitchen and poured that morning's cold coffee into a porcelain cup. With Christopher's penchant for answering mail, it could be a year before he read any message she sent him.

Rummaging through the crates spread out all over the room, she found a bottle of her father's prized brandy and dumped a few capfuls into her coffee.

Incredible sex indeed!

In his usual Donally reaction to glean only logic from an equation, Christopher had excluded the one single fact that ten years had not altered between them.

They were still in love with each other.

"I'll be working late tonight," Christopher told Stewart as he walked past the lobby desk and into his office.

"Yes, sir."

Removing his jacket, Christopher tossed it on the lounge in his office. "Has the list for the financial committee members arrived yet?" he asked Stewart from the doorway.

His secretary nearly jumped in response. "List?"

"L-i-s-t, Stewart. List. The one I requested this morning. I want to know all the way up the chain to Parliament who is exercising their authority over the Channel project."

"Yes, sir," Stewart replied to the papers he was reading.

Two things hit Christopher at once as his gaze went over his secretary, then hesitated on others who swiftly turned away. He wasn't a man prone to paranoid tendencies, but he could feel an undercurrent in his staff. He'd never witnessed a group of people working harder to appear busy.

Christopher walked to his desk to light his lamp. He had neither the time nor the patience to deal with this manner of nonsense from his staff. Light spilled over the desk. His gaze fell on a copy of *Vanity Fair*, then on two evening newspapers, opened to the latest *ton* gossip.

He should have been her escort to the art gala last week. He felt as if he'd abandoned her. He thought of Alex alone in some middle-class townhouse, fending for dinner herself when he could have easily fed her.

"Dammit, Alex." He stripped off his tie, flinching against the wrenching fury at himself as much as her. "What were you thinking?"

She was completely delusional when it came to society's strictures. He flipped through the messages on his desk and saw those she'd written to him. With a disgusted oath at himself, he dropped them. He'd been so bloody concerned about her since she'd left his estate with her father.

Whether Alex had intended to or not, she'd let loose an arena of jackals against her father. People who jumped to seize fault with the powerful aristocracy base. Not that Ware didn't deserve the agony, but Christopher was loath to play martyr for the day. Or the catalyst.

Even for her.

And now that people knew about his past with Ware's daughter, how long before someone discovered the other details? His military history, the records of his reprimands that had conveniently disappeared after his stint in India. Ware may have sent him off to hell, but he'd taken the blight off

Christopher's military career and practically made him a hero.

Worst of all, how long before someone learned that he and Alex had had a child?

The knowledge was so inherently private to him, so unsettled in his heart, that he wondered if he understood the depth of his own pain.

He threw aside the newspapers.

"People have too much time on their hands, sir, to bother with stories like that," Stewart said from the doorway. "But I thought that you would want to know. That's why I left them on your desk. Not that any of us here at D&B are prone to gossip, sir."

"Naturally." Christopher didn't look up from the correspondence he was flipping through. "Because that probably would get you fired."

"Yes, sir."

"You're not in the military, Stewart." He dropped the mail on his desk. "You've known me for years. Quit talking to me as if you're standing at attention."

"Yes . . . Mr. Donally, sir." Stewart handed Christopher the list he'd asked for. "Lord Ware's name is on there. He's been newly appointed to the Royal Commission overseeing all public works."

Christopher dropped into his chair.

"Sir?"

"Anything else you'd like to add to make my day any more pleasant?"

Nonplussed by Christopher's acerbic response, Stewart squared his shoulders. "This message arrived a few hours ago." He raised a slip of paper and read over his glasses. "Someone named Potter from the museum came by looking for you. He was quite insistent that you would want to see him and said he had information for you. In case you forgot who he was, he left me this card."

Christopher hadn't forgotten. He turned the calling card over in his hand. It was the one he'd given the security guard when he'd visited the museum some weeks ago. He'd wager certain parts of his anatomy that the museum security guard had learned about the dead maid.

"Sir." Stewart removed his spectacles. "About that article . . . ?"

"The answer is yes." Christopher was quite sure he didn't want to discuss that article. On the other hand, there wasn't a hell of a lot he could do about anything at this point. "Lady Alexandra Marshall used to be my wife. Our marriage was legally annulled. And yes, we are on speaking terms, so if she should show up here, I expect her to be treated with respect."

Most everyone was gone by the time Christopher finished his work at his desk. Finley should have been to Alex's flat by now to install the locks. Removing his waistcoat, Christopher walked to stand in front of the window. The night was never quiet. Across the river as far as he could see, lights dotted the landscape. A steamer blared. Rarely could he stare out at the Thames and imagine silence.

And as he looked across the river, Christopher struggled with all the reasons he'd walked away tonight. All the reasons she would never belong to his world, and the reasons he didn't want to belong to hers. Though he was a man who touted success, who had risen by sheer tenacity through the commoner ranks to touch noses with the wealthy, the emotions she evoked still managed to bring him crashing back to his roots.

The floorboards creaked. Christopher turned from his place in front of the window. Ryan walked into the room and dropped a pair of dossiers next to the slide rule discarded on Christopher's desk. "What are you still doing here?" he asked.

Christopher walked to the desk. "I like my work."

They had not spoken since both had left the committee yesterday after learning that D&B was no longer in the running for the Channel project. And since it was Christopher's presentation that had ultimately failed to win the board's confidence, he could see that there was a part of his brother that itched for a fight.

Christopher couldn't blame Ryan. Working for the prestigious project had been as much his brother's effort as it had been Christopher's ideas that put them in the running. Indeed, all of twenty-four years old, there wasn't a more capable civil engineer than Ryan, who also managed to combine a rare genius for rendering production specifications into lay terms when speaking before parliamentary committees. Their London operation was a success because Christopher had put Ryan in charge.

Christopher picked up the dossier Ryan had dropped, and held it nearer to the light. "We've problems at the Charing Cross site," Ryan said. "Our inspection team found cracks in the cofferdam spanning the Hungerford abutment."

Christopher swore. With five years' worth of work before the planning board, the recent loss of the Tunnel project, and his problems with Alex, this couldn't have come at a worse time.

"Are you going to continue to see her?" Ryan tossed the newspaper into the refuse container.

Christopher wanted to tell his brother it was none of his business. "Maybe."

"Do ye think Ware had a hand in our losing the Channel project?"

Christopher met his brother's gaze. "I don't know."

"We were close." Shoving a hand into his pocket, Ryan smiled ruefully. "Maybe we should pack up and help De Lesseps complete the Suez Canal. Show him how the Irish do it."

Christopher grunted. He tossed aside the dossier he was reading. "Isn't the Charing Cross site where the crew found the body of that O'Connell woman?"

"Half buried in the silt beneath the bridge. The place is covered at high tide. I was going to go there tomorrow—"

"I'll go," Christopher said.

"You? The esteemed lord of D&B?" Ryan narrowed his eyes. "We have a dozen engineers who can handle that job."

"I miss the outdoors. What difference does it make?"

Ryan gave him a considering look. "Stewart said that you've been keeping hours at the gym. How is Finley? Out of jail, I hope?"

"I'm not involved in anything illegal, if that's what concerns you."

Ryan's mouth crooked. "That's good to hear, Chris."

The concern in Ryan's face, concern that he'd put there, stopped Christopher's response. Christopher admitted to the problems he'd had in the past with opium and whiskey. It was something that would never leave him, and on the deepest level he knew that there would always be that part of his family that would be watchful. That would worry just a little bit more than they should about his capabilities, his state of mind.

And suddenly it was important that Ryan know how much Christopher appreciated his talent, his camaraderie, and his loyalty.

"We'll get past this with the committee," he said. "There will be other projects."

Ryan walked to the window. "Now that the Channel project meetings are finished, Rachel will be taking Brianna back to Carlisle soon. I promised my dearly betrothed that I would show her the sites before she left. Rachel is with us."

A dubious brow shot up. "You want me to entertain Rachel?"

"Have mercy on me, brother. We're attending Cremorne Gardens tonight. Later in the week, Kathleen wants a showing at the museum. I need your connections." A dark lock of hair tumbled over Ryan's brow. "Besides, Rachel thinks ye hate her. This will give you a chance to make nice to all of us after being such an ass all week."

Watching his brother play patty-fingers with his bride-to-be was not at the top of his list of entertainment tonight, but it beat the hell out anything else he had on his agenda. "In an hour?" he asked. "I'll change here."

"I'll be back with the carriage."

After Ryan left, Christopher fastened his fingers behind

his head and lounged back in the chair. His gaze fell on Potter's card. He sat forward and picked it up, idly flicking at the stiff corner. He walked to the door.

Stewart looked up from the desk. "Yes, sir?"

"Has a positive identification been made on the woman found at the Charing Cross site?"

Stewart rustled through his papers. "No, sir. Not that I know."

Christopher walked to the window and looked out over the city. Even knowing the big Irishman would remain near Alex's apartment tonight didn't take the edge off his mood.

His eyes turned as if compelled to the doorway. By slow degrees, he found that his will would indulge him more than his memories of her. His body burned with the need to go back to her.

With an oath, he pressed both palms against the glass as if that crystalline barrier could keep his will at bay.

Hell, someone should just take him outside and shoot him.

Get it over with now. Before Ryan or Johnny did it for him.

Chapter 16

Alexandra struck a match. The chilly draft raised bumps on her arms beneath the long sleeves of her silk gown. The sulfur flared to life. She held the flame to the chips of wood she'd scraped from the log. She repeated the action three more times before she burned her fingers.

The bloody wood would not start. Outside, rain spattered against the streets. Alexandra rubbed her brow against the soiled sleeve of her gown and sat back on her heels in displeasure. She eyed the pile of books, papers, and years of memorabilia spread like an unkempt carpet over the floor. Having decided to dedicate the last week to organizing her household, she'd been on her hands and knees until they were raw. She'd climbed the stairs to the third-floor attic a hundred times, and still it looked as if she'd barely touched this room.

With a sigh, she surveyed the messy dishes left over from a disastrous breakfast. Christopher could go to perdition.

She threw the useless matches at the log and climbed to her feet to retrieve her bucket of water. She'd worked diligently scrubbing the upper rooms before hanging the curtains she'd brought over from the cottage.

It shocked Alexandra to realize that Christopher really intended to stay away from her. She'd not seen him for days. He'd sent no messages, only Finley to fix her locks. She wondered why he'd bothered at all.

Still, she'd kept herself busy. Mary and Alfred had not yet arrived. She'd been working all week to ready their room. She'd wanted everything to be perfect.

By dint of will, she bent her head to tighten the knots on the kerchief she'd brought home from the anthropology lab. Then, eyeing a pair of dirty rags and the mop, she set to work once again.

Back straight, Brianna stood with her nose to Lady Alexandra's door, her thoughts askew. She prayed the door would open before anyone saw her standing in the shallow alcove. It was too cold and miserable for June. If Christopher knew that she'd left the townhouse, he would be furious. On the busy street behind her, a pedestrian shouted at a hansom driver. The weather had been beautiful all week until the day she'd chosen to go out.

Lady Alex suddenly appeared before her. Wearing a ratty gown, her hair hidden beneath a kerchief, she looked as if she'd been cleaning the fireplace.

"Good heavens." Lady Alex looked behind her. "You're the last person I expected to see. How did you find me?"

"It was not easy, my lady." Without being invited, Brianna stepped inside and swung her gaze over the set of rooms.

"I went to your house yesterday. Today I went to the museum. A security guard told me where you were. But I have used up all my money coming here. Christopher does not believe in giving me funds of my own," Brianna uttered, the tears that she'd been shedding all day just at the surface again. "I'm surprised to see you here as well, my lady. I wish I had someplace like this."

"Brianna." Lady Alexandra wiped a stray curl from Brianna's forehead. "What are you doing here?"

"I needed so desperately to talk to someone. You are the only one I could turn to."

"Where is your brother?" Lady Alexandra walked her into the adjoining parlor, a warm mellow room of browns and burgundy, with deep-buttoned armchairs and a matching settee set around a second fireplace. The curtains were opened to the iron fence that looked up to the street. Raindrops splashed against the windows.

"Christopher is at some construction site. He's been there all week." Brianna withdrew a lacy handkerchief. "Tonight they'll all probably go out again and leave me alone. But that is just ducky, because he is Christopher. Man of his own rules. Hypocrite extraordinaire!" Her chin lifted. "And you? How could you not tell me that you and my brother were . . . that you were more than mere acquaintances?"

Alexandra put her hand on the wall beneath the archway where she stood. "It wasn't my place, Brianna."

"Even after we became friends?" Eyes shimmering, Brianna sat down. "My brother never grants personal interviews. Yet, there have been four newspaper and magazine spreads the last few months. Not including that hubbub made over his endowment to the museum. Why the fascination with him? I don't understand."

"He is an interesting study in cultural defiance, I think."

"Rachel thinks it's because he is handsome, rich, and Irish." Brianna untied the bright fluffy ribbons on her hat. "He was furious when he found out about the *Vanity Fair* article and that you had actually talked to a writer about him. I think that my brother is not the man with the sterling character everyone thinks he is."

"Yes, I'm aware of that."

"Christopher is a liar by omission. And a tyrant by fact. It is not fair that I be condemned when such a double standard exists. I shall join the suffrage league. Or run away. That's why I came here."

"Brianna—"

"I hate him. I truly do. If I'm bad, it's Christopher's fault."

Alexandra sat next to the distraught girl. "I thought that you'd left London."

"Rachel didn't want to leave until after the hearings for the Channel project. And what Rachel wants, Rachel gets. She and Christopher have become quite close, all chitchat and laughs." Brianna's eyes flashed. "She dared to take Christopher and Ryan's side against me. Lectured me, as if she had rights over my life, by virtue of the fact that she is a Bailey. I shall never forgive her this digression against my person."

Alexandra managed not to look down at her hands folded in her lap. Christopher had been going out on the town with Rachel. The shock touched a quickness within her stomach. But if Christopher chose to dally with another woman, she could no more stop him than she could turn back time.

"Why are you here, Brianna?"

The girl lowered her gaze.

"I'm not your mother, Brianna. I'm not even a mother figure. And I'm too old to be your best friend. You cannot run away and you've put me in an awkward position coming here today."

Brianna still didn't reply. Alexandra knew that she'd hurt the girl's feelings, but Brianna didn't belong here.

Rising to her feet, Alexandra decided to offer tea. At least she knew how to boil water. It was the least she could do before she escorted Brianna back to Belgrave Square. Christopher would not want his sister to be seen alone in this neighborhood.

"My lady," Brianna said, when they'd sat at the table. Steam wafted from the porcelain teacups. "Do you know that you have the most beautiful eyes in the lamplight?" Her voice faded. "Except for Stephan's."

Alexandra smoothed the curls from Brianna's cheek. "Does your sudden mood have something to do with Mr. Williams?"

"It is not sudden, as you must know. My lady . . . I'm sorry that I came here. I know that I shouldn't have." Then all at once she was in Alexandra's arms, sobbing like a babe. "My whole life is over. I've lost Stephan. I didn't know where else to go."

"Nonsense." Alexandra stroked Brianna's hair. "Why do you think you've lost Mr. Williams?"

"He won't speak to me anymore." Her gaze fixed on the floral print of her sleeves. "You see, he and I used to meet after Christopher left. The only tree on the block grows in the courtyard out back of Ryan's townhouse. A swing hangs from the branches. We would sit there for hours and just talk. Once we even snuck out to Cremorne Gardens. Have you ever been there?" She lifted wet eyes inquiringly.

Unable to comprehend Brianna's actions, Alexandra shook her head.

"The place is a crystal fantasyland encased in light."

"Didn't you think that perhaps it was wrong for Mr. Williams to take you there? He is older than you are. He knows better, Brianna. If Christopher ever found out you did this, I guarantee you would probably never see the light of day again. Nor would Mr. Williams. If he survived the thrashing he deserved."

"It doesn't matter anymore." A ragged sigh escaped. "Stephan won't even come to my window. He is afraid of Christopher. How can I love a man who will not stand up for me to my brother?"

"Can he support you, Brianna?"

She dabbed at her wet eyes. "We love each other."

"Are you part of the same church, the same economic or social background? Do you have *anything* strong enough in common to build a whole life upon? To withstand public censure?"

"We love each other!"

"There are rules, and consequences when you break those rules. Maybe Christopher knows that love is not enough to stand up against sacrifice." The words arrested her thoughts and froze her voice for a dozen heartbeats before she focused on Brianna watching her. "Maybe Christopher wants more for your future. Maybe he's afraid for you."

"Maybe he doesn't know who I really am."

"When you're seventeen, everything in the world seems impossible. When you're twenty-eight, you realize why everything seemed impossible at seventeen." Alexandra took Brianna's hand, cradling the tender palm between her own. "Maybe your brother knows more than you think."

"Mr. Williams *has* been accepted to Cambridge." Brianna's sniffles lessened. "That is an honor, isn't it?"

"Very much so."

Brianna sat up straighter. "He will become a barrister."

"A most noble profession."

"I told him that I would wait for him. But I'm not sure he will still love me."

"If he doesn't, he will move on and so must you."

Brianna gently rubbed a tear off Alexandra's cheek. "Is that what happened to you and my brother?"

Alexandra contemplated her answer even as she changed clothes and took Brianna back to the townhouse. Because Christopher was doing exactly what her father had done, and she didn't want to empathize with her father, she found that neither did she want to feel compassion toward Christopher.

Yet, she found herself caught.

Christopher was wrong. Just as her father had been.

Yet, he was also right.

He had been right about so many things that she began to view his desire to stay away from her in a new light. One that picked at the sharp planes of her discomfort and gave back no warmth.

"My lady," Brianna said after they'd arrived at the Donally townhouse. Alexandra had bade the hansom to await her return. "You don't like me anymore, do you?"

Alexandra turned to her young charge. "That's not true." She cared a lot for this youngest Donally. Too much, in fact.

The wind wrestled with her skirts. Holding a hand against

her hat, she looked at the ugly sky, and felt a raindrop on her face. "Is Christopher staying here?"

"No, my lady." Brianna swept past the high iron porticos and turned. "The only reason he stayed here before was because of me."

So, he and Rachel were not sleeping beneath the same roof. Christopher was going home every night.

Alone.

And suddenly she smiled to herself.

Brianna's face lowered. "He's still a hypocrite, my lady."

"Understand this." Alexandra tipped a gloved finger beneath the girl's chin. "If I ever learn that you've gone out on your own at night again, I will not hesitate to tell your family. And, Brianna." Despite her desire to lecture the girl for her melodramatics, Alexandra kissed her on the cheek. "If I had a sister, I would wish her to be like you."

Brianna's face brightened. "Thank you, my lady."

What seemed like hours later, Alexandra finally stood on the ledge of the embankment site where Christopher was working. Brianna's conversation had stayed with her, more so because Alexandra found her heart plagued by the wisdom of her own insight.

Wooden fences partitioned the entire area for blocks, and picking her way over the rubble, she worked to get around the wall. The wind caught her skirts and she regretted that she'd not brought a wrap. A ferry sounded on the river. Her hand against her hat, Alexandra stopped to catch her breath, and slowly straightened. A menacing noise surrounded her as scaffolding, stories tall, was being erected and shaft holes sunk.

She could only stare in wonder at the world that met her eyes. Big Ben and Parliament stood framed by the churning skyline, a visual monstrosity of ancient beauty surrounded by a tapestry of modern progress. Scaffolding lined the riverbank for miles. In a matter of years, London's past would be reduced to little more than pictures in history books and Christopher's name would be engraved in stone forever as a contributor to London's new face. A keen sense of awe filled her.

Movement grabbed her gaze and she found Christopher. Balanced between two girders where once the river used to be, his collar open, he wore no tie or jacket. Dressed in slacks and a white shirt now plastered to his body from the drizzle, he was out of place, yet so perfectly at home in the massive chaos surrounding him. She was conscious of his height, and where his shirt sagged open. Men who looked like they hauled off brick houses for a living stood nodding as he spoke to them.

Indeed, he looked occupied, and she began to doubt the wisdom of coming here. Maybe she'd just wanted to see a little of his life. To understand more of the man he'd become. To understand his drive.

He had more at stake than she. More to lose.

While she'd sought to excavate her whole existence, he strove to make a difference with his. His reputation and that of his company needed public support to prosper.

She was already a scandal to her peers. In truth, she'd done far more than commit social suicide, and still a part of her thrived in her misanthropic defiance. Clearly, she was driven by forces that lacked regard for her welfare.

Christopher was not.

And therein lay the crux of their problem. The irony of their switched roles over the decade did not escape her. Yet, perhaps uncertainty of the future was nothing time wouldn't remedy. Could she not be an optimist at least when it came to matters of her heart?

She wanted to be seventeen again when everything in the world seemed possible.

She was still standing on the incline when someone yelled at her from down the bank, flapping his arms wildly at her. The *thug* of a steam engine drowned out his voice. A man standing next to Christopher saw her, and nudged his boss as he pointed in her direction. Christopher turned abruptly. His hair wet against his head, the wind whipping his sleeves, she saw his gaze snap to something behind her. Alarmed, Alexandra looked up. A crane was swinging its heavy load over her. It swept past, but even as she watched, a one-ton piling dropped into the riverbed a hundred feet from where she stood. The ground shook. She fell back into the rocks, and sat there as workers started to run toward her.

Then, just as she thought circumstances could get no worse, the sky let loose a furious downpour.

The carriage where Alexandra had been brought sat parked on a narrow side street. Outside, she heard Christopher's voice before the door swung open. Water splashed off his lashes and his face and sucked his shirt to every inch of corded restraint in his arms.

"Sir!" one of his men called from across the street. He jogged toward Christopher, his boots slapping in the mud. Raindrops pounded the ground. "You left this, sir." His bearded face ruddy, he was breathless as he turned over Christopher's jacket. "Down by the pilings. What shall I tell the men?"

Christopher tossed the jacket into the carriage, pausing only to wipe the mud from his shoes. "Get a message to Ryan that he needs to inspect everything that has come from the Galloway plant in the last two months. He's at the Southwark office, or will be"—he pulled out his watch—"in an hour."

"Yes, sir."

"I'll be finished here in a moment." Christopher shifted his attention to her. "Make that two."

The door slammed. Lowering himself on the bench seat across from her, he expelled a breath and ran his hand around the back of his neck. Neither spoke for a moment. Gathering her shattered poise by gritting her teeth, Alexandra folded her hands in her lap like a chastened child. Her clothes were sodden. Ruined. The feather from her hat lay plastered against her cheek. The only positive aspect of the whole fiasco was that she'd gotten a much-needed bath when it had started to pour.

"I've n-never seen what it is that you do," she spoke into the awkward silence.

Reaching below his seat, Christopher pulled out a woolen blanket. "The constable only just reopened the section where O'Connell was found. People dying on my site tends to slow progress." He tucked the blanket around her. "Are you all right?"

Her mouth quirked. She heard her teeth chattering from the cold. It required no mental feat to recognize her blunder. So, she did not defend her reasons for coming here. "I'm very proud of you." Clasping the corners of the blanket, she smiled. "I know that sounds trite."

His eyes halted on her lips before his gaze raised to find her watching him. He sat back in the seat. "Why are you here, Alex?"

A light burned next to the door casting a soft glow on his handsome face. She'd come here for a dozen reasons. None that seemed as particularly material as the fact that he was with her in the carriage. "Ever since you sent that man Finley to my townhouse, you've been avoiding me. Aren't you curious about my new locks?"

Christopher cocked a brow as if to tell her he knew that wasn't what brought her today. "He said you weren't pleased with his services."

"Perhaps you should visit my humble abode," she rebuked with much bravado. "I have beautiful doors, probably worth more than the whole townhouse, quite extraordinary, actually, considering the kind of man and his stable of delinquents who installed them. You should have warned me."

"So you've met the boys." A smile touched his mouth. "They didn't rough you up, did they?"

Her mood softened. "How is it that you know those people? Finley was less than forthcoming about his association with you."

He stretched his arm along the back of the seat. "What is it you wanted to talk to me about, Alex?"

She'd wanted to ask him about Rachel. But jealousy forbade any query. She needed to talk to him about her father, but here didn't seem the right time or topic. "You've ignored my messages," she said instead. "So I went to visit your sister today."

"You've sent no messages." He leaned an elbow on one knee, his eyes challenging hers. "I've taken to reading *all* of my daily correspondence. A quaint need if one wishes to avoid surprises. Did my sister fill your ear full of woe about how I won't allow her to see Mr. Williams?"

Beneath the blanket, Alexandra crossed her arms. "Brianna is a grown woman, whether you see her as that or not." She looked out the window at the broken London landscape. "If you ever learned anything from my father you should have learned that the quickest way to find your sister wed is to tell her that she can't see the man she loves."

He sat back, his knees spread in a casual slouch, and looked at her hard. "You're freezing. I need to get you home."

"Hark! You *d-do* care about me. Admit that you miss me."

"Care?" Leaning forward, he cupped her face in his palm. His skin was warm against her cheek. "What do you think this is about, Alex?" Scraping both hands through his hair, he slumped back. "You gave me a bloody stroke just now. Trust me, I'm doing Williams a big favor. He doesn't need a woman to complicate his life. Give a man the goddamn Inquisition any day."

"That is a *wretched* thing to say, Christopher Donally. Why don't you just ask me to hammer a stake through your heart and get it over with?"

He grinned, his teeth stark white against the shadow on his jaw. "Aye," he said consideringly, taking in her wet attire where the blanket had slipped, "a stake would be nice. A long metal one with a pointed end."

"You're the most unreasonable man I know, Christopher."

She threw the blanket at him and started for the door.

He barred the exit with his arm. A slow, dangerous smile crooked his lips as he settled his gaze where her breasts molded themselves to his arm, before raising his eyes to meet hers again. A blush warmed her face. "Am I? I thought I was being rather sociable."

Alexandra watched him throw open the door. "The carriage is yours, my lady." The sound of rain roared through the coach. One hand braced on the door, he hesitated. "If you have anything else about which you want to talk, my carriage will bring you back to my office, after you change."

"Where every word can be heard through the transom? I really do need to talk to you. It's about my father."

She met the quiet blue of his eyes. "I'll see if I can clear my schedule," he said noncommittally. "And Alex? Don't come to this site again. Do you understand?"

Slamming the door, he shouted something to the driver huddled beneath a tarp across the street. The carriage swayed with his weight as he climbed into the boot. Alexandra let down the window. "How will you get back?"

He thumped the carriage and sent it rolling into traffic. "I'll hire a cab."

Christopher remained in the street, his hair and shirt plastered to his body. Slamming the window shut, Alexandra dropped back into her seat.

Her former spouse could write the book on unreasonable behavior!

Christopher's jacket remained on the seat. For a long time, she ignored it. But like a shiny gold Roman coin, it kept pulling at her.

Finally, giving up her angry vigil, she dragged the sodden jacket into her lap. A thump sounded at her feet.

Alexandra picked up his money clip and, with widened eyes, thumbed through the thick pad of banknotes.

Poor Christopher. He wouldn't be hiring anyone to get him to his office. He'd be walking.

* * *

Alexandra opened her kitchen cupboards, slamming each one in turn. With all the hullabaloo today, she'd forgotten to go to the bakery. She stared at tins of tomatoes, peaches, and pears. She'd eaten the last apple she'd brought from a little girl on the street corner a few days before. Now that she wasn't taking her meals at the museum, she'd diminished her food supply this weekend. Her coffee ran out that morning.

Pacing to and fro in front of her useless fireplace, she shivered in her wrapper, appreciating even more the comforts servants had provided her throughout her life. She'd barely been able to get out of her sodden gown. She could *not* get out of her wet corset. The dull knife she'd used to pry the hooks loose had sliced her finger instead.

It was impossible not to feel sorry for herself and angry at Christopher for whatever reason she could seize. Christopher, with his penchant for survival, and leaping adversity in one bound, was probably faring better than she was. Even if he did have to walk back to the office.

With a deep breath, Alexandra gathered her composure and managed not to listen to the traitorous voice inside her head telling her that she'd been a fool to trade the luxury of her home for this awful place. She tightened the belt at her waist and walked to the door, opening it wider when she espied the foursome loitering across the street. She'd noticed the boys when she'd arrived home earlier before the bobby shooed them away the first time. They were the same youths who'd shown up with Finley when he'd come to fix her doors a few days ago.

She was faintly surprised when they crossed the street. In the fading daylight, she noted red hair beneath one grubby hat, a towheaded urchin, and two with black hair. All of them looked as if they could use a bath. Red seemed to be their leader.

"How would you like to make a shilling?" she asked.

They looked at each other, unimpressed.

"All right, two," she offered, her voice firm.

"Five," the red-headed waif said. "One for each of us."

"But there are only four of you."

The blue-eyed hustler grinned. "We don't know how to count, mum, seeing as we never been educated the way you have."

Alexandra narrowed her eyes. "Five shillings is bloody robbery. You don't even know what it is I want you to do."

"Don't matter. Five shillings. That's our price."

Behind them, the sun was already beginning to set. "I need food," she said. "I'll make a list." Her eyes hesitated on their grimy faces. "On second thought, can you remember if I tell you what I need?"

"Better than we can read, Missus Donally."

"Please don't call me that. That's not my name."

The towheaded scamp plunked a fist on his hip. "Finley says it is. He says you and Mister Donally was married a long time ago."

Rolling her eyes, Alexandra tossed her hands. Explanations were too complicated. Walking into her bedroom, she rummaged through her armoire. She'd let Christopher handle the name problem, sure that he would set the matter straight the instant he heard some misguided soul call her his wife.

Fishing out the needed shillings, Alexandra looked at her cash reserves. She gnawed her lip. Christopher's money clip sat on the table in her dining room where she'd thrown it earlier. She had not managed her self-imposed allowance well at all and would have to budget better. At this rate, she doubted her ability to live out the year.

"Only for a year and a half, Alexandra," she told herself as she shoved the pouch back into the dresser drawer. "A year and half and you will be of age for your inheritance." She'd scrub bloody floors before she went back to her father for anything.

The boys were standing inside when she came out of the bedroom. "Bloomin' 'ell, milady." Four pairs of youthful eyes were staring above her fireplace. "Can you use that thing?"

Her gaze raised to the wicked scimitar above the fireplace

she'd labored all morning to hang on stone. Light flashed off the silver blade. "Where did ye get that, mum?" a little boy no older than seven asked.

"Algeria," she said, studying each of them. Their eyes didn't move.

"Blimey," they cooed as if one.

"Have you ever killed anyone with it?" asked their leader.

"Yes, *many, many* times. See?" she pointed to a spot of rust near the gilded grip. "Blood," she said succinctly.

The interest on their faces turned to awe, and Alexandra knew she'd won four new friends for life. One boy saw her pile of matches on the floor and knelt beside the fireplace. Holes in his knees bore the evidence of a recent scrape. "You've green wood, milady," he informed her. "That's why it ain't much good fer lighting."

Alexandra joined him at the hearth, and they both looked at the pile of useless wood. "They cut the tree down outside. The roots were shoving up the street. I found the wood stacked beside my door."

A few moments later Red entered from the courtyard with a bucket of coal. He then showed her where to find it in her bin.

The boys gathered around her outside. "Ye have coal fer the stove, too, mum. But you'll be needin' to fill the bins soon. Them bein' nearly empty."

"Truly?" Alexandra leaned over and looked inside. She made a note to talk to her landlord about how to go about ordering coal.

Wrapping her arms around herself, she looked up and down the row of manicured gardens. Some people had not retrieved their laundry before the storm.

This existence was new for her. Until recently, she'd never even swept her own floor. Her gaze tracked up the brick façade to her second floor, where she'd pulled back the lace curtains.

"You've a nice place to live, mum," towhead said. "You've even birds in the trees."

Nodding, she looked around the small paved yard enclosed by a brick wall where the trash bins were kept. The previous tenant had tried to till a garden in the plot of dirt beside the wall.

The littlest boy stepped forward. "During dry spells, the water man's cart comes and fills the cisterns here. Don't he, Bob?"

"The milkmaid comes in the mornings," Bob added. "The vegetable wagon makes rounds later. And a cheese cart comes once a week."

They walked her back inside, then showed her how to light the fire efficiently before scampering off to the market. An hour later they returned with her items. "We brung ye candy, milady." Offering her a piece of horehound, they managed to talk her out of another shilling.

Later, with the golden cat watching from the sill outside, she ate a meal of eggs, potatoes, peppers, and cheese. She gazed at her new hand-carved mahogany door with its shiny brass latch with genuine fondness, despite the fact that Finley had probably robbed some house in Mayfair to get it.

A lightness of spirit encased Alexandra. She didn't know why entirely, except maybe it had something to do with the fact that she'd finished unpacking and cleaning. Her larder was full. After washing the dishes, she'd bandaged her hand again because her cut had started bleeding, and felt idiotic for having injured herself in the first place. She should have been more patient and waited for her stays to dry. They'd come off easily then.

Across the back courtyard, the resident ingénue played the piano as Alex read the latest museum periodical. A long sigh slipped from her as she propped her chin on her palm. For compared to this strange part of London, in the midst of her new life, she'd only now realized how silent her everyday world had once been. And how much she liked noise.

A tap sounded at her front door. She turned on her chair, her eyes going to the clock on the mantel. It was eleven o'clock: just the right hour for someone venturing out to enjoy London's colorful nightlife.

Aware that Christopher rarely missed a detail, especially a missing money clip, she guessed who her visitor might be. Her gaze touched the scimitar, and for a moment she wished she really could use the weapon.

Chapter 17

Alexandra's hand hesitated on the latch. She pressed her ear to the door and could feel Christopher on the other side of the panels. Every fiber in her being thrummed with new resiliency.

"Who is it?" she called.

A pause. Then, "It's me, Alex." Christopher's voice was low. "Just open the bloody door."

The key fumbled in the lock. Alexandra wriggled it noisily, taking her time, before finally opening the door. She half expected to find Miss Bailey standing behind him or awaiting his return in his carriage.

Christopher stood with his palm braced on the doorframe, his head bowed slightly. The long woolen coat pulled at his shoulders. He lifted his head and looked at her. She felt undressed by the dark glitter in his perusal.

"Nice door," he said.

A low mist had settled on the street behind him. The street was empty. "This is late for a visit, Christopher."

"And yet, here I am, standing before you. Your humble servant."

"Humble indeed?" Her brows arched doubtfully. "Or

maybe you're here because I have something very valuable of yours?"

"Aye." Christopher leaned a shoulder against the doorframe. "I could keep a mistress with what you found in my clip."

"Truly," she said, unimpressed. "Are you a libertine? I think not." She remained in the doorway. "Though you'd probably make an excellent rake if you ever set your mind to the task."

His gaze seemed to gentle on hers. "May I come in?"

Giving up her vigil, she stepped aside. "Where is your carriage?"

Christopher shut the door, taking in the ordered room, the fire, her appearance. An air of detached elegance clung to him. He'd changed into evening garb, and the black jacket beneath his coat both complimented his hair and contrasted with the stark blue of his eyes. He *wore* his clothes. They never seemed to wear him.

"Ryan wanted Kathleen to see the museum. Atler gave us a private showing of the Cairo exhibit. And dinner. One of the privileges of being a trustee. After dinner, the carriage took the others home."

And he'd remained. "What did you think of the exhibit?" she asked.

"Clearly those in charge possess a romantic flair for history."

She was perversely delighted by the *way* he'd said the words. "I'll take that as a compliment."

Christopher leaned closer. "It was more than a compliment, Alex."

He did not remove his coat as he walked to the fireplace and touched the domed clock that sat on the mantel. "You've done all right here. I'm impressed."

"Really, Christopher." She laughed. "I'm not entirely helpless." She moved to the table, where she'd thrown his clip next to the small wooden crate filled with produce that she hadn't washed or put away yet.

"I see you've even attended the market."

"It hardly takes an education to figure out how to get one's food from the market. There are stalls for everything. Even candy." She plopped a horehound candy drop in her mouth and turned.

Christopher stood directly behind her. She almost choked down the drop. He was removing his gloves, then reached around her and took the last piece of candy. He brushed her shoulder. Her lashes drifted upward to find his dark gaze on hers. She watched him slide the drop beneath his tongue. "I know the shop this came from." He put two steps between them. "Nice pair that runs the place. Best shop on Regent Street," he supplied.

"Regent Street!"

Those little hooligans had splurged her every shilling in one of the most expensive sweet shops in all of London.

Reaching into his pocket, Christopher withdrew a handful of shillings and dropped them on the table. "You paid them too much, Alex."

Alexandra looked on in astonishment. "I paid them to run errands. You had no right."

"They're already being paid to run your errands. They're being paid to watch this townhouse. They'll rob you blind if you let them."

"I thought you liked them."

"Which has nothing to do with reality. You need to keep your money."

She sighed mentally, but the sound slipped out. "You can be irritating, Christopher. Completely irritating."

"Among other things. I've been called worse."

She crossed her arms. "By your whole family, no doubt."

Christopher leaned against the table and crossed his arms. His coat hung loose around his calves. "You wanted to talk?"

Alexandra longed to look away from the man who seemed to make the fire burn hotter in this room. "Yes, now that you're here." She tucked a strand of hair behind her ear, only to startle as he caught her hand.

"I would have come here sooner, but I couldn't get away."

He scraped a thumb over her bandage. "What happened to your hand?"

"I cut it trying to get my corset off." She eased away and backed into a chair, which hit the table. Her coffee cup rattled. "The knife was dull, and slipped."

"You tried to cut off your corset?" His voice was incredulous.

Her chin went up. He was pushing her off subject. "My father thinks you're trying to publicly humiliate him. Maybe even blackmail him."

His hand went to his hip. "Over you?" She heard his quiet snort of disgust. "It's a little late for blackmail on that point."

"You think this is amusing?"

"Frankly, Ware is an arrogant bastard and I give you credit for walking out on him."

The words gave her pause. "You do?"

He took her hand again and she tensed. Pausing slightly, he turned her palm face up as he unraveled the bandage. "That doesn't mean I agree with the means you chose to fight him. But I admire your courage." They were both suddenly looking at her finger because it seemed the most neutral point between them. "It's but a scratch," he said, unimpressed.

"I didn't say that I'd sliced it to the bone."

"Hardly worthy of a bandage, Alex."

"Certainly it will leave no trophy scar like yours. It hurt."

"Maybe a kiss will make it feel better?"

"Pah!" She snatched away her hand. "And give me an infection?" Shoving the ill-used member behind her, she was suddenly furious to realize that he was laughing at her. "You've changed the subject."

He crossed his arms. "Is this the extent of your important news?"

"My father has lost a great deal of money," she said. "In the process, he borrowed against his London estate. It seems that you own the mortgage on the house and his notes at the clubs."

"I own a lot of mortgages." His expression was neutral. "I'm part of a lucrative conglomerate that invests in real estate."

"Is it possible you could be a lien holder to his London estate?"

"Did you see my name on the actual lien? Did he?"

"It was a letter from Papa's solicitor."

"And naturally, if my name was mentioned, he assumed the worst."

"Papa is on the Royal Commission that oversees public works. He thinks you've plans to blackmail him into voting your way on certain public works proj—"

A finger went to her lips and he was suddenly on his feet standing over her. "I know your father, Alex." His eyes held hers in a steady gaze. "And as for the other, my solicitor is the only one able to answer those questions."

"Then you intend to look into the matter?"

"I do."

Somehow she'd ended with her thighs pressed against the table. "So tell me." His hands went to the belt looped around her waist. "Did you get your corset off?"

The faint essence of bayberry fell over her. "Yes. But if I start gasping for breath, it's because you are making me suffocate." Without reminding him that he'd accused her once of being equal to an opium addiction or that any man would prefer the Inquisition to a woman, she slapped his money clip against his chest. "Go away, Christopher. I have nothing else to say." Alexandra slid past him and opened her front door. Her whole body hummed in outrage. "I mean it. Go away."

Christopher remained where she'd left him, looking devastatingly handsome and too bloody tempting.

A current of air blew in the scent of fog. Christopher walked to the door and paused in front of her.

Then his hand reached up and shut the door. The weight of his stare bore down on her. "I'm not unaware of the string of coincidences that have plagued both of us since we met." As if coming to a decision, he withdrew a business card from his inside pocket with someone's name scribbled on back. "Do you know the day watchman at the museum? Potter?"

Alerted by the change in him, she nodded. "I used to pass him every day outside the vaults. I believe he quit his post weeks ago."

"Or was terminated?"

She lowered her head. Her hair slipped over her shoulders. "Yes." She nodded. "I believe he was discharged. Is that where you've been tonight? Looking for Potter?"

"If I'm not mistaken, you're the only one connected to those thefts still working at the museum."

His observation startled her. "I hadn't thought about it that way."

"Why not? Doesn't it seem strange to you?"

"Put in that perspective, yes," she said defensively, unable to understand why Atler had not dismissed her yet, "but employee turnover is always high. Except among the scholars."

He pondered the card in his hand, his thumb flicking the corner. "Atler is completely loyal to your father. Why?"

"They both grew up in Ware. Believe it or not they've been friends for years." Attentive to his line of questioning, she raised her gaze. "Why the questions?"

"Your father was at Atler's residence tonight. We shared a dinner engagement."

Alexandra tightened her arms around herself. "That must have been entertaining."

"Aye, he's still alive."

Crossing her arms, she continued to eye Christopher. But some of the tension had left. "Is that why you were hesitant to talk to me? You're concerned about my loyalties?" Perhaps she was too close to both Richard and his father to trust herself to answer that question honestly. "If you must know, my father used his massive influence to force Professor Atler to hire me. I didn't know that until recently. But I'm guilty of remaining after I found out."

"I'm not accusing anyone of anything," he said flatly. "I'm certainly not questioning your professional integrity."

"I hope not, Christopher. Because I really do know what I'm doing." And suddenly she was defending Atler, because in doing so she defended herself. "Professor Atler is doing what he has to do to protect the museum. You said so yourself."

"Alex—"

"He has an impeccable reputation. To imply wrongdoing would only backfire against you. As for Richard, I've known him my whole life. He would never do anything to hurt me. He wouldn't."

He listened to her verbiage without expression. She tucked a strand of hair behind her ear, afraid without knowing why. "Where is the White Swan that I gave you? Have you received any information about the real jewel?" she asked, then managed to recover her composure. "Maybe I should just take it back and return it to the vault."

"Finley has the Swan." Replacing the card in his jacket pocket, he raked his gaze up her form to settle on her face. "It would be remiss of me not to go to the constable."

"But you swore that you wouldn't. You can't. I'll be ruined. We've still no proof of anything."

"There are coincidences here that can't be ignored any longer."

"Then you're concerned about what I told you tonight?"

His hand fell away from his pocket. "I wasn't entirely surprised by what you told me, because Ware and I had already exchanged dialogue tonight, brief as it was. About you, mostly."

"I see. Then you decided to waltz across the street because you knew that I would let you inside? And he would see you?"

He laughed, but it was such a gentle response that Alexandra was suddenly caught by the sound of it. "Ware left Atler's residence over an hour ago. No one saw me come over here. I went for a walk."

"You did?"

"Your father said that you were naïve and filled with romantic notions about life. Of course, that was after he offered to recommend D&B for various public works projects and before he threatened to have me imprisoned if I ever tried to blackmail him."

Alexandra wanted to bury her head in her hands in humiliation. Christopher's palm went to her nape, and pulled her head back. With the brush of his fingers, the moment filled with an ungovernable need to yield something of the fire inside her.

"I'm not the same man I was years ago, Alex," he said suddenly, his voice quiet and so filled with need that Alexandra could not look away. "Tangiers took something of me to the grave, and I had been content never to revisit those memories again."

She watched his struggle with a desperate sense of indecision.

"I only know that I've spent the past few hours weighing every argument it took to stay away from here."

A self-depreciating grin mocked his words. Even the intrepid Christopher Donally did not seem immune to a bout of sheepishness, and that she was the cause lent her courage. "You lost an argument." Her rasp, deliberately provocative, raised his brow. "Nor were ye run over by a beer wagon, were ye?" She affected his occasional brogue.

"I can't walk away from D&B." She was unprepared for the solemn intensity of his answer, the unguarded vulnerability. "And I won't live the kind of life that runs its schedule from hunting season to hunting season, that dissects me under a magnifying glass. I had enough of that kind of control in the army. My life is my own. And I've made it what it is."

"Have you ever watched people walk to work?"

Christopher's mouth quirked. "No, I can't say that I have."

"They go the same way. Every day. To and fro. The same routine. Familiarity fosters security. Most species share that behavior."

Looking at her face, he seemed to think about her words. Did he recognize only himself? Or did he see that she spoke about them both? They could continue to traverse the same path they'd been walking for years or make a right turn now.

"Do most species take their mates against the wall, Alex?" His rasp held a sharp razor edge of awareness no longer held in check. "You have no idea what I want to do with you at this moment."

His hand went to the door, only to be stopped by hers. Somewhere she'd lost the desire to see him leave. Nor was she unaware of what she could cost Christopher.

But her heart raced and her breath stilled as she felt the coiled strength of his arm beneath her hand. There was so much inside him beyond her touch.

And the ground she stood on suddenly seemed less solid.

"Tell me why you came here tonight."

His gaze dropped slowly to the cool pale fingers against the dark of his sleeve before raising his gaze back to hers.

He didn't move.

"Tell me."

Planting his hands against the wall behind her, he locked his gaze on hers. "In sordid detail?" His whisper breached her lips.

"Yes."

She wanted to remain forever cloaked in the firelight that burned in his eyes. He lifted her hair aside, brushed it back with his hands, and tipped her head.

He lowered his mouth, this time in abandon, his lips touching her like a hot brand. His tongue swept inside her mouth, dipped and savored, with increasing hunger. Sinking against him, she raised her arms around his neck, inhaling his heat, the scent that belonged to him. He splayed the bend of her narrow waist. His hands burning through the wrapper, he slid them down her hips, then over her bottom. He brought her flush against his erection. She made a ragged sound as his mouth moved across her jaw to flick over her ear. One kiss had the might to overpower the differences between them.

No one had ever made the blood hum through her veins the way Christopher did.

No one had ever made her more aware of her emotions. Or

possessed her so thoroughly. Or kissed her in such a mind-melting rush.

No one had the power to destroy her world as much as Christopher did.

Not even her own father.

She felt his gaze on her upturned face, as if he knew her thoughts. "Alex?" His voice was husky, promising, darkly possessive.

Her lashes lifted. "So how much does it cost to keep a mistress anyway?"

His blue eyes glittered like night itself. "Do you want to be kept?"

"I . . . don't know." Her chin lifted as she considered the possibilities.

Alexandra suddenly felt the constraints of her station and envied him his freedom. Both knew she would never be entirely free of her world.

Maybe Christopher had been right. Maybe he *was* her sin. Her rebellion. Her spark of daring in a world bound by too many strictures.

"Have you ever made love against a wall?" she asked.

He raised a brow as if he hadn't heard her correctly, but neither did he answer. "Christopher!" Her jealousy responded to his silence.

"What kind of question is that?"

"Who was she?"

His features were starkly handsome, his gaze unrepentant as his eyes held hers. "She was a major's wife in New Delhi."

Alexandra opened her lips to reply but found she could not.

"I did what I did, Alex," he said with detached formality. No humility, only a predatory stillness as he watched her face. "You were no longer in my life."

There was a darkness inside Christopher that she was beginning only now to understand.

"I want the wall," she whispered against his lips. The heat

of him seeped through her wrapper to touch her all over. "I've never made love standing."

He slid his hands down her sides. His voice was soft when he spoke again. "Turn out your lights and draw your curtains so I can move away from this door."

Heart beating wildly against her ribs, Alexandra fumbled to check the knot on her belt. One by one, she turned out the lamps. She shut the curtains in her living room and beside the table. When the rooms were dark, she turned to search for Christopher.

He stood in her bedroom entryway; his coat and jacket were off. He watched her, his arm bent at his waist as he worked the cuffs on his snowy white shirt, now unbuttoned and hanging open. She had not closed her bedroom drapes all the way. The pale amber tint from the streetlight outside cast a lacy pattern over the floor behind him.

He reached out his hand to her and she took it, remaining where she stood, entwining her fingers so closely with his, touching in silence.

Then he gave a little pull. "Come here," he whispered.

Walking into the fold of his arms, she tested the feral warmth of her name against her lips. The kiss he took from her was hot and languid and ended too soon. Then he was stepping out of his trousers. Her wrapper slid off her shoulders into a puddle at their feet. Deftly sliding her gaze over sharply corded sinew and the dark hair on his chest, she followed the scar down his muscled thigh.

He looked carved from shadows and stone. All of him.

Her flesh was flawless in the muted light. The locket flashed silver and was warm between her breasts.

Nothing of her was concealed from his eyes. Nothing of him was concealed from hers. He leaned his palm against the doorframe and traced his mouth over the pulse against her throat. "Any certain wall you'd prefer?"

Shivers went over her. She wanted him in her bedroom. Inside her. All around her. "Here," she whispered, unable to move.

Threading his fingers into the tangled mass of her hair, he pinned her with his gaze. "Here." His words warmed her lips, as if he wanted to do more than crawl inside her.

He kissed her in fevered pleasure, his arousal distinct against her stomach. Backed against the wall, she arched her spine when he took first one breast and then the other into his mouth, the feel of him hot and liquid. She dug her fingers into the hard muscles of his back. Everything else ceased to exist but the feel of his lips on her body, his tongue, the wondrous touch of his palms.

His hand slid up her inner thigh and moved between her legs. "Christopher—" She uttered a small cry.

Parting her, penetrating her, his fingers moved deep inside her. She was wet and slick to his touch. "You're so tight."

Stretched taut, she tossed her head sideways. Her blood was pulsing through her veins in fevered rhythm to his fingers. Propelled toward climax, she felt herself buckling. He tilted her bottom. "Take me inside you." His guttural groan rasped against her opened lips. "Take me, Alex."

Unfocused, except on the intensity of his invasion, she raised one leg to his hip until he was fully sheathed. He whispered her name, and she sank onto him. She had her hands in his hair, her legs wrapped around his waist. Braced against her, he stopped, his body rigid and thrumming with heat. The weight of his flesh throbbed inside her. His breathing filled her senses. Slowly she opened her eyes, her lashes lifting to find him watching her, caressing her face with his gaze as if she were the most precious thing in the world.

"You make me feel good, Alex." The words were strained, barely audible.

She smiled beneath lowered lids into his eyes. Passion was taking her. "You make me feel good, too, Christopher."

He shifted her bottom, lifting her high, locking his fingers with hers. She clung. He pressed her hands against the wall and began moving inside her. Slowly at first, his body moving over her, against her. He drew her around him, extracting every precious breath from her body. Where he touched her, she was hot.

Then he was loving her.

Passion took them. Her hair draping his arms, her breasts hard against his chest, his lips moved on her mouth, demanding, and she gave what he took, her nails digging in the solid muscled splendor of his arms. And with each powerful stroke of his body, the primal tempest bore her to the clouds and beyond.

Finally bearing her home.

Christopher lay with Alex in his arms. A smile teased the corners of her mouth as she ran her fingers through his hair. A sheen of sweat coated his body and hers. Still in the afterglow of their carnal marathon, she arched in his arms and fell back on her pillow, her hair a silken halo around her head. His gaze fastened on her face. Mesmerized by her beauty, he feathered his palm over her breast. She seemed fairylike in her beauty, ethereal, as if she belonged in some pagan forest.

"Will you stay the night?" She traced his lips with her fingernail.

"Yes."

They lay in the middle of her bed, one of her legs straddling his hip, cloaked in her musky heat. Pillows, the covers, and most everything lay on the floor. "I could do this all night." She gloried in a stretch.

His fingertips touched her cheek. "Perhaps so, but even I need some time to recoup, madam."

She laughed. A crack in the curtains gave them the only light in the room, and he watched, as she grew pensive. She stroked the hair from his forehead. "How is it that you know people like Finley and those boys?" she asked.

Christopher kissed her shoulder. "Finley and I have known each other since we were kids," he said after a moment.

She blinked. "How?"

His lips curved ruefully at her reaction. "When my da first moved us from Ireland, we didn't live too far from Holborn," he stated simply. "Not by choice. Through the aid of a man named Michael Bailey, Da had been offered an assistant fellowship in metallurgy at the university. I was five. By the time I was seven, the powers that be on the streets were using Finley, my brother David, and me to climb through windows and open doors so the houses could be robbed." His teeth flashed white. "It behooved us to learn to pick locks instead."

"What happened?"

"I spoke every language of every foreigner that lived on those streets. Most were laborers who worked on the docks. Because of my mother, I learned to read and became something of an asset." His eyes assessed her. "Then shortly after one of Da's inventions was published in a science journal, Bailey moved us. I was then stuck in a classroom with a nasty tutor for the next eight years. Eventually I scored high enough to get into the Royal Military Academy at Woolwich." He looked down at her face. "There, you have my life history."

"Why didn't you tell me this before now?"

"Finley owns the gym on Holborn," he said, studying the palm of his hand. "I sponsor him. I sponsor his boxing tournaments, his programs with the children. The kids have someplace to sleep and eat better than most have at home." He lifted his gaze and hoped she'd understand what was in his heart. "This is something personal between me and my Creator. Private business, ye might say. I owe Him."

Her eyes filled with love.

For him.

"Will you ever talk to me about your time in India?" She fixed him with a searching glance. "To help me understand."

"To help understand what?" Pressing her backward into the mattress, Christopher trailed his mouth down the moist curve of her neck. "I work every day. I eat. I sleep. On occasion, when time allows, I like to ride my horses and sometimes involve myself in criminal investigations. Lately I've even involved myself in a romantic liaison. Some would call that miraculous."

She lifted on her elbows and forced him back into the pillows. "Why?"

"Because . . . I thought it impossible." His finger traced the curve of her brow. "To feel this way again."

Whatever argument she'd been about to mount faded in her liquid green gaze. "Is she pretty? This romantic liaison?"

"Most of the time. When she's not just been pulled from the gaol or caught in a rainstorm."

Looking seductively petulant, her lips invited his complete attention. The corners of his mouth curled wickedly. "I find her . . . interesting."

She caressed his hair. "She finds you interesting, too."

On the other side of the courtyard outside her window, someone started playing the piano. Alexandra laughed. Christopher lifted his head and glared at the ghastly intrusion. "Does she know the hour?"

"She is quite lusty with her piano, is she not?" Giggling, Alex threaded a finger through the hair on his chest and waited until she could see his eyes again before she spoke. "Do you believe in fate?"

"Is that a rhetorical question?" His lips brushed her hair. "Or a launch into religious philosophy? If it is Philosophy, let me put on my clothes."

"Seriously." Alex pushed at him with her palms. "Have you ever thought that it was a coincidence that we should meet each other again after all these years? At the time that we did?"

"Neither of us planned to meet in front of the entrance exhibit."

"Papa and I had been invited that night to dine with Professor Atler and the newest trustee. Papa didn't know that you were the guest. I'd been late and we ended up not attending the meal. But that night, instead of going out the back of the museum, I'd left through the front. We met anyway. Fate."

Something seemed to flash through Christopher's mind. Perhaps it was his lack of belief in fate. Or maybe, like her, his mind worked over the question in more detail.

Christopher flinched at the warbly soprano that suddenly

joined the piano. "You're moving out of this place as soon as the Season ends. An acceptable place will open where you can let."

Alex stretched out against him. She sank deeper into her bed. "What if I don't want to leave?"

Brushing his palm over her hair, he kissed her temple. "You don't belong here, Alex. It's wrong. And don't tell me you're not here to defy your father. Defy him someplace more reasonable."

"He thinks that I can't do anything without him."

"So you intend to prove him wrong." It was a statement.

"No," she said quietly. "I intend to live."

His eyes were no longer hooded against her probe. "You've lived all over the world, Alex."

"Yes. And I never lived in one place for more than a few years my whole life. I never had girlfriends. I was so desperate for companionship that I used to force Richard to play tea with me. I even put a petticoat on his head to pretend he had long tresses, and told him that he had to be a girl if he was going to sit at my special tea table. He was five."

"And he allowed you to do that?"

Her smile curved her mouth. "He followed me everywhere. We were always going to be explorers together." She blinked up at him. "So you see . . . when you asked me tonight about Professor Atler's ties to my father, if I overreacted, I apologize. You have brothers, sisters, nieces, and nephews who love you. You'll never lose that."

His gaze gentled on hers. He didn't argue with her observation. Merely moved his hand over her breast and down her stomach, to claim the heat between her thighs. "Lying naked against you, I can think of a lot better ways for you to use your mouth than talk."

He moved between her legs, sliding inside her. Eyelids half lowered, Christopher cupped Alex's bottom in his palms and turned into the bed with her straddling him. She moved against him. "I like this position, too," she hummed against his lips.

His senses reeling, he opened his eyes, a satisfied smile on his lips as he discovered Alex watching him. "You're good, Alex. Very good."

Their gazes held and they loved with their eyes as well as their bodies. The words were not spoken but they were there between them all the same, undiluted and as strong as whiskey. And he was unsettled by how good it felt to drink.

A pounding rushed through his veins, his labored breathing the single hushed sound, her possession of him complete. She arched in his hands, her breasts, rose-tipped, filling in his palms. Their eyes continued to hold, her fingers joining his as she fell forward to take his mouth into hers. Somewhere a distant sound echoed like the drumbeat of his heart. Drawing her lips from his, she lifted her lids. It seemed as if reality wanted to intrude, and Christopher bade it leave.

He watched Alexandra's expression freeze. Lifting to his elbows, he realized the unending pounding was coming from her front door.

"Milady?" A muffled voice called from the other side of her window. A tap on glass followed.

Her frantic gaze whipped back to Christopher. "It's Mary and Alfred." She mouthed the words.

"Now?" he mouthed back in disgust.

"I'm coming, Mary," she called in what she clearly hoped was a sleepy voice, dislodging herself from him.

Christopher bit back a groan. "Not anymore tonight, you're not."

Her eyes snapped up. Christopher moved off the bed to retrieve his trousers, and Alex covered her mouth to keep from laughing. His own mouth crooked with a grin. Everything was suddenly inexplicably funny, and he was trying not to laugh aloud with her.

There was a certain release in feeling young again, the rush of being caught, and the thrill of doing the deed in the first place.

"Their rooms are above me," she whispered as she

shrugged into her wrapper. "You can leave when I get them upstairs."

He shoved his shirt into his trousers. "I haven't had to run like this in a long time."

"When was the last time you ran from anything?"

Christopher was suddenly in front of her, his shirt hanging open, his hands working the tiny buttons on her wrapper. "That day in the stables at the compound"—his voice was husky as he pulled her against him—"when you tried to run me through with a pitchfork. I do believe we both ended up in the hay. With the fleas."

She curved her hand around his nape. Eyes sparkling with laughter, Alex pressed her mouth against his. "You *do* remember."

Fluffing her hair, she flashed him a white grin, then emerged from the room like royalty. The door shut behind her. Christopher leaned his palm against its support, but he wasn't listening to the muffled voices on the other side. He was thinking about Alexandra's words.

He'd lied when he'd once told her that he hadn't ever thought of their past.

There wasn't a day they'd ever spent together that he didn't remember.

Chapter 18

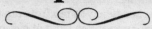

A burst of steam did nothing to illuminate the train's lead engine breasting the darkness. This was not the way Brianna had thought she'd be leaving London. With its gaslights and canary-gold street lamps, its gaily dressed *ton*, reading days at Lady Wellsby's, it was a whole world apart from where she was headed. She had not been kind to Christopher, and as she stood on the rail platform watching Rachel talk to the porter, she stole an involuntary glance over the crush of heads in the crowded depot.

Her brother stood with the handle of one of her brightly colored bags clasped in his hand as he talked to Kathleen and Ryan. Ryan, with his unfashionably queued hair, his dancing eyes, who epitomized his lack of moral certitude by the fact that he actually held his betrothed's hand in full view of all on the platform. Unlike Ryan, Christopher seemed even more distant than usual. Preoccupied.

Biting her bottom lip in frustration, Brianna turned away. Rachel had said in the quietest of tones last night at dinner that he'd been spending a lot of time with Lady Alexandra. Lady Alex the unmentionable, as if she were Christopher's dirty secret, and not someone who might actually make her brother happy. Brianna felt a tug of empathy where she least expected.

Brianna recognized that she'd behaved disloyally toward her family, Christopher in particular. She'd lived with each of her brothers since her father died, but it had been Christopher who'd seen to her education when most women never left home, who'd taken her to the boarding school in Edinburgh in the fall, and picked her up every holiday. Who supplied her with language lessons, arithmetic tutors, and the sense that she could do anything regardless of class or religious background, including having her debut in London.

Christopher took that moment to lift his gaze. Realizing that she was staring, Brianna blinked back tears.

Handing the bag to Ryan, he wove his way through the crowd, but before he reached her, the sound of his name drew him around. It was his solicitor, Mr. Joseph Williams.

And all at once, her heart stopped beating. Standing beside the distinguished gentleman, wearing a blue-checked wool overcoat and top hat, was his son.

Stephan was here!

His expression lit as he saw her.

Brianna's gaze flew back to Christopher. He watched her with warmth in his eyes, and she realized that Christopher had done this for her.

Then Stephan was standing in front of her, and the whole world suddenly seemed right again. "You came to see me off," she said with a laugh.

The shrill screech of a whistle blared. He took her to the bench nearby. "You look beautiful."

Smiling sheepishly, he pulled out a small packet. "I brought you this." He handed her a likeness of himself. "It was taken a few days ago." He looked into her eyes. "I hope that you don't think me presumptuous. I want one of you as well."

Brianna took the miniature from him and held it to her heart. He told her that he would visit her in Carlisle. She promised to write him every day. The crowd surged and bumped her elbow.

She suddenly could not see Christopher over the heads and hats of the crowd. "Is something wrong?" Stephan followed her gaze.

She came to her feet. "I have to see my brother before he leaves."

Then someone touched her arm. "Where are you going, imp?"

"Oh, Christopher." She flung herself into his arms. "Thank you."

The corners of his mouth turned up. "Try to go easy on Kathleen and Rachel when you get back to Carlisle. No pranks."

Wiping the tears from her face, Brianna nodded. His gaze found Stephan over her shoulder. "I trust that you will settle arrangements for your courtship with me sometime this week."

"Yes, sir."

Bending over her reticule in a rush, she withdrew a letter. "Will you give this to Lady Alex for me? If you think she won't mind?"

He slid the letter from her hand. "She'll want your letter."

"If she visited sometime, I wouldn't mind, no matter what the rest of the family thinks."

His gaze softened on her face. "Thank you, imp." He took Stephan into his gaze and nodded politely. "Mr. Williams."

Turning, he caught Ryan's gaze over the crowd, motioning something with his gloved hand, their sign language honed to a craft from the years of working around heavy machinery. "Now, if you'll both excuse me." He cupped Brianna's cheek, then without another word turned away.

"My father is working on an investigation for him," Stephan said with importance as they watched Christopher walk to Rachel, who was standing by herself.

Poor Rachel and her unrequited love. Brianna actually felt sympathy for the woman, and decided to be a little nicer even

if Rachel was under the misguided assumption that she was
Brianna's official chaperone.

She turned to Stephan. "Your father?" Her voice held a
layer of excitement. "What investigation?"

With a quick look around he said, "Since you're Mr. Donally's sister, he probably wouldn't mind if you knew." Then
proceeded to tell her about the thefts at the museum and the
investigations into the backgrounds of a few who might be
involved. "This could be the scandal of the decade," he concluded. "Very hush-hush."

More than impressed, Brianna lifted her gaze over the
crowd. Her prig brother was turning into a champion on all
fronts. And she would wager her left pinky that no one else in
the family knew.

Alexandra sat at the workbench in the anthropology lab,
feeling entirely too dreamy, her chin resting on her hand as
she stared off into space. She and Mary had varnished the
floor in her townhouse this week and Alexandra was thinking
about the paper that she wanted to put on the walls in her
room. She liked the color blue, the shade of Christopher's
eyes. Catching herself for the third time, Alexandra forced
her attention back to her notes on the next exhibit she was
working on. Barely an hour had passed since the last time
she'd eased the fob out of her pocket. Not that she had anyplace to go. She'd finished her hours in the Reading Room.
Christopher was working late tonight.

It had been a month of secret bliss for Alexandra. They'd
visited nearly every corner of London, unrecognized and free
to explore places the *ton* didn't frequent. He'd taken her to a
special play by the prolific Irish playwright Dion Boucicault,
to an antique auction house, and, after she'd pleaded prettily,
brought her to the gym where Finley held court in the boxing
ring. For all of her worldly travels, she'd never experienced a
more shocking, stimulating event than two men pummeling
each other to a pulp amid a screaming crowd of revelers,

most of whom she might find among the ruffians at the infamous Seven Dials or Whitechapel.

Footsteps sounded behind her as Richard emerged from his office. "Don't stay down here all day, doll." He breezed past her. "Or you'll be sharing my pitchfork and tail in no time at all."

"Very amusing, Richard." The door slammed shut behind him before she could ask where he was going now. Whatever was he so happy about?

Looking over the rim of her reading spectacles, Alexandra frowned. He'd become secretive and evasive of late. An entirely nonsocial entity.

The door suddenly creaked open again. Rusty hinges were only befitting of the shadows and dampness that pervaded the anthropology lab, where she and Richard were working on a new project.

"Lud, milady. This place gives me the frights, it does." Her secretary stood where Richard had just passed.

The room looked in a state of chaos. But then, the anthropology lab always looked in chaos. Richard's office was farther back. Tiers of large wooden drawers lined the walls, each dated sometime in the last half century. It was a massive human graveyard of skeletons, most found in digs here in London. Beyond the dusty boneyard lay the actual lab where two of the staff were currently working.

"Is something wrong, Sally?"

"Perhaps, milady." Her secretary advanced as if goblins would devour her. "I've come to tell you that I've been moved back upstairs to the office." She presented Alexandra with an affidavit. "You should see the room now, milady. It has a new coat of whitewash."

Her room had been painted? Forcing a lightness that she didn't feel in her voice, Alexandra read the note. "That's good, Sally. Maybe everything will return to normal soon."

Sally seemed to accept Alexandra's statement as a positive sign because she smiled. "I've heard that inventorying the vaults can take forever, milady. No one knows how much stuff we have here. Some of it has never been indexed and recorded," she babbled on, an expert because she had done so much of that with Alexandra.

"Sally, the entire contents of this museum are not being catalogued."

"Then I hope they finish soon. I don't know how you can stomach the basement, milady." Her secretary visibly shivered. "After what happened to poor Bridgett, I'm scared to come down the hallway alone."

"Nonsense," Alexandra snapped, attempting to divert the inane direction their conversation had turned. "Miss O'Connell was not murdered in this museum."

Alexandra had read the constable's report and the woman found in the Thames had drowned. Still, whether she'd been pushed or had jumped, no one may ever know.

After Sally left, Alexandra cleaned up. She marked and labeled the receptacle, filing it away with others that lined the musty shelves. She had never been afraid down here. She'd felt safe among these musty walls. Secure in her knowledge of this world and her life.

Now she wasn't sure that she knew either one anymore.

More than once Alexandra had inquired about the inventory and had been given the generic "everything is on schedule" statement.

Whose schedule? she was beginning to wonder.

Alexandra found Professor Atler in the second-floor corridor, his arms filled with papers. He slowed to let her catch up to him. He was tall and gangly, much like her father, and she practically had to chase him. "Just in time, dear," he said. "I need help with these books."

His face red with exertion, he dropped into her arms the load of books he was carrying. They stood in front of his office door, his name emblazoned in gold letters across the shiny wood. He stooped as he fumbled for his key. "What can I do for you today, dear?"

She despised when he patronized her. "Why didn't you tell me that you were going to clean out my office?"

"You don't own the space, Alexandra." Unlocking his office door, he removed the load from her arms. "I've made staff changes, as you are well aware, to accommodate the museum's expansion. Your belongings have been safely stowed."

"But what about my records?"

"I'm sure they've been moved to the basement." Swinging the door wide, he turned in his doorway. Behind him, his own office was being renovated. "As you can see, yours is not the only room undergoing work."

A workman interrupted them. Professor Atler walked to the desk and, setting down his load, directed the man to an adjoining room. It was as if there were no internal investigation at all, no worries, only an elevated sense of chaos that seemed worse than usual as makeshift construction was completed on the west wing to expand the gallery. Two more men entered carrying tin buckets of plaster. And Alexandra stood forgotten in the doorway.

Stripping off her apron and dumping it in the bin beside the stairs, she walked up another flight. She didn't see Professor Atler step out of his office and quietly watch her as she took the stairs.

Her gaze went down the long corridor to a memory of a young woman she'd last seen there.

The name on the brass plate beside the door had not been changed but everything else inside the office had. Alexandra stood over her old desk, staring at walls that no longer held her plaques, and shelves that no longer held her books. Paging aimlessly through the folder she'd picked up off the desk, she read the papers inside, turning when the door swung open. One of her former interns walked in. His cross-disciplinary studies while under her two years ago had led him to an assistant curatorship in mineralogy. He was a man who had a nose for museum politics. Now he occupied her office. Something else Professor Atler had neglected to tell her.

"So when will this be published?" she asked.

The younger man put the report back on the desk. "The

first of next year." His skin bore the copper tinge of too much sunlight. "Did you get a chance to read it?" he asked.

"It's very good." She looked around her old office, if only so he wouldn't see her face. Raw emotions shot through her. "It seems I have dutifully helped to train my replacement."

"Lady Alexandra . . ." The man looked embarrassed. "I expect that you need to speak with Professor Atler. I thought you knew."

Alexandra walked out.

After wasting time attempting to decide whether or not to face Professor Atler with her fury, Alexandra finally returned to her small workspace off the reading room. Leaning her palms flat on the desk, she closed her eyes. Her chest was tight. Her throat was tight.

For one desperate moment, she thought of going to her father.

Swinging around, she plopped on the desk, putting a hiatus on that thought before it took root. He wouldn't want to see her anyway. Not after the *Vanity Fair* fiasco. In addition to seeing his name mentioned prominently in the society sections of the papers, he was also taking a beating professionally as well. She knew this was the political arena in which they'd both lived for as long as she could remember, and the time of year when everything was at its worst.

Instead of running, Alexandra went out among the visitors and walked through the displays, looking one last time at each exhibit. Some people recognized her and took the time to talk. Later, she pinned her hat over her hair and walked outside, her resignation letter inked in black, delivered to Atler's office.

Sunlight hit her face and she looked up at the sky. She didn't return to her townhouse. She'd dressed somberly today, as she usually did when she worked, but a woman walking alone gathered unwanted attention. It was just something else in her life that she had to get used to now that she lived on her own. The streets were loud with the sound of traffic and the pounding of heavy machinery.

She shielded her gaze as she looked over the skyline. There was a curious juxtaposition of old and new in the contrasts between the dome of St. Paul's and the winches and machinery visible on the wrecked industrial landscape. Wasn't that what improvement was about? Eventually the chaos and catastrophe cleared into something orderly, more beautiful.

An hour later, stopping at the busy street corner, she eyed the red-brick building across the street. The breeze caught her skirts. She'd not made an appearance at Christopher's office since the first time months ago. A lot had changed since then. Smiling to herself, she ran across the street and up the stairs of the building to his office.

Stewart informed Alexandra a few minutes later that Christopher sat in a meeting. It was getting late, and she imagined the meeting would wind down shortly. She found a seat in the lobby to wait. At least he was still here. Hoping she wouldn't intrude too much, she sent him a note.

Before Alexandra had adjusted her skirts in one of the chairs in the lounge, Stewart returned and dutifully handed her back a reply. She hadn't expected a response. Certainly not one so fast.

Hesitantly, she unfolded the paper and read the bold scrawl. Blushing to the roots of her hair, Alexandra looked up quickly. Stewart thankfully seemed oblivious to her response.

"Excuse me." She cleared her throat and tried to appear offhand. "Who is in there with Mr. Donally?"

"Members of the public works committee, mum."

Her eyes went to the door. She wondered how Christopher could sit in that room with distinguished committee members and write something so explicitly graphic. "Perhaps you could take him another message, if you will?"

Christopher was fidgeting with a pen, his restless gaze turning out the window, when he heard the door to his outer office open again. He sat at the far end of the long conference table, his legs stretched out beneath, half listening to Ryan's

monologue on the sewer grid beneath the city. Clouds had
moved across the sunlight. Somewhere Christopher had
ceased taking notes. He was dwelling on Alexandra's message and his own response when Stewart reappeared at his
shoulder with another note. Down the table, Ryan continued
to talk over a plat map. The low drum of conversation now
fading completely in his mind, Christopher opened the scrap
of paper. Despite himself, he felt a grin tug at his lips.
Promptly firing off another reply, he sat back in his chair,
only to catch Ryan's dark gaze from across the table. There
was no break in his dialogue, but Christopher felt the admo-
nition in that brief glance nonetheless.

And it annoyed him.

It annoyed him that he had to be in this office bantering
about politics and bribes to corrupt city officials when D&B
was more economically fit and qualified than any other company in London to do the jobs presented to public works. It
annoyed him that the sky was clouding over. Or that Alex
might tire of waiting and leave.

He felt physically consumed by his need. It awakened him
at night. Intruded during meetings.

He wanted to take Alex home and make love to her in his
room, on his bed, bathed in moonlight and satin. To hell with
protocol and rumor or the fact that he had a household full of
servants. Darkly erotic and possessive, he wanted to watch
her climax beneath him, to see himself in her eyes when she
came.

A glance at the clock showed little movement from the last
time he'd looked. Five minutes before his agitation gave way
to visible frustration, the meeting ended and the committee
members departed.

"Do you want to explain to me what you're doing?" Ryan
closed the door between the rooms.

Christopher had already started packing his papers. "We
should have bloody thrown those jackals out an hour ago."

"We need their support, and you know it. Especially if
more investors pull out."

"We'll go before the Commons select committee, I don't really give a fig, Ryan. But we're not paying any more bribes to keep our name on the list of bids."

"What the blazes are ye doing, Chris?" Ryan's voice was gripped in frustration. "First that affectionate bit with Brea at the train station last month. Now you're writing bloody love notes? I don't even know who you are anymore."

Christopher was halfway through his packing when he stopped. He put his hand on hip, started to speak, then finally turned. "I'm bloody sick of politics. Of being in a constant stranglehold between policy and someone's personal agenda. As for Brianna, that was between her and I."

"And maybe you've got Ware's daughter on the brain and other parts of your anatomy that don't bear mentioning. I'm supposed to trust you with this operation when I leave for a month with my bride? Look at what you're saying."

"What is that exactly? What am I saying?"

"Investors are already leery because they're not entirely confident we'll be around in two years. With a few well-placed rumors, another scandal, it's not difficult to weaken the financial backbone of a company. Especially one that depends on government projects."

"We'll survive."

"I don't need you muddling my work here."

"Go to hell, Ryan. I've worked just as hard to make this company viable. You are not God's answer to civil engineers. Your as goddamn replaceable as the rest of us."

"Maybe I am." He swung open the heavy door, his jaw clenched as he brought his furious gaze back around. "But you're *not* replaceable. And right now, you're scaring the hell out of Johnny and me."

Ryan left the meeting room, the door swinging shut behind him. Christopher leaned his palms on the table. His gaze landed on the crystal decanters of brandy and strong Irish whiskey that remained on the table after the meeting. The biting scent of whiskey closed his eyes.

With an oath, he stripped off his tie and flung it onto the lounge. Nothing inside him yielded to Ryan's logic.

Why couldn't his family just leave him the bloody hell alone?

"Is there anything else you need, sir?"

Christopher was standing in front of the glass looking out over the busy city when Stewart entered. Without turning, he asked, "Is Lady Alexandra still here?"

"Yes, sir. She's out front."

Nodding, Christopher waited for Stewart to leave.

Early evening shadows had already begun to steal the light from the room, and he removed his jacket. The door from the outer office stood open to the hall. He heard Alexandra's voice, softly modulated as she said something to Stewart. He wondered how much of his argument with Ryan she'd heard. How much the whole staff had heard.

Christopher walked through his office as Alexandra and Stewart argued the engineering precocity behind the pyramids of Egypt. Leaning in the doorway, he listened as she spoke in mathematical terminology few people understood. He watched them both unobserved. His eyes swept downward over her breasts, then followed the curve of her neck to the smooth contours of her face, her brow furrowed in museful consideration. She took his breath away. But the emotion was so much more.

She made him happy.

As he continued to watch her, some intuitiveness brought Alex's gaze around, and she came to her feet, her eyes going over him with gentle concern, her smile tilting the corners of her comely mouth. His manner one of more ease than he felt, he returned her smile.

"Stewart and I have been debating the system of numerical notation used to lay out a pyramid," she said cheerfully to his silence. "Quite pragmatic, actually, compared to today's calculations."

Christopher was not unaware that his secretary and his

former wife had leaped the social boundaries of propriety and gone straight to a first-name basis. Feeling inexplicably territorial, he shifted his gaze. "I'll shut down the building, Stewart."

"Yes, of course. I was just leaving, sir." Stewart gathered up his hat and jacket. He slid his nervous glance toward Alex. "Milady, I enjoyed our discourse. It was most enlightening. Perhaps next time—"

"Good night, Stewart," Christopher said bluntly, knowing he was behaving poorly.

Alexandra pulled her stare from Christopher. "Thank you, Stewart," she said to the harried man just before the door closed behind him.

In the silence that followed, Alexandra shifted her gaze back to the doorway, where he remained leaning against the doorjamb.

"Are you all right?" she asked him.

He pushed off the doorjamb. "I've missed you today," he said, in a way that told her he wanted to put his hands all over her.

Forced to tilt her face up at him as he approached, Alexandra set her chin. He couldn't have missed her that much. They'd been with each other every night. "I'm not going to allow you to change the subject as you always do when you don't want to talk about something. Did you argue with Ryan?"

Splaying her ribbed bodice, he tugged her against him. "It had nothing to do with you."

She eluded his mouth. "Do you swear?"

"Terribly. All the time."

"Christopher!"

A grin pulled at his mouth, and she wondered how often he got his way with that not-so-innocent Donally smile. "I think the world doesn't know you for your truly wicked, wicked self." She let herself relax in his arms. "I couldn't bear to see you hurt. I do worry for you."

"I can handle my family, Alex."

Leaning into him, she wrapped her arms around his waist. "I resigned my post at the museum today."

He tipped her chin and looked intently in her eyes.

"What would you have done in my place?" she asked him.

His mouth crooked. "I would have told the whole board to go to hell a long time ago."

"Does that mean I can join your investigation? Because I want to find the person responsible for—for . . ."

"We will. I promised, didn't I?"

He eased his hands over her breasts. A low purr formed in her throat. "Did you mean it about dining in tonight? All of it?"

"Did I shock you?" The words were spoken into her hair. But she felt his mouth smile.

"Yes, you did, Christopher." Her palms traced the muscled span of his chest, stirring a trace of cologne. "I've never seen anyone eat a seven-course meal without utensils."

"Eight." His voice dropped to a hot whisper against her mouth, and her eyes drifted shut. "I forgot one." Descending the last millimeter, he took her lips in a hungry kiss.

Nine if she counted the fact that he'd swallowed her heart as well.

She was quite hopelessly in love.

Chapter 19

Alexandra stirred and opened her eyes as Christopher's carriage rolled to a stop. "Wake up." His voice touched her hair. "You're home."

"I don't want to be home," she groaned.

"Alex . . ." Dragging her gently across his lap, Christopher kissed her, before tapping on the carriage glass. "I have to leave." Handing her out to his driver, Christopher flinched as he climbed down behind her.

Fog had descended like a blanket on London. Though he knew there was a row of townhouses in front of him, he felt alone with Alex in a world void of sound.

"Is there anything you can do for your leg?" she asked when they'd reached her door.

"It's the dampness. It passes."

His tone told her in more than words that he didn't want to talk about his leg. She slipped her arms beneath his jacket. "I had a glorious time tonight. You certainly found a more creative way to use that conference table." Her mouth was hot on his.

His hands palmed her rib cage, and in a moment they were

doing their own private dance in each other's arms. "I know."
Brushing the hair from her face, he smiled down into her
sleepy eyes.

Before the air boiled around them all over again and he
was doing far more than kissing her on her porch, he reached
around her and opened her door, surprised when a gold cat
squeezed through their legs and bolted inside. "I think you
have company."

"Yes, he lives here now." She stepped across the threshold.

As if refusing to be the first to relinquish hold, their eyes
held. He leaned as the door narrowed the space between
them. "Lock your door."

Her cheek pressing against the door's edge, she smiled up
at him. "Good morning, Christopher."

He waited to hear the key turn in the lock. Hands in his
pockets, he hurried across the street to the brick walkway
that encircled the museum. The note he'd received from Finley an hour ago had been brief but to the point. Finley had a
break in the investigation.

Streetlights up and down the street glowed dimly in the
thick mist. Christopher barely discerned the palatial structure
behind the high wrought-iron fence. Turning on his heel, he
passed the museum, his presence like a shadow. His coat
slapped at his shins.

Finley suddenly appeared like a silhouette in the fog. Another man stood beneath a lamp, huddled in his jacket.

"Sorry to have interrupted your evening, Mister Donally."
The grin Finley wore told Christopher he wasn't too repen-
tant. "I have someone here who needs a word with ye."

The cryptic innuendo brought Christopher's gaze back to
the man standing beneath the lamp.

"Potter, *a mhic*," Finley hissed in Gaelic. "Tell him."

Stripping off the hat from his head, Potter stepped forward. "You remember me, don't you, Mr. Donally?"

"I gave up trying to find you."

"I was dismissed. They had no cause. No cause at all."

"What is it you want to tell me?"

Potter fidgeted. "Will it be worth twenty pounds, sir?"

Finley turned on the man. "Never mind." Christopher stopped Finley from grabbing Potter's throat. "Let him talk."

"I've not had a week's worth of steady work," the man grumbled at Finley. "He said he'd make my time worth his while."

"Twenty-five if the information is good," Christopher said.

"The girl, Bridgett O'Connell? It's a strange thing about her bein' dead and all, the way they say." He rolled the rim of his cap in his big palms. "She was a nice sort. Then she hooked up with some swell and got herself with his bastard."

"Potter." Christopher cut him off with the wave of his hand. "Get to the point."

"They said she'd been dead weeks. How can she have been dead for that long when I seen her a few days before she was found?"

The shock of Potter's revelation took several seconds to digest. "Where?"

"My sister lives in Sutton. I go there on Sundays to attend church. Be with the little ones. I saw her there. She was wrapped in a shawl. But I would know her anywhere."

Finley, clearly pleased with himself, handed Christopher a scrap of paper. It was a pawnbroker's duplicate. "The girl's uncle is a jeweler," Finley elaborated. "Quite popular until he went to jail ten years ago on charges of selling stolen gems. Now he works fairs and shows, and owns a small pawnshop and jewel store in Sutton. Goes by the name of Smith."

Christopher was looking at the address on the slip.

"The uncle was the same man who had your lady wife arrested after that riot at the fair for noggin' him in the head with a Buddha."

"Dammit, Finley, she's not my wife."

"Whatever ye say, Mister Donally."

Shaking his head, Christopher settled his growing irritation on Potter. "Is this where I can find this Smith?"

"His shop is near the square on Sheller Street," Potter said. "The address is in your hands."

"It might be nothing." Finley reached into his pocket and withdrew a pendant. Christopher recognized the White Swan. "Maybe Potter here only *thought* he saw Miss O'Connell. But there's no mistaking the coincidence of her uncle's occupation." Finley flipped Christopher the pendant. "I thought you might want to talk to him. Decide what to do."

Closing his gloved fingers around the Swan, Christopher lifted his gaze first to Finley, then to the thick seamless sky. He couldn't measure the time before dawn.

"You want I should go with you, Mister Donally?"

"No." There were others on the street at this time, packs of colorfully dressed fops headed for the local stews. This was not the best section in London, and he'd been loitering too long not to draw notice. Withdrawing his money clip, Christopher paid Potter.

A few minutes later, he reached his carriage where he'd left it down the block from Alex's townhouse. "Mr. Donally," his driver greeted, scrambling from the carriage boot as Christopher swung open the door.

Alex sat inside. Wrapped in a cloak, she lingered comfortably in the corner buried in shadows. "Hello, Christopher."

He arched one brow.

Fluffing her skirts in a major production of settling into her seat, she clearly refused to be intimidated. "Hmm, let me see." She examined her gloved hands. "Dark night. Mysterious meeting." She lifted her chin. "What did Finley have to say that was so important he wanted to meet you like this?"

Christopher looked at her without speaking, and something inside him relaxed. His gaze dropped to her nicely formed mouth. A huge wicked part of him had to admire that she was still game for any sort of adventure after the night they'd already shared.

Hell, if he didn't bring her, she'd probably just find a way to follow him. He eased his gaze over her expensive melon-green gown. "Do you have anything simpler to wear? You glow, sweetheart."

Christopher stared with gritty eyes at the end of the street. For a long time, he just studied his surroundings. There was no sense of organization to the brick-paved streets. Parking the carriage had been hampered by the gradient of a hill, so he'd left his driver to nap a few blocks back. Shop windows stood side by side with stone-fronted flats. Somewhere a church tower tolled the early hour.

"I should be the one to talk to that man." Alex scraped her knuckle over his bristly jaw. "You look like a criminal."

Bending nearer to her, Christopher felt her excitement. "I may look like a criminal, but you *are* one. If you go in that shop, he'll recognize you. Then everyone will know that I bribed a judge and two gaolers to lose you in the system."

His leg was beginning to cramp and he needed to walk. "There is a pub up the street and two tables set out beneath an awning," he said. "Why don't we see if we can talk them into opening for breakfast?"

After bribing a sleepy-eyed woman to open the pub for business, Christopher paid for coffee and crescent rolls to be delivered outside to his table.

"I'll pay you back for everything," Alex said after he joined her with coffee. "I hope you know that."

He didn't argue. He'd learned that she was incredibly strong-willed and probably kept an ongoing tabulation of her debt to him stuffed someplace in her many ledgers. "You're still not going in that shop."

"Really, Christopher." Her slipper fidgeted beneath her skirts. "Then why did you bring me?"

His fingers dallied over a stray lock of her hair. "For the ride over here. At least this way I can keep an eye on you."

"Then I think you should go in there now. He could escape."

"And go where? His livelihood his here."

"He might know we're here."

"He doesn't."

"I want to *do* something, Christopher."

Breakfast was delivered a few minutes later, and he suggested that she eat. Carriages and horse-drawn carts rumbled over the crumbling street, which had grown busier in the last hour as people shuffled to work. Christopher sipped his coffee.

"There could be a back door." Alex wiped crumbs from her lip. "He still might run," she said, clearly not a candidate for reconnoiter duty in the field. "What are we going to do if he doesn't talk?"

"I was thinking that we should kill him," he said with a straight face, taking his eyes off the second-story window above the shop to look at her. "Slowly, of course. In case he changes his mind and decides to talk."

She glared at him. Then laughed.

Christopher watched her and smiled. "You're impatient, Alex. Relax. I want to watch the shop for a while."

"Oh, Christopher." She tilted her head and breathed in the air. "This is truly what I've missed these last years. Change. Adventure."

And he knew that's what he was for her.

Change.

Adventure.

Even if she didn't recognize it, he did.

Where he'd settled safely into his life, she seemed to have broken free of hers. There was a certain invincibility in a person's spirit when she believed that she could take on the world and win.

His hand tightened around his cup. A vague discomfort had taken hold. He was beginning to feel that way himself.

"I received a letter from Brianna yesterday," Alex said over her coffee, quite oblivious to his silence. It took him a moment to hear her. "She said that you'll be going back to Carlisle for Ryan's wedding." These last words she spoke in her cup before she set it on the table. "She thought that once things settled you might allow her to return."

"I'm not going to deny her your company. But I'm *not* setting her loose in London with you again."

A slow-growing silence brought his gaze back around to hers. "You and my father would have gotten along just dandy, Christopher." Her voice was filled with hurt. "If he had not been so bloody insular."

"Your father had a right to his fury, Alex," he admitted, for the first time in his life. "You were seventeen. I was wrong with what I did and knew it. But did it anyway."

She crossed her arms. "For all of your Irish snobbery, sometimes I think you put me on a pedestal, Christopher. I knew my mind."

"Did you? Or were you merely broadening your experiences? The way you are now?"

She pulled back. But something had broken free inside him and he couldn't slam the lid back down. "Don't you think I know that I've been something exciting for you? That I offer you a life that you can't have anyplace else? That I've always been that for you?"

She swallowed. "And what have I been to you? If not the same thing?"

He sat forward. He didn't know how to talk to her about this. Not when everything inside had twisted and his heart was beating too damn hard for him to think.

"Respectability."

Her eyes softened on his. "But I'm not the least respectable."

"You are to me."

"I practically live in a tenement flat." She laughed.

"And look at everything that you've accomplished. Hell." He snorted at his own want to wax poetic over her. "For the first time in years, I'm confused about my own goals," he said with a wry twist to his mouth, leaning closer. "I'm in love with you. And I don't quite know what to do about it."

"You are?" Her lips parted.

Down the street, a door slammed. Annoyed by the distraction, it took a moment for Christopher's brain to register the sound. He heard Alex gasp. A young woman had exited the shop. A man followed her out, and they stood on the walk, their hands entwined as if saying goodbye.

"That's Bridgett O'Connell," Alex whispered.

A sick feeling building in his gut, Christopher was looking at the man whose back was to him. He wore a cloak, a thatch of wheat-blond hair visible beneath the hood. His height, his stance, were all too familiar, and Christopher went cold inside.

"No." At the same moment, Alex came slowly to her feet.

Christopher caught her arm and pulled her against the building out of sight.

"There's some sort of mistake." Panic laced her voice as the cloaked figure turned and walked briskly toward him. "Richard would never do anything illegal. He wouldn't. Let me talk to him first—"

Christopher stared at her, stilling her words. Did she think he would let her anywhere near the man? He removed her slim hand from his sleeve. "Stay here."

She grabbed his arm. "Don't hurt him. Please. . . ."

"Open your eyes, Alex." Christopher framed her face between her palms and forced her to look at him. He didn't know how to stop the hurt inside her, but he damn well wasn't going to listen to her defend the man. "He let everyone think that girl was dead. Including you."

Christopher stepped between the tables. The sun came out from behind the clouds. Squinting against the bright sky, he moved his attention back to the shop, to the young woman, before shifting murderously to the approaching man.

It took Richard Atler less than five more steps to see Christopher. A hand whipped out of the cloak and scraped off the hood that covered his head. A confused dawning spilling through his expression, he came to a halt. Thirty feet and a bench separated them.

Before Christopher could speak, Atler sprang off the walkway into the street, barely avoiding a collision with a carriage. He pushed through a crowd of men loitering on the corner and was running.

With an oath, Christopher followed. His leg was in no shape to chase Atler; still he managed to keep pace. The chase took him across the square, down a squalid alley. Atler leaped a puddle and dipped into the stables. Christopher leaped the same puddle, following Atler into the stables, a rash mistake, he realized at once. The darkened interior blinded him.

Before he could adjust to the dim light, a noise alerted him. He ducked aside. A bucket barely missed his head and glanced off his shoulder. He stumbled forward, not because he'd been hit, but because his leg wouldn't support his weight. Atler swung his fist. Christopher blocked the fist with his forearm and slammed him against a stall door.

"Do not . . . try to hit me again, you bastard." His elbow smashed against Atler's windpipe. "It makes me mad."

"I won't let you ruin everything," Atler rasped.

Atler kneed him in the thigh. White-hot pain shot through Christopher's body. He staggered back. Atler tore away from Christopher's grip and stumbled, then rounded for an attack.

Christopher ducked the man's wild swing. Atler's fist hit a wooden brace. "Jesus, Mary, and Joseph!" He stumbled back and tripped on the bucket. He fell against a bale of straw. "I broke my fugging wrist."

Bent with one hand on his thigh, Christopher regarded Atler's bloody limb through a haze of pain. Shit, he hurt like hell. "Maybe a knuckle," he said dispassionately, realizing through a wave of rolling pain that Atler had seriously hurt him. He could barely stand. "Better than your nose. Or your fooking teeth."

Gritting his jaw, Christopher slumped against the stall door. "Why don't you begin by explaining what you're doing with a former jewel thief? And a girl who is supposedly dead?"

Atler slumped. "You're not taking her anywhere."

The doorway filled with people. A pretty young woman, her fist balled against her lips, stared wide-eyed. "What have you done to him?" With a sob, she ran to Atler. "You've injured him. He's bleeding. Oh, my poor Dickie. You're hurt."

Atler struggled to one elbow. "Bridge, it's all right."

Alexandra shoved through the growing throng. As she stood in the doorway, her bright green gaze freezing first on him, then Atler, Christopher leaned against the stall door, his harsh expression cloaking the burning ache in his leg. He was in too much bloody pain to care whether she'd disobeyed him.

Her skirts billowing around her, she dropped onto the straw beside Atler. "You shouldn't have run, Richard." She dabbed at his knuckles with a handkerchief she'd pulled from her skirts. "Look what's happened to your hand. What is your father going to say?"

"My father can go to the devil." Atler turned to the girl sniffling over him and stroked the woman's pale hair. He glared past her to impale Christopher. "My father is the reason Bridge is here. Hiding."

"I don't understand." Alex sat back on her heels. "Was it you outside my cottage that night? Is it your footprint I cast?"

"No and no." He spoke over his swollen lip. "What do you take me for, a bloody voyeur?"

"I don't know." Exasperation laced her voice. "The two of *you* certainly had no qualms against my door that day in the museum. Lord, I should have connected who *Dickie* was." Alex looked directly at Bridgett. At her swollen belly, and blushed. "I'm glad that you're alive."

"That's real nice of you." Richard snatched the handkerchief and applied it to his knuckle. "I'm glad she's alive, too."

"This isn't like you at all, Richard," she whispered.

"What do you know about me? Nothing!"

Christopher had had enough. "Suffice it to say"—leaning heavily on his elbow against the stall, he looked at Alexandra—"the two of you have a lot to discuss. Might I suggest that this discussion be moved someplace less public?"

Alexandra didn't speak the entire walk back across the village square. Richard brought her and Christopher to the curio shop. A quaint little place filled with dolls, lace, and reproduction jewelry. It was the kind of place that Alexandra could lose herself in. But not today.

Christopher had been correct when he'd discerned the shopkeeper's reaction to her presence. The moment Bridgett's uncle recognized her, he'd decided that she'd come to the shop to rob him. To her surprise, Richard had laughed after he'd heard what had taken place at the fair and guaranteed Smith that she did not belong in Bedlam.

"She's a bona fide aristocrat," he'd reassured a nervous Smith, who clearly wanted nothing to do with the troubles she could bring down on this establishment.

After Smith left to prepare tea in the back room, Alexandra turned to Richard. He wore a simple brown plaid jacket and black trousers. Bridgett leaned against him, her cornflower-blue eyes wide and untrusting. They had not moved from the front of the shop.

"To think my father has held you up as the standard for exemplary behavior all these years," Richard said to Alex as his arm went around Bridgett. "I'm rather impressed that you have faults after all."

"That's not funny," Alexandra whispered.

"It wasn't an insult, I assure you. Now, your *ladyship*"—his arm swept across his torso—"I must beg your leave. Bridge needs to lie down."

With that, he lifted Miss O'Connell into his arms and carried her upstairs in his arms. The girl's pretty eyes lifted to look over Richard's broad shoulder, meeting Alexandra's gaze before she settled her cheek possessively against Richard's chest.

Forcing air into her lungs, Alexandra turned to the glass case filled with trinkets and laid her hands across the clear surface. Her throat tightened. Not because Richard, the carefree, take-no-responsibility scapegrace she'd known all her life seemed to be in love, but because he'd not seen fit to share his feelings with her.

What other secrets did he hide?

She didn't want the years of their friendship tested in this manner. He scared her. What was she supposed to do?

A sound behind her drew her around. Christopher stood in the doorway that led to the back rooms, his gaze unreadable as his eyes went over her face. He'd kept himself apart from the conversation, but not so far away that he'd left her alone with either Richard or the balding jeweler. Her emotions were untidy and suddenly unmanageable, a complicated muddle. Knowing how he felt about Richard, she hated that he saw her hurt reaction to him, and swallowed hard, only to discover a lump had rooted itself in her throat.

She could hear Richard's voice coming from upstairs. Her chin lifted. "Bridgett is with child," Alexandra murmured the obvious.

"Clearly she has been for a long time."

"Wait before you summon the authorities. Please. Let me talk to him first."

"Alex—"

"Do you know what happens to people who go to prison? They die, Christopher."

Christopher held a hand to his hip. He looked away before bring his gaze back to bear on hers. Angry. "Don't do this."

Alexandra's own anger momentarily wavered as she watched Christopher ease down onto the stairs that led from the main part of the shop to the sleeping quarters. He looked barely able to stand. "Why didn't you tell me that you'd injured your leg?"

His lashes lifted, revealing stark blue eyes. For a moment, he didn't say anything. "Because there's nothing you can do."

He was shutting her out. "You always do that," she whispered vehemently. "You pull away and go to that place inside that no one else can touch."

"What do you want from me, Alex?"

"I don't want you to bring in the authorities," she said irrationally, aware that she'd lost control of her temper. Her fists clenched. "I want you to trust *my* judgment for once."

He swore, a word she was fast learning, he used it so often. "You have a dirty mouth, Christopher Donally. I forget that you grew up on the streets and probably don't know better."

There was a dangerous glint behind his blue eyes. "Is that right?"

The lump in her throat grew bigger. "You're just like my father. Once your mind is set, you never change your reason. Ever."

Reading his darkening ire, she hastily lifted her skirts aside and brushed past him on the stairs. But he was quicker and grabbed her arm.

"I'm not the enemy, Alex."

She snatched her hand away, horrified to realize that for one minute she'd believed that he was. But he took her into his arms and let her weep against his shirt. She clung to him. "I'm afraid."

"I know." His lips touched her hair. "I'm sorry, Alex."

Sorry, because she wasn't thinking clearly. Sorry that her childhood companion had most probably betrayed her. Sorry because when it was all said and done, Christopher intended to have Richard arrested.

Teeth set, Christopher watched Alex ascend the stairs.

"He's a good boy, he is." A voice turned Christopher around.

Smith held two cups of steaming tea in his hand. Christopher grimaced. Why the hell couldn't today have been easy?

"I brought one for her ladyship as well," Smith said. "Maybe she don't need one, with her temper and all."

Christopher wrapped his palms around the cup and breathed in the aroma. He wore no jacket or tie. He hadn't shaved. He'd rolled his white sleeves off his forearms and, sitting on the stairs, imagined he looked about as conspicuous as a footpad. "She's exhausted and scared. Leave her alone." He wasn't going to drink, but the smell awakened him.

"Finley didn't say nothing about knowing her ladyship. He could have bloomin' warned me the two of you would show up here."

Christopher raised his head. "You talked to Finley?"

"Late yesterday."

Which explained why Finley wanted him to come here before going to the constable. Finley must have known about Atler. "I see. Old friends?"

"Finley and me, let's just say we've things in common from the old days. He came and asked a lot of questions. He was surprised I'd been living here all these years and staying legitimate. You must be the gent what hired him to look for some stolen jewels."

Christopher withdrew the White Swan from inside his vest pocket. "Then I suspect Finley asked you about this?"

Setting down the teacup on the glass countertop, Smith took the Swan. He wore a pair of baggy woolen trousers and a homespun shirt. He looked as if he'd been working in the back before the interruption this morning. "If he had, I'd have warned Richard. Smart man, Finley." He admired the Swan in the sunlight. "Some of my best work. We sell these for a lot of money." Handing the Swan back he said, "It's not illegal."

"Jewel theft is. Stealing from the museum is."

"Richard makes the mold and designs the metal for the jewelry. I make the synthetic jewel. Would you care to see what we've done?"

Smith walked through the curtained doorway to a back room. Christopher stood. His leg had swollen, and he could barely move without flinching. His gaze went to the rooms where Alex had disappeared.

"No need to worry about her ladyship, Mr. Donally." Smith had reappeared. "If Richard got testy earlier, it's because he's protective of Bridge."

Oaken cabinets lined the wall in the back room. Smith lit a lamp and set it on the table, directing Christopher to sit. "Seems you need that chair more than I do, Mr. Donally."

"You've been acquainted with Atler long?" Christopher set the cup at his elbow.

Smith moved to the wooden counters. "Two years now. My niece introduced us. My Bridge was always an independent sort. Moved to Bloomsbury a few years ago after her ma, my sister, passed on. She had some money and some schoolin', bein' the vicar's daughter, and she was able to get work at the museum. She and Richard . . . well, they was married last month. Civil ceremony. Couldn't post no banns for fear of his pa."

"Why did Miss O'Connell leave the museum?"

"She was forced to leave. She was home ill for a few days on account of the babe, and I suppose her friends started to worry. After that Richard's pa come bangin' on the door like he owned the place and her. Somehow he found out where she'd lived. Threatened all manner of harm to her if she ever saw his son again. Dismissed her on the spot. Without even paying her wages what was owed her. That night someone broke into her apartment and tore it up. Destroyed everything. I've been keeping her here ever since."

"And the body found at my site?"

"I don't know," he said. "Bridge's clothes and anything she had of value were all stolen from the flat. Who's to say? All I know is that Richard is afraid of his father finding Bridge."

Smith pulled out a stack of black velvet boxes and put them on the table. One by one, he opened the lids, revealing a collection of emerald rings and necklaces in one box, sapphire scarab broaches and pale ruby elephants in another. All the pieces were replicas from the museum.

"It is impossible to make synthetic diamonds. So we have none in our collection. The casts come from pieces at the museum."

"Taken from the originals without permission, I presume."

"Nothing ever left the museum. Richard cast the molds there."

"Who else has had access to Atler's work?"

"Richard kept a flat of these in his rooms where he lives with his pa. Sometimes he would have private showings and kept samples on hand. The piece in your hand was from that collection."

Christopher looked down at the White Swan. He'd pieced together enough puzzles in his lifetime to sense that his informal investigation had just turned into something far more complicated than jewel thefts.

"You'll have to tell the authorities that she's alive, Richard." Alexandra stood beside the window casement, softly fingering the pink muslin curtains. The sun bore down on her through the glass. "There's no reason to allow them to presume that there might be a murder connected to the museum."

"I imagine Donally will waste no time in setting the record straight."

Turning her head, Alexandra watched Richard fold a delicate chemise and place it gently into a trunk that sat on the bed. Miss O'Connell was comfortably disposed in another room and slept.

She looked away. Richard had said very little after she'd told him about the thefts at the museum. Miss O'Connell's uncle could even be implicated. She didn't know where Richard intended to go, but wherever it was, he intended to leave today. He was that afraid of his father.

"Christopher is involved in this because I asked for his help." She dropped the edge of the curtain. "Why didn't you tell me about Miss O'Connell?"

"You and I have known each other for a long time," he said without looking up. He had a visible bruise on his cheek and chin where Christopher had hit him. "But frankly, I don't trust you. When the constable talked to you, which eventually he'd have to, I didn't want you giving up the ship, so to speak. I don't want to defend my relationship with Bridge or be lectured by you. It's insulting."

They measured each other a moment in silence, and she felt only outrage for his judgment against her. For if she had been critical, she had also been supportive. If she had been

rash in some of her decisions of late, she had shown more
than her share of compassion.

"Someone died out there on the Thames, Richard."

"I didn't murder anyone." His hands stopped packing, and
he raised his gaze. "But neither was I going to dispute the
findings. Unlike Donally, I never claimed the market on
morality or ethical rectitude. The fact that a hapless individual chose to jump off a bridge on his site was an unfortunate
coincidence. But it took my father off Bridgett's trail."

Alexandra set her teeth and continued to watch him pack
with a gathering sense of frustration. "This is just an excuse
for you to quit everything. All your work . . ."

"I want to be an artist. I want to be free to explore my soul.
Not stuck in some bloody book job for the rest of my life.
That's all I've ever wanted. If you'd just looked, you would
have known."

Folding her hands tightly, she felt herself growing angry.
In truth, she was thinking in concrete terms, far more concerned about her own crisis than his desire to discover himself. "I need you with me, Richard." Alexandra rubbed one
temple. "I really do."

"Over alleged thefts at the museum?"

"They aren't alleged. I was the one who filed the report
with your father." Her voice started to fail her. Looking out
the window, she rubbed the hair out of her eyes. A sick feeling took hold, nauseous in its unerring traipse down her
spine. Professor Atler had cleaned out her office with all of
her original records. "Your father called people in from the
university to complete an inventory. I remained silent for as
long as I did to protect my position and the integrity of the
museum."

"Convenient, don't you think? Your silence?"

The sick feeling inside never abated. "Richard . . ."

Moving beside the bed, she told him about her inventory
list and index numbers that she had in her possession. Professor Atler had discarded the original copy of inventory sheets
she'd made of the artifacts that she'd found in question, but

she'd made another that very night. That's why she'd gone back to her office. To retrieve her records. Why she'd remained late at the museum that day when she'd met Christopher and Brianna standing in front of the odd-toed ungulates.

Did Professor Atler know she had a copy?

Was it he who had broken into the carriage house? Everything suddenly made sense. "If he's tampered with archives, then what I have is the only record of the original pieces in existence. I have every entry from my department logged into the museum inventory the last two years."

"Jesus . . ." Richard scraped both hands through his hair. "One does not accuse the head curator of the British Museum of misconduct. It just isn't done."

"Misconduct?" Leaning her brow against her hand, Alexandra shook her head. "Is that all it is?"

Richard laughed with something near bitterness in his voice. "Even with your list, the only way for you to exonerate yourself completely is to explain where those frauds came from and implicate me. My father is going to accuse you of misidentifying pieces to save himself and cover up his crime. Your credibility will be destroyed. In the end, he will be wealthier for the thefts. As much as I hate him at this moment, I have to admire him for thinking outside the circle."

"Your father and mine have known each other for so long. Why would he do this to me?"

"Because you're the only one who would protect me. Because in my stupidity and blindness, I never dreamed him capable of doing anything like this. Your father can't take exception to anything because you willingly quit the museum. Father has all the cards, Alexandra. And they are all aces."

She dropped her gaze to the pair of slippers lying on the bed. Christopher knew the truth. When the time came to report to the board, he would be sitting at that table. But what could he say in her defense? That she'd given him a forged piece of jewelry she'd stolen from the vaults? A piece that she had no real proof Professor Atler had even put there?

Worse . . . what would that do to Christopher's reputation?

Drawing in a deep breath, she tried to absorb the logic of everything. Whether it was some form of Richard's demented artistic mind that could create such a scenario, it didn't matter. Everything made too much sense for it not to be the truth.

Lifting her tear-veiled gaze, she found that Richard had almost finished packing. "You created the White Swan that I took from the vault?" she asked. "Your father must have thought it very good to use it in the display the way he did."

His eyes met hers. "I'm twenty-six years old. That's as close to a compliment he's ever given me my entire life. And now I could go to prison for it."

"You went through the photos and drawings in my file," she continued. "And while in my office, Miss O'Connell would remain in the hall to warn you if someone approached. Then you took the piece out of the vault to cast a mold?"

A hand on his hip, Richard finally nodded. "I know you think that I am some dandified buffoon most of the time. I'm the first to admit that I am. And heaven only knows that I've been bloody jealous of you my whole life. Call me reckless, but that's all. I swear I didn't destroy or steal anything. I cast molds."

"Most of those pieces were priceless, Richard." Her voice raised. "You could have ruined them in the casting process."

"Is this going to turn into another Alexandra Marshall lecture? Because if it is, I'm leaving this conversation."

Alexandra slapped the lid of the trunk down. "You already left a long time ago. If you want to hide your life away, that's up to you. I'm not going to stop you."

She walked past him out the door and into the hall. Christopher stood with his back against the wall. At her appearance, he straightened, lowering his arms to his side. Nodding as she stopped in front of him, she swallowed the inexplicable urge to cry in his arms.

His eyes seemed bluer amid the unshaven growth on his face. He didn't look over her shoulder into the room behind her. Or ask about Richard. He hadn't intruded.

He must think her such an utter, utter fool.

"I'm ready to go home," she said quietly, his warm presence dissolving the icy inrush of reality. Then, before he could hear the sob catch in her throat, she walked down the stairs and out the shop.

The ride back to London was accomplished in near silence. After what seemed only a moment, Alexandra opened her eyes, realizing she'd slept. Christopher sat on the opposite seat. He seemed to be looking outside the carriage window with careful concentration. She watched his tanned profile against the crisscross lines of sunlight that fell through the trees. As if aware of her gaze, he turned his head. But said nothing as he found her watching him.

Alexandra knew she could not hide in the sand like some doomed ostrich now that she was privy to Professor Atler's crimes. She had to determine which course she must take, how to conduct herself.

Christopher didn't appear overwhelmed by the silence and presently she inquired, "What are we going to do?"

"By discrediting you, have you considered that Professor Atler has more to lose financially and socially by forfeiting Lord Ware's support?" he queried, showing only the slightest inclination to emotion except in the way his eyes held hers. "What motive would prompt a man to alienate someone as powerful as Lord Ware?" he asked her. "Before I can possibly take this matter up with the authorities, I need to know that answer. Your father is the only one who could answer that question."

The blood drained from her face. He was asking her to go to her father. "He will never talk to me."

"Then again, Richard could have easily switched the jewels. Are you willing to talk to the authorities about that possibility? Because if you don't, you may as well hand Professor Atler a medal." He held out the White Swan for her to take. "Right now, I'm only thinking about you."

She attempted to turn away. "I'm sorry." To her disgust, tears leaked from beneath her eyes.

Alexandra was cognizant of the fact that by accusing someone of Professor Atler's position, Christopher was in danger of losing far more than she. He had to be cautious, or face condemnation by a society that held a man's honor above reproach.

She was suddenly desperately afraid for him. For what she had done to him.

"Come here." Christopher was holding his hand out to her.

Despite her aversion to shed tears, she did.

Silently.

Against his chest.

She didn't know which she should mourn first. The loss of Richard as a friend, her work as an archaeologist, or the fact that after today, Christopher might lose more than his future in his own firm.

Meager as her principles were, she could not allow him to go down with her.

Chapter 20

I t was still dark outside, not yet dawn three days later, when Alexandra turned over in bed and decided that she could not sleep.

Mary had yet to awaken. Climbing the stairs to her attic, Alexandra lit the glass lamp with a sulfur match and sat at her new desk. Then, pulling out the sheets of paper, she carefully read over the letters she'd penned last night to the Royal Geographical Society as well as the British Historical Society. Dissatisfied with what seemed like good work yesterday, she set about rewriting each letter, knowing that her current standing in the professional community would most likely hinder any appointment or interest they might have once had in her.

She suddenly didn't care. Crushing the letters in her hands, she dropped them in the garbage receptacle, noting the thing was overflowing onto the floor.

Somewhere dogs barked. In the thick darkness just before dawn, she could still hear singing from across the courtyard. Her gaze went over the freshly painted walls and shelves, the small desk and lamp, the muslin curtains she'd installed on the oval window overlooking the street. From up here she had an unimpeded view of the museum. A twig broom sat upright next to the door. Yesterday, she'd hired Finley and the boys to build shelves. Despite the fact that Finley had been forced to break up a fight between them three times, they'd done a superb job.

She'd not seen Christopher since he'd dropped her off at her townhouse three days ago. Not that he hadn't tried to see her twice. Alexandra had been at this desk when Mary had opened the door downstairs last night and lied that she was not here. She'd stood at the window and watched as he turned to look back at her house, pulling away from the curtain when his gaze had touched the place where she'd stood.

Wiping the moisture from her face, she forced herself to confront the paper that sat innocuously to her left. A letter of summons arrived before dinner last night. Professor Atler didn't confirm or deny her request for references or respond to her inquiry about the inventory, only requested a meeting with her. She knew that she would not avoid the inevitable meeting much longer.

Much earlier, while arranging her books and ledgers on the newly built shelves, Alexandra had found the copy of her inventory sheets buried in one of her unpacked crates. Thinking of everything Richard had said about her choices, she passed her hand over the sheets of thin paper that might have the power to salvage her reputation but certainly had the potential to implicate Richard of serious crimes. She gritted her teeth. After everything that she'd done for him, she resented his desertion.

But, in truth, Richard never had any pretentious illusions of his self-worth or enlightenment. She'd completed his university assignments for him because it made her feel superior, not because it helped him pass. She'd written his speeches and propped up his work at the museum because of her own arrogance, not because of her compassion or loyalty toward their friendship. He'd never pretended to be anything more than what he was. It was she who had done all the pretending.

Leaving her attic sanctuary, she chastised herself with bitter humor for the conceited person she was, who had so often congratulated herself for her intellectual abilities. Who, because of her social ineptness, considered herself too far above the mentality of her peers to take part in anything resembling social refreshment. Her paltry competition with the rest of the world not only left her isolated from her colleagues but also her peers. Until she'd met Brianna, she'd never realized how out of touch with the world she really was.

Until she'd met Christopher's family, she'd never resented that she was alone.

She opened her palm. The White Swan lay pressed in her hand.

Yet, these last months had given her back something she'd thought lost forever.

It had given her back Christopher as a friend.

No matter what he thought of the choices she was about to make, she had that link to him, and knew that he felt the same way about her. And it was that unequivocal honesty of emotion between them that had given her courage to do the right thing.

She would not allow him to forsake his future for her. She would rather end their relationship now than have him make a rash decision that he would regret in time. She couldn't bear ever becoming an object of his resentment.

These were all the things she'd told herself.

"Milady?" Mary's voice pulled her around, and Alexandra realized this was the second time Mary had spoken.

With the golden cat curled beside her, Alexandra sat on the window bench alcove in her parlor, her legs drawn to her chest, her chin on her knees. Half hidden by the red velvet window hangings, she turned her head. The clop of horses' hooves sounded outside on the brick streets.

Mary stood beside the bulbous crystal lamp, a cup in her hand. "I've brought you coffee, mum. You need to be eating something. You've been sitting here nigh on two hours, milady."

Smiling tentatively, Alexandra took the cup. "Your coffee is so much better than mine." She smiled over the steamy rim. "Thank you."

Mary cocked an experienced brow as she looked Alexandra over. "Are you feeling well, milady?"

Tipping the cup to her lips, she looked outside the window. Dawn was like a clear blue eye opening over the city. She could see the southern corner of the museum from where she sat. A pillar of stone bulked against the sky gave an impression of timelessness. "I miss my morning swims," she said, dropping her gaze to the hot coffee. "Taking a mere bath has become an exercise in privilege."

"Aye, mum. This place is not a palace, but it still sleeps three. You've a newfound strength in you, milady. Alfred and I trust that everything will work out."

Alexandra felt engulfed, humbled by Mary's belief in her and ashamed that it did not coincide with the same belief in herself. Her gaze held Mary's. "The truest satisfactions I have known in life have come from setting and working toward that goal, knowing that if I worked hard enough for something, and believed in it enough, that it would happen. Now I am faced with losing everything, and find myself hopelessly at odds with self-pity. I am afraid of uncertainty."

"None of us can know when or how things will end, milady."

Alexandra observed her elfish servant with a grin. "Do you think that I will grow to be one of those eccentric women with her pink turban who is forever flouting the rules and causing society matrons headaches?"

"Heaven forbid." Mary raised her eyes to the ceiling. "Turbans went out of style thirty years ago."

The absurd innocence of the remark astonished her, and they both suddenly laughed. A fierce determination to live her life the way she wanted filled her. She would never be happily dependent on anyone again.

"Do you think I will grow to be like my father? Unforgiving, cold, and a wretchedly bad judge of character," she asked when she'd taken the last sip of hot coffee.

"No, milady," Mary said quietly as she took the cup. "You've no danger of that. You're too kind."

Alexandra watched Mary go. Mary and Alfred were her

family these days, and Alexandra was the first to admit that their presence made her life much easier.

Alexandra left the narrow alcove. Once she closed the door to her bedroom, she reached behind her and unlatched the locket from around her neck. As she stood over her dresser, she stared at the silver filigree. Clicking a thumb beneath the latch, she flipped the lid. A dark curl of baby-fine hair was nestled inside.

Perhaps it was finally time to bury her past, and think now of her future. And of Christopher's.

Christopher's solicitor caught him between meetings. Feeling unfortunate to have found him at all, Joseph Williams reflected on the tight expression that was fast forming on his employer's face as he flipped through the packet of papers he'd been handed.

"How many people know about this?" Donally lifted his gaze from the papers.

"Only the man that you hired," Williams said. "The information was buried in the archives of some obscure church outside Ware. A former gardener on the Ware estate provided the tip."

Whatever inclination Donally had to comment on the matter of this new turn in the investigation was lost as he continued to flip through the pages. Williams had been Donally's man of affairs for six years and, until the recent rash of gossip, thought he'd known all there was to know about the young upstart Irishman who'd managed to throw more than one bureaucratic cog off its center since D&B came under his control. Donally's father had had a gift for science and invention, but it was the eldest son's application of his father's work that gave impetus to his father's genius. Williams didn't want to see D&B's charismatic head dishonored by the magnitude of the scandal this investigation would cause. But if Donally seemed worried by what he read, it didn't show on his dark implacable features, almost feverish in the dim light. Indeed, Donally was completely unemotional, ruthless, as he delved through each page of the report. He didn't look like the ostentatious social climber depicted by various recent gossip in the paper of late.

Someone bumped Williams. Feeling constricted in the narrow corridor where they stood at Whitehall, he was relieved when Donally moved them both out of the way of traffic and farther down the hallway. The rumble of a crowd filled a small antechamber to his left where the Commons select committee for public works currently sat. Mr. Donally and his brother, Ryan, had made an appearance this morning. His brother was still inside the room. Despising politics as much as he did, Donally looked to have grown impatient with waiting for his brother, and indeed he rubbed his thigh as if some pain harassed him.

"It seems the younger Atler is who he says he is," Williams said, returning his focus to the page Donally had just flipped through.

"Much to his father's disapproval," Donally replied without looking up.

"This year some of his drawings were featured in the art museum, under an assumed name, of course. He began designing jewelry four years ago, by the reports. His father found out and threatened to ship him off in the army."

Williams hovered closer. "Shortly after that, Richard Atler finished his studies at the university in the top of his class. At least he showed some promise with his education. Especially since he was sponsored by Lord Ware."

"Which all makes bloody sense now."

Over the metal rim of his glasses, Williams watched Donally shove the papers back into their packet, making it obvious their meeting was at an end. "What are you going to do?" he asked, hoping Donally would explain the look in his eyes.

If there was a gentle way to announce to someone of Lord Ware's stature that his manly parts sat wedged in a vise, Donally didn't appear as if he cared to be generous. Indeed, he looked furious enough to tighten the bloody contraption.

* * *

Christopher should have felt elation, but didn't. He'd arrived at Ware's state offices an hour later in a singularly unpleasant state, both physical and mental, handicapped by a low-grade fever he knew was caused by his swollen leg.

His suit jacket brushed aside, he rested his palm on his hip just above his suspender clip as he stared out the second of two windows and tried to keep the weight off his leg. The sun came out from behind the clouds. If Christopher hadn't been positive before about Professor Atler's guilt, there was no doubt now.

He'd sent the packet Williams had given him to Ware. After months of waiting, Christopher had finally produced something substantial.

Goddamn Ware and his blasted secrets.

When he'd first read the report, Christopher had been too angry to pay attention to anything else except throwing the packet in Ware's face and demanding retribution for what he had inadvertently done to his daughter. But somewhere between his meeting with Williams and the moment he'd entered this office, the reality of his position took hold.

A door clicked open, and Christopher turned. His smooth soles slid easily around on the carpet. Inside the adjoining chamber, Ware's impatient voice sounded an instant before he filled the doorway, his gaze slow and ponderous as he met Christopher's expressionless countenance.

From across the room, Christopher's pulse kicked over. No matter the years, a part of him still felt like the upstart military attaché in the crosshairs of his superior.

"Hold my appointments," Ware's gruff voice directed the secretary.

Christopher's former father-in-law stood aside in an unspoken command for him to enter the inner sanctum of his royal realm.

The room smelled of cigar smoke and aged leather. There was a pendulum clock in the corner that ticked away the seconds.

The door shut behind Christopher. Ware walked past him

to his massive desk, his steps muted by the dun-colored carpet. As tall as Christopher, he wore his authority in his stance, in the cut of his dark suit. Behind his mutton-chop whiskers already streaked with white, his mouth was flat. He dropped onto the chair behind his desk, clearly marking his disapproval as he kept Christopher standing.

Some things never changed, Christopher thought with a faint smile. He'd long since stopped caring what Ware thought of him.

"Damned impertinence." Dispensing with formalities, Ware flicked at the packet on his desk. Leaning back in the chair, he waved his other hand at Christopher in contempt. "Who the bloody hell do you think you are to have me investigated?"

"I had Richard Atler investigated." His gaze was direct. "If I'd had you investigated, I would never have found out anything."

"You had no business—"

Christopher came up against the desk. "Atler Senior was born to the daughter of the local vicar, five months before you were born to the countess." He launched into a recitation, filling in the blanks with intuition. He'd let Ware's reaction tell him if he hit the marks. "You two grew up together on the Ware estate. He was probably your only friend but never your equal. How it must have galled him to know that his mother had not been good enough, not socially placed enough, to become the wife of an earl. That but for a technicality of wedding vows, he should have been the rightful heir to your father's estate. That his son should be the one inheriting the title."

Ware's face was suddenly scarlet with rage. "If you think I'll allow you to bandy about the name of a good man, you've another thing coming, Donally. You do not know with whom you are dealing."

"And you don't know with whom you are dealing." Christopher had to pull back from his fury. "Trust me, my lord, I would not care if you were strung up by your thumbs and left to prune on the gallows in Wapping. Except you are the only one in a position to help your daughter."

Leather squeaked. Ware leaned an elbow on the desk. "I am aware my daughter has resigned her post. Her reasons for her actions are no longer my concern. Nor do I care. She is on her own, as she wanted."

"A pity, my lord," Christopher somehow managed with diplomacy. "Considering her current problems are not of her own making, but Atler's. No one has been able to get close to the investigation he has been supposedly conducting."

Ware's expression hesitated. "What are you talking about?"

And that's when it hit him. The full impact of Ware's virulent response. Ware knew nothing of the events of the last few months. The irony of it didn't fail to relieve the tautness in his gut.

"Almost four months ago your daughter discovered missing artifacts as well as tampered-with relics from her department. She went to Atler. Shortly after that, she was sent to work in the reading room. She didn't want you to know. But unfortunately circumstances have changed."

"Yet she told you."

"She asked me to investigate the source of the counterfeit jewels. I guarantee you that at the time, I was her last choice to ask."

Ware kept silent long enough for Christopher to detail the events that had taken over his life. In the quarter hour that followed, he informed Ware of the jewel thefts and the offensive implication that Alexandra had mislabeled antiquities, or that she might even be involved in the thefts themselves.

The more Christopher clicked the falling pieces into place, the angrier he became as he realized how much had been beneath his own nose the whole time. "Did you ever question where the newspapers received so much of their information about your daughter's past? Or how much money it would cost for someone to buy up your markers and your debt?"

"A coincidence," Ware replied, distracted, unwilling to admit to the implication that his own brother could hurt him. "Damned effrontery for you to imply that he would be involved."

Christopher set his teeth. Ware was blind not to see the threat to Alexandra. "Except you and your daughter are no longer speaking to one another. Divide and conquer. The oldest rule of attack. He's hit you where it hurts the most."

Ware blanched, and Christopher saw the first real hint of doubt as Ware cast a startled glance at the report on his desk.

"Do you know why I became involved with the museum? Atler invited me. He wanted me there. It was inevitable that Alex and I cross paths."

"Get out of here." Ware's voice was a malevolent rasp.

Christopher leaned both palms flat on the desk. "My guess is that Atler's actions entailed more than stealing from the museum. There is no profit in the treachery he has perpetuated. Which leaves one conclusion," he said laconically. "His target all along has been you. Your personal and professional life. And he doesn't care how he serves his vengeance. I'd say that your brother hates you enough to serve it very cold."

Something passed across the diplomat's gray eyes before they hooded, and he dropped his gaze to the desk. Clearly, Ware held genuine devotion to his brother that Atler did not reciprocate. Because of the affection for his own family, Christopher actually felt a spark of compassion for the tyrant. "It is not my desire to bring this in front of the public, my lord. The fact that you're Alexandra's father has kept me from taking this to the constable."

"What is it you *do* want, Donally?" Ware rasped.

"The board has the power to remove Atler from his post until all of the facts are available. I want the investigation opened to someone who can't be bought or bribed. Someone with the authority to investigate without fear of reprisals. You can do all of these things."

Ware looked etched from stone as he seemed to struggle for composure. Out of some unbidden sense of respect,

Christopher turned away. Whether Ware accepted it or not, his former son-in-law was right.

The well-appointed office was filled with the clutter of leatherbound books, some opened or marked in various places. Christopher removed his abstracted gaze and, without being dismissed, chose to leave. He'd said what he'd come here to say. He'd give Ware a few days to grapple with the reality of the situation. Not because of some indelible familial pity, but because Alex needed her father on her side.

Christopher opened the door.

"It's always a contest with you. To win." Ware's voice brought him up short. "To defeat the opposition any way you can, isn't it?"

His fingers tightening on the doorknob, Christopher slowly turned. Ware rose from the desk. "Even in Tangiers when your friends wagered you to walk across the ballroom and dance with my daughter, Lord Ware's plain, awkward daughter, authority held no sacred boundaries. She would not be at that museum now if you had not stolen from her any chance for a life with someone worthy of her station."

The hot rise of color went up Christopher's neck.

"You didn't think I knew about that wager? Or the vulgar cruelties people whispered behind her back? You used her innocence and her loneliness for your own self-seeking ends."

Christopher fought the talons of anger and shame that tore at him equally. It grated that he felt the familiar slice of pain pierce his gut. The mocking rendition of a past that would not go away. He'd served his queen. Put time in perdition for his sins. He'd spent the years since his return to England attempting to bring respect to his name. To make up for being Catholic, or Irish, or poor. For wanting more than he'd had.

None of which had ever mattered to Alex. The problem had always been deeply seeded inside him. Except for the one time in his life . . . that he'd imagined a different future for himself because of who she was.

Even now, the raw course of emotion gripped him as the

realization struck all over again that Ware was responsible for his absence when his son was born.

"You don't deny the accusation?"

Christopher seldom wasted words on the obvious. His lazy glance assessing Ware, he suddenly felt implacable pride for Alex that she had gone through the childhood she'd had and remained capable of loving anyone.

Christopher despised him.

He despised the pomposity of Ware's ilk. Despised the hallowed sanctum of authority that allowed such men to thrive in their conceit. He despised the inequality between him and Ware with a violence that had him aching to cut Ware off at the knees and put him to work in the sewers. The true underbelly of London. Not this citadel of bureaucracy where he roosted.

Ware had accomplished in five short minutes what ten years of restraint had managed to keep tightly coiled inside Christopher. "Are you expecting some revelation to the contrary, my lord?" It took all of his concentration to keep from balling his hand into a fist. "Some lie that would miraculously change my motives for thawing your *princess*?" The fact that he maintained power over Ware through Alex did not escape either of them. Let the bastard fester in his own sensibilities. Christopher didn't give a frog's bloody ass what he implied. "It must gall you to know that she has been with me for the last few months."

"She never knew you for what you really were."

"She's soft-hearted. Not a fool. You insult her intelligence."

"You overestimate her ability to read people."

"Naturally, you, who are all-seeing, can?" Christopher shot him a glance, his eyes hot with disgust. "You, his mighty lordship, who stands for duty and honor. To think that I ever for one second in my life admired what you stood for. Do you think I don't know what you did to my family?"

Lord Ware's expression darkened in grim silence.

"When I refused the annulment, you had my father dismissed from his place on the board of the Academy of Sciences. My father, who held a dozen patents in metallurgy and another dozen more in the iron industry. My parents lost their home in London. If it weren't for my father's partner, he would never have worked again. My mother became ill, and my father moved to Carlisle. Of course, by then I'd already been in India for almost two years. My mother was dead before my heroic return. Do you know what I want, my lord? From you? And the whole goddamn world?

"Peace. In here—" His fist hit his chest. "I want a life I can be proud to share with my children. A family who would be proud to call me their father, their brother, their uncle. I want you to stay the bloody hell out of my business. I want you to take yourself off the Royal Commission for Public Works. If I fail, it will be because of my actions, not yours."

His hand on the door, Christopher turned.

"Donally." Ware again stopped him. "Despite the best efforts of those in charge, businesses fail without necessary support. D&B is not immune to the political and financial whimsy of the market, as you are quite aware. Funding can stop. It happens that I know three of the members sitting on the board for the Tunnel project. I also know that a final decision will not be made until the end of the year. D&B can still be a contender."

Ware had hit him in the most vulnerable spot possible and, by the flare of triumph in his eyes, knew it. "If you feel anything for my daughter, you would see that it is in everyone's best interest to remove yourself from her affections."

"Indeed." Christopher laughed bitterly. It infuriated him that he was not immune to bribes or was willing to placate Ware in so unworthy a manner. "This has been a very liberating dialogue, my lord," he said in his most expressionless voice. "And my name is *Sir* Christopher. Sir Christopher Bryant Donally." Stepping back on his heel, he was no longer patient, or amiable to anyone's temperament but his own. Ware didn't deserve special consideration. "You have until tomorrow before I go to the other museum board members myself," he said flatly. "Then I'm going to the bloody authorities. Now, if you'll excuse me, my lord."

If there had ever been a second in time that they might have been allies united in any cause, the moment had passed into oblivion. Why in hell's name had he bothered with civility?

His only thought was to get out of the office. His leg ached. And despite his most concerted effort, he limped. Christopher walked through the door and stopped. Alexandra sat as if carved from ice in the chair against the wall. Who, along with the other half dozen staff in the outer office, had heard everything that had been said the moment the door had opened. Her leather satchel clenched against her chest, Alexandra slowly came to her feet.

"I'm sorry," she whispered, but he didn't seem to have any emotions, and she didn't know what else to say.

His face wiped clean of expression, he turned back to the door to complete his exit, leaving only the sound of a ticking clock and the river traffic outside the window in his wake.

Alexandra was sorry. But not about anything that had happened ten years ago.

She walked past the stunned secretary and stopped in the doorway. Her father sat slumped at his big desk cluttered with books and a lifetime of treasures he'd accrued on his travels, his head buried in his hands in a strange sort of despair. She had never seen him so defeated, so utterly worn.

His head lifted.

Papers lay across the floor as if tossed by an angry hand. She stepped into the room and shut the door. He watched her bend to retrieve the papers. He watched her read the report, one paper at a time. Then he watched her drop the report on his desk.

Unable to believe what she'd read, Alexandra raised her eyes. Tension coiled deep in her chest, her trust destroyed by his awful secrecy, his treatment of Christopher.

Of her.

That he could for one moment defend Atler over her.

Alexandra felt as if she were dying inside.

If there had ever been a time in her life that her father had shown her true affection, she didn't remember. Or whether

he'd joked or laughed or knew what it meant to love uncon-
ditionally. He'd even deprived her of knowing that she'd had
a family. All the years she'd grown up alone, she'd never really been alone at all. Richard was her family.

Somehow Christopher had discovered the truth. "Instead
of going to the authorities, he came to you, Papa. He was doing you a favor," she said. "Because he is decent."

She would not do her father the same favor. All information in her satchel would go to the constable. Turning away,
she walked to the door, the swish of her skirts a silent tribute
to restraint.

"Decent? Donally had the audacity to come here and
threaten me. *Me*." Her father came to his feet. Her hand hesitated on the latch. Unruffled, he appeared recovered, until
she looked closer into his eyes. "He'll make me regret every
bloody thing I said to him."

Alexandra realized that he was afraid of Christopher. "He
won't waste his time with a personal vendetta, Papa."

Her father favored her with a penetrating look. "You believe that? Even after everything you know about him?"

"If you're referring to the wager"—she laughed dryly,
then added with a hint of pride—"I hope he made a lot of
money. He certainly earned every shilling of it."

"Lexie . . ."

Holding on to her temper, Alexandra regarded him inquiringly. His stance rigid, he looked at her levelly, as if suddenly
realizing it was she who was standing in front of him. "Why
are you here?"

"I had an appointment." A barely perceptible shrug moved
her shoulder. "It was the only way I could talk to you."

Silence hung over the room.

His suit was rumpled from where he'd sat slumped in his
chair. A hand had settled in his pocket, and he suddenly
looked remarkably vulnerable standing alone behind his
desk with pieces of his life torn and exposed from the scarred
archives of his past. He had always been so much larger than
life, and that she felt pity for him now shocked her. Whether

he had the courage to face Atler and do what was morally right even amid public scrutiny no longer seemed important.

Something inside her broke free of him.

"I'm sorry for you, Papa." Her chin lifted as she fought to keep her voice steady, aware that they would probably both be alone until they died. "Your whole life you've taken everything that you couldn't control and crushed it. You've had the power and the influence to back your threats. Except you couldn't break Christopher. Not that you haven't tried. I'm ashamed that his only crime was that he once loved me."

"That was not his crime."

"You thought that he could not love someone like me. There had to be an ulterior motive. You couldn't stand the possibility that you might lose anything. He intimidated you. He was a brilliant strategist, ambitious, a man who was beginning to be recognized for his work. He scared you because he was flagrantly indifferent to protocol. Unafraid. Even of you."

Her father had not looked away. She continued to look at his haggard face, aware that for the first time in her life he had not threatened or interrupted her. He had not walked away in fury. "I love him, Papa. He is my life. In that respect, I hope that doesn't void the possibility that D&B could be tossed back into the running for the Channel project," she said with sarcastic irony. "If his company were put back into the project through your influence, it would be only poetic justice that you put it there."

She wagged a hand at the report on his desk. "Whatever you choose to do is up to you, but know that I will be doing all I can to aid in the investigation that I started. Not Christopher. But me. I've resigned my position at the museum. I want to do something more with my life than remain buried in the basement with the dead and the dust of the past." For the first time, she finally understood Richard. "I want to live, Papa."

Her hand on the door latch, she hesitated, fighting to control her emotions, not comprehending why she waited those extra heartbeats before throwing the door wide to the lobby. Perhaps she waited for a sign that her father loved her, or for him to say something to vindicate the way she felt. He'd turned away to stare out the window, his pride back in place like a metal rod bracing his spine against her. It was the first familiar behavior he'd displayed. Looking at his stiff back, she was sorry that he would never truly know her.

"Goodbye, Papa."

She walked out the door into the hallway, each step taking her farther away from her old life. Increasing her gait, she was suddenly flying down the stairs. By the time she reached outside, her heart was racing as she searched for Christopher. The streets were crowded with a mixture of farm carts and broughams, people in suits, common laborers, and women strolling with children. High tide on the Thames brought with it a tangy, cooling breeze. A drill pounded in the distance. The whole world was alive with sight and sound, and she wanted to be a part of it all.

Turning in a slow circle, she let her gaze follow the arc of billowy clouds. Snowy seagulls drifted on invisible currents of air, wings outstretched as they hovered against the bright dome of blue sky. She walked barefoot on a small patch of protected grass until a bobby ran her off. Then she caught a crowded omnibus. She'd never ridden one of the lumbering vehicles. The bus plodded down streets she'd never visited, snaking around the narrow tenuous avenues that formed the city. Her silk maroon gown of mousseline de chine flowing gracefully around her, she was oblivious to the color in her cheeks. Chestnut curls fell from their anchor beneath her hat and tossed in the breeze. When she suddenly recognized the road to Sutton, she hopped off the vehicle at the next stop, leaving people to crane their necks as they watched her departure.

Opening her reticule, Alexandra counted the notes inside, then flagged down a hansom. Once at the shop she learned from Smith that Richard was no longer there.

"They'll most likely be out of the country, mum." Smith

stood at the door wiping his hands on a dirty rag, looking abashed in her presence. Tossing the rag over his shoulder, he looked past her. "My apologies, mum. But I wasn't expectin' guests."

Alexandra glanced at her cab. She'd promised the driver a bonus if he waited. "I need to leave Richard a letter," she said stiffly. "Do you have paper and a pen that I can use?"

Standing aside, he let her pass. He slapped paper and ink on the counter, leaning an elbow against the ledge as he handed her a pen. Dipping the nib in the standish, Alexandra started to write, then raised her lashes. "Do you think I can have some privacy, sir?"

He shrugged his shoulders and leaned back against the shelves, his arms crossed. "I don't usually have ladies of quality visit this store. Maybe I can interest you in some jewelry?"

She lifted her head, her hand freezing. "Richard's?"

He nodded. While he went to the back of the store to retrieve his cases, she finished the letter. Smith set out the jewelry.

Gently laying the pieces on a black velvet cloth for showing, he slid the display in front of her. Alexandra studied the pieces. Forged in sterling and gold, they were exquisite. "Richard designed these?" She held them to the light. He would consider her purchase of anything charity, but she didn't care. He *was* a charity case, and with a baby on the way, she would personally box him in the ears if he placed pride above the welfare of his child. A man who had once worn candy stripes could surely swallow a little charity.

Besides, the jewelry was truly beautiful. "How much does he make if I buy everything in this case?"

"Half. He makes half of what we sell."

"You will be honest and give him the money?"

He placed a palm on his chest. "Bridge is my niece, milady."

"Finley will know if you've cheated Richard, and I'll have no qualms ordering him to break both your hands."

The man's mouth opened, and she felt a smug satisfaction knowing that she was capable of carrying out the threat.

"You can deliver them to my townhouse, and will be paid in full then." Alexandra scratched out her address on the bottom section of the letter she'd written. She assumed since Smith had both pen and paper in his shop that he could read. Then, carefully tearing it off, she handed the slip to Smith. "A wedding gift for my cousin. And recompense for you."

Smith looked blankly at the scrap of paper, then back at her. She said, "Call us even for my hitting you over the head with a Buddha."

At that, he rubbed the balding spot on his head and reddened. "Yes, mum. This will do nicely." He opened the front door for her before she reached it. A bell tinkled. "You're not like those other hoity 'ristocrats I've met, mum."

Alexandra arched her brows at him. She was very much a product of her upbringing. "Some would beg to differ, Mr. Smith." She reapplied her gloves to her hands. "Tell Richard to stay out of London for a while. And tell him . . . tell him that I understand his choice."

She hoped that he would understand what she was about to do.

Chapter 21

❧

Ryan Donally turned at the tap on his bedroom door. "Sir, there is someone here to speak to your brother," his steward said.

Still working his left cuff, Ryan descended the stairs. He had not expected a visitor at this early hour. Certainly not a man he disapproved of and disliked. For whatever reason, Chris had found it necessary to continue his association with a notorious felon.

"Finley." He snapped the silver clip in place. "What can I do for you at this time of the morning?"

If Finley recognized Ryan's animosity, he ignored it. Bowler in hand, the big man stood inside the townhouse entryway.

"I came to have a word with yer brother? Have ye seen him?"

Ryan smoothed the cuff. "Once or twice in my lifetime, Finley."

"You have a sense of humor." Finley's mouth broke into an unpleasant grin. "But that doesn't help me find Mister Donally."

Ryan elected not to ask if Finley had tried contacting her

royal ladyship, and he certainly wasn't about to send this
criminal to the Westminster office where he and Chris were
scheduled to meet with the commission in two hours. In
truth, his own calendar had not permitted him to see Christopher in nearly four days. Not since all the rumors began circulating about the showdown he'd had with Lord Ware.

Ryan could only plead for mercy from the Almighty and ·
pray that Chris had not just ruined the future of D&B.

"What is it you want with him?"

"The *Times* is trying to set up an interview. Someone
tipped them off that he is at the gym most evenings. Guess no
one told them he hasn't been in for a week. Which, mind ye,
isn't like him. They been askin' questions whether Lord
Ware recommended him for the board at the museum."

"Ware?" Ryan's laugh was short. "Are they insane?"

Finley hesitated. "Sir, have ye not seen the morning paper?"

Ryan reached Christopher's estate outside London as the
sun set. He dismounted on the drive, tossing the reins to a
young stable boy as he hurried up a gravel path. "Rub him
down, lad." Ryan had ridden the dun hard.

Removing his gloves, he let his gaze go over the front of the
house. Standing cloaked and booted in black, he was no more
than a shadow in the evening mist. Nearly every window in the
manse was ablaze with light. He took the front stairs, reaching
for the door as it swung wide. Barnaby stood on the threshold.

"It's taken me all bloody day to get here." Ryan stepped
past him into the tall corridor. "Where is he? He hasn't
shown up at the Westminster office in days! And I'm only
just apprised of this?"

"Sir, your brother hasn't been himself. He came home
from London last week in the blackest mood I've ever seen,"
Barnaby said. "He's been ill. His leg has swollen. He hasn't
slept in days. He wouldn't let me contact anyone, or I would
have asked you to come here sooner."

Ryan paused as he handed his cloak and gloves over to
Barnaby.

"Yesterday, he emptied every cabinet in this house looking for something to drink. Last night I sent for the physician."

"God blast it, Barnaby. Ye know how he despises doctors."

"Indeed." The man stiffened his spine. "You would not believe what your brother told us we could all do with ourselves. Then he discharged us, sir."

Ryan strode past him. "Is he in the library?"

"Upstairs, sir. He'd demanded to see a newspaper. But under the circumstances, we considered it best not to give him one. Sir Donally cannot dismiss me twice." He sniffed in indignation.

"Do not allow him to read a single bloody paper unless I tell you."

"Sir." Barnaby stopped him halfway up the stairway. "The physician said if he didn't stay off his leg . . ."

Taking the stairs two at a time, Ryan walked down the carpeted corridor. Christopher stood with his back to the room. Wearing only a morning robe, he faced the long mullioned window. His military regalia lay strewn over the floor. Drawers were opened as if someone had rifled through each one.

"Christopher . . ." The words died in Ryan's throat.

His brother pivoted. He could barely walk and favored his lame leg. A short-barreled pistol was in his hand. "You're not bloody keeping me here. And you're not bringing that damned surgeon back to this house. Do you understand?"

This was not a man Ryan recognized, and alarm went down his spine. A week's growth of black stubble rendered Christopher feral. Uncivilized. Quite capable of shooting him. If the gun were loaded.

"Old military-issue?" Ryan moved to stand in front of his brother. "You'll need to hold that pistol straighter if you're going to shoot me."

"Go to hell, Ryan. I *should* shoot you." Flagging the pistol around, Christopher turned back to the bed in disgust. "Do you know there's not a single bloody bottle of anything to drink in this whole goddamn house?"

Ryan motioned toward the pistol. "Do ye think to scare the surgeon off with that popgun?"

Christopher looked at the pistol in his hand and seemed to stare as if attempting to comprehend why he was holding an unloaded weapon. Last night he'd had the recurring nightmare.

His brain was murky, as if he had yet to sleep off a drunk. The goddamned doctor had poked and prodded his thigh like he was a raw brisket. He'd warned him not to touch him, but it hadn't mattered. Six years ago he'd held a gun on the surgeon who would have amputated his leg. He'd remained conscious until they'd started to sew him up. He'd been barely alive. When he'd awakened it had been to a nightmare of pain. The pistol was still in his hand, but he'd kept his leg.

"I'll have Barnaby draw up a bath."

"The hell you will. I've dismissed him. Along with every servant in this house. I can't even get a bloody newspaper."

Ryan's slow smile was an omen any other man would have heeded. All Christopher wanted to do was knock it off his brother's face. "Naturally, insolence will not be tolerated," Ryan said. "Especially since they put your welfare above their livelihood. Lie down, Chris." Ryan spoke with quiet authority. "You're going to let me look at your leg."

An ache throbbed in his head. It felt as if someone had laid a wet blanket over his senses. The gun still clutched in his hand, Christopher moved his gaze impassively to the doorway behind Ryan. "You don't have a chance of getting past me." Ryan's casually spoken words broke into Christopher's thoughts. The look in Ryan's eyes, and his own state of weakness predetermined the outcome of any argument. "Lie down, Chris."

Christopher stumbled. A curse sprang from his lips. "This doesn't change a bloody goddamned thing."

The pressure eased off his leg the moment Christopher laid down, and he almost sighed. Despising his own helplessness, he didn't respond when Ryan moved aside the edge of the robe.

Silence ensued. The kind of empty void that bespoke sickening volumes. Christopher knew what his brother would see, and what he would most likely conclude. His thigh had swollen to twice its size. The scar was stretched taut and white against the purplish marring. The injury was serious.

Ryan slumped back on the chair beside the bed and clawed a hand through his hair. A look of fury entered his eyes. "How long have you been like this?"

Christopher refused to answer.

"You need a specialist."

"I *need* a drink."

"I've heard that damage caused by shrapnel can manifest itself years later. A well-known war surgeon lives in Edinburgh. He fought in the Crimea—"

"I know who he is."

"Why didn't you tell anyone about this?"

Christopher braced his forearm across his stubbled face and didn't reply. Ryan snatched the pistol from where Christopher had dropped it beside his pillow. "Being dependent on anyone eats at ye like a meal of rusty nails, doesn't it?" Walking to the door, he yelled for Barnaby. His tall riding boots clipped on the floor. "I'm hiring everyone back," he told the old servant. "All of you work for me now."

"Don't you do it, Barnaby," Christopher warned.

Ignoring him, Ryan ordered new linens, a hot meal, and a bath brought upstairs. Barnaby shot Christopher a smug look. "It will be my pleasure, sir."

Two hours later Christopher had bathed and eaten, and was promptly put back to bed. Like some demented Florence Nightingale in trousers, his brother had dutifully overseen the whole process, then helped prop his leg on a pillow and cover him.

Christopher struggled to find some comfort. He didn't want any damn covers and kicked them off. "Get me something to drink, Barnaby," he said behind his sleeve, so exhausted, his eyes closed. "I'm through being ignored in my own bloody house."

Ryan leaned indolently against the bedpost. "They work for me now. Remember?"

Christopher lowered his arm to find Ryan watching him with shrewd eyes, the color of night. His youngest brother was the worst person on this earth to have found him. He was not a man to let him die in peace.

"It's bloody unfortunate I can't dismiss *you*. You're enjoying this too much."

"Bravo! He grins."

"Go to hell, Ryan."

"Your mood isn't just about your leg, Chris. Though that's bad enough. I heard about what happened at Lord Ware's office."

Christopher's forearm remained across his brow. "I don't want your condolences. I'm not that bloody weak."

"You? Condolences? Ha! You don't deserve commiseration. Since your reacquaintance with her ladyship, you've gone from a responsible businessman and talented engineer to a raging lunatic."

Yes, he had. He didn't argue.

But nothing erased his own overwhelming sense that he had failed her. First by trying to hide their relationship, then by walking away from her at her father's office, when he should have gone down on one knee and explained everything that she'd heard.

Now he couldn't go to her at all.

"Let me assure you." Ryan braced his foot on the mattress. "The best help you can give her now is to heal and stay out of her way. Personally, I think her ladyship deserves a commendation for having more guts than I ever gave her credit for."

Caught by something in Ryan's tone, Christopher pushed himself up on his elbows. "What are you talking about?"

Ryan leaned forward on his elbow. "After ye left Lord Ware's office, though I don't know which one of ye can claim to be the winner," he said in an aside, "it seemed her ladyship finished the job you started. She tore into the old wolf like a lion. Over you. From the gossip, it sounds as if his whole staff was listening with their ears pinned to the door. Then her ladyship went to the constable and reported the thefts of some priceless artifacts from the museum. She filed misconduct charges against the head curator and demanded an investigation be opened. Even Atler's own son returned yesterday to swear a deposition against him. She then hired your solicitor to defend her after Atler attacked her professional credibility."

"How do you know this?"

"Her ladyship went to the Westminster office today looking for you. Stewart told her that you were having your work sent here. She remained to bring him up to date. I didn't even know the two knew one another."

"Then Stewart and Williams have both seen her?"

"As well as Finley," Ryan added. "I had the pleasure of riding with your old friend to the office in search of you. It seems that some chap named Smith contacted him with information about one of his cohorts. The other man had bragged of receiving certain stolen jewels after hearing about the museum thefts in the newspaper. Does all of this make sense? Because it sure as hell didn't to me."

Trying to ignore the rush of his pulse, Christopher shut his eyes. "Yes," he murmured. Alex was waging a war in London and doing a sight better than Atler in the battle. In fact, the old bastard would be on his way to prison before the year was out. "Anything else?"

"On the positive side, museum attendance has increased twentyfold. Newspapers sales are up, and your ladylove has become the new darling for the women's suffrage league." Ryan raised his brow. "And somehow, through it all, your name has not been mentioned once."

Ryan pulled the blankets over Christopher. "Do you still want to drink yourself into a stupor? Or do I have your permission to tuck you into bed and call the physician back?"

"You said that she saw Stewart?" He pushed back to his elbows. "Ask Barnaby if I've received anything from the office today."

Ryan looked as if he might argue. Christopher fell back on the pillows, his strength depleted. "Just ask, Ryan. You can extract all manner of promises from me later. I'll see your damn doctor."

The brown paper packet arrived ten minutes later on a tray, sharing space with a bowl of chicken broth. Christopher tore open the packet. As he skimmed through daily notes, various project analyses reports, his fingers stopped. A slow grin formed. And if it was possible for his heart to stop beating, it would have. The nearly illegible penmanship was so unlike a woman's that, had Christopher not known her hand so intimately, he would have skipped the paper entirely on the first pass. Discarding the packet, he withdrew the single paper. He twisted to hold it beneath the lamp beside the bed.

Alex may not possess the flowery scrawl of a poet, but she did possess a way with the English language that made a man want to leap fences to see her. Even a lame man. And he didn't give a fig if Stewart had read any of it.

Her vulnerability wrapped around his chest and clenched.

The last two lines were an awkward attempt at raunchy innuendo, managing to be remarkably carnal even in all its ineptness, and, falling back on his pillow, he read the letter twice more.

He loved her.

Completely.

He was humbled by her artlessness, her loyalty, and every ounce of her misplaced nobility. How could she think she was protecting him, when the thought of losing her again made it hard just to breathe?

His hand rubbed over his swollen thigh. He'd replayed over and over in his mind the look on her face when he'd left her standing in the lobby of her father's office. He should have stayed to explain. He'd wanted to tell himself that he had not run from her.

Christopher Donally ran from nothing.

But there it was, plain as the nose on his face: He had.

He'd been running from himself his whole life.

The sole author of his state of mind, he'd taken his inexperience and become rebellious and arrogant. So full of his own self-importance, constantly fighting the establishment to prove that he was more than Irish Catholic or poor. That he was every bit as talented as his father had been. Always so bloody mutinous. And yet, that very defiance had also been his greatest strength.

Closing his eyes, Christopher gave a short breathless laugh, and felt the first hint of warmth in his veins that he'd felt in days.

Admitting to his fears, he also realized that he had risen above them and his own high expectations.

Alex had brought him full circle. She'd given him a sense of peace with his past. Détente with his darker side, so to speak.

His eyes still closed, he thought about her now. There were the obvious reasons why he wanted her. The physical aspect was certainly a driving force. His libido had increased tenfold since she'd walked back into his life, and he hadn't yet seemed to get a grasp on that. Then there were the questions his family would raise. Convincing them to accept his feelings for her would be more difficult. With the exception of Brianna, who was a radical romantic, no one would understand. Then there was the real question of whether what he and Alex shared could sustain them past the societal discourse that would surely follow if he wed her. Or whether he would end up with his heart ripped out and bleeding all over the polished floor of aristocratic incertitude.

Love alone would not conquer all obstacles, but Christopher was damn sure money might help. And he had money. It would get him married in the church. It would even buy him a capable surgeon. Now all he had to do was convince Alex that their future was worth fighting for.

"I look forward to the day my work can make me so blissful." Ryan watched him from the doorway, and Christopher appreciated his generosity, for the momentary concern in his brother's eyes also held a grim sense of the inevitable. "Are you going to marry her?"

Christopher would do all in his power to lessen the blow of his decision, but he would have his bloody way in this. "She is my heart, Ryan. The family will have to accept that."

Ryan nodded. "It will be hellish uncomfortable at first," he said with a deliberate casualness he clearly did not feel. "Give her a few years and she might actually beat one of us at croquet."

Alexandra popped the wafer on the blank envelope and hastily unfolded the letter that Mary had just handed her. It had arrived at her door just as she sat down to breakfast. The strong smell of biscuits and ham wafted from the kitchen. Outside, the weather had continued to be an absolute bore, with its low-hung clouds and humidity. The dining room was dark and Alexandra moved the letter nearer to the light.

"Who delivered this, Mary?"

With the exception of her raw-raw support from the suffrage league, social leprosy had taken on new meaning since the museum scandal broke in the papers, and she was half afraid to read the letter.

"A courier, mum. I think he said he was from Mr. Williams's office."

Her heart was already racing when Mary answered.

"Will you be needing more coffee, mum?"

"Save some ham for the boys, Mary," she answered, her eyes attached to the letter. "They'll be here shortly with items from the market."

The perfectly bold calligraphy belonged to Christopher.

Alexandra wasn't sure afterward if she had acknowledged Mary's question. Her heart hammered at her ribs. It was no use fending off the warm feeling whirling inside her. It had attacked her in full force. Christopher had responded to her letter.

Three pages worth!

His letter left her physically yearning to touch more than those words on the paper. It left her questioning all the ridiculous notions she had logically laid out for staying away from him. When the longing, the intense need to see him again was overmastering.

Suddenly surrendering to the chaos of her world seemed a little easier. There was something so completely male about the brisk, no-nonsense way he dealt with her.

He loved her.

He asked her to marry him.

Her legs took her to her bedroom, where, she closed the door and, in a hot rush of emotion, read the pages again. He had become the consummate hunter again, and there was something wildly exciting about being pursued.

He knew about her case against Atler—but then who in London didn't?—and he'd been informed of Richard's return. He'd given Mr. Williams full authority to release any information obtained during his investigation.

And he waited for her answer to his question.

Doubts pervaded. She wanted him here, but he assured her in another letter the next day that she didn't need him there. He was right, of course, in not coming to rescue her when she did not need rescuing. There was a sense of pride that he believed in her. She knew that his presence would only give the press fodder to feed on and further vilify Professor Atler's public opinion of her moral integrity.

But he was sharp as a tack when it came to business and legal savvy. He gave her strategic advice, which she used two days later to request an appearance before the museum board of trustees.

And he waited yet another day for an answer.

His response to her obvious silence on the matter of his proposal came that night.

Marry me, Alex. Don't you think it is time we put this foolishness behind us? C.

Closing her eyes, Alexandra fell back on the mattress. The bed ropes creaked against her weight.

How could you be so blind? Have you no ken what this can do to you? You are usually more rational. A.

That afternoon, while it stormed outside, she waited impatiently for Christopher's reply. By then, between the boys, Finley, and Mr. Williams's office, she and Christopher had managed to set up a personal courier service. Red delivered the latest letter, put out because the rain had soaked him clean through, adorning him with a fresh-out-of-church look. After assuring him that he didn't look the least pious, Alexandra brought him inside and fed him crumpets while Mary dished out soup. Hurrying upstairs to her office, she unfolded the damp letter.

Is it that you're afraid for me or for yourself? You are being headstrong. But then, you always were. C.

If I am headstrong, it is for both of our sakes. I will not let myself be your anchor. This was not the purpose of my original letter. Why can't you see that it is better the other way? A.

Barely a day had passed before she received his response. Once alone in her bedroom, Alexandra tore open the letter.

There can be no other way. Not anymore. And let me now ask your forgiveness for ever putting you in a place where you deserved so much more. I have loved you since the first day I looked across a glittery ballroom and saw you standing alone beside the refreshment table, tapping your slippered foot to the music as you watched others dance. You had on a silver gown. I had never seen you before that night. But I'd known who you were. I was not kind to approach you for the reason that I did, but soon it didn't matter. I wanted you. I wanted what I would be because of you. You gave me something more of myself to believe in. I have known loneliness but never more than the years after I lost you. I have seldom known companionship of the kind that we share, and I have tortured myself into believing that this is enough to build a marriage. I do not believe that I am wrong. And if I could come get you now, I would. C.

Don't think about coming here. Have you not been reading the papers? The press has been covering this case like leeches. I will sneak out and find a way to see you. I wish to tell you my answer in person. And by the by, I knew who you were before that night in the ballroom. I saw you twice in my father's office. I had set my cap on you before you even looked my way. A.

That's good to know, sweetheart, which makes my goal all the more important. Our meeting will have to take place after Ryan's wedding in September. There are other reasons it is best you stay in London and win your battle. I don't mean to sound cryptic. I await your answer, my lady. My heart.

> *Yours always,*
> *Christopher*

Christopher's handwriting no longer held the bold flourish she was used to seeing. Her finger traced the letters.

"Richard will be here in an hour, mum," Mary said from her doorway some time later.

She was lying in bed, on her stomach, her forehead resting on her palm as she stared at the letter, aware of the new tension inside her. "Thank you, Mary," Alexandra answered absently.

She'd received a message from the constable this morning asking her to come to the museum. Richard had received a similar reply.

Alexandra hurriedly pulled out her stationery, prepared to demand that Christopher explain his tone, that it was indeed cryptic, and she didn't like it one bit. Her pen froze as a knock sounded on the front door. Twisting around, she found the clock on her nightstand. Richard was not due for another half hour. Forbidding to her ear, a voice in the living room drew her out of bed. She hastily stepped into a wrapper just as Mary returned to her bedroom door.

"Milady," she said urgently, " 'tis 'his *lordship*. Your father!"

Her father was sitting in the parlor when Alexandra appeared a few minutes later. The old barrier that had surrounded him her whole life was gone. His long legs were crossed in front of him, and two fingers rapped quietly on the gilt edge of the chair. She stopped half in the parlor, half out, straddling the invisible line, staring through the invisible walls dividing them, aware that she could go no farther. His gaze lifted; then he unfolded his long form and came to his feet.

"Papa," she said, leaving the question of why he was here hanging in limbo between them.

"You're not dressed." His voice was curt, so old school that Alexandra looked down at herself. "Do you not have a meeting with the constable this morning?"

She straightened when she realized he intended to go with her. "How did you know?"

"Atler announced his resignation this morning to the board and to the press," he replied. "He's agreed to sign a confession."

Alexandra stared at him in dismay. "I . . . don't understand."

Without turning, her father quietly said, "Sir Donally was correct when he ascertained . . . my brother's motives. He despises me. And because of me, he wanted to hurt you." His expression wavered slightly as it went over her. "He might have gotten away with it had you acted in any other way than what you did. What shames me is that if you had come to me months ago, I would not have believed you. For that, I have no excuse."

"So you've managed to make a deal instead. How fortunate for him." So, he'd managed in his autocratic way to once again take control.

His gray eyes pierced her. "I'm paying for his incarceration. He could either sign a confession by this morning or take his chances with the courts later. Justice would not have been kind and he would not have wanted to live out the remainder of his days where I would make sure they sent him. This way, he does receive some measure of guaranteed comfort. And you will not go through a trial."

In her mind, she would have gone through ten trials, no matter how wretched and awful she knew them to be. Atler deserved a prison barge. He deserved to wear an iron collar for the rest of his life. "You didn't do this out of some noblesse of character, Papa. You were afraid of the scandal that would come out in a trial."

"Whether you will it or not, this is about you, Lexie. Donally as well. I didn't solve or right anything. You did," he said quietly. "You and Richard, and Sir Christopher. I've taken responsibility for seeing that a proper investigation is conducted. It will be the last thing I do before I resign."

Staring at the floor, she felt frustration well through her. That he was being unusually polite about Christopher did not pass over her. Yet, despite his attempt to bridge the chasm between them, Alexandra shuddered. She could not dismiss what her father had done to Christopher. She didn't think that she ever could.

"Papa, Richard will be escorting me today, and so is Mr. Williams." She stepped into the parlor. "You wish to make a united front, when we are not united. I'm truly sorry that you have no family left. But you did this to yourself. So, if there is nothing else . . ."

Her father turned to face the window. He was no longer the powerful diplomat in charge of his world. In his dark, almost formal attire, he looked old, displaced, his autocratic manner dimmed among the feminine furnishings. A sense of his vulnerability shrilled through her like a scream, and she had to clamp down the urge to ask if he'd been taking his heart pills.

Clearing his throat, he faced her directly. "Four days ago, I sent word to the consulate in Tangiers asking about . . . my grandson. They have ways to find the records of where the church might have moved him before it was torn down. I thought to have your son brought home to Ware."

Before Alexandra could think or respond, her throat tightened against a sob. "You know where his grave is? Where, Papa?"

He started to say something, then, as if coming to a decision, reached inside his jacket and produced an aged packet. He stared at the tattered edges of the brown package, then set it down on the tea table beside the settee, clearly for her dissection. "I don't know why I kept them all of these years. But I did."

Alexandra lifted the packet and looked inside. Letters.

Letters dated ten and eleven years ago. Dozens posted from Christopher. And from her.

Her vision wavering behind tears, she looked up at her father.

"You'll find every letter you wrote him while living at the consul, and all that you'd received from him while he was in India." His voice lowered as some emotion seemed to overtake him. "I knew of no other way to protect you, Lexie. You were seventeen years old. He was a hard-drinking . . . How does a father fight something like that?"

Partly to keep pace with the violent churning of her thoughts, she dropped down on the settee.

"He wrote to you almost every week. He wrote when he received no response from you. He wrote even after he received the annulment papers with the letter saying that you would not contest it."

"Only because I thought that was what he wanted." Anguish tightened her chest. "Oh, Papa. All those years, he thought that I didn't love him enough to fight for him."

"He sent the last letter days before the uprising, just before his cantonment went under siege."

"Why would you give this to me now?"

"I'm a diplomat and cannot even negotiate a truce with my own daughter."

"Truce?" She wanted to laugh at his arrogance.

The past didn't vanish just because her father had decided to clear his conscience. Or because he had second thoughts about a man that he'd nearly destroyed. In his way, she imagined that her father was even attempting to grab on to the last vestige of his dying legacy by bringing his grandson home.

"What happened to him there?" she whispered without looking up.

Her father sat on a chair. He leaned his forehead against his cane.

"Tell me, Papa. What happened to Christopher in India?"

"Donally proved to be one of Sir Lawrence's greatest assets to the garrison at Cawnpore. Even I can't deny the man's courage."

Alexandra didn't know the names her father seemed to intimately banter about her. It didn't matter. But she did know the disastrous events that took place there. Who in the whole world did not? The garrison had surrendered after a three-month siege and had been subsequently slaughtered. Men, women, and children.

"Captain Donally was one of four men who survived the entrenchment. He made it out amid the butchery. Even surviving that, he went on to fight until the war was over. He was an intelligence officer beneath Brigadier General Neill working on the front line. . . . Donally was injured while saving the general's life, but not before he'd already earned three commendations. I cleaned up his military jacket and forwarded his records to the necessary people. A year after his return to England, he was knighted by the queen."

"And you thought that would be enough, Papa?" Her voice was a rasp.

"Under the circumstances at the time, I would not change what I did. It wasn't my intent to send the boy to war. He could have been court-martialed and imprisoned for what he did in Tangiers, or gone to the Crimean or the Frontier. He was a career soldier, Lexie. He would have eventually gone to one of those places anyway."

"Did you have anything to do with D&B losing the Channel project?"

"No," he said earnestly. "But it seems that one of the contenders has since proven to be financially insoluble. The engineering firm of Donally & Bailey was dismissed because of inexperience and for no other reason. Frankly, in my opinion the military will halt the project before it ever comes to fruition. A tunnel beneath the Channel to the continent is a significant risk to national security. Absurd."

"Lord in heaven." She glared at the ceiling. "I can't believe we've veered to talking about national security." Wiping her face, she sat straighter. "Christopher told you to stay out of his business. Now that I think about it, I believe he was quite serious."

She came to her feet and started to pace.

She only knew that she loved Christopher with all of her heart, and her father had been the one who had made her choose between them. Something like that just didn't go away over a few words.

But something else nagged at the edge of her thought as she began to pace faster. She paused in her peregrination and faced her father. Why would her father suddenly be on Christopher's side? By giving her these letters, that was exactly where he put himself. The color draining from her face, she looked at the packet in her hands, realization dawning.

"You've found out something about my son, haven't you?"

Her father grunted a reply and gathered up his hat with that dismissive tone that told her he was finished talking. "The constable is waiting, Lexie."

"Papa . . ." She stepped in front of him. "Where is he buried?"

"By Jove," he grumbled furiously beneath his breath, "Donally is a first-rate Irish son of a bitch. He has been a goddamn burr in my side for over a decade. I could even find something illegal in what he did and have him prosecuted if that's what you wanted."

"Papa!"

"Still, it's difficult not to respect the man's motives."

The words were probably more than he had ever meant to say. He glared at her as if he were about to break one of the seven sacred sacraments. He composed himself quickly. "Your son is buried in Carlisle, Lexie. Donally had him moved years ago before the old cantonment church was razed."

The air seemed to leave her. There was a huge lump in her throat that she didn't know how to swallow without giving away all of her pain. "You must be mistaken." Her hand clasped the locket she wore again.

His eyes told her he hadn't mistaken anything. That he was probably as thorough in his search as Christopher had ever been in his.

Which made her want to plow a fist into her fantasy world. A world built these last months on trust, honor, and integrity.

Christopher had known for years? He had known!

But her father for once wasn't grinding an I-told-you-so heel in her face. The annoyance faded from her expression as she realized something vitally important. Her voice was ragged and tight. "You *admire* what he did? That's why you brought that packet here today."

Grumbling something incoherent, he flipped open his watch fob. "I don't expect to be invited to the wedding. But I imagine you'll have one anyway with or without my blessing." Snapping his fob shut, he turned on his heel. "We'll be tardy if you do not get yourself dressed. I have a newspaper in the carriage. I'll await you there."

Alfred had the door open for him as he stalked from the parlor. But her father turned to look at her as he reached the door. There were so many things mingled in that one look before he clamped his hat on and left. Calm. Acceptance. Approval.

He had never looked at her like that. Not in her whole life.

It still didn't make up for his past sins. She doubted anything he ever did would. But she was no longer terrified of him. Of failing him.

She would survive never working at the museum again. The *ton* could have their way with her reputation. She would survive that as well.

Richard appeared behind her. "I still don't know if I'll ever be able to call your father uncle," he said.

She laughed at that because otherwise she would have cried. She loved Richard. He had come back to her and done the right thing.

"Bridgett is with Mary in the kitchen," he said. "We saw his lordship's carriage out front and came in through the back door."

Richard brushed back her hair, then wrapped her in his arms. "I should say something here, but unfortunately I'm fresh out of satire."

"Why when I need it the most do you fail me?" she lamented over a broken laugh. Dabbing her eyes on his jacket, she looked up at him. "Have I thanked you for returning?"

"Many times."

"I'm sorry about your father—"

He stopped her words. "I'm not."

The house smelled of braised pork. Lively chatter emanated from the kitchen. "Milady." Mary rose to her feet when she entered. Brushing off her white apron, Mary hurried to the stove. "Will ye be needing to dress now?"

The trestle table in front of the cooking stove was full. The boys were there. Looking cleaner than she'd ever seen them, they were bent over a bowl of Mary's hot custard, slurping down every last treasured drop. Bridgett sat at the other end, her golden ringlets captured by red ribbons. Alexandra returned her greeting and smiled. Mary and Alfred sat at the other end. Even the golden cat lounged indolently in front of the doorway. And for the first time in weeks, the tension ebbed out of her muscles. She looked at those gathered around her table.

Her table.

And realized that their camaraderie included her.

"Yes," she answered Mary. "I need to dress."

Pensively, Alexandra laid on her bed the packet she still carried. Her mind was no longer on the proceedings today.

But on going home. Going to her real home.

Chapter 22

❧❧❧

"**D**id Williams say where she had moved?" Christopher threw the latest correspondence from his solicitor onto the floor, where a breeze from the opened balcony door scattered the pages.

Colin sat comfortably on one side of his bed, playing secretary. It was late afternoon at the family estate in Carlisle and the floor was awash in amber. Trees stirred gently beyond the bastions of the Donally stronghold, and for the last week the house had been filling with family and friends arriving in celebration of Ryan's upcoming nuptials.

Christopher flinched as the surgeon poked at the wound in his thigh, enduring the abuse only because he wanted everyone out of the room. "Will he be walking in Ryan's wedding processional?" Johnny asked. "Or will Rachel have to wheel him down the aisle?"

"The stitches are out." The old doctor raised to his full height and glared down his hawkish nose at Christopher. "Though for all the trouble you've caused me, I should have left them in longer!" His gaze took in Ryan and Johnny, who were leaning against the bedstead watching the proceedings. "As you can see, he is alive and quite well."

Gathering up his leather satchel, he reached inside and removed a thin sliver of metal visible in a glass vial. "For you." He handed Christopher the souvenir. "The injury that young Atler fellow gave you must have dislodged the piece of shrapnel you've had embedded in your thigh all these years. It finally worked its way to the surface. I barely had to cut into your thigh to retrieve the culprit."

Christopher regarded the piece with distaste. That such an insignificant scrap could have made his life hell for so long seemed incomprehensible. He supposed he owed Richard Atler for the well-placed knee to his thigh.

Three weeks ago, Christopher had returned to Carlisle to undergo the risky surgery. Now all he wanted was for everyone to leave him the hell alone so he could get back to Alex. His tyrannical siblings had taken shifts to see that he remained an invalid for the last month.

He had not heard from Alex. Not in all the time since he'd been here. As a museum trustee, he'd received a formal letter two weeks ago announcing Professor Atler's arrest. There had been quotes from Lord Ware in the papers that health concerns prompted Atler's removal from London. He was being moved to Mayfair asylum.

In addition, Ware had taken responsibility to see that a proper investigation was conducted and restitution paid. Within weeks, the scandal had faded to the third page of the London *Times*.

Perhaps he would have been more relieved that the ordeal was over but for the fact that he longed impatiently to hear something from Alex.

With the physician's prognosis behind him, his recovery imminent, he asked his jovial, protective family to leave, and summoned Barnaby. He and the old steward had not spoken since Christopher had dismissed the man, and now Christopher was in the unfortunate position of making a formal plea for his loyal service. In a house run by tyrants, he needed an ally. Even Brianna had proven to be stubborn and uncooperative when it came to allowing him outside, or in sneaking him a decent meal, or any other manner of freedoms he should have had in his own house.

Barnaby appeared a moment later. "Can I help you, sir?"

Christopher waited until they were alone before throwing back the covers and sliding from bed. His leg was stiff but in working order. Unbeknownst to his jailers, he'd been walking on it steadily since the surgery.

"Barnaby, I wish to apologize for my behavior a few weeks ago." He locked the door. He wore only his underclothes and managed to find a morning robe in his armoire.

"That's not necessary, sir." He helped Christopher into the robe.

"It is. I was temperamental and wrong."

"You are always temperamental, sir. I thought nothing of it."

"I see." Christopher lashed the belt on his robe. "Then I have worried about having offended you for nothing."

"Apparently so, sir. None of us took you seriously when you dismissed us."

"Indeed."

"You have not been yourself . . . for many months now, sir."

Christopher was surprised how much of himself *had* emerged these last months. He was more himself than he'd been in years.

"I wish to leave this house. I need clothes, Barnaby."

Barnaby's bushy brows raised. "Clearly you would have clothes if your family thought it necessary, sir."

"Barnaby—" He rubbed the kink in his neck and forced himself to breathe. "It's important that I get to London."

Unimpressed with Christopher's plea, the old steward waited to be let out of the room. "I suggest that you talk to your family, sir. They are the ones who gave express orders that you were to be given no clothes until after your wound has healed. Clearly they do not trust you to mind your own health. Lunch will be served downstairs if you would like to go down and join everyone."

Several newspapers were scattered over the sofa. Snatching up a pair of spectacles and a handful of papers, he walked downstairs. Children played outside on the lawns, their laughter bringing him onto the veranda. Very shortly, he was placed like an invalid in a chair, his leg propped on an ottoman, where he sat in state, like royalty overseeing court from his own porch.

"Ye really should take better care of yourself." Rachel tucked an afghan around his shoulders.

"It's August, Rache." Ryan laughed from the doorway behind Christopher. "He doesn't need a bloody blanket."

Rachel's back snapped straight. "The problem with you, Ryan Donally, is that ye have too much time on your hands. You've become an ogre." In a whirl of bright yellow muslin, Rachel sidestepped a potted plant.

"Rachel—" Ryan plowed his fingers through his hair and swore.

Raising his eyebrows, Christopher looked up at Ryan.

"Uncle Fer?"

Christopher pulled his gaze around. Little Katherine stood beside him with a ball in her hands. All ribbons and ruffles, her cheeks were pink from running. "Will you play catch?"

He looked past Johnny's little girl to the lawn, where the boys were engaged in a very physical form of catch the ball and kill the opponent.

"They're mean," Katherine announced with four-year-old fervor.

"Won't let you play, will they?"

Ryan scooped the little girl up. "I'll play catch with ye, poppet. We'll show those boys what fun they're missing."

Christopher met his brother's gaze over the girl's head. Katherine laughed. Wiggling out of Ryan's arms, she bounced out onto the lawn.

"Do you want to tell me what that was all about with Rachel?" Christopher asked.

Ryan bounded down the stairs. "Frankly, no." With an athletic agility, he turned midstride. "Some of us understand commitments and responsibility better than others."

"You're out of line, Ryan." Johnny stepped onto the veranda. "This isn't the time—"

"Hell, maybe it is." Ryan regained two steps. "Why are we always protecting him?"

Christopher edged out of the chair. "I wasn't aware that you were."

"I don't want you back in the London operation. Johnny and I have talked about this. Productivity has dropped ten percent since you've been there."

Christopher faced Johnny, who suddenly seemed too silent. A muscle worked in Christopher's jaw. His hand went to his hip. The laugh he felt churning just below the surface was not a pleasant one, but neither was it filled with the anger he should have felt.

"Where are Brianna, Rachel, and Colin in this little self-serving consensus?"

"Self-serving?"

Johnny stopped Ryan. "Brea went with Colin to pick up David from the train station," he said. "She doesn't know. Rachel thinks Ryan is an ass. I won't go into where that argument went this morning. Colin . . . it's not that he thinks you're incapable."

"The hell it's not," Ryan snapped. "Rachel doesn't know anything about the business. Colin knows the income and loss numbers. Brianna can't vote yet."

Johnny's gaze narrowed on his brother. "What is the matter with you? Chris isn't responsible for market fluctuations—"

"I resign." Christopher looked at both of his brothers. "I quit."

Johnny's expression tightened. "That's not what either of us intended."

"Uncle Ryan!" Katherine called impatiently.

Ryan looked over his shoulder. The breeze caught the sleeves of his shirt. He turned back to Christopher, his eyes hard. "If the partnership doesn't buy ye out, then I will do it alone." With that, he turned on his heel and trotted off to play with Katherine.

"Jaysus," Johnny groaned. "He can be such a bloody bastard. I do not know what has gotten into him."

"Maybe he knows he's marrying the wrong woman."

Folding his arms, Johnny leaned back against the newel post and raised his brows in supposition. Then he sobered and looked away. "Ryan is impulsive and determined. He gets something in his craw and it won't let him go."

"I know what Ryan is." Christopher watched his brother throwing Katherine in the air. Besides the fact that Ryan blamed him for the loss of the Channel project, there was a long-standing history of competition that Christopher had never understood. "If it weren't for him, I would not have seen a surgeon. He cared enough to get me help."

"Are you really resigning? Just like that?"

Christopher brought his gaze around. Looking at his brother's strained face, he grinned, but it wasn't pleasant or particularly brotherly. "Yes." And it felt good to say the word. "Today."

He limped back into the house, his heavy robe brushing his legs.

"Don't do this, Chris."

"Are you worried that you can't handle the helm? Or that Ryan will snatch the operation from you?"

Johnny stopped him before he reached the drawing room door. "I'm worried what this might do to the family."

"I am not the glue that holds this family together, Johnny. There are five of us on that board. Six when you count Rachel. David was smart to bow out years ago, and I have Brianna's proxy."

"What of this house? Are ye going to sell your shares in this house as well? Da's home?"

Christopher looked around him. Officially, the house belonged to the family, but Christopher and Brianna had taken up residence here the last few years. Richly paneled walls and fine marble mantels installed last year gave the impression of extravagant wealth. A fine collection of Chinese porcelain was housed in various cabinets all over the room. At each end of the room a small fire burned, but only one of the Venetian crystal chandeliers was lit, which he now stood below.

It was strange how he'd once thought it all so important. That a man's importance was weighed by his wealth. That nobility was more a birthright than a man's true character. "It's only a house, Johnny."

He wouldn't be bringing Alex here to live.

Outside, a burst of excited laughter filled the room. Christopher went to the long window and looked out over the gardens while Johnny walked onto the veranda. David had arrived. Except for his black priestly garb, his wild, once rakehell brother didn't seem to have changed much in the two years since he'd put on that robe. He knelt and scooped up Katherine and was suddenly inundated by the rest of the family. They adored him. Especially the children.

Christopher strolled out onto the veranda. He and David had been in a fiery correspondence these last weeks, and Christopher's expression remained neutral. Johnny stood beside him on the veranda. Ryan came to the steps and stopped. David raised his face and glimpsed him.

"You had a comfortable trip?" Christopher asked.

His brown eyes twinkling, David walked to the bottom of the stairs. "It's na every day a man of the church gets his own private railcar. One would think I was the holy pope himself." David mounted the steps one at a time. "But I didn't travel alone." Handing Katherine off to her mother, he continued to climb the steps. "At the train station, I met a very interestin', very well dressed young lady who just arrived from London." His hands on his hips, he said, "Imagine my surprise when she approached and asked if I was any relation to you. She knows ye quite well. Over a decade, I believe is what she said."

Christopher stepped down a stair. "Alex is here?" He suddenly found himself the target of all eyes. "Where?"

"She asked to go to the cemetery. Brea took her there."

"The cemetery?" His heart thundered. He should have known it would only be a matter of time. . . . "How long ago?"

"A half hour."

Christopher was down the stairs. He couldn't run, but he sure as hell wasn't going to walk leisurely, either. Before he reached the edge of the property, he realized that he was being followed. His whole family trailed in his wake, clomping through long grass, an overgrown path frequented by few. Brianna wouldn't know where his son was buried . . . unless David had told her.

He found his sister fifteen minutes later, standing with her head bowed at a respectful distance from the lone woman kneeling beside the headstone of her son. Brianna saw him. Whatever judgment she held toward him didn't show in her blue eyes as she turned and walked away, leaving him alone with Alex.

In his turmoil, he remained frozen. Seeing him, Alex rose slowly to her feet. They stood facing each other across the emptiness in what had suddenly become an entire lifetime. She was beautiful in the broken sunlight weeping through the splayed branches of trees that hovered over the lone grave. She wore blue.

"Christopher." Wiping one eye, she lowered the handkerchief. "Why are you wearing your robe and slippers?"

Christopher looked down at himself as if unable to comprehend her words. His black hair was mussed. Beard stubble covered his jaw. But his eyes when they lifted back were clear with purpose. In a short time, she'd become his life all over again.

"I had a problem with my leg."

Her eyes went at once to the limb in question. "What happened?"

"It seems Richard did me a favor when he kicked me. Somehow he dislodged shrapnel from my old wound. I had a small surgical procedure—"

Her eyes flared wide. "How could you not tell me? How could you not tell me anything?"

"Alex—"

When he reached for her, she stepped away from him. "Don't touch me!" Tears watered her eyes. "Or I'll . . . I'll just cry." Her hands flapped in front of her face as if to keep the tears at bay. "You keep too many secrets, Christopher Donally. I should throw something at you. Like my fist."

"Alex. Please." He pulled her into his arms, where she cried against his robe. "I should have told you about our son. I would have told you as soon as I saw you again."

She shook her head.

"You have to believe I meant no deception."

"You don't understand. . . ."

Her tears soaked through the cloth of his robe. He was helpless to stop them. There was so much he'd wanted to tell her. But he was desperately afraid he'd lost the chance. Then she raised her head, her eyes wet and shining. "You don't understand, Christopher." She cupped his face. "I'm not unhappy. You brought him home. Don't you know what that means to me? Even when I thought I'd lost you forever and that you hated me—"

"I never hated you." His voice was a rasp.

"Then forgotten me."

"I forgot for a while, Alex. I needed to forget. But he was my son, and I wasn't going to see him buried in some forgotten grave in a godforsaken country, and never at Ware. But here. I didn't tell you because I didn't want a fight. I had to make sure—"

Her hands wrapped around his head and pulled him down to her mouth. She kissed him.

Hard.

And if any of his family were still standing on the ridge, then they watched his arms enclose her and crush her to him. He trailed his lips over her cheek and buried his face in the mass of her fragrant hair. "Whatever we had is worth saving,

Alex." He stroked her hair and tilted her face. "It's worth enduring ten scandals. It's worth fighting for."

"But I can never give you another child."

"I want *you,* Alex. I want a woman who knows what a Sommelier boring machine is, who appreciates *Kama Sutra* art—in all its forms. Who is not afraid of her passion or stepping up to do the right thing no matter the price." He leaned his forehead against hers. When he spoke his voice was low and fierce. "I want to wake next to you in the mornings. I want your face to be the last thing I see at night before I close my eyes. I want you to step out of my dreams and into my future." He framed her face with gentle palms. "We don't have to live here in England. They need engineers in the Suez. We can go to Egypt. You can study history to your heart's content. Write books that will set the scholars back on their heels. Make love to me every night." He crooked his infamous Donally smile, and Alexandra was lost. "I'm lonely without you."

She laughed. It was a novelty to see the powerful head of D&B looking so uncertain of himself.

"Besides, you've seen me wearing my robe." He kissed her brow, her lips, her nose. "You have to marry me. I've compromised you."

"I love you." She laughed.

"I know," he declared in a teasing voice. His words brushed her temple. "It was one of the factors in my favor."

Wiping her eyes, she leaned her cheek against his heart. "What about D&B, Christopher? What about your dreams?"

"Ryan will buy out my partnership. It was arranged today. A unanimous decision."

She raised her face. "Are you sure?"

His casual shrug was more felt than seen. "I've enough to keep us living in the lap of luxury until you receive your inheritance."

She knew, no matter his carefree words, he would never allow her to support him. Still, he probably had no idea how truly wealthy he'd be just by marrying her. As her husband, he would become executor of her estate. And everything would belong to him.

"I love you, Alex," he whispered. "I love you so much I ache. Are we worth the fight?"

She leaned into his strength, and found that he also leaned into hers. "I think you've taught me a little about fighting."

They were suddenly looking at the marble headstone. Only a single date carved in its surface bore any hint of the life buried there. His arm around her shoulder, together they stood at their son's grave, hands entwined, observing the moment in silence. They were parents who had suffered a loss. Who had mourned separately and now shared the moment together. It was a long time before they left the cemetery.

Christopher did not return to the house by way of the main path.

"I apologize that it took so long to get back to you." Alexandra leaned her head on his shoulder as she helped him walk. He had a noticeable limp now. "There were ends to tie up with the investigation, and I needed a new place to live."

Easing her quietly through the servants' door, he quietly snuck her up the back stairs. "Where did you go?"

"We moved into your house."

Christopher stopped on the stairs. "You moved into my house?"

"I know it was brazen of me. But I knew you would be busy here for a few weeks with Ryan's wedding. I left Mary and Alfred there." Her fingers splayed his upper arms. "The boys even visit. They aren't that bad once they clean up. And Mary is very good about seeing to that before they step inside. Are you angry?"

"Angry?" His gaze on her lips, he pressed her against the wall. He had all but declared in the past that he was no gentleman, and his hands boldly proved the fact. "I've been thinking about you for weeks," he rasped, walking her backward up the stairs. "Worried sick because you had not responded to my letters."

"I should have written. But what I wanted to tell you needed to be said in person."

"God, I love you," he whispered against her lips.

"Christopher," she whispered back, her palms firmly planted on his chest. "Why are we sneaking into your house?"

"Because he's at war with the Donally clan." Brianna sat on the top stair, her chin propped on her elbow, watching them.

With an oath, Christopher dropped his hands away from Alexandra, but their position on the stairs left little room to maneuver away..

"For which I don't blame him." Brianna came to feet, her rose-silk skirts rustling.

Catching the look between brother and sister, Alexandra wasn't prepared as Brianna stepped forward and gave her a hug. "I think you are the bravest person I know, my lady. I like you very much." She turned her blue gaze on Christopher. "And you—" Brianna flung her arms around Christopher. Alexandra watched him flinch against the pressure he applied to his leg as he caught her weight. "I am going to come live with you."

"Thank you, Brea. I shall certainly feel peace of mind in your presence." He winked at Alexandra.

"I just wanted you to know where I stood," she said when she pulled away.

"Thank you, Brea."

"You've had a fight, haven't you?" Alexandra demanded after Brianna left.

A few moments later, Alexandra and Christopher were alone in his bedroom, where he shut the door firmly. "Let me explain something to you," he said to the accusation in her eyes. "I don't do anything unless I damn well want to. I have no regrets about D&B. As for my family? We argue all the time. You'll just have to get used to it. But right now—" His hand reached over to the door handle beside her. The big key in the lock clicked with the flick of his wrist. "All I can think about is getting you naked beneath me."

A knock sounded on the door.

"Shit." Christopher glared at the door. "What is it now?"

"My apologies, sir," Barnaby said from outside the door. "Her ladyship's trunks have arrived from the station—"

"Take them to the inn, Barnaby." Christopher splayed her waist and pulled her against him. "That includes my clothes as well. Her ladyship and I will be spending the night there. Tell my brother, the priest, that I want to see him."

The room where she stood was filled with windows that faced a lake. White curtains as soft as gauze billowed in the fragrant breeze. There was only a breath between his smile and her anticipation. "I love you."

Their eyes met and loved in a timeless embrace before he lowered his mouth to her lips. A long time later, when he'd finally raised his mouth and she opened her eyes, Alexandra smoothed a lock of dark hair from his brow. "You no longer have D&B. You and your family are at odd ends. I no longer have a career. Where exactly did you say that leaves us in this equation?"

"I'd say that leaves us right where we started."

And it was a wonderful place to begin.

Christopher and Alexandra were married that night bathed in moonlight and the soft glow of lanterns the same way they were so many years ago. They would marry again later in a public ceremony surrounded by her friends and his family, but tonight belonged to them alone.

The diplomat's daughter had discovered more than a young Irish soldier's love so long ago beneath the stars. She had discovered her destiny.

The days may be getting longer, but the nights are definitely getting hotter with these sizzling titles, coming in May from Avon Books.

A DARK CHAMPION by Kinley MacGregor
An Avon Romantic Treasure

Stryder of Blackmoor has never desired the comforts of home and hearth—until he gazed upon the exquisite face of Rowena. He dares not succumb to her sensuous charms, but when treachery and danger threaten, the noble knight must stand as the lady's champion—though it could cost him his honor, his heart . . . and his forbidden dream of happiness.

WHAT MEMORIES REMAIN by Cait London
An Avon Contemporary Romance

Cyd Callahan has no memory of the terrible event of her childhood, and she'd rather the truth remain buried. Ewan Lochlain, however, is determined to unravel the mystery of his parents' deaths—and he's convinced Cyd holds the key. But Ewan realizes too late that his personal investigation may have just cost Cyd her life . . .

ONCE A GENTLEMAN by Candice Hern
An Avon Romance

Nicholas Parrish had no intentions of taking a bride, but when Prudence falls asleep in his townhouse, her irate father demands satisfaction. Being a true gentleman, Nicholas agrees to do the proper thing. But he may need to reconsider his plans for a "marriage in-name-only" when his bride decides to make him fall in love with her!

THE PRINCESS AND THE WOLF by Karen Kay
An Avon Romance

Married by proxy to a European prince she doesn't love, the princess Sierra will not believe her husband died in far-off America—and crosses an ocean to discover the truth. But she will need a scout in this wild land, and puts her life in the hands of High Wolf, the proud Cheyenne brave she once loved . . . and should rightly have wed.

REL 0404